PENGUIN CLASSICS

MAX HAVELAAR

Multatuli was the pseudonym of Eduard Douwes Dekker. He was born in 1820 in Amsterdam, the son of a Dutch sea captain. In 1838 he went to the Indies and joined the East Indian Civil Service. Despite being involved in various disputes with his superiors, his outstanding abilities were recognized and he rose steadily in rank. He married Everdine, Baroness van Wijnbergen, in 1846 and they had two children. Increasingly unable to accept the brutalities of colonial rule, he resigned from the service in 1856. Years of poverty followed, during which he wandered around Europe, struggling to survive by his writing and endeavouring to improve the situation of the Javanese. *Max Havelaar*, his powerful indictment of colonialism, was written during 1859 and caused a sensation in Holland when it was published in 1860. He spent his later years involved in political and economic polemics and died in 1887.

An Englishman by birth, Roy Edwards married a Dutch-speaking wife and settled in the Low Countries in his later years. During the 1950s and 1960s he translated the works of many of the Netherlands' greatest authors and was awarded the prestigious Martinus Nijhoff Prize in 1962 for his translations from the Dutch. Roy Edwards died some years ago.

R. P. Meijer was born in the Netherlands and took his first degree at the University of Amsterdam. For several years he taught at the University of Melbourne, and was Professor of Dutch Language and Literature at the University of London, first at Bedford College and later at University College, from 1971 until 1988. His publications include *Literature of the Low Countries* (1978), *Dutch Grammar and Reader* (with Jacob Smit, 1976) and *Post-war Dutch and Flemish Poetry* (1974). He is a regular reviewer for *NRC Handelsblad* and an editor of *Neerlandica extra Muros*.

MULTATULI

MAX HAVELAAR

Or the Coffee Auctions of a
Dutch Trading Company

Translated with Notes by Roy Edwards
Introduction by R. P. Meijer

PENGUIN BOOKS

PENGUIN BOOKS

Published by the Penguin Group
Penguin Books Ltd, 27 Wrights Lane, London W8 5TZ, England
Penguin Putnam Inc., 375 Hudson Street, New York, New York 10014, USA
Penguin Books Australia Ltd, Ringwood, Victoria, Australia
Penguin Books Canada Ltd, 10 Alcorn Avenue, Toronto, Ontario, Canada M4V 3B2
Penguin Books (NZ) Ltd, 182–190 Wairau Road, Auckland 10, New Zealand

Penguin Books Ltd, Registered Offices: Harmondsworth, Middlesex, England

First published 1860
This annotated English translation first published by Sijthoff, Leyden/William
Heinemann Ltd, London/London House and Maxwell, New York 1967
Published in Penguin Classics 1987
5 7 9 10 8 6 4

The Introduction by R. P. Meijer is a slightly revised version of a commemorative
address delivered at a Public Meeting of the Netherlands Cultural Committee held at the
University of Melbourne on 19 May 1960 and published by the Dutch Section of the
Department of Germanic Languages, University of Melbourne

Printed in England by Clays Ltd, St Ives plc

CONTENTS

TRANSLATOR'S INTRODUCTION

Eduard Douwes Dekker, who wrote under the pseudonym Multatuli, was born in 1820 in Amsterdam, the son of a Dutch sea captain. In 1838 he went to Java, where he entered the East Indian Civil Service. Although he had many disputes with his superiors his outstanding capacities seem to have been recognized, and he rose steadily in rank.

In 1846 he married Everdine, Baroness van Wijnbergen, the Tina of *Max Havelaar*. A son, Eduard, the 'little Max' of *Havelaar*, was born to him in 1854, and a daughter in 1857.

In January 1856 he took up the appointment of Assistant Resident of Lebak. However, within three months he had resigned from the East Indian Civil Service altogether, and left Lebak, following the events narrated in *Havelaar*. Then came years of poverty-stricken wandering for the family in Holland, Belgium and Germany, during which Multatuli struggled with his pen to obtain rehabilitation for himself and justice for the Javanese.

In 1859 he wrote *Max Havelaar*, under the circumstances described in his introductory note to the edition of 1875 (pp. 321–27). The manuscript was entrusted for publication to Jakob van Lennep, a well-known lawyer, journalist and historical novelist. Van Lennep recognized the value of *Havelaar*; but the possible consequences of such a literary bombshell obviously frightened him. Not only did he subject it to drastic editing (scrapping and disguising proper names, etc.), but, by circulating it only cautiously, he also did his best to prevent it from coming quickly into 'the wrong hands', contrary to the vehemently expressed intention of the author.

Nevertheless the book caused a great sensation—sent a 'shudder' through the whole body of the Dutch nation, as Multatuli was later contemptuously to recall (p. 324). Contemptuously . . . for the success of *Max Havelaar* did nothing to improve the lot of ex-Assistant Resident Eduard Douwes Dekker. He was not reinstated; nor did the Javanese receive immediate justice, although *Havelaar* eventually led to many reforms. Multatuli spent the rest of his life in polemics over a variety of political and economic subjects, and died embittered in 1887.*

It is interesting to compare him with the other figure of world stature produced by the Netherlands in the last century—Vincent van Gogh.

To an outsider's eye, Van Gogh and Multatuli—the one so internationally famous, the other so little known—bestride the narrow world of the Dutch nineteenth century like colossi. Both were egocentric reformers intensely concerned for the human condition. Multatuli swore an official oath to protect the Javanese, and took it literally, with the effects recorded in *Havelaar*. Van Gogh went as evangelist to the brutalized miners of the Borinage and tried to follow Christ literally by giving all he had to the poor and sleeping on the ground, until he was sacked by his horrified superiors in Brussels. To the end of his life Multatuli swore he was a man of action and not a writer (p. 323); and Van Gogh always remained an evangelist at heart.

In the art they practised, both were autodidacts. In Multatuli's case it is a wonder he ever managed to struggle out of the morass of sentimental, parochial thinking that prevailed in the Holland of his day and whose influence is seen in his embarrassing poems (though he fully recognized their badness—see note, p. 16). Both men had the first prerequisite of genius—vitality. This vitality, this energy surges in every line of *Havelaar*, for instance in the tempestuous use of italics, stresses and capitals, which has been faithfully reproduced in the present translation. Although Multatuli fared much better than Van Gogh, neither was properly appreciated in his own day. And even now, in spite of the great Van Gogh collections in the Netherlands, and the Multatuli Society and Multatuli Museum there, one sometimes suspects that the Dutch, at any rate, do not quite see the difference in *kind* between these two and all the other painters and writers of their time in Holland—that difference which we can only call genius. D. H. Lawrence, in the Introduction to W. Siebenhaar's translation of *Max Havelaar* published in 1927, senses this lack of perspective when he says:

> If you ask a Hollander for a really good Dutch novelist he refers you to the man who wrote: *Old People and the Things that Pass* (Louis Couperus)—or else to somebody you know nothing about.

* *However, he wrote at least one more book that could interest non-Dutch readers—the unfinished* Woutertje Pieterse *(Wally Peters), the story of a child's life in Amsterdam, which aroused the admiration of Sigmund Freud.*

viii

As regards the Dutch somebody I know nothing about, I am speechless. But as regards *Old People and the Things that Pass* I still think *Max Havelaar* a far more real book. And since *Old People* etc. is quite a good contemporary novel, one needs to find out why *Max Havelaar* is better.

Finally, both men died in exile—Multatuli in Germany, Van Gogh in France.

This brief account has been written purely to supply the minimum of background knowledge necessary for a real understanding of the book and the author's notes on it. Multatuli's full life-story is far more absorbing, though painful. Anyway . . . after more than a hundred years, his book is as fresh as ever; and the words with which Lawrence concluded his review of Baron Corvo's *Hadrian the Seventh* are equally applicable to *Max Havelaar*: 'The book remains a clear and definite book of our epoch, not to be swept aside. If it is the book of a demon, as the contemporaries said, it is the book of a man-demon, not of a mere poseur. And if some of it is caviare, at least it came out of the belly of a live fish.'

ROY EDWARDS

INTRODUCTION BY R. P. MEIJER

Max Havelaar was published in Amsterdam in 1860 and immediately gen-
erated heated discussions. And controversial it has remained. One would
be hard put to find a novel of this vintage which still has the effect of
dividing its readers into two camps, for or against, and of raising stormy
debates among otherwise placid people. These clashes of opinion are not
in the first instance provoked by a disagreement about the literary value
of the book, but rather by non-literary criteria. From 1860 till today the
discussion about *Max Havelaar* has centred mainly on the question of truth
or untruth in the case which is presented in the novel. For the book
presents a case, a report of what happened to Eduard Douwes Dekker,
Assistant Resident of Lebak, in the year 1856. And it is not a neutral
presentation of a case but an attempt by the author to explain and justify
his actions when he was this Assistant Resident of Lebak. So the book
is an autobiographical novel, which means that it cannot be properly
understood without some knowledge of the man who wrote it.

Who was this ex-Assistant Resident, this unknown author who published his book under the romantic, self-pitying pseudonym of Multatuli,
meaning 'I have endured much'?

He was forty years old when he published his book, having been born
in 1820, in Amsterdam, the son of a sea-captain. His home background
seems to have been that of a reasonably well-off middle-class family. When
Eduard was twelve years old, he went to the Latin School in Amsterdam
in order to become a minister of the Church, like his elder brother Pieter.
But he did not finish school; after three years he left, for unknown reasons.
He went to work in an office, a textile business, until he was eighteen,
when he went to Indonesia. Why he went, or was taken, to Indonesia, is
also uncertain. There is a story that he had taken some money from the
petty cash to help a friend in need, that his parents were very upset when
this was discovered, and that Eduard then asked to be taken to Indonesia
so that he could start afresh. It is a pretty story, and a useful one, because
it satisfies both parties: Multatulians and Anti-Multatulians. The Anti-

Multatulians cheerfully hail it as the first of Dekker's many financial débâcles, whereas the Multatulians say: 'But he did it to help a friend.' It is a pretty story, but unfortunately the evidence for its authenticity is very slight. Yet Eduard did go to Indonesia, on his father's ship and with brother Jan as second mate. We do not know much about their voyage, only one little anecdote which gives us an idea of what kind of young man Eduard was. One day, when his brother Jan was holding forth about the difficulties of climbing the mast, Eduard suddenly ran to the mast and climbed to the top, although he always suffered badly from fear of heights and dizziness. This anecdote links up with another, which refers to one of his first days in Indonesia. Eduard and Jan were yachting near Jakarta, and Jan kept on warning him not to fall overboard. Eduard finally had enough of it, and told Jan to stop being such a bore or he would jump overboard. 'You would not do that,' said Jan. 'The place is full of sharks.' Whereupon Eduard jumped overboard. It took a while to turn the boat and pick him up, and when Eduard had climbed on board again, Jan took him severely to task for his recklessness. Whereupon Eduard jumped overboard for the second time. After that, one presumes, Jan was silent. One must be careful, of course, not to make too much of anecdotes of this kind, but they do show young Dekker as having an independent and recalcitrant nature and as resentful whenever somebody talked to him like a Dutch uncle.

After his arrival he became clerk at the office of the Auditor-General. He did good work there, was generally appreciated and was quickly promoted. In those first years in Indonesia he fell violently in love with a girl called Caroline Versteegh. He wanted to marry her, but there were several obstructions in his way. First, she was a Roman Catholic and he was not, and she made it quite clear to him that she would marry him only if he also became a Roman Catholic. He was passionately in love, and gave in. This impressed Caroline but not her father, who did not want Dekker as a son-in-law even after his conversion. He intercepted Dekker's letters to Caroline, because, as she herself wrote, 'He has heard such bad reports about you.' Dekker then wanted to know what they knew about him, and she seems to have received this letter, for she wrote back: 'You want to know what we have heard about you: in the first place you seem to have shown too much indifference to money, especially in playing billiards, your wallet must be very well filled if you can afford to lose 100 guilders every week. Furthermore: you have fought: I had better not say more, as you will understand how annoyed Papa is about this . . . although I am sure that everything has been exaggerated and magnified, it hurts me terribly to hear of such accusations about you.' So Dekker was a gambler and a fighter, and he was not allowed to marry his Caroline. Her informants may have been right: there are also later stories about his fighting—he was once taken to court and convicted for a fight—and there is all too much evidence that he was an inveterate gambler. But all this does not seem to have worried the administration a great deal, for a year later, in 1842, he was appointed District Officer at Natal, on the west coast of Sumatra. Even when one realizes that promotions were generally quick, and that the west coast of Sumatra was unpopular because of the bad reputation of the Governor, Colonel Michiels, Dekker's career was a rapid one for a young man of twenty-two without much schooling and without much specific training.

His stay at Natal was an unhappy one, and it began ominously with his proa being wrecked in the roadstead, so that he arrived swimming. Natal was a small place, and his functions there were manifold: he was head of police, judge, registrar of births, deaths and marriages, postmaster, manager of the salt and rice stores, collector of taxes, auctioneer and a few other things. Small though the place was, this cumulation of functions made bookkeeping complicated, particularly for a man who was anything but a born bookkeeper. Things did go wrong, and in 1843 he was suspended by the Governor, Michiels, because of irregularities in his bookkeeping and suspected fraud. The suspicion was that he had embezzled about 2,000 guilders. He was suspended, and his salary was stopped while his case was investigated. This situation lasted for about a year, probably the worst year of his life, during which he had no income and was reduced to absolute poverty. When the final verdict came, it was found that he had made a mistake but had in no way been dishonest. He was rehabilitated and appointed, in a temporary capacity, to bring order to the administration of an Assistant Resident in Java who had become an alcoholic. Dekker, bad bookkeeper though he may have been, seems to have been a good administrator otherwise, for when his task was finished he received a magnificent testimonial. After that he held posts in the administration in various places. In the meantime he had married Everdine, Baroness van Wijnbergen. Together they went to Poerworedjo, his next post, then to Menado and to Amboina. There is not a great deal to say about his service in those places because we do not know a great deal about it. The most important thing we know is that the official reports mentioned him as a very capable, industrious and intelligent civil servant, but with a rather

3

too independent mind and with a streak of eccentricity. On the whole, he was a man of whom much was expected, not only by himself but also by his superiors.

After his service in Amboina he was entitled to two years of European leave, and in 1852 he left for Holland. If all the stories about his leave are true, he must have had a very hectic time, full of adventures, festivities and excursions to casinos where he lost all his money and fell heavily into debt, in spite of what he regarded as an infallible system of playing roulette. He did not want to go back to Indonesia before he had recovered his financial losses, either by bringing off a big coup at roulette or by clearing up the mysterious case of his wife's lost millions. He managed to get an extension of his leave of more than a year but did not succeed in either of his enterprises. Finally he had to go back and arrived in Jakarta in the second half of 1855. A few months later, in January 1856, he was appointed Assistant Resident of Lebak, in west Java, where he arrived at the end of that month.

His appointment at Lebak was an unusual one, as it was made over the heads of the Council of the Indies, which always drew up recommendations for such appointments. Dekker was appointed by the Governor-General personally, without regard to the recommendation of the Council. The Governor-General, Mr Duymaer van Twist, knew Dekker personally and had been impressed by him because of his interest in the welfare of the Indonesian population. It was an unusual appointment and also an important one, for Lebak was known as a difficult district: it was poor, and it was known that the population was oppressed by one of the native princes, although this had not officially been proved. Dekker's predecessor knew it and had been busy collecting evidence in order to lodge an official complaint against this prince, the Regent, who seemed to be the main culprit. Dekker's predecessor in Lebak, Mr Carolus—known as Slotering in the novel—had not been able to bring the case officially before the administration, as he had died before he had finished his investigations. But he had talked about it to the Resident, Mr Brest van Kempen—who in the book appears as Slymering—and had apparently received no worthwhile support from him. Such was the situation in which Dekker arrived, and this was also the situation in which the series of events which form the body of *Max Havelaar* were to take place.

When Dekker arrived in Lebak, he was under the impression that he was being sent there by the Governor-General personally in order to carry out a special mission: that is, to put things right, to remove the oppression

4

from which the population suffered. He arrived in Lebak with the romantic-quixotic feeling of being the chosen protector of the poor. He felt that action was expected of him, and that if he did not act, he would betray the Governor-General's confidence. So he carried on from where Carolus had left off and began investigations into the abuses of power of which he suspected the Regent. He had collected some evidence when he heard from Mrs Carolus that she was convinced that her husband had not died a natural death but had been poisoned by order of the Regent. These things together—the evidence that he had found in Carolus's files, the evidence that he had collected himself, the suspicion that Carolus had been poisoned and the fear of being next on the Regent's list and being poisoned himself—led Dekker to bring a charge against the Regent exactly one month after he had arrived in Lebak. In view of this short period, the Resident was of the opinion that the charge was hasty and ill-considered, and he asked Dekker to withdraw it. Dekker refused, and when it was clear to him that he would not get any support from the Resident, he went over his head and addressed himself to the Governor-General. This was a very unusual thing to do, but Dekker must have reasoned that he stood in a special relationship to the Governor-General. He knew him; he was his protégé to a certain extent; he had been appointed by the Governor-General in a way which ran contrary to tradition; and he thought that he could approach the Governor-General in a similarly unconventional way. He also felt that the Governor-General would agree with his point of view and would support him against the weakness of the Resident. But there he was entirely wrong. He received no support—on the contrary, he was sharply rebuked for his actions. The Council of the Indies recommended his dismissal, but the Governor-General softened the blow, relieved him of his functions at Lebak and transferred him to another district. After some hesitation Dekker then handed in his resignation. It seems, from the letters that we have left, that he was inclined at first to accept the transfer when he received notice of it. But with the second mail delivery of that same day he received the covering letter of the Governor-General, in which he was severely taken to task for his 'undue haste and lack of cautiousness' and in which the Governor-General expressed his doubts as to whether Dekker was really fit to hold a position in the administration. When Dekker received that letter, he wrote his letter of resignation, deeply shocked, apparently, for the draft of his letter which has been preserved shows a nervous and hurried handwriting, quite unlike his usual style. Five days later he received word that his resignation had been accepted, and a fortnight after that he left Lebak for Jakarta. All in all he had been there for just under three months.

But Dekker did not really regard his resignation as final. He wrote a letter to the Governor-General requesting an audience. In that letter he asked for an opportunity to explain and justify his actions. To this letter he received a negative reply. The Governor-General was preparing to go back to Holland, was busy and could not receive him. Dekker tried again, this time through the Governor-General's secretary, whom he knew. He was then given to understand that the Governor-General was suffering from a boil on his foot and that he could not receive him. Dekker tried once more and was told that the Governor-General was busy and could not receive him. Finally, on the eve of the Governor-General's departure, Dekker wrote him a passionate letter, bitter with indignation and despair, in which he told him, among other things, that there was blood on the savings which he was taking home. If Dekker had thought that this type of approach would bring the Governor-General round, and that he could shock him into sympathy for his case, he was as wrong as he had been before. For there was no reply, and the next morning Duymaer van Twist sailed home. This last letter of Dekker was a literary work of art rather than a tactful request for an audience; Duymaer van Twist, after all, was not a literary critic and was used to being addressed in different terms. But, quite apart from this last letter, the fact remains that Duymaer van Twist repeatedly refused Dekker a chance to explain what had happened, repeatedly denied a hearing to Dekker, whom he had appointed himself, whom he himself had singled out for this particular post and whom he now let down and abandoned completely. Even those who criticize Dekker for his actions in Lebak will have to concede that Duymaer van Twist showed distinct signs of moral cowardice when he chose to ignore Dekker in May 1856.

After the Governor-General had left, Dekker stayed for another year in Java, trying to find a job, making one plan after the other, thinking about starting a business or settling on a plantation, but all without any success. Then he decided to go back to Europe. He travelled around, through France and Germany. We do not know much about this period of his life, but he seems to have had as hectic a time as during his European leave. There is the story of Eugénie, for example. Dekker bought her freedom and released her from the brothel to which she was tied, and she followed him for a while. When they split up, he gave her money to start a new life. Dekker went on his way, to the Casino at Homburg, where he lost everything and contracted considerable debts. The only solution which presented itself to him was to get in touch with Eugénie again and to ask her whether he could borrow his money back. In later years he would still remember with great satisfaction how generously and proudly she had paid his debts with the money that he had given her a few days before. There are more anecdotes about the time of his travels, but they are almost all we have. At last we hear that he settled in Brussels. His wife had also left Indonesia and was staying in Holland with relatives, for financial reasons. This separation between Dekker and his wife has been very fortunate for the literary historian because he wrote her a great number of letters which would otherwise not have been written and from which we can reconstruct the period of his life immediately preceding the writing of *Max Havelaar*.

For in Brussels he began to write. When I say 'began to write', I actually give the wrong impression, for he had written before. During the time of his suspension in Sumatra he had written a play. At another time, earlier on, he had written a fictional diary. He had written quite a few poems and, furthermore, he had always been a great letter-writer. He had often toyed with the idea of becoming an author, and during his European leave he had shown his play to a publisher and had asked him whether he had the makings of a writer. The reply had not been particularly encouraging at the time, but now, in Brussels, he began to rewrite his play, with the firm intention of having it performed and published. Then, in the same letter in which he reports to his wife that the play is finished, copied out and bound, he also says, for the first time, that he is writing a book. 'For many days,' he says, 'I have been writing a thing that will perhaps be as much as three volumes. It is strange how often during this work I change my opinion of it. There are moments when I am very satisfied with it, and then again it seems only worth tearing up. I think I have about a hundred pages of print ready. But it is a pity that I do not know myself whether my work has any value. Often it seems so insignificant to me, and then again it doesn't.' This feeling of uncertainty about the value of what he was writing was to remain with him for a long time. He kept his wife informed of all his ups and downs, of his hope and belief that this book would help them out of their misery, that the king would give him justice (for he was going to dedicate it to the king), of his fear that it was worthless. He told her of the circumstances in which he was writing, of his fight against starvation, cold and lice. There were days, he wrote, when he worked very quickly, but on other days he could not write one page. That last statement is surprising, for when one pieces together the evidence that we have, it appears that he wrote the book within four weeks, which works out at an average of at least fifteen pages of print a day. An average! If there were days in which he did not write, there must have been others in which he wrote much more than fifteen pages, which is a great deal indeed. Some critics have said that the greater part of the book had been written earlier, and that when he was working at it in Brussels, he was only putting it together, but they have not been able to produce any worthwhile evidence for this claim. On 13 October 1859 Dekker wrote triumphantly to his wife: 'Darling, dearest, my book is finished, my book is finished!' Then he had to find a publisher, and just as almost everything that Dekker touched turned into tragedy, the publication of the book also became near-tragedy. Through a mutual friend he got in touch with Jakob van Lennep, the celebrated novelist and a very influential man in Dutch letters. He sent the book to Van Lennep, in the hope that he might like it and might recommend it to a publisher. Van Lennep liked it very much and wrote to Dekker that he thought it 'd— beautiful, there are no other words for it'. And he would use his influence to get it published, just as he had done for several other Dutch writers.

The strange thing now is that while Dekker was asking Van Lennep's help for the publication, he was at the same time hoping that the book would *not* be published. He was hoping to be offered a position in the colonial administration which would rehabilitate him, which would 'crown a principle', as he called it, and which would remove the necessity to publish the book. For the book had been written with a double purpose, as he had said before: improvement in the position of the Javanese and rehabilitation for himself, and he had never made any bones about this second purpose. So he asked Van Lennep to pass the book on to the Minister for the Colonies to see what he had to say about it, and to see whether any offer would be forthcoming. In the meantime he formulated for himself the following four conditions. '1. Residency in Java. Particularly Passaroeang, in order to pay my debts. 2. Recognition of years of service, for my superannuation. 3. A liberal advance. 4. Knighthood (*Nederlandse Leeuw*).' If those four conditions were fulfilled, he would not publish the book.

'That is blackmail,' says one critic. 'Most disappointing,' says another. 'Quite right,' says a third. 'That's the way to deal with them.' To my mind, all three reactions are wrong. This was not the way to deal with them, as the outcome showed. But it was not blackmail either. One hardly associates blackmail with the publication of something that the would-be blackmailer has written himself. He had written the book to obtain justice; if he could obtain justice on the basis of the manuscript, by what moral code was he bound to publish it? And 'disappointing'? Only to those who have made a demi-god out of Multatuli, and who cannot see him as the man he was, with weaknesses and inconsistencies, as a man who scorned society and at the same time craved its recognition, with all the complexity of motives which goes with this situation. The fact that he asked so much suggests to me that he was only half-serious about it. With the other half of his mind he must have realized that those claims would never be granted. And he did not really want them to be granted, for he wanted to be an author so badly that he would give up the idea only at the price of those four points, which would mean rehabilitation, honour and security for the rest of his life. His motives in drawing up these conditions were complex, and I believe that awareness of this complexity is the only key to the understanding of Dekker's personality.

However, nothing came of it. The Minister for the Colonies refused to re-appoint him in Indonesia but offered him an 'honourable, independent and lucrative' position in the West Indies, which Dekker indignantly refused. So the book was to be published. Van Lennep had his contacts and found a publisher for it. But Van Lennep, who combined his literary pursuits with an active political life, found himself in a dilemma. On the one hand, he had great admiration for the book and its author; on the other hand, he feared political repercussions. He wanted to publish it, but at the same time he wanted to soften the blow that it was going to deal to the Government. To be able to do that, he first pilfered the copyright of the book from Dekker in a very underhand way. Then he changed the book in many places, left out place names and dates to make it seem less realistic, toned down expressions and rewrote several passages. Furthermore, whereas he had at first agreed with Dekker that it would be published in a cheap, large edition and that a great many copies of the edition would be reserved for Indonesia, he now had it published in a limited edition, at the high price of four guilders, and saw to it that only a few copies were sent to Indonesia. Dekker took Van Lennep to court for this, but lost, appealed and lost again, and it was several years before he got the copyright back.

The birth of the book had been a painful one but, once published, its success was enormous. This success, in 1860, can, of course, be explained to a certain extent by the topical nature of its subject-matter. But that does not explain why the book lasted. It was, moreover, a novel with a message, and those are the ones which date most quickly. And, one could add, nineteenth-century disputes about points of colonial policy appear to us particularly dated. If the book were only a novel of purpose, or if the author had done nothing but grind his axe in public, then, I think, the book would have been forgotten a long time ago. But it was more than just a case history of a civil servant who was disappointed with his Government, more also than an indictment of Dutch colonial policy of the 1850s. The book is still read because it is a literary masterpiece of the first order, although several critics have had reservations. They miss a unity in it; they call it a medley, a medley of fascinating writing, but a medley. D. H. Lawrence, in his Introduction to the American edition of 1927, made the same criticism: 'As far as composition goes,' he says, 'it is the greatest mess possible.' On the face of it, this criticism does not seem unjustified. The book certainly appears to be a medley of situations and characters. It is set alternately in Java and Holland, in Lebak and Amsterdam. For a long time the author does not seem to be able to make up his mind as to who is going to be his main character: from the title we should have said Max Havelaar; in the first four chapters we are led to believe that it will be Droogstoppel, the Amsterdam coffee-broker; then we think for a while that it may be Scarfman (Sjaalman in the original), the down-and-out ex-colonial; and it is not until the sixth chapter that we realize that it must be Havelaar after all, the new Assistant Resident of Lebak. Apart from all this, there is a great variation of styles, ranging from everyday colloquial to the heights of biblical parable style, from the dry officialese of the documents and letters to the emotional outburst at the end of the book, from the matter-of-fact style of the historical surveys to the sentimental poetry which appears every now and then in the book. There is more, but this is enough to suggest that there seems to be some justification in the criticism that the book lacks unity and that the composition is 'messy'. Actually, Dekker himself got in first, when he, obviously to cut the ground from under future critics' feet, introduced an imaginary critic in one of the last pages of his book and made him say: 'The book is chaotic . . . disjointed . . . striving for effect . . . the style is bad . . . the writer lacks skill . . . no talent . . . no method . . .'

And yet, when one has a closer look, there appears to be far more method than one had thought at first glance. The use of the various styles proves to be clearly functional and an essential factor in the characterization. It becomes clear that Droogstoppel characterizes himself by what he says and how he says it, and the same applies to Havelaar, to Scarfman, to Blatherer (Wawelaar in the original), to Slymering, etc. On the whole, Dekker does not describe his characters but makes them characterize themselves. The author remains in the background when he presents his characters. This makes his intrusions much more effective and enables him to produce a tremendous impact at the end of the book, when he, as the author, suddenly appears on the scene and kicks his characters off the stage one by one, to finish the book himself.

After close reading it also becomes clear that there are certain elements in the book which hold it together, which link up the various scenes and put them in perspective, so that some apparently disconnected scenes are not at variance from the point of view of composition but become mutually explanatory. An example of this is to be found in the approach to Max Havelaar and the Rev. Blatherer, two characters who apparently have nothing in common. But both make a speech in the book: the Rev. Blatherer preaches a sermon; Havelaar gives his famous address to the Heads of Lebak. The text of the preacher's sermon is 'God's love as apparent from his wrath against the unbelieving'. This love turns out to be nothing but hatred; it is shown only in terms of damnation and hell and then disappears entirely in the grand climax, in which a graphic description is given of what hell will be like for the unbelieving Indonesians. The tenor of Havelaar's address is also love, love for one's neighbour, which Havelaar sees as the only possible basis for a mutual understanding. Thus there is a parallel between the two speeches, and this parallel exists also in the language which is used by both speakers. Blatherer's language is biblical, and so is Havelaar's but with a difference. The sermon is constructed almost entirely of biblical clichés; Havelaar's address has a biblical flavour, but nearly all his phrases and images are original—they are reminiscent of biblical images but are not derived from the Bible. When one reads the sermon after Havelaar's speech, one is reminded of the speech because of similarities of theme and language, and one realizes then that Blatherer's sermon is a perversion of Havelaar's address. This has the effect of setting off Havelaar's speech, of giving it an extra dimension of meaning. And just as the sermon perverts Havelaar's address, so the preacher's name perverts the name of Havelaar. In the original the names Wawelaar and Havelaar are very close, the only differences being the initial consonant and the middle 'w' instead of the 'v'. But Wawelaar is derived from the verb *wawelen*, meaning 'to twaddle', so that he is introduced to us as the Rev. Blatherer. The preacher, therefore, in his name, in what he

11

says and in the way he says it, is presented as a perversion of Havelaar. When one realizes this, he ceases to be merely a caricature but has an additional function, that of placing the figure of Havelaar in clearer perspective.

Similar treatment is given to Droogstoppel. Droogstoppel, of course, is a recognized caricature, probably the best-known in Dutch literature. At first he is presented to us as nothing but a caricature. His name, Droogstoppel (Drystubble or Dry-as-dust), indicates this, as does his patriotic-sounding Christian name Batavus, which, to my knowledge, is not really a personal name at all and which contributes to making him into a type. Droogstoppel characterizes himself right at the beginning of the book as the worst possible philistine, as callous, heartless, hypocritical, narrow-minded and unshakeable in his prejudices. There are two principles which guide his life, he always says, and they are devotion to his work and devotion to the truth. But, later on in the book, we find that those are also the principles which guide Havelaar. Their principles are the same, but Droogstoppel perverts Havelaar's idealism, as Blatherer the preacher does. Droogstoppel debases Havelaar's ideals to an extremely pedestrian level; the preacher debases them in a religious context. In the novel these three characters are linked, as are the situations in which they appear, which are presented in such a way as to put one another in perspective. The question of whether this was done on purpose or by intuition is immaterial. Only the effect counts. And the effect is to give the book coherence, so that instead of being a rambling novel, it appears as a very well-constructed unity. Because of this firm construction (beneath its chaotic appearance) I have no hesitation in calling this novel a masterpiece. There is more, of course, to warrant this judgement. I could mention the humour of the book, the sarcasm and satire that one finds in it, or the beauty of the descriptive passages, or the lyricism of the 'Saidjah en Adinda' story, or the masterly portrayal of Havelaar who, though overdrawn and slightly larger than life, yet remains entirely convincing.

At this stage one should consider the actual effect of the book. To quote a speaker in the House of Parliament shortly after its publication, 'It sent a shiver through the country.' When he said that he was referring not to the literary quality of the book but to the shock that the Dutch reading public received when it heard of the state of affairs in the colonies. The book was discussed in Parliament, and questions were asked there. There is no doubt that it did have an influence on colonial policy. The main object of Dekker's criticism was the so-called *Kultuurstelsel* (Culture System), whereby it was compulsory to grow certain products prescribed by the Government. This Culture System, which dated from 1830, had been under heavy fire for some time when Dekker published his book, but the opponents of the system had not yet achieved any results. Dekker's book gave them a mighty weapon, which they used to advantage, so that after 1860 we see the gradual abolition of the Culture System: in 1862, two years after *Max Havelaar*, it was abolished for the cultivation of pepper, in 1863 for cloves and nutmeg, in 1865 for tea, in 1866 for tobacco, and so on. I do not want to say that *Max Havelaar* was responsible for the abolition of the Culture System—when the book was published, the system had had its day and would have disappeared sooner or later, even without *Max Havelaar*—but the book certainly deserves the credit of having hastened it. Perhaps more important was the fact that the book, through the effect it had on many future colonial civil servants, created an atmosphere in which a new colonial policy could develop.

So, looking back on the 1860s, one would be inclined to say, with a final note of optimism, that everything had turned out well and that Dekker had every reason to be satisfied: his first book was hailed by most critics as a masterpiece; from an unknown he had overnight become Holland's best-known writer; and even the politicians were taking notice of his ideas. For a while, overwhelmed by all the attention which he received, he basked in the sun of his success. But it was of short duration. The second object of his dual-purpose novel was never attained: he was not rehabilitated, and he was never offered re-appointment. Shortly after his resignation the Government held an official inquiry into the situation at Lebak, found that Dekker's allegations had been true, but did not accept him back into the administration. Nor was he offered re-appointment after the publication of the book. Dekker was never able to resign himself to this. He saw it as the greatest possible injustice. It continued to rankle in his mind, and it coloured every page of the thousands which he wrote after *Max Havelaar*.

MAX HAVELAAR

TO THE REVERED MEMORY OF
EVERDINE HUBERTE, BARONESS VAN WIJNBERGEN
FAITHFUL WIFE, HEROIC, LOVING MOTHER,
NOBLE WOMAN

'I have often heard the wives of poets pitied; and undoubtedly, they cannot have too many good qualities if they are to fill that difficult post in life with dignity. The rarest collection of excellences is no more than is strictly necessary, and is not even always sufficient, for common happiness. To have the Muse playing gooseberry during all your most intimate conversations; to take in your arms and cherish the poet you have for a husband when he comes back to you harrowed by the disappointments of his task; or else to see him fly off in pursuit of his chimera ... these are everyday occurrences for a poet's wife. But the chapter of hardships can also be followed by that of rewards—the hour of laurels won by the sweat of his genius, and which he lays reverently at the feet of the woman he lawfully loves, in the lap of the Antigone who acts as guide to the blind wanderer through this world.

For ... make no mistake: nearly all Homer's grandsons are more or less blind, in their way. They see what we do not see; their gaze pierces higher and deeper than ours; but they cannot see the homely highroad which is straight in front of them, and they might stumble and come to grief over the merest pebble if they had no support in plodding through these valleys of prose in which the lines of human life are laid.'

(HENRY DE PÈNE)[1]

COURT OFFICER. My Lord, this is the man who murdered *Babbie*.

JUDGE. That man must hang. How did he do it?

COURT OFFICER. He cut her up in little bits and pickled her.

JUDGE. That was very wrong of him ... he must be hanged.

LOTHARIO. My Lord, I haven't murdered *Babbie*! I have fed her and clothed her and looked after her ... I can produce witnesses to testify that I am a good man, and no murderer.

JUDGE. You must hang! You aggravate your crime by conceit. It's not seemly for a person who is ... accused of something to consider himself a good man.

LOTHARIO. But, my Lord, I have witnesses to confirm it. And since I am accused of murder ...

JUDGE. You must hang! You've cut *Babbie* up, pickled her, and you are self-satisfied ... three capital offences! ... Who are *you*, my good woman?

WOMAN. I am *Babbie* ...

LOTHARIO. Thank God! My Lord, you can see I haven't murdered her!

JUDGE. Hm ... aye ... perhaps! But what about the pickling?

BABBIE. No, my Lord, he hasn't pickled me. On the contrary, he has been very kind to me. He is a noble man!

LOTHARIO. You hear, my Lord, she says I am a good man.

JUDGE. Hm ... so the *third* charge stands. Officer, take this man away, he must hang. He is guilty of conceit. Recorder, cite in the preamble the judgment of *Lessing's* Patriarch ...

(Unpublished play)[2]

I am a coffee broker, and I live at No. 37 Lauriergracht,⁴ Amsterdam. I am not in the habit of writing novels or things of that sort, and so I have been a long time making up my mind to buy a few extra reams of paper and start on the work which you, dear reader, have just taken up, and which you must read if you are a coffee broker, or if you are anything else. Not only have I never written anything that resembled a novel, I don't even like reading such things, because I'm a businessman. For years I've been asking myself what is the use of them, and I am amazed at the impudence with which a poet or story-teller dares to palm off on you something that never happened, and usually never *could* happen. If I, in *my* line—I am a coffee broker, and I live at 37 Lauriergracht—gave a statement to a principal—a principal's someone who sells coffee—which contained only a small portion of the untruths that form the greater part of all poems and novels, he would transfer his business to Busselinck & Waterman at once. They're coffee brokers too, but you don't need to know their address. So, then ... I take good care not to write any novels, or make any other false statements. And I may say I have always noticed that people who go in for such things generally come to a bad end. I am forty-three years old, I've been on 'Change for twenty years, so I can come forward if anyone's called for who has experience. I've seen a good many firms go down! And usually, when I looked for the reasons, it seemed to me that they had to be sought in the wrong course most of the people had taken in their youth.

Truth and *common sense*—that's what I say, and I'm sticking to it. Naturally, I make an exception for *Holy Scripture*. The trouble starts as far back as Van Alphen,⁵ and in his very first line, the one about those 'dear little mites'. What on earth made that old gentleman want to pass himself off as an adorer of my little sister Gertie, who had sore eyes, or of my brother Gerard, who was always picking his nose? And yet he says: 'he sang those little verses, urged by *love.*' As a child, I often thought: 'My good man, I should like to meet you, and if you refused me the marbles I asked for, or wouldn't give me my full name—I'm called *Batavus*—in pastry letters, I'd pronounce you a liar.' But I never saw Van Alphen. He was already dead, I believe, when he told us that my father was my best friend—I was fonder of Paulie Winser, who lived next door to us in Batavierstraat[6]—and that my little dog was so grateful. We ... never kept any dogs, because they are so dirty.

Nothing but lies! And that's how education goes on. 'Your new little sister came from the vegetable-woman in a big cabbage.' 'All Dutchmen are brave and magnanimous.' 'The Romans were only too glad the Batavi spared their lives.' 'The Bey of Tunis always got the gripes when he heard the Dutch flag flapping.' 'The Duke of Alva was a monster.' 'The low tide in ... 1672, I believe ... lasted a little longer than usual specially to protect Holland.' Lies! Holland has remained *Holland* because our old folk attended to their business, and because they had the true faith. That's all there is to it!

And later on we're told more lies. 'A young girl is an angel.' Whoever first discovered that never had any sisters. 'Love is bliss.' One flies with some object or other 'to the end of the earth.' The earth has no ends, and that love they talk about is nonsense, too. No one can say I don't live decently with my wife—she is a daughter of Last & Co., coffee brokers—no one can find fault with anything in our marriage. I am a member of 'Artis',[7] she has a shawl which cost ninety-two guilders, and yet between *us* there's never been any talk of such an idiotic sort of love, that won't rest till it lives at the end of the earth. When we got married, we took a little trip to The Hague—she bought flannel there, and made vests out of it, which I still wear—and farther into the world than that, love never drove us. So: it's all nonsense and lies!

And is *my* marriage, now, less happy than that of people who fret themselves into a decline for love, or tear their hair out by the roots? And do you think my household is any less well run than it would be if I'd told my sweetheart in *verse* that I wanted to marry her, seventeen years ago? Nonsense! And yet I could have done so just as well as anybody else, because versifying is only a trade like any other, and an easy one at that—certainly less difficult than ivory-turning. Otherwise, how would crackers with rhyming mottoes in 'em be so cheap? ... Frits calls them 'bonbons', I don't know why ... But just ask the price of a set of billiard balls!

Mind you, I've no objection to verses in themselves. If you want words to form fours, it's all right with me! But don't say anything that isn't true. '*The air is raw, the clock strikes four.*' I'll let that pass, if it really *is* raw, and if it really *is* four o'clock. But if it's a quarter to three, then I, who don't range my words in line, will say: '*The air is raw, and it is a quarter to three.*' But the versifier is bound to four o'clock by the *rawness* of the first line. For him, it has to be exactly four o'clock, or else the air mustn't be raw. And so he starts tampering with the truth. Either the weather has to be changed, or the time. And in that case, one of the two is false.

And it is not only verses that tempt young people into untruthfulness. Just go to the theatre, and listen to all the lies that are served up there. The hero of the piece is pulled out of the water by someone who's on the point of going bankrupt. For this, he gives him half his fortune. That *can't* be true. A short time ago, on Prinsengracht, when my hat was blowed—Frits says: 'was blown'—into the canal, I gave a couple of stivers to the man who brought it back to me, and he was quite satisfied. I'm well aware I should have had to give him more if he had fished *me* out of the water, but certainly not half my fortune, because it's obvious that, in that way, you only have to fall into the water twice to be reduced to beggary. And the worst thing about such shows on the stage is that the public gets so accustomed to all these untruths that they admire them and applaud them. I should just like to throw the whole pit into the water, to see which of them had honestly meant his applause. I am a man who loves truth; and I warn whoever it may concern that I won't pay such high salvage to anyone who fishes *my* person out of the water. Those not satisfied with less may leave me where I am.

Only on Sunday I'd be prepared to give a little more, though, because then I wear my braided gold watch-chain and a different coat.

Yes, that same stage corrupts many people—more, even, than the novels do. Seeing is believing! With a little tinsel, and lace cut out of paper, it all looks so very alluring. For children, I mean, and for persons who aren't in business. Even when those actor-people want to represent poverty, the picture they give of it is always dishonest. A girl whose father's gone smash works to support the family. All well and good. You see her sitting there, sewing, knitting, or embroidering. But just you count the stitches she makes, in the course of a whole act. She talks, she sighs, she runs to the window, she does everything but work. The family that can live from *her* labour doesn't need much. That girl is, of course, the heroine. She's thrown several seducers down the stairs, she never leaves off crying 'Oh Mother, Mother!', and so she represents virtue. What kind of virtue is that, which takes a whole year to make a pair of woollen stockings? Doesn't all this give false ideas of virtue, and of *'working for a living'*? All nonsense and lies!

Then her first love—he used to be a copying clerk, but now he's rolling in money—suddenly comes back, and marries her. More lies. A man with money doesn't marry a girl from a firm which has gone bust. And if you think that might pass muster on the stage as an exception, I still stick to what I say, that in that way the feeling for truth gets blunted among the people, who take the exception for the rule, and that public morality is sapped by accustoming them to applauding something on the *stage* which, in the *world*, every respectable broker or businessman regards as ridiculous lunacy. When *I* married there were thirteen of us in the office of my father-in-law—Last & Co.—and there was plenty doing, I can tell you!

And still more lies on the stage. When the hero goes off to save his country, with his stiff mountebank's step, why does the double door at the back always open for him of its own accord?

And again ... how can a person talking in verse foresee what answer the other has to give, so that he can make rhyming easy for him? When the General says to the Princess: '*Madam, to close the gates your enemies have dared,*' how can he know in advance that she will say: '*To arms then, undismayed, and let the sword be bared*'? For just suppose that, hearing that the gates were closed, she replied that in that case she would wait a while until they were opened again, or would come back another time, what would become of metre and rhyme? So isn't it acting an arrant lie, when the General looks in-quiringly at the Princess, to learn what she intends to do now that the gates are closed? And again: suppose the good lady had felt more like retiring to bed for the night, instead of baring something? Nothing but lies, I tell you!

And then, this business about virtue rewarded! Oh, oh, oh! I've been a coffee broker for seventeen years—37 Lauriergracht—so I've seen quite a bit in my time; but I can't help always getting frightful-ly annoyed when I see God's precious truth so shamefully distorted. Virtue rewarded? If it was, wouldn't that make virtue an article of commerce? Things just aren't *like* that in the world, and it's a good thing they're not. For what merit would there be in virtue if it was rewarded? So why do people have to invent such infamous lies?

Take, for instance, Luke, our warehouseman, who was already working with the father of Last & Co. (the firm was Last & Meyer then, but the Meyers are out of it). *He* was what I would call a virtu-ous man. Never a bean was short; he went regularly to church; and he didn't drink. When my father-in-law was in the country, at Drie-bergen,[8] Luke looked after the house, the cash, everything. One day the Bank gave him seventeen guilders too much, and he took them back. Now he's old and rheumatic, and can't work any more. So now he starves, for we do a deal of business, and we need young people. Well, then ... I consider Luke *very* virtuous; but is he re-warded? Does any prince come along to give him diamonds, or a fairy to butter his bread? Not on your life! He is poor, and he stays poor, and that is as it should be. *I* can't help him—we need *young* people, since we do so much business—but supposing I could, where would his virtue be if he could have an easy time in his old age? Then every warehouseman would become virtuous, and everyone else too, which can't be God's intention, because in that case no special reward could remain for the good in the hereafter. But on the stage they twist that around ... all lies, abominable lies!

I'm virtuous myself, but do I ask a reward for it? If my business flourishes—and it does ... if my wife and children are healthy, so that I have no bother with doctors and apothecaries ... if I can put something by, year after year, for my old age ... if Frits grows up a smart boy, so that he can take my place later on, when I retire to Driebergen ... then, you see, I shall be quite content. But all this follows naturally from the circumstances, and because I attend to my business. For my virtue I claim nothing: virtue is its own reward!

And, the fact that I *am* virtuous can be seen from my love of truth. That is my strongest characteristic, after my devotion to the Faith. And I should like you to be convinced of this, reader, because it is my excuse for writing this book.

A second trait of mine, which is as strong in me as my love of truth, is my passion for my profession. I am, let me say, a coffee broker, 37 Lauriergracht. Well then, reader, it is my unimpeachable love of truth, and my enthusiasm for business, that you have to thank for these pages. I'll tell you how it came about. But since, for the moment, I must take leave of you—I have to go to the Coffee Exchange—I invite you to partake of a second chapter presently. So *au revoir!*

Oh, wait a bit, be so kind as to put this in your pocket ... oh, I assure you, my dear Sir, it's no trouble ... and you never know, it may come in handy ... ah, here it is: my card! That 'Co.' is me, since the Meyers have been out ... old Last is my father-in-law.

> LAST & CO.
> *COFFEE BROKERS*
> 37 Lauriergracht

Things were slack on 'Change, but the spring auction will no doubt put matters right. You mustn't think there's nothing doing with us! With Busselinck & Waterman, things are even slacker. It's a queer world. You see a thing or two when you've been on 'Change some twenty years. Just imagine, they tried—Busselinck & Waterman, I mean—to take Ludwig Stern off me. Since I don't know whether you're familiar with the Coffee Exchange, I'd better tell you that Stern is a first-class coffee firm in Hamburg, who've always been served by Last & Co. By pure chance I found out about it ... I mean, about Busselinck & Waterman's undercutting. They offered to drop a quarter of a per cent of the brokerage—scabs, that's what they are, nothing else!—and now see what I did to knock *that* on the head. Anyone else in my place might have written and told Ludwig Stern that he would drop something too, and that he hoped for consideration in view of the long services of Last & Co., etc., etc. ... I've calculated that in the last fifty years or so our firm has made £40,000 out of Stern. The connection dates from the time of Napoleon's Continental System, when we smuggled goods in from the colonies via Heligoland. Yes ... who can tell what anyone else might have written? But no, you can say what you like, I don't undercut. I went to 'Poland',[9] called for pen and paper, and I wrote:

That the great expansion which our business had undergone recently, especially through the many esteemed orders from Northern Germany ...

It's the absolute truth!

... that that expansion necessitated some increase in our staff.

It's the truth! Only last night our book-keeper was in the office after eleven o'clock, looking for his spectacles.

That above all the need had made itself felt for having respectable, well-brought-up young men for the German correspondence. That, admittedly, many German youths already in Amsterdam possessed the requisite qualifications, but that a self-respecting house ...

It's the truth, so help me God!

... in view of the increasing frivolity and immorality among the young, and the daily growth in the number of adventurers, and with an eye to the necessity of combining integrity of conduct with integrity in the execution of orders ...

On my oath, it's all nothing but the truth!

... that such a house—I mean Last & Co., coffee brokers, 37 Lauriergracht—could not be careful enough in the matter of the employees it engaged.

All this is the plain truth, reader! Did you know that the young German who stood at pillar 17 at the Exchange has run off with Busselinck & Waterman's daughter? And our Marie will be thirteen in September!

That I had had the honour to learn from Mr Saffeler—Saffeler travels for Stern—that the esteemed head of the firm, Mr Ludwig Stern, had a son, Mr Ernest Stern, who was desirous of being employed for some time in a Dutch house with the object of perfecting his commercial knowledge. That I, mindful of this ...

Here I repeated all that immorality stuff, and told him the tale of Busselinck & Waterman's daughter. It can't do any harm for them to know that, I should think.

... that I, mindful of this, would like nothing better than to see Mr Ernest Stern responsible for the German correspondence of our firm.

Out of delicacy, I refrained from making any reference to honorarium or salary. But I added:

That, if Mr Ernest Stern would be content to make our house—37 Lauriergracht—his home, my wife had expressed herself willing to look after him like a mother, and his linen would be mended on the premises.

This is the honest truth, for Marie darns and mends very nicely. And finally:

That in our house we serve the Lord.

He can put that in his pipe and smoke it—the Sterns are Lutherans. And I sent that letter. You'll understand that old Stern can't very well transfer his business to Busselinck & Waterman while his boy is in our office. I'm very curious to have his answer.

And now, to come back to my book. A short while ago I happened to be passing through Kalverstraat one evening, and I stopped to look in the shop of a grocer, who was busy sorting a quantity of *Java, middling, fine yellow Cheribon-type, a little broken, with sweepings,* which greatly interested me, for I always keep my eyes open. All of a sudden I caught sight of a gentleman who was standing in front of the bookshop next door, and whom I thought I knew. He seemed to recognize me too, for our eyes kept meeting. I must confess that I was too much taken up with the coffee sweepings to notice at once a thing which I did notice later, and that was that he was pretty shabbily dressed. Otherwise, I would have left matters at that. But suddenly the idea occurred to me that he might be a traveller for a German firm, in search of a trustworthy broker. He really had a touch of the German about him, and of the traveller, too. He was very fair, had blue eyes, and in his bearing and rig-out there was something that betrayed the foreigner. Instead of a decent winter coat he had a sort of scarf dangling over his shoulder—we call it a *sjaal* in Dutch, so Frits has to call it a 'shawl', which isn't even right, just to show off his English—as if he—the scarf-man, I mean—was just back from being on the road. I thought I could smell a client, so I gave him one of our cards: *Last & Co., Coffee Brokers, 37 Lauriergracht.* He held it up to the street gas lamp, and said: 'Thank you very much, but I find I've made a mistake. I thought I had the pleasure of seeing an old schoolfellow before me, but ... *Last?* That's not the name.'

'Excuse me,' I said—for I'm always polite—'I'm Mister Droogstoppel, Batavus Droogstoppel.[10] *Last & Co.* is the name of the firm, coffee brokers, 37 Lauriergr......'

'Well, Droogstoppel, have you forgotten me? Just take a good look at me!'

The more I looked at him, the more I remembered having seen him before. But, strange to say, his face had the effect of making me smell outlandish perfumes. Don't laugh, reader, presently you'll see why that was. I am sure he hadn't a drop of scent on him, and

27

yet I smelt something agreeable, something strong, something that reminded me ... I'd got it!

'Is it *you*,' I exclaimed, 'the person who rescued me from the Greek?'

'It certainly is,' he said. 'And how are *you*?'

I told him there were thirteen of us at the office and that there was a lot doing. And then I asked him how *he* was, which I afterwards regretted, for he didn't appear to be in flourishing circumstances, and I don't care for poor people, since there's usually some fault of their own at the bottom of it—the Lord would not forsake anyone who served Him faithfully. If I had said quite simply 'There are thirteen of us and ... I wish you good evening!' I should have been rid of him. But all those questions and answers made it more and more difficult—Frits says: 'the more difficult'; but I don't—more and more difficult, then, to shake him off. On the other hand, though, I must admit that if I *had* shaken him off you would not have got this book to read, because it's the result of that meeting. I like to look on the bright side of things, and people who don't do that are discontented creatures, whom I can't bear.

Yes, indeed, it was he who had rescued me from the hands of that Greek! Now, don't think I was ever captured by pirates, or had a quarrel somewhere in the Levant. I've already told you that when I got married I went with my wife to The Hague. There we saw the pictures in the Mauritshuis gallery, and bought flannel in Veenestraat. That is the only outing our business has ever permitted me to take, because there's so much doing in our firm. No, it was here in Amsterdam that he gave a Greek a bloody nose, on my account, for he always meddled in things that didn't concern him.

It was in 1833 or 34, I think, and in September, because the fair was on. Since my people intended to make a clergyman of me, I learnt Latin. Afterwards I often asked myself why you have to know Latin in order to say 'God is good!' in your own language. Enough, I went to the Latin School—they call it the *Grammar School* now—and there was a fair on ... in Amsterdam, I mean.

There were stalls in the Westermarkt, and if you are an Amsterdammer, reader, and about my age, you will remember that there was one among them which was conspicuous for the black eyes and the long plaits of a girl dressed in Greek fashion. Her father was a Greek, too—at any rate he looked like a Greek. They sold all sorts of scent.

I was just old enough to think the girl pretty, but without having the courage to speak to her. Not that I should have got very far if I had, for girls of eighteen look on a boy of sixteen as a child, and very right they are, too. Nevertheless, we boys of the Fourth always went to the Westermarkt of an evening simply to see that girl.

Now, on one of these occasions, the man who at that moment stood before me with his scarf was with us, although he was a couple of years younger than the others and so still too much of a child even to look at the Greek girl. But he was top of our class—for he *was* clever, I can't deny that—and he was fond of games, horseplay and fighting. That was why he was with us. And so, as we—there were quite ten of us—stood a fair distance away from the stall, looking at the Greek girl and debating how we should go about trying to make her acquaintance, it was decided that we should put our money together to buy something at the stall. But then the problem was to find the bold spirit who would speak to the girl. Everyone wanted to but no one dared. We cast lots, and the job fell to me. Now, I candidly admit that I don't like running risks. I'm a husband and a father, and I regard anyone who deliberately seeks danger as a fool—come to that, it's in the Scriptures, too. It is indeed a pleasure to me to notice how, in my views on danger and such-like, I have been consistent all my life, since even now I still hold exactly the same opinions about these things as I did that evening when I stood there in front of the Greek's stall, clutching the twelve stivers we had got together in my hand. But, you see, through false shame I dared not say I dared not, and besides I couldn't help going forward, for my mates hustled me, and I was soon standing in front of the stall, whether I liked it or not.

I did not see the girl, I saw nothing! Everything went green and yellow before my eyes. I began to stammer out an aorist of some verb or other ...

'*Plaît-il?*' she said.

I recovered a little, and continued:

'Μῆνιν ἄεισε, Θεά',[11] and ... that Egypt was a gift of the Nile.[12]

I am convinced I should have succeeded in getting to know her if at that moment one of my mates, out of childish mischievousness, had not given me such a shove in the back that I collided mighty roughly with the showcase-cum-counter which shut off the front of the stall to half the height of a man. I felt a grip on the scruff of my neck ... a second grip, much lower down ... I floated in the air for a moment ... and before I clearly understood what was going on I was inside the Greek's stall, and he was telling me in intelligible French that I was a *gamin*, and that he would call the police. True, I was now close to the girl, but I got no pleasure out of it. I cried, I begged for mercy, for I was terribly scared. But it didn't do a bit of good. The Greek held me by the arm, and kicked me. I looked around for my mates—only that morning we had had a great deal to do with Scaevola, who put his hand in the fire, and in their Latin compositions they'd all found that so *very* fine—oh yes! But never a one stayed behind to put his hand in the fire for *me* ...

So I thought. But, lo and behold! Suddenly my Scarfman rushed into the stall through the back door. He wasn't tall or strong, and only about thirteen years old, but he was a nimble, plucky little chap. I can still see his eyes flashing—they were usually dull—he gave the Greek a punch, and I was saved. Later on, I heard that the Greek had given him a drubbing, but because it's a firm principle of mine never to meddle with things that don't concern me, I ran away immediately. So I didn't see it.

That, then, was the reason why his features reminded me so much of scent and of how you can get into a brawl with a Greek in Amsterdam.

At subsequent fairs, whenever that man was in the Westermarkt with his stall I always sought my entertainment elsewhere.

Fond as I am of philosophical observations, I really cannot refrain from remarking, reader, how wonderfully the affairs of this world are ordered. If that girl's eyes had been less black, if her plaits had been shorter, or if someone had not knocked me against that showcase, you would not now be reading this book. So be thankful that everything happened as it did. Believe you me, whatever is, is right; and discontented people who are always complaining are no friends of mine. Take, for instance, Busselinck & Waterman ... But I must get on, my book must be finished before the spring coffee auction.

Speaking frankly—for I'm a man who loves the truth—it gave me no pleasure to see that person again. I at once realized that he was not a sound connection to have. He was very pale, and when I asked him what o'clock it was, he didn't know. Those are the sort of things a man notices, when he's been on 'Change around twenty years, and witnessed so much in his time. I've seen a good many firms go down!

I thought he would turn to the right, so my business took me to the left. But, you see, he turned left too, and so I could not avoid conversation with him. But I constantly remembered that he did not know the time, and I also noticed that his shabby jacket was buttoned right up to the chin—which is a very bad sign—and so I kept the tone of our conversation a bit non-committal. He told me he had been in the East Indies, that he was married, that he had children. I had nothing against that, but I saw nothing important in it either. We approached Kapelsteeg—as a rule, I never go through that alley, because it doesn't do for a respectable man, in my opinion; but this time I meant to turn to the right, down Kapelsteeg. I waited till we had nearly passed the wretched little street, so as to make it quite clear to the man that *his* road lay straight on, and then I said very politely ... for I am always polite, you never know how you may need somebody later:

'I was delighted to see you again, Mister ... er ... er! And ... and

'... and ... your humble servant, Sir! I have to go in here.'

Then he looked at me very queerly, and sighed, and suddenly took hold of a button on my coat ...

'*Dear* Droogstoppel,' he said, 'there's something I'd like to ask you.'

A cold shiver ran down my spine. He didn't know what o'clock it was, and there was something he wanted to ask me! Naturally, I answered that I had no time, and had to go on 'Change, although it was evening. But when you've been on 'Change for twenty years ... and a man wants to ask you something, a man who doesn't know what o'clock it is ...

I disengaged my button, saluted most politely, for I'm always polite, and ... entered Kapelsteeg, a thing I never do otherwise, because it is not respectable, and I rank respectability above everything. I hope nobody saw me.

3

Next day, when I got back from 'Change, Frits said someone had been to see me. From his description, it was the Scarf-man. How had he found me? ... of course, the card! It made me seriously think of taking my children away from school, for it's a bit too much, after twenty or thirty years, to be dogged by a schoolmate who wears a scarf instead of an overcoat and doesn't know what time it is. Anyway, I have told Frits not to go to the Westermarkt when there are any stalls there.

The day after that, I received a letter, together with a big parcel. I will let you read the letter:

'*My dear Droogstoppel!*'

I really think he might have said: '*My dear Mr Droogstoppel*'—after all, I *am* a broker.

'*I called at your house yesterday with the intention of asking you a favour. I believe you are in comfortable circumstances ...*

That's true: there are thirteen of us in the office.

... and I should like to make use of your credit, in order to carry out a project which is of great importance to me.'

From reading that, wouldn't you think it was a question of an order at the spring auction?

'*Owing to a variety of circumstances, I am at present somewhat in need of money.*'

Somewhat? He had no shirt on. That's what he calls '*somewhat*'!

'*I cannot give my dear wife all that is necessary to make life pleasant, and the education of my children, too, is not what I would wish it to be, for pecuniary reasons.*'

To make life pleasant? Education of the children? Wouldn't you think from this that he wanted to rent a box at the Opera for his wife, and send his children to boarding-school in Geneva? It was late in the year, and pretty cold ... well, to cut a long story short, he was living in a garret, and hadn't even a fire. I didn't know that when I received the letter, but I did later on when I went to see

him, and to this day I'm still annoyed by the silly tone of his ef-
fusion. Hang it, when a man's poor, he may as well say he's poor!
The poor are always with us, that's necessary in society. Provided
he doesn't beg for alms and doesn't bother anybody, I have no objection whatever to a man's being poor; but he has no right to dress
it up in fine words. Listen further:

> *'Since it is my duty to provide for the needs of those dependent on me, I*
> *have decided to make use of a talent which, I believe, has been given to me.*
> *I am a poet ...'*

Pooh! You know, reader, what I and all sensible people think about
them.

> *'... and writer. Ever since I was a child I have expressed my emotions in*
> *verse; and later, as well, I wrote down every day what went on in my soul.*
> *I feel sure that among all these writings there are some articles of value,*
> *and I am looking for a publisher for them. But that is just the difficulty.*
> *The public does not know me, and publishers, in judging work, go more by*
> *the established name of its author than by its content.'*

Just as we judge coffee by the repute of the brand. And what's
wrong in that?

> *'So, if I may assume that my work is not entirely without merit, that*
> *would naturally only be proved after its publication, and publishers ask*
> *for payment in advance of printing costs, etc. ...*

And they're quite right.

> *... which does not suit me at the moment. Since, however, I am convinced*
> *that the proceeds from my work would cover expenses, and would confi-*
> *dently pledge my word on that, I have, encouraged by our meeting the day*
> *before yesterday ...*

He calls that 'encouraged'!

> *... resolved to ask you whether you would stand surety for me with a pub-*
> *lisher for the cost of a first printing, were it only of a small volume. I*
> *leave the choice of this first sample entirely to you. In the accompanying*
> *parcel you will find many manuscripts, and from them you will see that I*
> *have thought, worked, and witnessed much, ...*

I never heard he was in business.

... and if the gift of expressing myself well is not altogether wanting in me, it will certainly not be owing to lack of impressions that I do not succeed.

In anticipation of a favourable reply, I sign myself your old school-fellow ...
And his name was written underneath. But I shall not give it, because I don't like getting a man talked about.

Dear reader, you can imagine how taken aback I was, at this sudden suggestion that I should be elevated to the position of verse-broker. I feel sure that if 'Scarfman'—I think I may as well stick to calling him that—had seen me in the daytime, he would not have addressed such a request to me. For then, gentility and respectability cannot be hidden. But it was in the evening, so I'm not unduly worried about it.

It goes without saying that I wanted to have nothing to do with this nonsense. I would have got Frits to take the parcel back, but I did not know Scarfman's address, and I heard nothing further from him. I thought he might be ill, or dead, or something.

Last week it was the Rosemeyers' turn to give the weekly party. The Rosemeyers are in sugar. Frits went there with us for the first time. He is sixteen years old, and I think it's a good thing for a youth of that age to start getting out and about in the world. Otherwise he may go to the Westermarkt, or something of the sort. Before dinner the girls had been playing the piano and singing, and during dessert they were teasing each other about something that appeared to have happened in the drawing-room while we were in the back room having a game of whist. It was something which seemed to concern Frits.

'Yes, yes, Louise,' exclaimed Betsy Rosemeyer, 'you *did* cry! Papa, Frits has made Louise cry!'

My wife said at once that if that was so Frits would not be allowed to come again. She thought he had pinched Louise, or done something else unseemly, and I was just about to put a strong word in myself, when Louise exclaimed:

'No, no! Frits has been very nice! I wish he would do it again!'

Do *what* again? He had not pinched her; he had recited something, that was it!

Of course, the lady of the house always likes to see her guests amused during dessert. It fills a void. Mrs Rosemeyer—the Rosemeyers insist on being called 'Mrs',[13] because they're in sugar and part-owners of a ship—Mrs Rosemeyer realized that what had made Louise cry would entertain us too, and asked Frits for an encore; he had gone as red as a turkeycock. I couldn't for the life of me think what he had treated them to—I knew his repertoire from A to Z: 'The Wedding of the Gods', 'The Books of the Old Testament in Rhyme', and a bit from 'The Wedding of Camacho', which boys always enjoy because there's something in it about a lavatory seat.[14] What there could be in any of those to draw tears, was a mystery to me. Young girls cry easily, though.

'Come, Frits! Oh yes, Frits! Do, Frits!' So they went on, and at last Frits began. I don't hold with deliberately keeping the reader in suspense, so I may as well say at once that before leaving home Frits and Marie had opened Scarfman's parcel and extracted from it a mass of sententiousness and sentimentality which afterwards brought no end of trouble down on my head. Yet I have to admit, reader, that this book before you also came out of that parcel, and later on I shall render proper account of this fact, for I am jealous of my reputation as a man who loves the truth and knows his business. (Our firm is *Last & Co., Coffee Brokers, 37 Lauriergracht*.)

Then Frits recited something which was a tissue of nonsense from beginning to end. No, tissue you couldn't have called it—it didn't hang together at all. A young man was writing to his mother that he had been in love, and that the girl had married someone else—and very right too, in my opinion—but that he, notwithstanding, had always loved his mother. Are these last few lines clear or not? Do you consider many more words are necessary to say that? Well ... I ate a cheese roll, then I peeled and ate two pears, and I had half finished munching a third, before Frits had done with his yarn. But Louise was blubbering again, and the ladies said it was very, very beautiful. Then Frits, who I do believe thought he had achieved something quite out of the ordinary, told us he had found the thing in that parcel from the man who wore a scarf, and I explained to the gentlemen how it came to be in my house. But I didn't say anything about the Greek girl, because Frits was there, and I didn't say anything about going down Kapelsteeg either. Everyone considered I had done right in getting shut of the fellow. You will see presently that there were other things in that parcel, but things of a more solid nature, and some of them will go into this book, because they are connected with the *Coffee Auctions of the Dutch Trading Company*.[15] For my profession's my life to me.

Later on, the publisher asked me whether I wouldn't put in here what Frits had recited. I don't mind, provided it's clearly understood that normally I never have anything to do with this sort of thing.[16] Lies and tomfoolery, from beginning to end! But I'll abstain from commenting, otherwise my book will get too long. I will only say that the rigmarole seems to have been written about 1843 in the neighbourhood of Padang, and that that's an inferior brand. Of coffee, I mean.

> Mother, far, oh far from me
> Is the land of my first years,
> Is the land of my first tears,
> Where your love and charity,
> Where your faithful mother's heart
> Lavished care upon your boy,
> Shared all with him, tears and joy,
> Prompt in healing every smart ...
> Folk might think Fate cruelly tore
> In two the bond that made us one ...
> True, I stand on a strange shore
> With myself and God, alone ...
> But yet, whatsoe'er the grief,
> Pleasure or pain I may have had,

Mother, hold to your belief
In the love of your own lad!

Scarcely twice two years ago
I was in the dear homeland,
Gazing, silent on the strand,
Into future weal and woe—
Then I summoned unto me
All the beauty there in store,
Present times' dull round forswore
For paradises soon to be ...
Then the heart in youthful pride
Boldly trod life's wilderness,
Sweeping barriers aside
And, dreaming, deemed itself in bliss ...

But the four years that have gone
Since our last fond, farewell meeting,
Swift as lightning, past as one,
Like a wraith in daylight fleeting,
Left in their mysterious race
Marks time never can efface!
Through mingled joys and injuries
I have prayed and I have thought,
I have exulted, I have fought,
Through days that seemed like centuries!
I have found and I have lost,
For life's jewel I have striven,
Still a child, by suffering riven,
Hours to me whole years have cost!

But still, Mother, oh believe me,
By our God's all-seeing eye—
Mother, Mother, yet believe me,

You dwell in my memory!
I loved a maiden. Life's whole burden,
Through that love, seemed light as air.
In my eyes she was a guerdon,
A crown of laurel waiting there,
Offered me by God's dear care.
Blissful through the spotless treasure
Given as life's aim for me
As a token of his pleasure,
I thanked Him on bended knee.
Love and religion—they were one ...
And the soul in exaltation
Rose in thanks for *her* creation,
And in prayer for *her* alone!

That love brought me carking care,
Torture broke my heart in twain—
Man cannot endure the pain
When such wounds the soft soul tear.
Fear and grief alone, in foison,
Took the place of highest pleasure,
And instead of long-sought treasure
Was my part but woe and poison.

Silent suffering was delight!
Firmly I stood, hoping madly
Against hope, fighting the fight—
For her sake I suffered gladly!
Misery by Fortune meted
Made the prize but brighter shine,
Every hardship had I greeted,
Had Fate only left her mine!

But that image, which I bore—
Loveliest in the world to me—
In my poor heart's inmost core,
As a blessing beyond fee ...
Love for her was *strange* to me!
And, although that love will stand
Till the opening of Death's door
Her to my arms shall restore
In a better Fatherland ...
Love had just *begun* to be!

What is love that must *be born*
To the love that God impresses
In the child at its own dawn,
Speechless still, amid caresses?
When in mother's breast it first,
Hardly come from mother's womb,
Finds the dew to slake its thirst,
In her eyes, first light thro' gloom?

No, no bond more tightly chains,
Be life's ocean ne'er so wild,
Than the bond that God maintains
'Twixt the mother and her child!

And a heart whose blazing fires
Were for beauty's transient gleam,
Plaiting but a crown of briars,
Not one garland for my dream—
Should *that* heart forget devotion
Of the faithful mother's heart?
And the woman's deep emotion,
Taking straight her darling's part,
Soothing me in childish grief,

Hearing my first childish cries,
Kissing the tears from my eyes,
Nurturing me with her own life?

Mother! You may not believe me;
By our God's all-seeing eye,
Mother! Still you must believe me,
You dwell in my memory!

Here am I far, oh far away
From home's abundance of fair and gay,
And the joys of youth's first spring,
Often vaunted, rich and rare,
Will not fall to me elsewhere:
The lonely heart can never sing.
Steep and thorny is my road,
Trouble bows me to the earth,
And the dead weight of my load
Kills in me all peace, joy, mirth ...
Be my tears the only witness
That so many hours of pain
Drive your son, for very sadness,
Nature's breast to seek again ...

Often, when my courage fled,
This was all but forced from me:
'Father! Give me 'mid the dead
What in life was not to be!
Father! Give me over yonder—
When I feel the kiss of death—
Father! Give me over yonder
Rest ... unknown while I drew breath!'

But that prayer found no release,
Rose not to the Lord on high ...
I did kneel on humble knees,
But the burthen of my sigh,
Was: '*Not yet, O Lord, thy bliss—*
Grant me first my mother's kiss!'

4

Before I go on, I must tell you that young Stern has arrived. He's a nice enough young fellow. He seems to be quick and capable, but I believe he's a dreamer—'*schwärmt*', as those Germans say. Marie's thirteen. His wardrobe is very neat. I have set him to work on the copybook, so that he can get some practice in Dutch style. I am curious to see how soon it will be before we get orders from Ludwig Stern. Marie is going to embroider a pair of slippers for him ... for young Stern, I mean. Busselinck & Waterman have missed the boat. A respectable broker doesn't undercut, say I!

The day after the party at the Rosemeyers', the sugar people, I called Frits and told him to bring me that parcel of Scarfman's. You must know, reader, that I am a stickler for religion and morality in my family. Well, the evening before, just after I had peeled my first pear, I could see from the face of one of the girls that there was something in that poem which was not as it should be. I hadn't listened to the thing myself, but I had noticed that Betsy crumbled her roll of bread, and that was enough for me. You will realize, reader, that you have to do with a man of the world. So I got Frits to show me that precious piece he had read last night, and I very soon found the line that had crumbled Betsy's roll. It mentions a child at the mother's breast—that can pass, I suppose—but: 'hardly come from mother's womb', you see, I didn't think that was right —talking about it, I mean—and my wife didn't think it was right either. Marie is thirteen. In our house, we don't talk about 'the new little sister coming from the vegetable-woman in a big cabbage', or 'the stork' or suchlike, but I don't think it necessary to be so blunt about it either, because I set great store by morality. Frits unfortunately already knew the thing 'outwardly' as Stern calls it, meaning by heart; but I made him promise he would never recite it again— at any rate, not before he was a member of 'Doctrina', since no young girls are allowed in that club—and then I put it away in my desk, the poem, that's to say. But after this I felt I ought to know

43

whether there wasn't anything else in that parcel which might give offence. So I started looking through the papers. I could not read them all, there were languages in them which I did not know; but suddenly my eye fell on a packet: 'Report on Coffee-growing in the Residency of Menado'.

My heart leaped up, because I am a coffee broker—*37 Laurier-gracht*—and Menado is a good brand. So, then—this Scarfman, who wrote such immoral verses, had been in coffee too! That made me look again at his parcel, with quite different eyes; and I found articles in it which, it is true, I did not entirely understand, but which showed genuine expert knowledge. There were lists, statements, calculations with figures that I couldn't make head or tail of, and everything had been worked out with such care and exactitude that, speaking frankly—for I love truth—it occurred to me that, should our third clerk drop out at some time—which is quite on the cards, he's getting old and doddery—Scarfman might very well take his place. It goes without saying that I should first have to make inquiries about his honesty, religion and respectability, for I will have no one in the office until I am certain on those points. This is a fixed principle with me, as you have seen from my letter to Ludwig Stern.

I did not want Frits to see that I was at all interested in what was in the parcel, so I sent him away. It really made my head swim when I took up one bundle of papers after another, and read the titles. Granted, there were many poems among them, but I found many useful things too, and I was amazed at the diversity of the subjects. I must admit—for I love truth—that I, who have always been in coffee, was not qualified to assess the value of all these things; but even so, the list of titles alone was remarkable enough. I have told you the story of the Greek, so you already know that in my youth I was something of a Latinist. And, although I strictly abstain from giving classical quotations in my correspondence—a thing which would be out of place in a broker's office, anyway—I could not help thinking when I saw all this: '*de omnibus aliquid, de toto nihil*',[17] or '*multa, non multum*'.[18]

But that was really more out of a kind of irritation, and of a certain urge to address this mass of learning before me with a Latin phrase, than because I genuinely meant it. For, when I looked a little further into some of the articles, I had to admit that the writer appeared quite equal to his task, and even that his reasoning was very sound.

I found dissertations and essays:

On Sanskrit *as the mother of the Germanic languages.*

On the penalties for infanticide.

On the origin of the aristocracy.

On the difference between the concepts 'infinite time' and 'eternity'.

On the theory of probabilities.

On the Book of Job. (I found something else about Job, but that was in verse.)

On protein in the atmosphere.

On Russian statecraft.

On the vowels.

On cellular prisons.

On the theories concerning the horror vacui.[19]

On the desirability of abolishing penalties for slander.

On those causes of the Dutch revolt against Spain not *arising from the desire for religious or political liberty.*

On perpetum mobile, *squaring the circle, and the square root of surds.*

On the gravity of light.

On the decline of civilization since the rise of Christianity. (What?!)

On Icelandic mythology.

On Rousseau's 'Emile'.

On civil law in commerce.

On Sirius *as the centre of a solar system.*

On import duties as ineffectual, offensive, unjust and immoral. (I never heard anything about this.)

On verse as the oldest language. (I don't believe that.)

On white ants.

On the unnaturalness of schools.

On prostitution in marriage. (A scandalous piece of work.)

On hydraulics in connection with the cultivation of rice.

On the apparent ascendancy of Western civilization.

On cadastral surveying, registration and stamp duty.

On children's books, fables and fairy tales. (I think I'll read that, because he insists on the need for truth.)

On the middleman in trade. (This doesn't appeal to me at all. I believe he wants to do away with brokers. However, I have picked it out and put it aside, because there are one or two things in it which I can use in my book.)

On death duties, one of the best taxes.

On the invention of chastity. (Don't understand this.)

On multiplication. (This title sounds quite simple, but there are a good many things in the article which had never occurred to me.)

On a certain kind of French wit, a consequence of the poverty of the French language. (Quite true, I should say. Wit and poverty ... he ought to know.)

On the connection between the novels of August Lafontaine *and phthisis.* (I'll read that, there are some books by this Lafontaine up in the attic. But he says the influence doesn't appear until the second generation. My grandfather didn't read.)

On the power of England outside Europe.

On trial by ordeal in the Middle Ages and now.

On arithmetic among the Romans.

On lack of poetry in composers of music.

On pietism, hypnotism and table-turning.

On infectious diseases.

On Moorish architecture.

On the power of prejudice, as evident from illnesses attributed to draught. (Didn't I say the list was remarkable?)

On German unity.

On longitude at sea. (I don't suppose things at sea are longer than they are on land.)

On the duties of the Government regarding public entertainments.

On the similarity between the Scottish and Frisian languages.

On prosody.

On the beauty of the women of Nîmes and Arles, and an inquiry into the colonization system of the Phoenicians.

On agricultural contracts in Java.

On the suction power of a new kind of pump.

On the legitimacy of dynasties.

On national literature in the form of Javanese rhapsodies.

On the new method of reefing.

On percussion as applied to hand grenades. (This article is dated 1847, i.e. before Orsini.)[20]

On the idea of honour.

On the Apocrypha.

On the laws of Solon, Lycurgus, Zoroaster *and* Confucius.

On parental authority.

On Shakespeare *as a historian.*

On slavery in Europe. (Don't understand what he means by this.)

On Archimedean screws.

On the sovereign right of pardon.

On the chemical constituents of Ceylon cinnamon.

On discipline aboard merchantmen.

On the opium-licence system in Java.

On regulations for the sale of poisons.

On the cutting of the Suez Canal, and its consequences.

On payment of land tax in kind.

On coffee-growing in Menado. (I have already mentioned this.)

On the partition of the Roman Empire.

On the Gemüthlichkeit *of the Germans.*

On the Scandinavian Edda.

On France's duty to herself to counterbalance England's influence in the Malay Archipelago. (This was in French, I don't know why.)

On the manufacture of vinegar.

On the veneration for Schiller *and* Goethe *in the German middle classes.*

On man's claims to happines

On the right of rebellion against oppression. (This was in the *Javanese* language. I only found out the title afterwards.)

On ministerial responsibility.

On some points in criminal law.

On the right of a people to demand that the taxes they pay shall be applied for their benefit. (This again was in *Javanese*.)

On the double A and the Greek ETA.

On the existence of an impersonal God in the hearts of men.

On style.

On a constitution for the Empire of INSULINDE.[21] (Never heard of that empire.)

On the absence of ephelcystics in our rules of grammar.

On pedantry. (I think this article was based on a good deal of expert knowledge.)

On Europe's debt to the Portuguese.

On the sounds of the forest.

On the combustibility of water. (I think he must mean *aqua fortis.*)

On the milk sea. (I've never heard of this. It seems to be something near Banda.)

On seers and prophets.

On electricity as motive power, without soft iron.

On the ebb and flow of civilization.

On epidemic corruption in national economies.

On privileged Trading Companies. (This contains various things I need for my book.)

On etymology as an aid to ethnological studies.

On the bird's-nest cliffs on the southern coast of Java.

On the place where day begins. (Can't understand this.)

On personal views as standard of responsibility in the moral world.

On gallantry towards women.

On Hebrew versification.

On the Marquis of Worcester's Century of Inventions.

On the fasting population of the island of Rotti, near Timor. (Living must be cheap there.)

On the cannibalism of the Battak and head-hunting among the Alfuros.
On lack of confidence in public morals. (I believe he wants to abolish locksmiths. I'm against it.)
On 'law' as opposed to 'rights'.
On Béranger as philosopher. (This, again, I don't understand.)
On the Malays' antipathy to the Javanese.
On the worthlessness of the teaching in the so-called universities.
On the loveless spirit of our ancestors, as manifest from their ideas of God. (An impious piece of writing!)
On the interrelation of the senses. (True enough, when I saw him I smelt attar of roses.)
On the conical root of the coffee tree. (I have put this aside for my book.)
On feeling, sensitiveness, sentimentality, SENSIBLERIE, EMPFINDELEI, *etc.*
On the confusion of mythology with religion.
On the gomuti-palm wine of the Moluccas.
On the future of Dutch trade. (It was this article that impelled me to write my book. He says there won't always be such big coffee auctions, and my profession's my life.)
On Genesis. (An infamous piece!)
On Chinese secret societies.
On drawing as the natural form of writing.
On truth in poetry. (Tell us another!)
On the unpopularity of rice mills in Java.
On the connection between poetry and the mathematical sciences.
On the Chinese shadow-shows.
On the price of Java coffee. (This I put on one side.)
On a European currency.
On irrigation of common lands.
On the influence of racial intermarriage on the mind.
On the balance of trade. (In this, he talks about premiums on bills of exchange. I put it on one side for my book.)
On the persistence of Asiatic customs. (He maintains Jesus wore a turban.)

On Malthus's theories about the ratio of population to means of subsistence.

On the original inhabitants of America.

On the piers and jetties of Batavia, Semarang and Surabaya.

On architecture as the expression of ideas.

On the relationship of the European officials to the Regents in Java. (One or two things from this are going into my book.)

On cellar-dwellings in Amsterdam.

On the power of error.

On the idleness of a Supreme Being, in view of the existence of perfect natural laws.

On the salt monopoly in Java.

On worms in the sago palm. (They eat them ... ugh!)

On Proverbs, Ecclesiastes, the Song of Solomon, and the pantuns *of the Javanese.*

On the Jus primi occupantis.[22]

On the poverty of the art of painting.

On the immorality of angling. (Whoever heard of that before?!)

On the crimes of the Europeans outside Europe.

On the weapons of the weaker animals.

On the jus talionis. (Yet another detestable paper! There was a poem in it which I know I should have thought absolutely scandalous if I had read it to the end.)[23]

And that was by no means all! Besides the poems—there were poems in several languages—I found a number of small bundles with no title on them, romances in Malay, war songs in Javanese, and Heaven knows what else! I also found letters, many of them in languages I did not know. Some were addressed to him, others had been written by him, or rather they were copies of letters written by him; yet he seemed to have some purpose in mind with these, for everything had been signed by other persons as: *Certified true copy.* In addition, there were extracts from diaries, notes and odd jottings ... some of them indeed very odd.

As I have already said, I put some of the articles on one side, since it seemed to me that they might come in handy in my profession, and my profession's my life. But I must admit I was at a loss what to do with the rest. I could not return the parcel to Scarfman, for I did not know where he lived. And it *had* been opened. I could not deny that I had looked into it, and I should not have denied that anyway, because I am a man of truth. Besides, try as I might, I could not tie it up so that it looked exactly as it had been before. And I had to admit that some of the articles, dealing with coffee, interested me, and that I wanted to make use of them. Every day I read a few pages here and there, and I became more and more—Frits says 'all the more', but I don't —more and more, I say, convinced that you have to be a coffee broker in order to find out in *this* way what goes on in the world. I am cert, in that the Rosemeyers, who are in sugar, never set eyes on anything like this in their lives.

Now I was afraid that that fellow Scarfman might suddenly appear before me again, and that he might again have something to say to me. I began to regret turning down Kapelsteeg that evening, and I realized one should never leave the straight and narrow path. Of course he had wanted to ask me for money, and to talk about his parcel. I might perhaps have given him something; and *then* if he had sent me his mass of scribble next day it would have been my lawful property. I could then have separated the wheat from the chaff, I would have kept out the items I needed for my book, and burnt the rest, or thrown it into the wastepaper basket, which I could not do now. For if Scarfman returned I should have to give the parcel up, and he, seeing that I was interested in one or two articles from his pen, would be strongly tempted to ask too much for them. Nothing gives the seller more advantage than the discovery that the buyer needs his wares. So a merchant who knows his job will do his utmost to avoid getting into such a position.

Another idea—though I have already mentioned it—which goes to show how susceptible life on 'Change may leave one to humane impressions, was this. Of late, Bastiaans—that's the third clerk, the one who is getting so old and feeble—has scarcely been in the office twenty-five days out of thirty, and when he does turn up he often works badly. As a man of probity I feel I owe it to the firm—*Last & Co.*, since the Meyers left it—to see that everyone does his work properly, and I am not at liberty to squander the firm's money from a mistaken idea of pity or from squeamishness. Such are my principles. I would sooner give this same Bastiaans three guilders out of my own pocket than go on paying him the seven hundred guilders a year which he no longer earns. I have calculated that, during the last thirty-four years, the man has enjoyed in income—both from *Last & Co.* and from *Last & Meyer*, but the Meyers are out—the amount of nearly fifteen thousand guilders, and for a simple office worker that's quite a nice little sum. There aren't many in his station in life who have as much as that. So he has nothing to complain of. I was prompted to this calculation by Scarfman's article on multiplication.

This Scarfman writes a good hand, I thought. He looked shabby, and didn't know the time … suppose I gave him Bastiaans's place? I should tell him, of course, that he would have to call me Sir, but he probably wouldn't need telling anyway, for naturally a clerk cannot address his employer by his surname; and in that way he might be settled for life. He could start on four or five hundred guilders— our Bastiaans also had to work a long time before he got up to seven hundred—and I should be doing a good deed into the bargain. Why, there was no reason why he shouldn't start on three hundred guilders —since he has never been in business before, he could look upon the first few years as 'prentice time, which is no more than reasonable, for he can't expect to put himself on the same level with people who have done a lot of work. I feel quite sure he would be satisfied with two hundred guilders.

But I wasn't easy about his record … he wore a scarf, you know. And besides, I didn't know where he lived.

A couple of days after this, young Stern and Frits went to a book auction in 'Het Wapen van Bern'. I had forbidden Frits to buy anything, but Stern, who has plenty of pocket money, came home with some rubbish or other. That's *his* business. But would you believe it, Frits told me he had seen Scarfman, who seemed to be employed at the auction. He took the books down from the shelves as they were wanted, and pushed them along the long table to the auctioneer. Frits said he looked very pale, and that a gentleman who appeared to be in charge there had sworn at him for dropping some bound volumes of *Aglaia*; I certainly think it was very clumsy of him to drop such a charming collection of fancy-work patterns for ladies to do. Marie goes halves in it with the Rosemeyers, who are in sugar. She tats from it ... from *Aglaia*, I mean. But during the row Frits heard what Scarfman earned. 'D'you think I'm going to throw away fifteen stivers a day on you?' the gentleman had said. I calculated that fifteen stivers a day makes two hundred and twenty-five guilders a year—I don't suppose Sundays and holidays count, otherwise he would have named a monthly or yearly salary. I'm quick to make up my mind—when you've been in business as long as I have, you always know at once what to do—and early next morning I was at Gaafzuiger's.[24] He was the bookseller who had held the auction. I asked for the man who had dropped the *Aglaias*.

'He's got the sack,' said Gaafzuiger. 'He was lazy, cocky and sickly.'

I bought a box of wafers in the shop, and at once decided to give our Bastiaans another chance. I could not bring myself to turn an old man out into the street just like that. Firm but, where possible, gentle—that's always been my principle. Still, I never omit to learn anything that may be useful in business, so I asked Gaafzuiger where that Scarfman fellow lived. He gave me the address, and I wrote it down.

I was constantly mulling over my book. But, since I'm a man of truth, I must frankly confess that I didn't know how to set about it. One thing was certain: the material I had found in Scarfman's parcel was very useful to coffee brokers. The only question was, how was I to sift that material and put it together aright? Every broker knows how important it is to grade the various lots of coffee properly.

But ... writing—apart from correspondence with principals—is not much in my line. And yet I felt I ought to write, because the future of the whole profession might depend on it. The information I had found in Scarfman's papers was not such that *Last & Co.* could keep it for their own sole use. If it had been, anyone can understand that I should not take the trouble to have a book printed which Busselinck & Waterman would also get to read; for the man who helps a competitor on his way is a fool. That is a fixed principle of mine. No ... I realized that danger threatened the entire coffee market—a danger which could only be averted by the united efforts of all brokers, and that it was even possible that those efforts would not be sufficient, and that the sugar refiners, *raffinadeurs* as we say in Dutch—Frits says *raffineurs* but I say *raffinadeurs*; the Rosemeyers do too, and they're *in* sugar. I know one talks about a *geraffineerd* scoundrel, and not a *geraffinadeerd* scoundrel, but that's because everyone who has to deal with scoundrels gets shut of them as quickly as possible, without wasting a syllable—well, then, that the sugar *raffinadeurs*, and the indigo merchants, will also have to be in on it.

When I ponder the matter like this as I write, it seems to me that even shipowners are affected by it to some extent, and the mercantile marine ... certainly they are, there's no doubt about it! And sailmakers, too, and the Minister of Finance, and poor-law guardians, and the other Ministers, and pastrycooks, and haberdashers, and women, and shipbuilders, and wholesalers, and retailers, and caretakers, and gardeners.

And—it *is* strange how things will occur to one, while one's writing—my book also concerns millers, and the clergy, and the sellers of Holloway's pills, and distillers, and tilemakers, and the people who live from gilt-edged securities, and pumpmakers, and ropemakers, and weavers, and butchers, and brokers' clerks, and the shareholders in the Dutch Trading Company, and, in fact, properly speaking, everyone else too ...

And the King, as well ... yes, the King above all!

My book *must* go out into the world. There is nothing for it! No matter whether Busselinck & Waterman read it too ... envy is not in my nature. But they remain chisellers and scabs—that's what *I* say! In fact, only to-day I said it to young Stern, when I put him up for membership of 'Artis'. And he's welcome to write and tell his father so.

Well, then ... only a few days ago I was still in a proper quandary about my book, but now, thank Heaven, Frits has helped me out. I didn't tell him that, for I don't approve of letting people know you're beholden to them—that's one of my principles—but it's true all the same. He said Stern was such a smart lad, that he was making such progress in learning our language, and that he had even translated some German verses of Scarfman's into Dutch. As you see, the world's topsy-turvy in my house; the Dutchman had written in German, and now the German was translating it into Dutch! If each had stuck to his own language, it would have saved trouble. But, I thought—suppose I got Stern to write my book for me? If I should have anything to add, I could write a chapter now and again myself. Frits can help, too, I thought. He has a list of the words you write with two e's. Marie can make a fair copy of everything; and that will give the reader a guarantee against any immorality. For you will understand that no respectable broker would put into his daughter's hands anything that was not wholly in keeping with morality and decency.

So I spoke to both the boys about my project, and they thought it was a good one. Only it appeared that Stern, who has literary leanings—like so many Germans—wanted a say in the way it was carried out. To be honest, this did not altogether please me; but as the spring auction is at hand, and I still haven't had any orders from Ludwig Stern, I didn't want to cross him too much. He said that: 'when his breast glowed with feeling for truth and beauty, no power on earth could keep him from striking the notes which harmonized with such feeling, and that he would rather be silent than see his words shackled by the degrading fetters of the workaday world.' (Frits says 'everyday', but I don't—after all, there's nothing wrong with work.) I thought this was all very silly on Stern's part, but my profession comes first and foremost with me, and the old man's is a good firm. So we agreed:

1. That Stern should produce a few chapters for my book every week;
2. That I should change nothing of what he wrote;
3. That Frits was to correct the grammar;
4. That I should be entitled to write a chapter myself from time to time, so as to give the book an appearance of respectability;
5. That it should be called: *The Coffee Auctions of the Dutch Trading Company*;
6. That Marie should make the fair copy for the printer, but that we should have patience with her on the days when the laundry came home;
7. That the finished chapters should be read aloud every week at the party;
8. That all immorality should be avoided;
9. That my name should not appear on the title page, because I am a broker;
10. That Stern should be authorized to publish *German*, *French* and *English* translations of my book, because—so he maintained —such works are better understood in foreign countries than in ours;
11. *(Stern emphatically insisted on this.)* That I should send Scarfman a ream of paper, a gross of pens, and a bottle of ink.

I acquiesced in everything, since my book was very urgent. The following day, Stern had finished his first chapter; and here, reader, is the answer to the question how a coffee broker—*Last & Co., 37 Lauriergracht*—comes to be writing a book that looks like a novel.

However, no sooner had Stern set to work than he ran into difficulties. Besides the problem of selecting and arranging the necessary materials out of so much, words and expressions which he did not understand, and which I did not know either, cropped up again and again in the manuscripts. They were mostly Javanese or

Malay. And here and there abbreviations had been used which were difficult to decode. I realized that we could not do without Scarfman, but, since I don't think it a good thing for a young person to form undesirable connections, I did not wish to send either Stern or Frits to him. Taking with me some sugarplums that had been left over from the last party—for I always think of everything—I went to look him up.

His abode was not exactly sumptuous; but equality for all men, which would, of course, include their dwellings, is surely a chimera. Scarfman had said so himself, in his essay on human claims to happiness. Besides, I don't like people who are always discontented.

It was a back room in the Lange-leidsche-dwarsstraat. The ground floor was occupied by a second-hand dealer, who sold all kinds of junk, cups, saucers, furniture, old books, glassware, portraits of Van Speyk,[25] and so forth. I was scared to death of breaking anything, because if you do people always demand more money for the things than they were worth. A little girl was sitting in the stoep, dressing her doll. I asked whether Mr Scarfman lived there. She ran away, and her mother came out.

'Yes, 'e lives 'ere, Sir. Just go up the stairs to the first landin', and then up another lot of stairs to the second landin', and then up another lot, and you're there. Minnie, just go and tell 'em there's a genulman called. 'Oo shall she say it is, Sir?'

I said I was Mr Droogstoppel, coffee broker, from the Lauriergracht, but that I would announce myself. I climbed as high as she had said, and on the third landing I heard a child's voice singing: 'Presently Father comes, dearest Papa.' I knocked, and the door was opened by a woman or a lady—I really didn't know quite what to make of her. She was very pale. Her features showed signs of fatigue, and reminded me of my wife when she has just finished with the laundry. She was dressed in a long white shirt or jacket without a waist, that hung down to her knees and was fastened in front with a black pin. Under that, instead of a proper dress or skirt, she wore a piece of dark linen with a flower pattern, that seemed to be wound several times round her body and fitted rather tightly round her hips and knees. There was no trace of any folds, width or amplitude, as there surely ought to be in a woman's dress. I was glad I hadn't sent Frits, because her get-up struck me as very immodest, and its strangeness was aggravated by the free way she moved about, as though she felt quite at her ease like that. The creature didn't seem to be in the least aware that she didn't look like other women. I also had the impression that she wasn't at all embarrassed by my visit. She hid nothing under the table, moved no chairs about—in a word, she did none of the things that are customary when a stranger of genteel appearance drops in on you suddenly.

Her hair was combed straight back like a Chinese, and tied behind her head in a kind of knot. (I learnt afterwards that her dress was a sort of East Indian costume, which they call *sarong* and *kabaya* out there; but I thought it very ugly.)

'Are you Juffrouw[26] Scarfman?' I asked.

'To whom have I the honour of speaking?' she said, and in a tone that seemed to imply that I could have introduced some *honour* into *my* question.

Well, I'm not fond of paying compliments. It's a different thing with a principal, and I've been in business too long not to know my world. But I didn't see the necessity of mincing matters on a third floor. So I said bluntly that I was Mr Droogstoppel, coffee broker, 37 Lauriergracht, and that I wanted to speak to her husband.

She motioned me to a cane chair, and took on her lap a little girl who had been playing on the floor. The little boy I had heard singing stared fixedly at me, looking me up and down from head to foot. *He* didn't seem at all shy, either! He was about six years old, and likewise dressed peculiarly. His baggy trousers came hardly halfway down his thighs, and his legs were bare from there to his ankles. Most indecent, I thought. 'Have you come to see Papa?' he asked abruptly; and I immediately realized that the education of that child had left much to be desired, otherwise he would have spoken in the second person plural, as behoves a little boy addressing his elders and betters, and not used the form reserved for equals and inferiors. But as I felt a bit awkward myself, and was disposed to talk, I answered:

'Yes, my little man, I've come to see your Papa. Do you think he'll soon be home?'

'I don't know. He is out, looking for money to buy me a paintbox.' (Frits writes it as two words, but I don't, then it's sooner over.)

'Be quiet, child,' said the woman. 'Go and play with your pictures, or with your Chinese musical box.'

'How can I? You know perfectly well that that gentleman took everything away with him yesterday?'

He even addressed his mother in the second person singular, and it seemed that there had been a 'gentleman' who had 'taken everything away' ... a cheerful visit that must have been! The woman did not seem very happy either—she furtively wiped her eye as she got up and took the little girl across to her young brother. 'There,' she said, 'you play with Nonni.' A queer name. But he did.

'Well, Juffrouw,' I asked, 'do you expect your husband back soon?'

'I cannot say for certain,' she answered.

Suddenly the little boy, who had started to play at rowing boats with his little sister, left her and asked me:

'Sir, why do you call Mama "Juffrouw"?'

'What do you mean, laddie?' I said. 'What else should I call her?'

'Why ... the same as other people do! The woman downstairs is "Juffrouw", she sells cups and saucers.'

Now *I* am a coffee broker—*Last & Co.*, *37 Lauriergracht*; there are thirteen of us in the office—fourteen if you count Stern, who gets no salary. Very well then ... *my* wife is still 'Juffrouw' and yet I was to say 'Mevrouw' to *this* person! Surely that was absurd? Everyone must know their station, and what was more, only yesterday the bailiffs had taken away all the valuables. So I considered my 'Juffrouw' quite correct, and stuck to it.

I asked why Scarfman had not called at my house for his parcel. She seemed to know about that, and said they had been away, to Brussels. There he had worked for the *Indépendance*, but he had not been able to stay there because his articles so often caused the paper to be turned back at the French frontier. They had returned to Amsterdam several days before, because Scarfman was to get a job here ...

'With Gaafzuiger, I suppose?' I asked.

Yes, that was it. But it had been a failure, she said. Well, I knew more about that than she did. He had dropped the *Aglaias*, and was lazy, cocky and sickly ... *that* was why he had been kicked out.

And, she went on, he would certainly come and see me soon, perhaps he was at my house at that very moment, for an answer to the request he had made me.

I said that Scarfman had better call some time, but that he was not to ring the bell, for that gave the servant so much trouble. If he waited a while, I said, the door was bound to be opened sooner or later when someone had to go out. And then I left, and I took my sugarplums back with me, because, speaking frankly, I didn't like it there. I did not feel comfortable. A broker isn't a porter, and I maintain that I look respectable. I was wearing my fur-trimmed coat, and yet she sat there as casually, and talked to her children as calmly, as if she had been alone. Besides, she seemed to have been crying, and I can't bear discontented people. Again, it was cold and uncomfortable—probably because most of the furniture had been taken away—and I like a room to be cosy. On my way home I decided to give Bastiaans another chance, for I don't like putting anyone out into the street.

Now comes Stern's first week's work! It goes without saying that there are a lot of things in it which don't please me. But I have to abide by Article 2 of our agreement, and the Rosemeyers approved of it. I believe they are buttering up Stern because he has an uncle in Hamburg who is in sugar.

Scarfman had indeed called. He had seen Stern, and had explained to him some words and matters which he didn't understand. Which Stern didn't understand, I mean. I must now ask the reader to wade through the following chapters, and then, I promise him, later on he will get something more solid, from *me*, Batavus Droogstoppel, coffee broker, of *Last & Co.*, *37 Lauriergracht*.

5

One morning at about ten o'clock there was an unusual bustle and stir on the highroad in Java that connects the Divisions of PANDEG-LANG and LEBAK. 'Highroad' is perhaps a slight exaggeration when applied to the wide footpath which, out of courtesy and for want of a better, is called 'the road'. But when, in a coach and four, you leave SERANG, the main township in the Residency of BANTAM, with the intention of going to RANGKAS-BETUNG, the new centre of LE-BAK, you can be fairly sure of arriving there at some time or other. So it *is* a road. Admittedly, again and again you get stuck in the mud, which in the lowlands of BANTAM is heavy, clayey, and sticky: admittedly, time after time you will be forced to enlist the help of the inhabitants of the nearest village—though that is not *very* near, for villages are not numerous in those parts; but when at last you do succeed in getting together a score or so of peasants from the vicinity, it is usually not very long before coach and horses have been brought back on to terra firma. The driver cracks his whip, the runners (in Europe, I suppose, you would call them footmen—but no, there is nothing in Europe like them), those incomparable runners, then, with their short, thick whips, resume their trotting beside the four horses, utter indescribable shrieks, and beat the steeds under the belly to encourage them. And in that way you will jolt along again for some time, until once more the fateful moment comes when you settle down into mud over the axles. And then the shouts for help go up once more. You wait until help arrives, and ... struggle on.

Often, coming along that road, I felt as though in one place or another I might find a coach full of travellers left over from the last century, who had sunk into the mud and been forgotten. But that never happened to me. So I assume that all who ever came that way eventually got to where they wanted to go.

It would be a great mistake to judge the main road through Java from the character of this road in LEBAK. The real highway, with its many branches, which Marshal Daendels caused to be built with considerable sacrifice of life, is indeed a magnificent piece of work; and one is amazed at the energy of the man who, in spite of all the obstacles which envious rivals and opponents in the motherland placed in his path, dared defy the unwillingness of the population and the discontent of the native chiefs in order to create something which excites and merits the admiration of every visitor even to this day.

Consequently, no post-horse service in Europe—not even in England, Russia or Hungary—can compare with that in Java. Across high mountain ridges, skirting abysses which make you shudder, the heavily laden mail coach flies onward at an unremitting gallop. The driver sits on the box as though nailed to it, for hours, nay for whole days at a stretch, and wields his heavy whip with an iron hand. He can calculate exactly where and how much he must rein-in the plunging horses in order that, after a headlong flight down a mountain slope, at yonder turning …

'My God, the road is … gone! We are going down into the abyss!' screams the inexperienced traveller. 'There is no road … there is only a precipice!'

Yes, so it seems. The road bends, and just when one leap more by the galloping animals would send the leaders into space, the horses turn and swing the coach round the corner. They fly up the mountain slope, which you did not see a moment before, and … the abyss lies behind you.

On such occasions there are moments when the carriage rests on nothing but the wheels on the inside of the curve it is describing: centrifugal force has lifted the outside wheels from the ground. You have to be coolheaded not to shut your eyes; and the man travelling thus for the first time writes to tell his people in Europe that he has been in danger of his life. But the old hands in Java laugh at him.

It is not my intention, especially at the beginning of my story, to take up much of the reader's time with descriptions of places, landscapes or buildings. I am too much afraid that I might put him off by anything that smacks of prolixity; only later, when I feel I have him properly on my side, when I see from his look and attitude that he is interested in the fate of the heroine who is leaping from some balcony four floors up—only then, with a bold contempt for all the laws of gravity, shall I leave her floating between heaven and earth until I have relieved my feelings in a detailed picture of the beauties of the countryside, or of a building that seems to have been placed there to supply a pretext for an essay of several pages on mediaeval architecture. All those castles look alike. Their style is invariably heterogeneous. The keep always dates back to a few reigns earlier than the annexes that were added under some later king. The towers are dilapidated ...

Dear reader, there are no such things as towers. 'Tower' is an idea, a dream, an ideal, a fiction, intolerable bragging! There are only half-towers, and ... *miniature* towers.

The fanaticism which thought it a duty to place towers on edifices erected in honour of this saint or that did not last long enough to complete them, and the spire which is intended to point the faithful to heaven usually rests a couple of stages too low on its massive base, reminding one of the man without thighs at the fair. Only the *little towers*, the *little steeples* on village churches, have ever been completed.

It is decidedly not flattering for Western civilization that the ambition to create a great work has seldom persisted long enough to see that work completed. I am not speaking now of enterprises which *had* to be finished to cover expenses. If anyone wants to know exactly what I mean, let him go and look at Cologne Cathedral.[27] Let him consider the grand design of that building in the soul of the architect ... the faith in the hearts of the people, which enabled him to begin and continue that labour ... the influence of the ideas which required such a Colossus to serve as visible image of invisible religious feeling ... and let him compare this tremendous tension with the movement which, a few centuries after, gave birth to the moment in which the work was suspended ...

64

A deep gulf lies between Erwin von Steinbach and our builders!
I know, of course, that for years people have been trying to obliter-
ate this gulf. And in Cologne they are again working on the cathedral. But will they be able to join the broken thread? Will it be possible to find again in *our* day what *then* constituted the power of the
prelate and the patron of architects? I do not think so. Money will
no doubt be obtainable; and money will buy bricks and mortar. The
artist who makes the plans, and the mason who lays the stones, can
be paid. But no money will buy the lost yet admirable sentiment
that saw in a building a poem, a poem in granite that spoke loudly
to the people, a poem in marble that stood there as an immovable
eternal prayer ...

On the boundary, then, between LEBAK and PANDEGLANG, there
was an unusual commotion one morning. Hundreds of saddled
horses blocked the road, and at least a thousand people—a lot for
that place—were walking up and down in lively expectation. They
included the chiefs of the villages and the chiefs of the Districts of
LEBAK, all with their retinues, and, to judge by the beautiful Arab
cross-breed which, richly caparisoned, stood champing at its silver
snaffle, a chief of higher rank was also present. This was indeed the
case. The Regent of LEBAK himself, RADHEN ADHIPATTI KARTA
NATTA NEGARA,[28] had left RANGKAS-BETUNG with a large following and, in spite of his great age, had made the journey of twelve
to fourteen miles which separated his home from the borders of the
neighbouring Division of PANDEGLANG.

A new Assistant Resident was expected, and custom, which has
the force of law in the Dutch East Indies more than it has anywhere
else, dictates that an officer charged with government of a division
shall be given a festive reception. The Controleur, a middle-aged
man who had, as next in rank, performed his late chief's duties for
some months after the death of the previous Assistant Resident, was
also present.

As soon as the date of arrival of the new Assistant Resident had
become known, a *pendoppo* had been hastily erected, a table and

some chairs had been brought there, and refreshments placed in readiness. In this *pendoppo* the Regent and the Controleur awaited their new chief.

Next to a broad-brimmed hat, an umbrella, or a hollow tree, a *pendoppo* is undoubtedly the simplest representation there is of the concept 'roof'. Imagine four or six bamboo posts, driven into the ground and connected at the top by further bamboos, on which a cover has been fixed made of the long leaves of the nipa palm, called *atap* in those parts; and then you have a picture of such a *pendoppo*. As you see, it is as simple as can be; and, in fact, it was merely meant here to serve as *pied-à-terre* for the European and native officials who came to welcome their new chief on the divisional boundary.

In saying that the Assistant Resident was also the Regent's chief, I have not expressed myself quite correctly. To enable you to understand what is to follow, I shall have to make a digression here regarding the machinery of government in these regions.

NETHERLANDS INDIA or the Dutch East Indies—the use of the word *Dutch* appears incorrect to me, but it has been officially adopted —can be divided into two very different main portions as regards the relationship of the mother country to the population. One portion consists of tribes whose princes and princelings have recognized the Netherlands as *suzerain*, but where direct government still remains more or less in the hands of the native Chiefs themselves. The other portion, comprising—with one very slight, perhaps only apparent, exception—the whole of JAVA, is immediately subject to THE NETHERLANDS. There is here no question of tribute, or levy, or alliance. The *Javanese* is a *Dutch subject*. The King of the Netherlands is *his* king. The descendants of his former princes and lords are *Dutch* officials. They are appointed, transferred, promoted, dismissed by the Governor-General, who rules in the name of the *King*. The criminal is convicted and sentenced under a law made in THE HAGUE. The taxes the Javanese pays flow into the Exchequer of THE NETHERLANDS.

It is only with this portion of the Dutch possessions, which thus forms an integral part of the KINGDOM OF THE NETHERLANDS, that these pages will mainly deal.

The Governor-General is assisted by a Council, which, however, has no *decisive* voice in his decisions. In Batavia the various branches of government are divided into Departments, headed by Directors, who form the link between the supreme authority of the Governor-General and the Residents in the provinces. However, in cases of a *political nature*, Residents communicate with the Governor-General direct.

The title *Resident* dates back to the time when the NETHERLANDS still ruled the population only *indirectly*, as *overlord*, and was represented by *Residents* at the courts of the then still reigning Princes. Those Princes are no more, and the Residents have become rulers of regions, like provincial governors or *prefects*. Their task has changed, but the name remains.

It is these Residents who actually represent Dutch authority in the eyes of the Javanese population. The people know neither the Governor-General, nor the Council of the Indies, nor the departmental Directors in Batavia. They only know the *Resident*, and the minor officials who rule them under his direction.

Each Residency—some contain nearly a million souls—consists of three, four, or five Divisions or Regencies, at the head of which are placed the Assistant Residents. Under them, again, the administration is carried out by Controleurs, Inspectors and a number of other officers necessary for collection of taxes, supervision of agriculture, public works, the police, and administration of justice.

In each of these Divisions the Assistant Resident is helped by a native chief of high rank with the title of Regent. Such a Regent, although his relation to the Government and his function are entirely those of a *paid official*, is always of the highest nobility of the land, and often comes from the family of the princes who in the past ruled independently over that region or the neighbouring regions. Very shrewd political use is thus made of their ancient feudal influence—which, in Asia, is generally of great importance, and is regarded by most of the peoples as part of their religion: because, by appointing these chiefs as officers of the Crown, a hierarchy is created, at the summit of which stands Dutch authority, exercised by the Governor-General.

There is nothing new under the sun. Were not the Landgraves, Margraves, *Gau*-graves and Burgraves of the Holy Roman Empire similarly appointed by the Emperor, and mostly chosen from among the Barons? Without wishing to expatiate on the origin of aristocracy, which is rooted in nature itself, I must nevertheless interject here that in our own part of the world and yonder in the distant Indies the same causes have had the same effects. A country governed from a great distance away requires officials to represent the central authority. Under the system of military despotism, the Romans chose for this purpose the *Prefects*, who were usually the commanders of the legions that had subjugated the land in question. Such regions therefore remained *provinces*, i.e. *conquered* regions. But later, the central power of the Holy Roman Empire felt the need to bind some distant peoples to it by other means than mere brute force; and as soon as a far-off region was considered to belong naturally to the Empire through similarity of origin, language and customs, the direction of affairs there was entrusted to somebody who was not only a native of that country but whose rank elevated him above his fellow-natives, so that obedience to the commands of the Emperor should be made easier for them by enlisting their automatic instinct to obey the person charged with execution of those commands. By this means, at the same time, the cost of a standing army was entirely or partially avoided, and with it a burden on the Imperial treasury, or, as was mostly the case, on that of the provinces which had to be watched over by such an army. Hence the first Counts (*'Graven'*) were chosen from among the Barons of the country, and therefore, strictly speaking, *Count* is not a title of nobility at all but only the designation of a person charged with a certain *office*. And I believe that in the Middle Ages the Holy Roman Emperor was generally considered to have the right to appoint Counts, i.e. *provincial governors*, and Dukes, i.e. *army leaders*, but on the other hand the Barons held that they were the equals of the Emperor as far as birth was concerned, and owed allegiance only to God, and to the Emperor provided he had been elected with their consent and from their ranks. A Count filled an *office* to which the Emperor had called him. A Baron considered himself a Baron '*by the grace of God*'. The Counts represented the Emperor, and as such carried *his* banner, i.e. the standard of the Empire. A Baron raised men under his own colours, as a *banneret*.

Now the circumstance that Counts and Dukes were usually selected from among the Barons caused them to throw the weight of their office into the scale along with the influence they derived from their birth; and from this, apparently—especially when the offices had become hereditary—sprang the precedence those titles subsequently took above that of Baron. Even nowadays, many a baronial family (without imperial or royal letters patent, i.e. a family that traces its nobility back to the origin of the country, one that was *always* noble *because* it was noble—*autochthonous*) would decline elevation to the rank of Count as derogatory. There are instances of this having actually occurred.

Naturally, the persons entrusted with government of such a 'county' sought to obtain from the Emperor the assurance that their sons, or, failing these, other relatives, would succeed them in their office. And that in fact usually happened, though I do not believe that the right to such succession was ever *organically* recognized, at any rate as regards these functionaries in THE NETHERLANDS, for instance the Counts of Holland, Zealand, Flanders and Hainault, the Dukes of Brabant, Gelderland, etc. This form of hereditary privilege started as a favour, soon became a custom, and finally a necessity; but it never became law.

More or less in the same manner—as regards choice of persons, since here there is no question of the same duties, although a certain correspondence is noticeable—a Regency in Java is headed by a native official who combines the rank given him by the Government with his *autochthonous* influence, in order to facilitate the rule of the European officer who represents *Dutch* authority. Here, too, hereditary succession, without being established by law, has become the custom. As a rule, the matter is already settled in the Regent's lifetime, and the promise that he will be succeeded in his post by his son counts as a reward for zeal and faithful service. Very weighty reasons are required for a departure from this rule, and, even so, the successor is still generally chosen from among the members of the same family.

The relation between European officials and such highly placed Javanese grandees is of a very delicate nature.

The Assistant Resident of a Division is the responsible person. He has his instructions, and is considered to be the head of the Division. Yet in spite of this the Regent, by virtue of his local knowledge, his birth, his influence on the population, his financial resources and corresponding way of life, is in a much higher position. Moreover the Regent, as the representative of the *Javanese* element of an area, and being understood to speak in the name of the hundred thousand or more souls that form the population of his Regency, is, even in the eyes of the Government, a much more important person than the simple *European* official, whose discontent need not be feared, since many others can be found to take his place, whereas the displeasure of a Regent might become the germ of unrest or rebellion.

All this, then, results in a strange situation whereby the *inferior* really commands the *superior*. The Assistant Resident orders the Regent to furnish him with reports. He orders him to send labour to work on the bridges and roads. He orders him to have taxes collected. He calls upon him to attend the Divisional council, over which he, the Assistant Resident, presides. He reprimands him when he is guilty of dereliction of duty. This most peculiar relationship is only rendered possible by extremely courteous forms, which, however, do not necessarily exclude either cordiality or, on occasion, severity; and I think the tone which should prevail in the relationship is fairly well indicated in the official instructions on it: 'the *European* official is to treat the *native* officer who assists him as his *younger brother*.'

But he must not forget that this *younger brother* is greatly beloved —or feared—by their parents and that, in the event of differences between them, his greater 'age' would be a reason for blaming him for not having treated his *younger brother* with more indulgence or tact.

However, the innate courtesy of the Javanese grandee—even the lower-class Javanese is far more polite than his European equivalent—makes this apparently difficult relationship more tolerable than it otherwise would be.

Let the European be well-bred and discreet, let him behave with friendly dignity, and he may rest assured that the Regent, on his part, will make government easy for him. The—otherwise distasteful—command, when issued in the form of a request, will be carried out to the letter. The difference in rank, birth, wealth, will be effaced by the Regent himself, who raises the European to his own level, as being the representative of the King of the Netherlands; and in the end a relationship which, superficially considered, would seem bound to provoke conflict, very often becomes a source of pleasant intercourse.

I have said that one of the things which gave such Regents precedence over the European official was their wealth; and this is only to be expected. The European, when called upon to rule a province equal in area to many a German duchy, is usually a person of middle age or more, married, and a father. He fills the office *for a living*. His income is barely sufficient, often even insufficient, to provide for his family. The Regent is TOMMONGONG, ADHIPATTI or even PANGÉRANG, i.e. Javanese *prince*. With him, the question is not one of merely living; he has to live in the manner which the people are accustomed to see among their aristocracy. Whereas the *European* occupies a house, the *Regent*'s residence is often a *kraton*, with many houses and villages inside it. Whereas the *European* has one wife, and three or four children, the *Regent* maintains a number of women, with all that that implies. Whereas the *European* rides out followed by a few officials, not more than are required on his round of inspection for furnishing information en route, the *Regent* is accompanied by the hundreds belonging to the retinue which, in the eyes of his people, is inseparable from his high rank. The *European* lives like a middle-class citizen, the *Regent* lives—or is supposed to live—like a prince.

But all this has to be *paid for*. The Dutch Government, which has based itself on the influence of these Regents, knows that, and therefore nothing is more natural than its raising their income to a height which would appear exaggerated to the *non*-East Indian, but which in reality is rarely sufficient to meet the expenses connected with the mode of living of such a native chief. It is nothing unusual for Regents with an income of two or three hundred thousand guilders a year to be in financial difficulties. This is largely due to the truly princely carelessness with which they squander their revenues, their negligence in supervising their subordinates, their mania for buying things, and *especially* the advantage often taken of these weaknesses by Europeans.

The revenue of such a Javanese chief may be broken down into four parts. Firstly, his fixed monthly salary. Secondly, a specific sum as compensation for rights transferred to the Dutch Government. Thirdly, a bonus in proportion to the quantity yielded by his regency of products such as coffee, sugar, indigo, cinnamon, etc. And finally, the arbitrary use of the labour and property of his subjects.

The last two sources of revenue require some explanation. The Javanese is naturally a husbandman. The soil on which he is born, which promises much for little work, lures him to this, and, above all, he is devoted heart and soul to the cultivation of his rice fields, in which he accordingly shows particular skill. He grows up amidst his *sawahs* and *gagahs* and *tipars*,[29] and goes with his father to the field at a very early age, to assist him there in labouring with plough and spade, and on dams and channels for the irrigation of his land.

He counts his years by harvests, he calculates time and season by the colour of his standing crop, he feels at home among the comrades who cut the *paddy*[30] with him, he seeks his wife among the girls of the *dessah*[31] who at eve, to the sound of merry singing, pound the rice in order to remove the husk ... possession of a yoke of buffaloes to draw his plough is the ideal that beckons him ... in a word, rice is to the Javanese what the grape is to the wine growers along the Rhine and in the south of France.

But strangers came from the West, who made themselves lords of his land. They wished to benefit from the fertility of the soil, and commanded its occupant to devote part of his labour and time to growing other products which would yield greater profit in the markets of EUROPE. To make the common man do this, a very simple policy sufficed. He obeys his Chiefs; so it was only necessary to win over those Chiefs by promising them part of the proceeds ... And the scheme succeeded completely.

On seeing the immense quantity of Javanese products auctioned in the Netherlands, one must be convinced of the effectiveness of this policy, even though one cannot consider it noble. For, if anyone should ask whether the man who grows the products receives a reward proportionate to the yields, the answer must be in the negative. The Government compels him to grow on *his* land what pleases *it*; it punishes him when he sells the crop so produced to anyone else but *it*; and *it* fixes the price it pays him. The cost of transport to Europe, via a privileged trading company, is high. The money given to the Chiefs to encourage them swells the purchase price further, and ... since, after all, the entire business *must* yield a profit, this profit can be made in no other way than by paying the Javanese just *enough* to keep him from starving, which would decrease the producing power of the nation.

The European officials are also paid a bonus in proportion to the production.

It is true, then, that the poor Javanese is lashed onward by the whip of a dual authority; it is true that he is often fetched away from his rice fields to labour elsewhere; it is true that famine is often the outcome of these measures. But ... merrily flutter the flags at Batavia, Semarang, Surabaya, Pasaruan, Besuki, Probolingo, Pachitan, Chilachap, on board the ships which are being laden with the harvests that make Holland rich!

Famine? In rich, fertile, blessed Java—*famine?* Yes, reader. Only a few years ago, whole districts died of starvation. Mothers offered their children for sale to obtain food. Mothers ate their children ...

But then the Motherland took a hand in the matter. In the council-chambers of the people's representatives in Holland there was dissatisfaction, and the Governor-General of that day had to issue instructions that in future the output of what were called the *European-market products* was not to be pushed to the point of causing famine ...

I see I have been bitter. But what would you think of someone who could write such things *without* bitterness?

It now remains for me to speak of the last and principal source of revenue of the native Chiefs: their arbitrary disposal of the persons and property of their subjects.

According to the idea generally held over almost all Asia the subject, with all he possesses, belongs to the Prince. The descendants or relatives of the former Princes gladly make use of the ignorance of the people, who do not clearly understand that their TOMMON-GONG or ADHIPATTI or PANGÉRANG is now a *paid official* who has sold his own rights and theirs for a fixed income, and that therefore the poorly paid labour in coffee plantation or sugar-cane field has taken the place of the taxes which were formerly exacted from the dwellers on the land by their lords. Accordingly, nothing is more normal than that hundreds of families should be summoned from a great distance to work, *without payment*, on fields that belong to the Regent. Nothing is more normal than the supply, unpaid for, of food for the Regent's court. And should the horse, the buffalo, the daughter, the wife of the common man find favour in the Regent's sight, it would be unheard-of for the possessor to refuse to give up the desired object unconditionally.

There are Regents who make only moderate use of such arbitrary powers, and do not exact from the humble more than is absolutely necessary to support their rank. Others go a little further. Nowhere is this illegality altogether absent. And undoubtedly it is difficult, if not impossible, to extirpate such an abuse *entirely*, since it is deeply rooted in the very nature of the population which suffers by it. The Javanese is generous, especially when it is a matter of proving his attachment to his Chief, to the descendant of those his forefathers obeyed. He would even think he was failing in the respect due to his hereditary lord if he entered the *Kraton* without bringing gifts. These gifts are, admittedly, often of such small value that to refuse them would be tantamount to humiliating the giver; and often, therefore, this custom might rather be compared to the homage of a child, who seeks to express his love for his father by offering a small present, than be conceived as a tribute to tyrannical despotism.

But ... in this way the existence of a *charming custom* makes it difficult to abolish an *abuse*.

If the *alun-alun*[32] in front of the Regent's residence was in a neglected state, the neighbouring population would be ashamed of it, and considerable authority would be required to *prevent* them from buckling to and ridding that square of weeds, putting it into a condition commensurate with the rank of their Regent. And to offer them any payment for this would be generally considered an insult. But alongside this *alun-alun*, or elsewhere, lie *sawahs* that are waiting for the plough, or for a channel to bring the water to them, often from miles away ... and these *sawahs* belong to the Regent. In order to till or irrigate *his* fields, he summons the populations of whole villages, whose own *sawahs* are just as much in need of being worked ... therein lies the *abuse*.

This is known to the Government; and when you read the official gazette containing the laws and instructions and advice for the functionaries, you applaud the humanity that appears to have presided at their framing. Everywhere the European who is clothed with authority in the interior is enjoined, as one of his most sacred duties,

75

to protect the population against their own docility and the rapacity of their Chiefs. And, as though it were not sufficient to prescribe this obligation *in general*, the *Assistant Residents*, when assuming administration of a Division, are required to take a *separate oath*, to the effect that they will consider this paternal care of the population as a primary responsibility.

Assuredly, theirs is a noble vocation. To stand for justice, to protect the lowly against the exalted, to defend the weak against the strong, to demand the return of the poor man's ewe-lamb from the pen of the *princely* robber ... is it not enough to make a man's heart glow with joy, the thought of being called to so glorious a task? And if at times the official in Java should be dissatisfied with his station or his reward, let him turn his gaze to the sublime duty devolving upon him—to the supreme delight which fulfilment of *such* a duty brings with it; and he will desire no other reward.

But ... that duty is not easy. First of all, he has to decide precisely where *use* has ceased and made room for abuse. And ... where abuse *does exist*, where robbery or tyranny *has* indeed been practised, the victims themselves are only too often accomplices, either from excessive submissiveness, or from fear, or from lack of confidence in the will or power of the person appointed to protect them. Everyone knows that the *European* official may be called away at any moment to take up another post, whereas the *Regent, the powerful Regent*, remains. Besides, there are so many ways of appropriating the possessions of a poor, ignorant man. If a *mantri*[33] tells him that the *Regent* would like his horse, the animal is soon after to be found in the Regent's stables; but this by no means proves that the Regent does not intend to pay a high price for it ... sometime. If hundreds of people are working in a Chief's fields without receiving payment, it by no means follows that this is being done for *his* benefit. May it not have been his object to make the harvest over to them, from the purely philanthropic calculation that his land was better situated and more fertile than theirs, and so would reward their labour more liberally?

Furthermore, where is the European official to find witnesses with the courage to make a statement against their lord, the dreaded Regent? And, were the official to risk a charge *without being able to prove it*, what would become of the relationship of an *elder brother* who would then have impugned his *younger brother's* honour without good cause? What would become of the good opinion of the Government, which gives the official bread for his service but would deny him that bread, dismiss him as incapable, if he should lightly suspect or accuse of wrongdoing one so highly placed as a Tommongong, Adhipatti or Pangérang?

No, no, the official's duty is not an easy one! This is already evident from the fact that everyone knows that every native Chief oversteps the limit of permissible use of the labour and property of his subjects ... that all Assistant Residents take the oath to combat this ... and that nevertheless it is only very rarely that a Regent is charged with tyranny or misuse of power.

So it appears that almost insurmountable difficulties prevent the official from keeping his oath *'to protect the native population against exploitation and extortion'*.

6

Controleur Verbrugge was a good man. When you saw him sitting there in his dress uniform of blue broadcloth, with oak- and orange-tree branches embroidered on collar and cuffs, you could hardly fail to recognize in him the type that prevails among the Dutch in the East Indies ... a type, incidentally, which is very different from the Dutch in Holland. Indolent as long as there was nothing to do, and quite free from all the fussiness which passes in Europe for zeal, but zealous where action was necessary ... simple but cordial towards everyone about him ... informative, helpful and hospitable ... well-mannered without stiffness ... open to good impressions ... honest and sincere, but without any inclination to become a martyr to these qualities ... in short he was a man who, as they say, would be in the right place anywhere, without, however, making one think of naming the century after him—an honour which, if it came to that, he would not have wanted anyway.

He sat in the middle of the *pendoppo*, at the table, which was covered with a white cloth and an abundance of dishes. From time to time, with decided impatience, he addressed the *mandoor* (the head of the police and office staff under the Assistant Resident), asking him, in the words of Mrs Bluebeard's sister,[34] whether he didn't see anyone coming yet? Then he would get up, try in vain to make his spurs jingle on the hard-trodden clay floor of the *pendoppo*, light his cigar for the twentieth time, and sit down again. He spoke little.

And yet he could have spoken if he had wanted to, for he was not alone. By this, I do not simply mean that he had the company of the twenty or thirty Javanese servants, *mantris* and other attendants squatting on the ground inside and outside the *pendoppo*, nor the many who were constantly running in and out, nor the large number of natives of all ranks and conditions who held the horses or rode around on them ... No; but the Regent of Lebak himself, RADHEN ADHIPATTI KARTA NATTA NEGARA, was sitting opposite him.

Waiting is always wearisome. A quarter of an hour seems an hour, an hour half a day, and so on. Verbrugge might have been a little more talkative. The Regent of LEBAK was a cultured old man, who could speak on many subjects with intelligence and judgment. You only had to look at him to be convinced that the majority of the Europeans who came into contact with him could have learnt more from him than he from them. His lively dark eyes contradicted by their fire the lassitude of his features and the grey of his hair. What he said was usually well considered—a characteristic which, for that matter, is general among orientals of breeding; and when you conversed with him, you felt you had to look upon his words as memoranda, minutes of which he kept in his archives for reference if required. This may seem disagreeable to people who are not accustomed to intercourse with Javanese aristocrats. But it is not difficult to avoid *all* topics that may give offence, especially as the Javanese themselves will never brusquely change the subject, because that would be contrary to Eastern ideas of good form. Accordingly, anyone who has reason to avoid touching upon any special point need only talk about insignificant trifles and he may rest assured that a Javanese Chief will not take him where he would rather not be taken by giving an undesired turn to the conversation.

There are, it is true, differing opinions on the best manner of dealing with these Chiefs. But it seems to me that natural straightforwardness, without any attempt at diplomatic circumspection, is the manner to be preferred.

However this may be, Verbrugge began with a trivial remark about the weather and the rain.

'Yes, it is the south-west monsoon,' said the Regent.

That, of course, Verbrugge knew perfectly well: it was January. But what *he* had said about the rain was equally well known to the Regent. This was followed by another brief silence.

The Regent, with a scarcely perceptible movement of his head, beckoned one of the servants who was squatting at the entrance to the *pendoppo*. It was a little boy, charmingly attired in a blue velvet coatee and white trousers, with a gilt girdle which held his costly *sarong*[35] round his loins and on his head the attractive *kain kapala*,[36] beneath which his black eyes peeped roguishly out. He crept squatting to the feet of the Regent; put down the gold box containing the tobacco, lime, *siri, pinang*, and *gambier*;[37] made the *slamat* by raising both hands joined as in prayer to his deeply bowed forehead; and then offered his master the precious box.

'The road will be difficult after so much rain,' said the Regent, as though giving an explanation for the long wait. While speaking he spread some lime on a betel leaf.

'In PANDEGLANG the road is not so bad,' answered Verbrugge, who, if he really did not want to touch on any sore subject, was surely somewhat thoughtless in replying. For he should have remembered that a Regent of LEBAK would not be pleased to hear the roads of PANDEGLANG praised, even if they *were* better than those in LEBAK.

The *Adhipatti* did not make the mistake of answering too quickly. The little *maas* or page had already crept backwards, still crouching, as far as the entrance to the *pendoppo*, where he took his place again among his mates ... the Regent had already dyed his lips and few remaining teeth brown-red with the juice of his *siri*, before he said:

'Yes, there are a good many people in PANDEGLANG.'

For those who knew the Regent and the Controleur, for those to whom conditions in LEBAK were no secret, it would have been clear that the conversation had become a conflict. An allusion to the better state of the roads in a neighbouring Division could be interpreted as following unsuccessful attempts to get such better roads constructed in LEBAK as well, or to get the existing ones kept in better repair. But in this respect the Regent was right. PANDEGLANG was more densely populated, especially in proportion to its much smaller area, and therefore labour on the main roads, with united forces, was much easier than in LEBAK, a Division which covered some hundreds of square miles but had only seventy thousand inhabitants.

'That is true,' said Verbrugge, 'we haven't many people here. But ...'

The *Adhipatti* looked at him as though expecting an attack. He knew that that 'but' might be followed by something which would be disagreeable to hear for him, who had been Regent of LEBAK for thirty years. However, it appeared that Verbrugge had no desire to continue the fight for the moment. At any rate he broke off the conversation, and again asked the *mandoor* whether he saw no one coming?

'I still see nothing in the direction of Pandeglang, Sir, but over there, on the other side, there's someone coming on horseback ... it is the TUAN KOMMANDAAN.'

'So it is, Dongso,' said Verbrugge, looking out, 'it's the Commandant! He's been hunting around here, he went out early this morning. Hi! Duclari ... Duclari!'

'He has heard you, Sir, he's coming this way. His boy is riding after him, with a *kidang*[38] behind him across the horse.'

'*Pegang kudahnya Tuan Kommandaan*,'[39] Verbrugge ordered one of the servants squatting outside. 'Morning, Duclari: are you wet? What's the bag? Come in!'

A robust-looking man of about thirty, and of soldierly appearance although there was no trace of a uniform about him, entered the *pendoppo*. It was Lieutenant Duclari, Commandant of the small garrison of RANGKAS-BETUNG. Verbrugge and he were friends, and their intimacy was all the greater as Duclari had been staying in Verbrugge's house for some time already, while awaiting the completion of a new fort. He shook hands with him, saluted the Regent courteously, and sat down with the question: 'Well, what have you got to offer?'

'Would you like some tea, Duclari?'

'Oh no, thanks, I'm quite warm enough! Haven't you any coconut milk? That's fresher.'

'You're not getting any. When you're warm, I think coconut milk is very bad for you. It makes you stiff and rheumatic. Just look

81

at the coolies who carry those heavy loads across the mountains: they keep themselves fit and supple by drinking hot water, or *koppi dahun*. But ginger tea is even better ...'

'What? *Koppi dahun*, tea made from coffee leaves? Never heard of it in my life!'

'That's because you haven't served in Sumatra. There it's quite the custom.'

'Very well, give me tea, then ... but not from coffee leaves, nor from ginger either. Of course, you've been in Sumatra ... and the new Assistant Resident has too, hasn't he?'

They had been talking Dutch, a language the Regent did not understand. Either because Duclari felt that there was some discourtesy in thus excluding him from the conversation, or for some other reason, he suddenly broke into Malay, and addressed the Regent:

'Did you know, ADHIPATTI, that Mr Verbrugge knows the new Assistant Resident?'

'No, no, I didn't say that!' Verbrugge interrupted. 'I *don't* know him—I've never seen him. He was stationed in Sumatra some years before me. I only told you I heard a great deal about him there, that was all!'

'Well, it comes to the same thing. You don't exactly need to see a man in order to know him. What do *you* think, ADHIPATTI?'

At that moment the ADHIPATTI had to call a servant. So a few minutes passed before he could say: 'I agree with you, Commandant, but still, in many cases it is necessary to see a person before you can form an opinion about him.'

'Generally speaking, that may be true,' Duclari went on in Dutch —either because he was more familiar with that language and considered he had done enough to satisfy the requirements of good manners, or because he wished to be understood by Verbrugge alone—'Generally speaking, that may be true, but when it comes to Havelaar, you certainly don't have to have met him ... he's a fool!'

'I didn't say that, Duclari!'

'No, *you* didn't, but I do, after all you've told me about him. I call a man who jumps into the water to save a dog from sharks a fool.'

'Well, it certainly wasn't sensible, but ...'

'And look here, that lampoon against General van Damme ... that was bad form!'

'It was witty.'

'True! But a young chap has no business to be witty at the expense of a General.'

'Don't forget, he was *very* young ... that was fourteen years ago. He was only twenty-two then.'

'And what about the turkey he stole?'

'That was to annoy the General.'

'Precisely! A young man has no business to annoy a General, who was his chief too, in this case, being the civil governor. That other little rhyme I thought amusing enough, but ... those everlasting duels of his!'

'They were usually on behalf of someone else. He was always taking the weaker fellow's part.'

'Well, let everyone fight his own duels, if he really must fight duels! In my opinion they aren't often necessary. If it was unavoidable I should accept a challenge, and in certain cases I should even be the challenger, but to make that sort of thing an everyday business ... no, thanks! Let's hope he's changed on that point.'

'Most certainly he has, there's no doubt about it! He's so much older now, and he's been married for years, and an Assistant Resident. Besides, I always heard it said that he had a good heart, with a warm corner in it for justice.'

'That will come in very handy in LEBAK! Something happened this morning that ... do you think the Regent can understand us?'

'Probably not. But show me something from your gamebag, then he'll think we're talking about that.'

Duclari took his bag, fetched out a couple of wood pigeons, and, handling the birds as though he was talking about shooting, he told Verbrugge that, while he was out hunting, a Javanese had run after him and asked him whether he could do nothing to lighten the load under which the people groaned?

'And,' he went on, 'that means a lot, Verbrugge! Not that I'm surprised by what he actually said. I've been in Bantam long enough to know what goes on here; but your humble Javanese is usually so cautious and reticent about his Chiefs, it amazes me that he should ask such a thing from someone who's in no way concerned with it!'

'And what did you answer, Duclari?'

'Well ... I said it was not my business! I told him to go to you, or to the new Assistant Resident when he arrives at RANGKAS-BETUNG, and make his complaint there.'

'*Ini apa tuan-tuan datang!*' the *mandoor* Dongso suddenly called. 'I see a *mantri* waving his *tudung!*'[40]

All rose to their feet. Duclari did not wish his presence in the *pendoppo* to be interpreted as meaning that he too was at the division-al boundary to welcome the Assistant Resident, who, though his superior, was not his chief, and was moreover 'a fool'. So he mount-ed his horse and rode off, followed by his servant.

The ADHIPATTI and Verbrugge stationed themselves at the en-trance to the *pendoppo* and saw a coach coming, drawn by four horses and in a pretty muddy state. The vehicle stopped near the little bam-boo structure.

It would have been difficult to guess all that that coach contained before Dongso, assisted by the 'runners' and a number of servants belonging to the Regent's retinue, had unfastened all the straps and knots that kept the carriage enclosed in a black leather case remind-ing one of the caution with which in earlier days lions and tigers were brought into town, when the Zoological Gardens were still travelling menageries. Now, there were no lions or tigers in the coach. It had only been carefully closed up in this way because of the south-west monsoon, which made it necessary to be prepared for rain.

To descend from a carriage in which you have been jolting along the road for a long time is not so easy as people who have never or rarely travelled in one might imagine. More or less like the poor prehistoric Saurians, which, by dint of waiting long enough, have at last come to form an integral part of the clay in which originally they had not settled down with the intention of remaining permanently, so also, with travellers who have sat too long in a coach, closely packed and in a cramped position, something takes place which I propose to call 'assimilation'. Eventually one no longer knows precisely where the leather cushion of the carriage ends and where the ego begins; in fact, the idea has sometimes occurred to me that in such a coach one might have a toothache or cramp which one mistook for moth in the cloth, or vice versa.

There are few circumstances in the material world that do not give a thinking man occasion to make observations on the intellectual plane. Hence I have often asked myself whether many errors which have the force of law among us, many obliquities which we mistake for rectitude, might possibly result from the fact that we have been sitting with the same company in the same coach for too long? The leg which you had to stick out to the left, between the hatbox and the basket of cherries ... the knee you kept pressed against the carriage door, so that the lady opposite might not think you intended an attack on crinoline or virtue ... the foot with corns which was so scared of the heels of the commercial traveller next to you ... the neck you were compelled to turn to the left so long, because the rain was dripping in on the right of you ... all these, you see, must in the end become necks, knees and feet that have something distorted about them. I think it is a good thing to change carriages, or seats, or fellow-passengers, from time to time. It enables you to turn your neck in another direction, now and again you can move your knee, and perhaps sometimes your neighbour will be a lady wearing dancing shoes, or a little boy whose legs do not reach the floor. You then have a better chance of seeing *straight* and walking *straight* as soon as you have firm ground under your feet again.

Now I do not know whether, in the coach which stopped in front of the *pendoppo*, there was anything that opposed the 'dissolution of continuity'. But it certainly took a long time for anything to emerge. A conflict of courtesies appeared to be in progress. One could hear the words: 'After you, Mrs Havelaar!' and 'Resident!'. Anyway, at last a gentleman got out, whose bearing and appearance decidedly put one in mind of the Saurians I have just mentioned. Since we shall be seeing him again, I may as well tell you at once that his immobility could not be attributed exclusively to assimilation to the travelling carriage, because, even when there was no carriage about for miles, he still displayed a calmness, a slowness, and a circumspection which would have made many a Saurian jealous, and which, in the eyes of a large number of people, are the hallmarks of gentility, composure, and wisdom. Like most Europeans in the Indies he was very pale, though in those parts this is in no way considered as a sign of poor health; and he had delicate features which bore testimony to some intellectual development. But there was something cold in his glance, something that reminded you of a table of logarithms; and though in general his appearance was not unpleasing or repellent, one could not help suspecting that his rather large thin nose felt bored on that face, because so little happened on it.

He politely offered his hand to a lady, to assist her in alighting from the carriage; and when she had taken a child, a fair-haired little boy of about three, from a gentleman still sitting inside, they entered the *pendoppo*. After them came the second gentleman just referred to, and people acquainted with Java would have noted as something singular the fact that he waited at the carriage door to help an old Javanese *babu* to get out. Meanwhile, three other servants had managed to extricate themselves from the patent-leather cupboard that was stuck on the back of the coach like a young oyster on the back of its mama.

The gentleman who had alighted first offered his hand to the Regent and to Controleur Verbrugge, and they shook it respectfully; their whole demeanour indicated that they felt themselves to be in the presence of an important person. He was Mr Slymering, Resident of BANTAM, the extensive region of which LEBAK is a Division, a Regency, or, as it is called officially, an *Assistant Residency*.

In reading works of fiction I have more than once been irritated by the little respect shown by authors for the public's taste; and this has been especially the case whenever they were concerned with producing something that was supposed to be droll or burlesque, not to say *humorous*, a quality which people almost always confuse with *comical* in the most wretched fashion. They introduce a speaker who either does not understand the language or pronounces it badly; for instance, they make a German say: 'Co kvickly to ze great Ganal', or 'Certy is not cood at srowing sings avay.' Failing a German they take someone who stammers, or they 'create' a person who works to death a couple of constantly recurring words. I have seen an idiotic vaudeville 'make a hit' because there was a man in it who kept on saying 'My name is Meyer'. In my opinion, this sort of wit is rather cheap, and, to tell the truth, I should be angry with you if you found it amusing.

But now I myself must put something of the kind before you. From time to time I have to make someone 'walk on'—I promise to do it as little as possible—who actually did speak in a way which, I fear, will draw upon me the suspicion of an abortive attempt at making you laugh. And therefore I must emphatically assure you that it is not *my* fault if the eminently dignified Resident of BANTAM, who is here referred to, had something *so* peculiar in his mode of expressing himself that I find it difficult to reproduce it without appearing to be trying to make a witty effect by using a *tic*. For he spoke as though there was a full stop after each word, or even a prolonged rest; and I can think of nothing better with which to compare the space between his words than the silence following the 'Amen' after a long prayer in church, which, as everyone knows, is a signal that one has time to shift in one's seat, cough or blow one's nose. What he said was usually well-considered, and if he could have broken himself of the habit of making these untimely pauses his sentences would mostly have appeared sound enough, at any rate from a rhetorical point of view. But that piecemeal delivery, all that jerking and jolting, made it irksome to listen to him. And often it tripped you up. For usually, when you had begun to answer, under the impression that the sentence was finished and that he was leaving completion of the part omitted to the sagacity of his audience, the missing words would come along behind like the stragglers of a defeated army, and made you feel you had interrupted him, which is always a disagreeable experience. The people of the chief town in the Residency, SERANG, at any rate those not in Government service —a position which tends to make the majority rather cautious—described his discourses as 'slimy'. I do not consider this a very tasteful word, but I am bound to admit that it expressed the main feature of the Resident's style of eloquence pretty accurately.

I have said nothing as yet about Max Havelaar and his wife—for these were the two persons who got out of the coach with their child and the *babu*, after the Resident—and it might perhaps be sufficient to leave the description of their outward appearance and character to the course of events and the reader's own imagination. However, since I have started describing anyway, I will tell you that Mrs Havelaar was not beautiful, but that her way of looking and speaking had something very sweet about it, and by the easy unconstraint of her manners she gave unmistakable testimony of having moved in the world and of belonging to the higher classes of society. She had none of the stiffness and unpleasingness of middle-class gentility, which imagines it must needs torment itself and others with a show of shyness in order to pass as 'distingué'; hence she attached but little importance to the outward forms which seem to have value for some other women. In her dress, too, she was a model of simplicity. A white *baju* of muslin, with a blue girdle—I believe that in Europe a garment of this kind would be called a *peignoir*—was her travelling costume. Round her neck she wore a thin silken cord, to which were attached two little lockets, which, however, could not be seen as they were concealed in the folds that covered her breast. For the rest, her hair was arranged *à la chinoise*, with a small spray of *melati*[41] in her *kondeh*[42] ... such was all her toilet.

I have said she was not beautiful, and yet I should not like you to think she was the opposite. I trust you *will* find her beautiful as soon as I have the opportunity of presenting her burning with indignation over what she called 'neglected genius' when her adored Max was concerned, or when she was animated by an idea connected with the well-being of her child. The face has been described as the mirror of the soul too often for anyone to value the portrait of an impassive face which has nothing to mirror because no soul is reflected in it. Let me say, then, that *she* had a beautiful soul, and that one would have had to be blind not to see beauty also in the face in which that soul was to be read.

Havelaar was a man of thirty-five. He was slim, and quick in his movements. There was nothing remarkable in his appearance except his short and mobile upper lip, and his large, pale-blue eyes, which had something dreamy about them when he was in a calm mood, but shot fire when a great idea took possession of him. His fair hair hung lank over his temples, and I can very well understand that people seeing him for the first time would get the impression that they were in the presence of one of the rare ones of the earth as regards both head and heart. He was a 'vessel of contradictions'. Sharp as a razor, yet tender-hearted as a young girl, he was always the first to feel the wound his bitter words had inflicted, and he suffered more from it than the injured party did. He was quick on the uptake; he grasped at once the most exalted, most complicated matters; he delighted in solving difficult problems, for which he found no labour, study or exertion too much ... And yet often he could not understand the simplest thing, which a child could have explained to him. Full of love for truth and justice, he frequently neglected his nearest, most obvious duty, in order to redress a wrong that lay higher, further, or deeper, and that drew him by the probable need for greater effort in the struggle. He was chivalrous and brave, but, like that other Don Quixote, often wasted his valour on windmills. He burned with an insatiable ambition which made all normal distinction in society seem worthless to him, and yet he considered his greatest happiness to lie in a calm, secluded home life. A poet in the highest sense of the word, he dreamt solar systems from a spark, peopled them with beings of his own creation, felt himself lord of a world which he himself had called into existence ... and yet, immediately afterwards, he was perfectly capable of carrying on, without the slightest dreaminess, a conversation about the price of rice, the rules of grammar, or the economic advantages of an Egyptian poultry farm. No science was wholly foreign to him. He divined what he did not know, and he possessed in a high degree the faculty of applying the little he knew—everyone knows but little, and he, though perhaps knowing more than some others, was no exception to this rule—applying the little he knew in a way which multiplied the measure of his knowledge. He was precise and orderly, and withal extremely patient; but all that was self-discipline—preciseness, order and patience did not come naturally to him, since his mind had a tendency to extravagance. He was slow and circumspect in judging, although he did not seem it to those who heard him expressing his conclusions so rapidly. His impressions were too vivid for people to look upon them as lasting, and yet he often proved that they *were* lasting. All that was great and sublime attracted him, and at the same time he was as simple and naïve as a child. He was honest, especially where honesty could become generosity, and would leave unpaid hundreds of guilders that he owed because he had given away thousands. He was witty and entertaining when he felt that his wit was understood, but otherwise curt and reserved. Warmhearted to his friends, he made—sometimes too readily— friends of all that suffered. He was sensitive to love and affection... true to his word, once given ... yielding in small things, but firm to stubbornness where he deemed it worthwhile to show character... modest and obliging to those who acknowledged his mental superiority, but difficult when people attempted to dispute it ... candid out of pride, and reticent by fits and starts when he feared that his candour might be taken for foolishness ... as susceptible to sensual as to spiritual pleasure … diffident and clumsy in expressing himself when he thought he was not understood, but eloquent when he felt that his words were falling on fertile soil … sluggish when he was not urged on by any spur from his own soul, but zealous, ardent when that was the case … Finally, he was affable, well-mannered, and blameless in his behaviour: such, more or less, was Havelaar!

I say: more or less. For, granted that all definitions are difficult in themselves, they become even more so when it is a question of describing a person who greatly deviates from the everyday norm. No doubt this is why novelists usually make their heroes devils or angels. Black and white are easy to paint; but it is more difficult to reproduce the exact shades and nuances that lie between them when one is bound by the truth and may therefore not tint the picture either too dark or too light. I feel that the sketch I have tried to give of Havelaar is extremely incomplete. The materials before me are of so diverse a nature as to impede my judgment by '*embarras de richesse*'; and so I shall probably revert to them, to complete the picture, in the course of unfolding the events I wish to relate. One thing is certain: Havelaar was an uncommon man, and well worth the trouble of studying. (I notice already that I have omitted to mention, as one of his principal traits, that he grasped the ludicrous and the serious side of things with equal rapidity and simultaneously, which gave his style of conversation a kind of 'humour' without his knowing it, leaving his audience in continual doubt as to whether they had been struck by the deep feeling that prevailed in his words or ought to laugh over the absurdity which suddenly checked that earnestness.)

It was remarkable that his appearance, and even his emotions, showed so few traces of the life he had lived. To boast of experience has become a ridiculous commonplace. There are people who for fifty or sixty years have drifted along with the little stream in which they claim to swim, and who would be able to tell you little else about all that time except that they moved from A-Square to B-Street. Nothing is commoner than to hear the very people pride themselves on their experience who have come by their grey hairs the most lightly. Others again presume to found their claims to experience on vicissitudes they have really undergone, but without there being anything to show that those changes deeply affected their mental lives. I can imagine that to witness, or even to participate in, important events may make little or no impact on a certain type of disposition which has not the capacity for receiving and absorbing impressions. If anyone doubts this, let him ask himself whether he would be justified in crediting with 'experience' all the inhabitants of France who were forty or fifty years old in 1815. And yet all of these were persons who had not only seen the stupendous drama that began with 1789 but had even played in it, in some more or less important role.

And, vice versa, how many people undergo a whole series of emotions without outward circumstances appearing to give occasion for them? One may recall the Robinson Crusoe novels; Silvio Pellico's *My Prisons*; Saintine's enchanting *Picciola*;[43] the struggle in the breast of an 'old maid', who all her life long cherishes one love without ever betraying by a single word what is going on in her heart; or finally, the feelings of a friend of humanity who, without being outwardly involved in the course of events, nevertheless takes a burning interest in the welfare of his fellow-citizens or fellow-men. One may imagine how that humanitarian hopes and fears alternately, how he watches every change, how he enthuses over a fine idea and blazes with indignation when he sees it pushed aside and trampled on by the multitude, who, at any rate for a moment, are stronger than fine ideas. Think of the philosopher who, from out his cell, tries to teach the people what is truth, when he has his voice drowned by pious hypocrisy or money-grubbing quackery. Think of Socrates—not while draining the cup of hemlock, for here I refer to the inner experience of the soul, not to that which comes from outward circumstances—and how deeply grieved his heart must have been when he, who strove to find goodness and truth, heard himself called 'a corrupter of youth and denier of the gods'.

Or even better: think of Jesus, gazing so sadly down on Jerusalem, and lamenting that her people 'would not' take heed.

Such a cry of grief—before the cup of poison or the Tree—comes not from an untried heart. It is *there* that suffering has been, great suffering ... *there* is true *experience*!

This outburst has escaped me unawares ... well, here it is, and here it can stay. Havelaar had experienced much. Do you want something to set against the move from A-Square? He had been shipwrecked—more than once. In his diary there were fire, riot, assassination, war, duels, wealth, poverty, hunger, cholera, love and 'loves'. He had visited many lands, and had mixed with people of all races and conditions, customs, prejudices, religions and colours.

Hence, as far as the circumstances of his life were concerned, he *could* have experienced much. And that he *had* really experienced much, that he had not gone through life without *seizing* the impressions it offered him so abundantly—for that, the nimbleness of his mind might go bail, and the receptiveness of his heart.

All those who knew or could guess how much he had seen and been through were amazed that so little of it was to be read in his face. His features undoubtedly expressed something like weariness, but this suggested too early maturity rather than approaching age —and yet it should have been approaching age, for in the East Indies a man of thirty-five is no longer young.

As I have said, his emotions had also remained young. He could play with a child, and like a child, and he often complained that 'little Max' was still too young to fly kites, because he, 'big Max', was so fond of that. With boys he would play at leapfrog, and he delighted in drawing embroidery patterns for girls. He would even take the needle out of their hands and amuse himself with such work, although he frequently said they could be doing something better than 'mechanically counting stitches'. With lads of eighteen he was a young student who gladly joined them in singing '*Patriam canimus*' or '*Gaudeamus igitur*' ... in fact, I am not quite certain whether, only a short time ago, when he was on leave in Amsterdam, he

did not pull down a signboard that displeased him because it showed a negro in chains, at the feet of a European with a long pipe in
his mouth, and under it the inevitable words: 'The Smoking Young
Trader'.

The *babu* he had helped out of the coach resembled all the other
babus in the East Indies when they are old. If you know this type of
servant, I do not need to tell you what she looked like. And if you
do not know, I cannot tell you. There was only this to distinguish
her from other nursemaids in the Indies ... that she had very little
to do. For Mrs Havelaar was a model in caring for her child, and
whatever had to be done for or with little Max she did herself, to
the great astonishment of many other ladies, who did not approve
of a mother being 'a slave to her children'.

7

The Resident of BANTAM introduced the Regent and the Controleur to the new Assistant Resident. Havelaar greeted both officials courteously. With a few cordial words he put the Controleur at his ease —there is always something painful in meeting a new chief—as though he wanted at once to establish a kind of intimacy which would make subsequent relations between them easier. His meeting with the Regent was such as was fitting in the case of one entitled to the golden *payong*[44] but who was at the same time his 'younger brother'. With courtly affability he chid him for his excessive conscientiousness, which had brought him out in such weather to the frontier of his Division; for, strictly speaking, according to the rules of etiquette the Regent need not have done this.

'Really, ADHIPATTI, I am cross with you for having gone to so much trouble on my behalf. I had not expected to see you until I got to RANGKAS-BETUNG.'

'I wished to meet the Assistant Resident as soon as possible, in order to make friends with him,' said the ADHIPATTI.

'Of course, of course, I am greatly honoured! But I do not like to see one of your rank and years exerting himself too much. And on horseback, at that!'

'Yes, Mr Havelaar! When the Service calls, I am still swift and strong.'

'Ah, but you are asking too much of yourself! Isn't he, Resident?'

'The ADHIPATTI. Is. Very...'

'True, but there are limits.'

'Zealous,' the Resident drawled along behind.

'True, but there are limits,' Havelaar had to reiterate, almost as though he were swallowing his previous words. 'If you don't mind, Resident, we'll make room in the carriage for the ADHIPATTI. Our *babu* can stay here, and we'll send a *tandu*[45] from RANGKAS-BETUNG for her. My wife will take Max on her lap ... won't you, Tina? That way, there will be enough room.'

'I. Have. No...'

'Verbrugge, we'll give you a lift too; I don't see...'

'Objection!' said the Resident.

'I don't see why you should splash through the mud on horse-back without good cause ... there's room enough for us all, and then, we can get to know one another. What do you say, Tina—we'll manage all right, won't we? Come here, Max ... look, Verbrugge, isn't he a nice little chap? This is my son ... this is Max!'

The Resident had sat down in the *pendoppo*, with the ADHIPATTI. Havelaar called Verbrugge, asking him who the white horse with the red saddle-cloth belonged to. But when Verbrugge came to the entrance of the *pendoppo* to see which horse he meant, Havelaar laid his hand on the Controleur's shoulder and asked:

'Is the Regent always so conscientious?'

'He's hale and hearty enough for his years, Mr Havelaar, and you'll understand he wants to make a good impression on you.'

'Yes, I understand. I've heard many good reports of him ... He's a cultured man, isn't he?'

'Oh yes...'

'And he has a large family?'

Verbrugge looked at Havelaar as though he did not see the connection. And that was, indeed, often difficult for those who did not know the man. His mental agility often made him skip some links in the chain of reasoning during a conversation, and no matter how gradually the transition took place in *his* thoughts, people who were less nimble-witted, or not used to his nimbleness, could not be blamed on such occasions for staring at him with the unspoken question on their lips: 'Are you mad... or what?'

Something like this could be read in Verbrugge's face, and Havelaar had to repeat the question before he answered:

'Yes, he has a very large family.'

'And are any *mejeets* being built in the Division?' continued Havelaar, again in a tone which, in contradiction to the words themselves, seemed to indicate a connection between those mosques and the Regent's 'large family'.

Verbrugge answered that a great deal of mosque-building was certainly going on.

'Yes, yes, just as I thought!' exclaimed Havelaar. 'And, tell me now, are the people very much behind with their land tax?'

'Yes, things could be better...'

'Exactly! Especially in the District of PARANG-KUJANG,' said Havelaar, as though he found it easier to answer his questions himself. 'What's the assessment for this year?' he went on; and when Verbrugge hesitated as though considering what reply to make, Havelaar anticipated him, continuing in the same breath:

'All right, all right, I know ... eighty-six thousand and a few hundred ... fifteen thousand more than last year ... but only six thousand above '55. Since '53 we've only gone up by eight thousand... and the population's very thin, too ... yes, of course, Malthus and all that! In twelve years we've only increased by eleven per cent, and even that's doubtful, the earlier censuses were very inaccurate... come to that, they still are! In '51 the number even went down. And the livestock figures aren't progressing either ... that's a bad sign, Verbrugge! Good Lord, look at that horse capering! I believe it's got the staggers ... come and look, Max!'

Verbrugge realized that he would not have to teach the new Assistant Resident much, and that there was no question of ascendancy through 'local seniority'—which, to do him justice, the good fellow had not desired anyway.

'But it's only natural,' Havelaar went on, taking Max in his arms. 'In CHIKANDI and BOLANG[46] they're very glad of it, and so are the rebels in the LAMPONG DISTRICTS. I shall be grateful for your co-operation, Mr Verbrugge! The Regent's getting on in years, so we must ... tell me, is his son-in-law still District Chief? All things considered, I think we should be lenient with him ... the Regent, I mean. I'm very glad everything here is so backward and poverty-stricken, and ... I hope to be here a long time.'

So saying, Havelaar shook hands with Verbrugge, who, returning with him to the table at which the Resident, the ADHIPATTI and Mrs Havelaar were seated, already realized a little better than five minutes before that 'that Havelaar wasn't such a fool' as the Commandant believed. Verbrugge was by no means lacking in intelligence, and, knowing the Division of LEBAK about as well as one man *can* know a region which is extensive but where nothing is printed, he began to see that, after all, there *was* a link between the seemingly disconnected questions of Havelaar, and also that the new Assistant Resident, although he had never set foot in the Division before, knew something about what was going on in it. Admittedly he still did not understand Havelaar's rejoicing over the poverty in LEBAK; but he persuaded himself he had misinterpreted the man's words. Afterwards, however, when Havelaar often repeated them, he saw how much greatness and nobility there was in that rejoicing.

Havelaar and Verbrugge sat down at the table and, talking trivialities over their tea, they waited until Dongso came to tell the Resident that the fresh horses had been harnessed to the carriage. The travellers packed themselves in as comfortably as they could, and drove off.

The jolting and shaking made conversation difficult. Little Max was kept quiet with a *pisang*,[47] and his mother, who had him on her lap, absolutely refused to admit that she was tired when Havelaar offered to relieve her of the heavy child. During a moment of enforced rest in a mudhole, Verbrugge asked the Resident whether he had yet spoken to the new Assistant Resident about Mrs Slotering.

'Mister. Havelaar. Says ...'

'Certainly, Verbrugge, why not? The lady can stay with us. I shouldn't like ...'

'That. It. Is. All right,' the Resident dragged out with great effort.

'I shouldn't like to close my door to a lady in her circumstances! Such a thing goes without saying ... doesn't it, Tina?'

Tina also considered that it went without saying.

'You have two houses at RANGKAS-BETUNG,' said Verbrugge. 'There's room and to spare for two families.'

'But even if there wasn't …'

'I. Could. Not. Promise …'

'Oh, Resident!' exclaimed Mrs Havelaar, 'there is no doubt about it!'

'It. To. Her. Because. It. Is …'

'Even if there were ten of them, so long as they're willing to take us as they find us.'

'A. Great. Inconvenience. And. She. Is …'

'But it's impossible for her to travel in her condition, Resident!'

A violent jerk of the carriage as it came out of the mud set an exclamation mark after Tina's assertion that travelling was impossible for Mrs Slotering. Everyone had uttered the usual 'Whoah!' that follows such a jerk; Max had found again in his mother's lap the *pisang* he had lost through the jolt; and they were already well on the way to the next mudhole, before the Resident could bring himself to conclude his sentence by adding:

…'A. Native. Woman.'

'Oh, that makes no difference,' Mrs Havelaar tried to tell him. The Resident nodded, as if to say he was glad the matter had thus been settled; and since conversation presented such difficulties, they dropped it.

The Mrs Slotering referred to was the widow of Havelaar's predecessor, who had died two months before. For the time being Verbrugge, who had thereupon been appointed Acting Assistant Resident, would have been entitled to occupy the spacious house which, at RANGKAS-BETUNG as in every Division, had been built by the Government for the head of the Divisional administration. However, he had not done so, partly perhaps from fear that he would have to move out again too soon, and partly in order to leave the use of it to Mrs Slotering and her children. Not that there would not have been room enough for him: in addition to the fairly large official dwelling itself, there stood next to it, in the same 'compound', another house, which had formerly served the same purpose and which, though somewhat dilapidated, was still perfectly fit to live in.

Mrs Slotering had asked the Resident to speak to her husband's successor on her behalf and obtain his permission for her to live in the old house until after her confinement, which would take place in a few months' time. It was this request which Havelaar and his wife had so readily granted, as was quite typical of them, for they were hospitable and helpful in the highest degree.

We have heard the Resident say that Mrs Slotering was a 'native woman'. This remark requires some elucidation for the non-East Indian reader, who might otherwise readily (and wrongly) come to the conclusion that the lady concerned was a full-blooded Javanese.

European society in the Dutch East Indies is rather sharply divided into two parts: the real Europeans, and those who—although legally enjoying exactly the same rights—were not born in Europe, and have more or less 'native' blood in their veins. In fairness to the conceptions of humanity in the East Indies I hasten to add here that, however sharp the line which is drawn in social life between the two classes of individuals who, for the genuine natives, both equally bear the name of *Hollander*,[48] this distinction has nothing of the barbarous character which prevails in the American status differentiation. I cannot deny that, even so, there is still much in this mutual relationship which is unjust and repellent, and that the name *liplap* (half-caste) has often grated on my ear as proof of the distance which separates many a non-half-caste, a 'white' person, from real civilization. It is true that only in exceptional cases is the half-caste admitted into European society, and that generally, if I may use a very slangy expression, he is not regarded as 'one hundred per cent'. But few people would present or defend such exclusion or disparagement as a *just principle*. Everyone is, of course, at liberty to choose his own environment and company, and one cannot blame the full European for preferring to mix with his own kind rather than with persons who—irrespective of their greater or lesser moral or intellectual value—do not share his impressions and ideas, or—and this, in a presumed difference in *civilization*, is perhaps very often the main thing—whose *prejudices have taken a different direction from his*.

A *liplap*—if I wanted to use the official, more polite term, I should have to say a '*so-called native child*', but I beg leave to keep to an idiom which seems born of alliteration; *I* intend nothing impolite by it, and what does the word mean anyway?—a liplap may have many good qualities. The European may also have many good qualities. Both have many that are bad, and in this too they resemble each other. But the good and the bad qualities inherent in both are too divergent for commerce between them to be, as a rule, mutually satisfactory. Besides—and for this the Government is largely responsible—the liplap is often ill educated. We are not concerned here with what the European would be like if his mental development had been thus impeded from his youth; but it is certain that *in general* the liplap's poor schooling hinders his being placed on an equality with the European, even when some *individual* liplap may perhaps deserve to be ranked above some *individual* European, as regards culture or scientific or artistic attainments.

In this too there is nothing new. It was, for instance, the policy of William the Conqueror to raise the most insignificant Norman above the most accomplished Saxon, and every Norman would appeal to the superiority of the Normans *in general*, in order to assert himself *in particular*, where he would have been the inferior *without* the influence of his countrymen as the dominant party.

Such a state of affairs naturally gives rise to a certain awkwardness in social intercourse, which nothing could remove except philosophical, broad-minded views and measures on the part of the Government.

It is obvious that the European, who is the gainer by such a relationship, feels perfectly comfortable in his artificial ascendancy. But it is often ludicrous to hear someone who acquired most of his culture and grammar in ZANDSTRAAT in Rotterdam jeer at the liplap because, in speaking Dutch, he makes *glass* or *government* masculine, or *sun* or *moon* neuter.

A liplap may be well-bred, well-educated, even learned—there are such! But no sooner has the European who shammed sick in order to stay away from the ship on which he washed dishes, and who bases his claims to good manners on "ow are yer?' and 'Beg pardon', become head of the commercial undertaking which made such 'stupendous' profits out of indigo in 1800-and-something ... nay, long before he becomes owner of the *toko*, the general store in which he sells hams and fowling-pieces—no sooner has this European noticed that the most well-bred liplap has difficulty in distinguishing between *h* and *g*, than he laughs at the stupidity of the man who does not know the difference between *hot* and *got*.

But, to take the grin off his face, our European would have to know that in Arabic and Malay those two consonants are expressed by one letter, that *Hieronymus* passes via *Geronimo* into *Jerôme*, that from *huano* we make *guano*, that our *hand* fits into a French *gant*, that *kous* in Dutch is *hose* in English, and that for *Guild Heaume* we say in Dutch *Huillem* or *Willem*. So much erudition is too much to ask from someone who made his fortune 'in' indigo and got his education from success in throwing dice ... or worse!

And such genuine Europeans surely cannot be expected to hob-nob with liplaps!

I understand how *Willem* comes from *Guillaume*, and I must admit that, especially in the Moluccas, I have often met liplaps who amazed me by the extent of their knowledge and who gave me the idea that we Europeans, in spite of all the resources at our disposal, are often—and *absolutely*, not merely *relatively*—far behind these poor pariahs, who have to contend from the very cradle with artificial, studied, unjust subordination and with silly prejudice against their colour.

But Mrs Slotering was preserved once and for all against making mistakes in Dutch because she could not speak anything but Malay. We shall get to see her later, when we take tea with Havelaar, Tina, and little Max on the front verandah of the Assistant Resident's house at RANGKAS-BETUNG, where our travellers, after much jolting and bumping, finally arrived in safety.

The Resident, who had only come to install the new Assistant Resident in his office, expressed the wish to return the same day to SERANG:

'Because. I...'

Havelaar also expressed his readiness to lose no time...

'Am. So. Busy.'

... and it was arranged that they would meet for the inaugural ceremony on the spacious front verandah of the Regent's house within half an hour. Verbrugge was prepared for this; days before, he had instructed the District Chiefs, the PATTEH, the KLIWON, the JAKSA,[49] the Tax Collector, some *mantris*, in fact all the native officials who had to attend the function, to assemble at the Divisional 'capital'.

The ADHIPATTI took his leave, and rode off home. Mrs Havelaar looked round her new house, and was very pleased with it, especially because it had a large garden and that struck her as fine for little Max, who needed to be a great deal in the open air. The Resident and Havelaar had retired to their rooms to change, for official uniform was obligatory at the coming ceremony. The house was surrounded by hundreds of people, who had either accompanied the Resident's carriage on horseback or belonged to the retinues of the assembled chiefs. The police- and office-orderlies hurried to and fro; in short, everything showed that the monotony of existence in this forgotten corner of the earth had been broken by a little life for a moment.

The handsome carriage of the ADHIPATTI soon drove across the open space before the house, and up to the door. The Resident and Havelaar, glittering with gold and silver but in danger of stumbling over their swords, got into it and were conveyed to the Regent's home, where they were received with the music of *gongs* and *gamelangs*.[50] Verbrugge, who had likewise put off his muddy costume, was already there. The lesser Chiefs sat on mats on the floor, in a wide circle, according to Oriental custom; and at the end of the long verandah stood a table at which the Resident, the ADHIPATTI, the Assistant Resident, the Controleur, and two or three of the Chiefs took their places. Tea and cakes were served, and the simple ceremony began.

The Resident rose and read out the Order of the Governor-General by which Max Havelaar was appointed Assistant Resident of the Division of BANTAN-KIDUL (South Bantam), as LEBAK is called by the natives. Then he took the *Official Gazette* containing the text of the oath laid down for the assumption of offices in general, which runs: *'that, in order to be appointed or promoted to the office of ......, [the person concerned] has promised or given nothing to anyone, nor will he promise or give anything; that he will be loyal and faithful to His Majesty the King of the Netherlands; that he will obey His Majesty's Representative in the East Indian Dominions; that he will strictly observe and cause to be observed the laws and regulations made or to be made, and that in all things he will act as behoves a good ...* (in this case: Assistant Resident).'

This was, of course, followed by the sacramental: *'So help me God Almighty.'*

Havelaar repeated the words as they were read out. Properly speaking, the promise *to protect the native population against exploitation and oppression* should have been considered as implicit in this oath. For, when swearing to uphold the existing laws and regulations, one only had to cast a glance at the numerous provisions they contained to that effect in order to see that a special oath for the purpose was really quite superfluous. But the legislator seemed to have considered that one cannot have too much of a good thing; at any rate, a separate oath is required of Assistant Residents in which this obligation towards the lowly is again explicitly stated. Havelaar therefore had once more to take 'God Almighty' as his witness, to the pledge that he *'would protect the native population against oppression, ill-treatment and extortion'*.

A keen observer would have found it interesting to note the

difference between the attitude and tone of the Resident and of Havelaar on this occasion. Both had attended such functions before. Hence the difference to which I allude did not consist in one or the other being more or less struck by the novelty or the unusual character of the scene, but was solely due to the dissimilarity between the natures of the two men. It is true that the Resident spoke slightly faster than usual, as he only had to *read* the Order and the oaths, which saved him the trouble of having to search for his final words. But, nevertheless, everything on his part was done with a stateliness and solemnity which were bound to give the superficial onlooker a very high idea of the importance he attached to the affair. Havelaar, on the other hand, when, with uplifted finger, he repeated the oaths, showed something in his face, voice and bearing that seemed to intimate: 'This goes without saying; I should do this even *without God Almighty*.' And anyone with some knowledge of human nature would have felt more confidence in his unconstrained manner and apparent indifference than in the official gravity of the Resident. For is it not absurd to think that a man who is called upon to administer justice, a man in whose hands is placed the weal or woe of thousands, would consider himself bound by a few spoken sounds if his own heart did not impel him to do right, even without those sounds?

We believe that Havelaar would have protected the poor and oppressed wherever he found them, even if he had promised the *opposite* by 'God Almighty'.

Then followed an address to the Chiefs by the Resident, who introduced the Assistant Resident to them as the head of the Division, asked them to obey him, to carry out their obligations conscientiously, and more such commonplaces. After this, the Chiefs were presented one by one to Havelaar. He shook hands with each of them, and the 'installation' was over.

Lunch was taken at the house of the ADHIPATTI, Commandant Duclari also being invited. Immediately after the meal the Resident, who wished to be back in SERANG that evening

Because. He. Was. So. Extremely. Busy.

... re-entered his travelling coach, and RANGKAS-BETUNG soon relapsed into the quiet to be expected at a Government station in the interior of Java where but few Europeans live and which, moreover, is not on the main road.

Duclari and Havelaar were soon at ease with each other. The ADHIPATTI likewise gave evidence of being well pleased with his new 'elder brother', and shortly afterwards Verbrugge mentioned that the Resident, whom he had escorted part of the way back to SERANG, had also spoken very favourably of the Havelaars, who had spent some days at his house en route for LEBAK. He had added that Havelaar, being highly thought of by the Government, would most probably ere long be promoted to higher office, or at least transferred to a more 'attractive' Division.

Max and 'his Tina' had only shortly been back from a voyage to Europe, and were tired of 'living in trunks', as I once heard it very curiously termed. So they considered themselves lucky, after long wanderings, to find themselves at last in a place which they could call home. Before their trip to Europe Havelaar had been Assistant Resident of Amboina, where he had had numerous difficulties to contend with because the population of that island was in a state of ferment and rebellion owing to the many mistaken measures that had recently been taken there. By exerting considerable energy he had succeeded in quelling this spirit of revolt; but, chagrined by the scant assistance given him by the authorities, and irked by the bad government which for centuries has depopulated and ruined the glorious region of the Moluccas ...

If the reader is interested in this subject, he should try to get hold of what was written about it as long ago as 1825 by Baron van der Capellen. He can find the articles of this friend of humanity in the *East Indian Gazette* for that year. The situation has not improved since then!

... anyway, Havelaar did what he could in Amboina, but, through fretting over the lack of co-operation he received from those whose first duty should have been to assist him, he became ill, and that had led to his going to Europe on furlough. Strictly speaking, on his reposting he had been entitled to a better place than the poor, by no means thriving, Division of LEBAK, because his office in Amboina had been of greater importance, and he had been entirely independent there, without a Resident over him. Moreover, before he left for Amboina his promotion to the rank of Resident had already been mooted, and some were surprised that he was now charged with the administration of a Division which yielded so little in the way of plantation bonuses, because many people measure the importance of a post by the income attached to it. However, he did not complain of this in the least, for his ambition was not of a kind to make him beg for higher rank or more money.

And yet more money would have stood him in good stead! For he had spent the little he had saved over the past years on his travels in Europe. He had even left some debts there, and he was, in a word, poor. But he had never looked on his profession as a money-making business, and on his appointment to LEBAK he had contentedly determined to wipe out his arrears by economy, knowing that his wife, who was so simple in her tastes and wants, would willingly second him.

But economy did not come easily to Havelaar. As far as he himself was concerned, he was able to limit his requirements to what was strictly necessary. In fact, he could restrain himself in this way without the slightest effort. But when other people needed assistance, it was a veritable passion with him to help, to give. He was well aware that this was a weakness; with all the common sense he had, he reasoned how *unjust* it was of him to succour anyone else when he himself had a stronger claim to his own support ... He felt this injustice still more acutely when 'his Tina' and Max, both of whom he loved so much, suffered from the results of his liberality... He reproached himself for his good nature as a weakness, as vanity, as a desire to pass for a prince in disguise ... He privately vowed to mend his ways, and yet ... every time someone or other succeeded in representing himself as a victim of misfortune, he forgot all good intentions in his eagerness to help. And that despite bitter experience of the consequences of this virtue of his become vice through excess! A week before the birth of little Max he had lacked the wherewithal to buy the iron cot that was to hold his darling, and yet only a short time previously he had sacrificed his wife's few jewels to come to the rescue of someone who was undoubtedly better off than himself.

But all this was already far behind them when they arrived in LE-BAK! In cheerful peace of mind they moved into the house 'where they really hoped to stay for some time'. They took a peculiar delight in ordering in Batavia the furniture that was to make everything so *comfortable* (sic) and cosy. They showed each other the places where they would breakfast, where little Max would play, where their books would stand, where, in the evening, Havelaar would read to Tina what he had written during the day, for he was always working out his ideas on paper ... and: 'some day that would be printed,' thought Tina, 'and then people would see what sort of man her Max was!' But never yet had he sent to the press any of the things that passed through his brain, for he was possessed by a kind of diffidence which was not unlike chastity. He himself, at any rate, was unable to describe this diffidence better than by asking those who urged him to publish: 'Would *you* send your daughter out into the street stark naked?'

This, again, was one of the many sallies that made people around him say: 'Really, that Havelaar *is* a peculiar type!' And I will not say they were wrong. But if you had taken the trouble to translate his unusual mode of expression you would probably have found, in his strange question about a girl's costume, the text for a treatise on that chastity of the spirit which shrinks from the stare of coarse passers-by and would fain cloak itself in a mantle of maidenly modesty.

Yes, they would be happy at RANGKAS-BETUNG, would Havelaar and his Tina! The only cares that still weighed on them were the debts they had left behind in Europe, together with the still unpaid costs of the voyage back to the East Indies, and the expense of furnishing their new house. But they would live on half, on one third, of his income, wouldn't they? Perhaps, again, in fact probably, he would soon be made a Resident, and then everything would come right in no time at all ...

'Though I should be very sorry to leave Lebak, Tina, because there's a lot to be done here. You must be very economical, sweetheart, and then we may be able to pay off everything, even if I don't get promotion ... and if we manage that, I would hope to stay in Lebak a long time, a very long time!'

This exhortation to economy, however, need not have been addressed to *her*. If they had to be careful, it was certainly not *her* fault. But she had so completely identified herself with her Max that she felt the admonition in no way as a reproach. Nor was it meant to be; for Havelaar knew perfectly well that it was only *he* who had failed, through being too openhanded, and that *her* mistake—if mistake there was in her case—had only been her love of him, which had always made her approve everything he did.

Yes, *she* had approved of his taking two poor women, who lived in Nieuwstraat and had never left Amsterdam and never had an 'outing', round the fair at Haarlem, on the amusing pretext that the King had charged him with: 'the entertainment of old ladies who had lived an exemplary life'. *She* had approved of his treating the orphans of all the institutions in Amsterdam to cake and almond milk, and loading them with toys. *She* fully understood that it was up to him to pay the hotel bill for the family of poor singers who wanted to go back to their own country but did not want to leave their belongings behind, including the harp and the violin and the double-bass which they needed so badly for their poverty-stricken profession. *She* could not consider it wrong that he should bring to her the girl who had accosted him in the street one evening ... that he gave the girl food and lodging, and did not address to her the all-too-cheap admonition 'Go, and sin no more!' before he had made it possible for her not to 'sin'. *She* greatly admired her Max for having the piano returned to the drawing-room of the father whom he had heard say how much it hurt him that his girls had had to do without their music 'since my bankruptcy'. *She* understood perfectly that her Max had to buy the liberty of the slave family at Menado, when they were so heartbroken at having to mount the auctioneer's block. *She* thought it natural that Max should give other horses to the Alfuros in MINNAHASSA, when theirs had been ridden to death by the officers of the BAYONNAISE.[51] *She* did not object when he called before him, at MENADO and at AMBOINA, the castaways from the American whalers, and looked after them and felt too much of a *grand seigneur* to present an 'inn-keeper's reckoning' for it to the American Government. *She* thought it quite normal that the officers of every man-of-war that arrived mostly stayed with Max, and that his house was their favourite *pied-à-terre*.

Was he not *her* Max? Would it not have been too petty, too trivial, too absurd, to bind him, who thought on so princely a scale, to the rules of economy and thrift which apply to others? And besides, even though at times there might be some disproportion between their income and their expenditure, was not Max, *her* Max, destined for a brilliant career? Would he not soon be in circumstances which would enable him to give free rein to his generous inclinations without exceeding his income? Would not *her* Max be Governor-General of her beloved Indies some day, or even ... a King? In fact, was it not strange that he was not a King already?

If any faults could be found in her, they were due to her infatuation with Havelaar; and if ever it was true to say that much must be forgiven to those who have loved much, it was true in her case!

But she had nothing to be forgiven for. Without sharing the exaggerated notions she cherished about her Max, one may still assume that he had a promising career before him; and if those well-founded prospects had been realized, the unpleasant consequences of his generosity really might have been remedied. But a further reason, of an entirely different nature, excused the Havelaars' seeming carelessness.

Tina had lost both parents when she was very young, and had been brought up by relatives. When she married they told her that she possessed a little money, which they paid to her. But from some letters of earlier date, and from some stray notes and jottings which she kept in a casket that had belonged to her mother, Max discovered that her family had been very wealthy, on both her father's and her mother's side; yet he could not make out where, when or how that wealth had disappeared. Tina had never taken any interest in money matters herself, and could say little or nothing when he pressed her for details of the former possessions of her kinsmen. Her grandfather, Baron van W., had followed Prince William the Fifth into exile in England, and had been a cavalry captain in the army of the Duke of York. He appeared to have led a gay life with the exiled members of the Stadholder's family, and many people said that this was how he had lost his fortune. He afterwards fell at Waterloo, in a charge with the Boreel Hussars. It was touching to read the letters of Tina's father—then a youth of eighteen, who, as a lieutenant in the corps, took part in the same charge and received a sabre-cut on the head, from the consequences of which he was to die insane eight years later—letters to his mother, in which he lamented that he had searched the battlefield for his father's body in vain.

As regards her mother's side of the family, Tina remembered that her grandfather had lived in great affluence, and it was evident from some of the papers that he had owned the postal service in Switzerland in the same manner as, even now, this branch of revenue is an appanage of the Princes of TURN AND TAXIS in large parts of Germany and Italy. This suggested a large fortune, but here again, for entirely unknown reasons, nothing or only very little had come down to the second generation.

Havelaar did not learn what little was to be learnt about the matter until after his marriage, and during his investigations he was surprised to find that the casket which I have just referred to—and which, with its contents, Tina had kept out of filial piety, without guessing that there might be documents in it which were of importance from a financial point of view—had unaccountably disappeared. Though in no way mercenary Havelaar could not help forming the opinion, from this and many other circumstances, that a *roman intime* lurked behind it all; and, with his expensive proclivities, one can hardly blame him for the fact that he would very much have liked that novel to have had a happy ending. Now, whatever may have been the truth about this *roman*, and whether or not 'spoliation' had taken place, there is no doubt that in Havelaar's imagination something had arisen that might have been called a *rêve aux millions*.

But again, it was strange that he, who would most meticulously and keenly have ferreted out and defended the rights of others, however deeply buried under dusty documents and thick-spun chicaneries—here, where his own interests were concerned, he carelessly let pass the moment at which the matter might perhaps have been tackled with the best chance of success. He seemed to feel something like shame, because here his own advantage was at stake; and I firmly believe that if 'his Tina' had been married to someone else, who had appealed to him to lend a hand in breaking the cobwebs in which her ancestral fortune had got tangled, he would have managed to restore to 'the interesting orphan' the fortune that was rightfully hers. But now that this interesting orphan was *his* wife, and her fortune was *his*, he felt there was something shopkeeperish, something degrading, about asking in her name: 'Are you sure you don't owe me something?'

And yet he could not shake off this dream of millions of money, even if it was only to have an excuse handy to answer his oft-recurring self-reproach that he spent too much.

Not until shortly before they returned to Java, when he had already suffered considerably from shortage of cash, when he had had to bow his proud head under the yoke of many a creditor, had he succeeded in conquering his lethargy or his reluctance, and taken up the matter of the millions he fancied might still be due to him.

And he was answered with an old unpaid bill ... an argument which is unassailable, as everyone knows.

But oh, they were going to be so careful in LEBAK! And why shouldn't they be? In such a barbaric country no girls wander about the streets at night, with a little honour to sell for a little food. There, you meet no stray people who live by dubious professions. There, no family is suddenly ruined by a change of fortune ... and such, after all, were usually the rocks on which Havelaar's good intentions foundered. The number of Europeans in that Division was so insignificant as to be negligible, and the Javanese in LEBAK were too poor to become interesting through still greater poverty, no matter what vicissitude befell them. Tina did not exactly consider all this—if she had, she would have had to go into the causes of their reduced circumstances more precisely than her love of Max made her want to do. But their new surroundings had about them something that breathed calm after the storm, and an absence of all the occasions—of course, with a more or less falsely romantic tint —which had in the past so often made Havelaar say:

'Tina, this surely is something I can't possibly get out of, can I?'

And to which Tina had always answered:

'No, certainly not, Max, you can't possibly get out of it!'

We shall see, however, how this simple, apparently humdrum place of LEBAK cost Havelaar more than all the past excesses of his heart put together. But that they could not know! They looked to the future with confidence, and felt so happy in their love and in the possession of their child ...

'What a lot of roses there are in the garden,' exclaimed Tina, 'and *rampeh* and *chempaka* too, and so much *melati*, and just look at those beautiful lilies ...!'

And, children as they were, they revelled in their new house. And that evening, when Duclari and Verbrugge, after visiting the Havelaars, returned to the home they shared together, they talked a great deal about the childlike gaiety of the new arrivals.

But Havelaar went to his office and stayed there all night.

8

Havelaar had asked the Controleur to request the Chiefs who had come to RANGKAS-BETUNG to remain there until next day and attend the *Sebah*, the council meeting, he wished to hold. These meetings were usually held once a month, but either because he wanted to save some of the Chiefs from unnecessary travelling to and fro, since they lived rather far from the main centre and the Division of LEBAK is very extensive, or because he wanted to speak to them earnestly at once, without waiting for the appointed day, he fixed the first *Sebah* for the morning after his installation.

In front of his house, to the left of it but in the same compound and opposite the house in which Mrs Slotering lived, stood a building partly given up to the offices of the Assistant Residency, including the local Treasury, and partly consisting of a fairly large open verandah, which offered a very suitable venue for such a meeting. And there it was that the Chiefs assembled, early that morning.

Havelaar entered, greeted them, and sat down. He was given the written monthly reports on agriculture, police and justice, and laid them on one side for further perusal.

After this, everyone expected an address like that which the Resident had delivered the day before. And it is not altogether certain that Havelaar himself intended to say anything different; but you had to have heard and seen him on such occasions to realize how, during speeches of this kind, he was carried away, and by his peculiar style of speaking imparted a new colour to the most familiar things; how then he would stiffen and rise erect, his eyes would shoot fire, his voice would change from caressing softness to lancet sharpness; how from his lips would flow metaphors as though he were strewing around him jewels which, however costly, had cost *him* nothing; and, when he ceased, how everyone gazed at him open-mouthed, as though asking: 'Heavens above, who *are* you?'

It must be admitted that he, who on such occasions spoke like an Apostle, a seer, could not remember afterwards exactly what he had said; and so his eloquence was more fitted to astonish and move than to convince by succinct argument. If he had been in Athens after the Athenians had resolved on war against Philip of Macedon he might have fired their martial spirit to frenzy; but he would probably have been less successful if his task had been to persuade them into the war by logical reasoning. His address to the Chiefs of LEBAK was, of course, in Malay, and this lent it an additional peculiarity, since the simplicity of the Eastern languages gives many of their expressions a force which our idioms have lost through literary sophistication; again, the mellifluousness of Malay is difficult to reproduce in any other tongue. It should likewise be remembered that the majority of his hearers were simple though by no means stupid people, and also that they were Orientals, whose reactions are very different from ours.

Havelaar must have spoken something like this:

'RADHEN ADHIPATTI, Regent of BANTAN-KIDUL, and you, RADHENS DHEMANG, who are Chiefs of the Districts in this Division, and you, RADHEN JAKSA, whose office is to see to justice, and you also, RADHEN KLIWON, who exercise authority in the Divisional centre, and you, RADHENS, MANTRIS, and all who are Chiefs in the Division of BANTAN-KIDUL, I greet you!

'And I say unto you that I feel joy in my heart, seeing you all assembled here, listening to the words of my mouth.

'I know that there are those among you who excel in knowledge and in goodness of heart. I hope to add to my knowledge from yours, for my store thereof is not as large as I would wish. And though I love goodness, yet often am I made aware that in me there are faults which overshadow my heart's goodness, and stunt its growth ... You all know how the large tree supplants the little one, and kills it. Therefore I shall look to those amongst you who excel in virtue, that I may seek to become better than I am.

'I greet you all most warmly.

'When the Governor-General commanded me to come to you as Assistant Resident of this Division, my heart was rejoiced. It may be known to you that I had never set foot in BANTAN-KIDUL. Therefore I caused to be given to me writings dealing with your Division, and I have seen that there is much that is good in BANTAN-KIDUL. Your people possess rice fields in the valleys, and there are rice fields on the mountains. And you wish to live in peace, and you do not desire to dwell in lands inhabited by others. Yes, I know that there is much that is good in BANTAN-KIDUL!

'But not only because of this was my heart rejoiced. For in other regions also, I should have found much that was good.

'But I perceived that your people are poor, and for this I was glad in my inmost soul.

'For I know that Allah loves the poor, and that He gives riches to those whom He will try. But to the poor He sends the one who speaks His word, that they may lift up their heads in the midst of their misery.

'Does He not give rain where the ears are withering, and a dewdrop in the cup of the thirsty flower?

'And is it not glorious to be sent to seek them that are weary, who lag behind after the day's labour, and sink by the wayside since their knees are no longer strong enough to bear them to the place where their hire is to be paid? Should I not rejoice to be allowed to hold out a helping hand to him who falls into the pit, and to give a staff to him who climbs the mountain? Should not my heart leap up to see itself chosen from among many to turn lamentation into prayer, and weeping into thanksgiving?

'Yes, I am overjoyed at being called to BANTAN-KIDUL!

'I have said to the woman who divides my troubles and multiplies my happiness: "Rejoice, for I see that Allah heaps blessing on the head of our child! He has sent me to a place where not all the labour has yet been accomplished, and He has judged me worthy to be there before the harvest time. For the joy lies not in the cutting of the *paddy*, but in the cutting of the *paddy* one has planted oneself. And the soul of man grows not from the hire, but from the labour that earns the hire." And I said to her: "Allah has given us a child who will one day say: 'Do you know that I am *his* son?' And then there will be those in the land who will greet him with love, and who will lay their hands on his head, and say: 'Sit down at our table, and dwell in our house, and partake of all that we have, for we knew your father.'"

'Chiefs of LEBAK, there is much work to do in your region!

'Tell me, is not the husbandman poor? Does not your *paddy* often ripen to feed those who did not plant it? Are there not many wrongs in your land? Is not the number of your children small?

'Is there no shame in your souls when the dweller in BANDUNG, that lies yonder to the eastward, visits your land, and asks: "Where are the villages, and where the husbandmen? And why do I not hear the *gamelang*, that speaks gladness with its mouth of brass, nor the pounding of the *paddy* by your daughters?"

'Is it not bitter for you, to journey hence to the south coast and see the mountains that bear no water on their flanks? Or the plains where never a buffalo drew the plough?

'Yes, yes ... I say unto you that your soul and mine are sad because of these things! And for that very reason are we grateful to Allah that He has given us the power to labour here.

'For in this land we have acres for many, though the dwellers in it are few. And it is not the rain which is lacking, for the tops of the mountains suck the clouds from heaven to earth. And it is not everywhere that rocks refuse room to the root, for in many places the soil is soft and fertile, and cries out for the grain, which she wishes to return to us in the bending ear. And there is no war in the land, to trample down the *paddy* while it is yet green, nor sickness to render the *pachol*[52] useless. Nor are there sunbeams hotter than is needed to ripen the crop that shall feed you and your children, nor *banjirs*[53] to make you lament: "Show me the place where I have sown!"

'Where Allah sends floods to wash away the fields ... where He makes His sun burn even to scorching ... where He sends war to devastate the land ... where He smites with sicknesses that make the hands hang heavy, or with drought that kills the rice in the ear ...

there, Chiefs of LEBAK, we bow the head in meekness, and say: "His will be done!"

'But it is not so in BANTAN-KIDUL!

'I have been sent here to be your friend, your elder brother. Would you not warn your younger brother if you saw a tiger in his path?

'Chiefs of LEBAK, we have made many mistakes, and our land is poor because we have made so many mistakes.

'For in CHIKANDI and BOLANG, and in KRAWANG, and in the regions round Batavia, there are many who were born in our land and who have left our land.

'Why do they seek labour far from the place where they buried their parents? Why have they fled from the *dessah* where they were circumcised? Why did they choose the coolness under the tree that grows *there* rather than the shade of our forests?

'And even yonder in the north-west, across the sea, there are many who should have been our children, but who have left LEBAK to wander round in alien regions with *kris* and *klewang*[54] and rifle. And they perish miserably, for the power of the Government is there, which strikes down the rebels.

'Chiefs of LEBAK, I ask you, why have so many gone away to be buried where they were not born? Why does the tree ask: "Where is the man I saw playing at my foot as a child?"'

Havelaar paused. In order to have any idea of the impression his words produced, you would have had to hear and see him. When he spoke of his own child there was in his voice something soft, something indescribably moving, which made you ask: 'Where is the little one? I cannot wait to kiss the child that makes his father speak like this!' But when shortly afterwards, with little apparent transition, he passed on to ask why LEBAK was poor, and why so many of its inhabitants left to go elsewhere, his tone reminded you of the sound of a gimlet being forcefully screwed into hard wood. And yet he did not speak loudly, nor did he lay any stress on particular words, and there was even a certain monotony in his voice; but, whether it was studied or natural, this very monotony imprinted his words the more deeply in hearts that were peculiarly receptive to such language.

His metaphors and images, always taken from the life around him, really were to him instruments for making his meaning exactly clear to his audience, and not, as is so often the case, the irksome appendages that encumber the periods of orators without helping to illuminate the matter they profess to be explaining. We are nowadays quite accustomed to the absurd expression 'strong as a lion'. But the person who first used that simile in Europe showed that he had not drawn it from the poesy of the soul, which reasons in pictures and *cannot* speak otherwise, but had merely copied his commonplace image from some book or other—perhaps the Bible—in which a *lion* occurred. For none of his hearers had ever experienced the strength of the lion; and consequently it would have been more to the point to make them realize *that* strength, by comparing the lion with something whose strength was known to them from experience, than vice versa.

One cannot but acknowledge that Havelaar was a true poet. One cannot but feel that, when he spoke of the rice fields on the mountains, he raised his eyes to them through the open side of the 'hall', and really saw those fields. One cannot but realize that, when he made the tree ask where the man was who had played at its foot as a child, that tree actually stood there and, in the imagination of Havelaar's audience, really did gaze around it in search of the departed inhabitants of LEBAK. He invented nothing: he *heard* the tree speak, and considered he was only repeating what he had so clearly heard in his poetic inspiration.

If anyone should remark that the originality of Havelaar's style of address was not altogether indisputable, since his language recalled that of the Old Testament prophets, I would remind him that I have already said that in moments of exaltation he really became more or less a seer. Fed on the impressions communicated to him by a life in forests and mountains, and by the poetry-breathing atmosphere of the East, he would not have spoken otherwise even if he had never read the sublime poems of the Old Testament.

In verses dating from his youth, do we not already find lines like the following (written on SALAK—one of the giants, though not the greatest, among the mountains of the PREANGER REGENCIES), in which, again, the opening portrays the tenderness of his emotions but suddenly passes on to echo the thunder he hears beneath him?

'Tis sweeter here to praise aloud one's Maker ...
Prayer sounds more fair by mountainside and hill ...
The heart ascends higher than it does yonder—
On mountains one is nearer to God's will!
Here He created temple-choirs and altar,
Where foot of man brings no impurity,
Here He makes to Himself the tempest for his psalter ...
And rolling roars His thunder: Majesty!

... And do we not feel that the last lines could not have been as they are, if he had not really heard God's thunder dictating them to him, in periods reverberating from the mountain walls?

But he did not really like writing verse. 'It was a nasty corset,' he said; and if he was induced to read anything he had 'committed', as he put it, he took a delight in spoiling his own work, either by reciting it in a tone calculated to make it ridiculous, or by suddenly stopping, especially in a highly serious passage, and throwing in a quip which was painful to his audience but which, to him, was nothing else than a satirical comment, wrung from the heart, on the disproportion between that corset, that straitjacket, and his soul, which felt so cramped in it.

Few of the Chiefs partook of the refreshments that were served when Havelaar, with a sign, ordered that tea with *maniessan*,[55] the inevitable accompaniment to such an occasion, should be brought in. It seemed as though he deliberately wished to provide an interval after his last sentence. And he had good reason for that. 'Why,' the Chiefs were meant to think, 'he already knows that so many have left our Division in bitterness of heart! He already knows how many families have emigrated to neighbouring regions, to escape the poverty that prevails here! And he even knows there are so many *Bantammers* in the gangs that have raised the banner of rebellion against Dutch authority in the LAMPONG DISTRICTS! What does he want? What does he mean? Who does he have in mind, with his questions?'

And some of them looked at RADHEN ..., the District Chief of PARANG-KUJANG. But most of them looked at the ground.

'Come here, Max!' called Havelaar, noticing his son playing outside in the compound; and the *Regent* took the child on his lap. But little Max was too restless to stay there for long. He jumped down, and ran round the wide circle, amusing the Chiefs with his prattle and playing with the hilts of their *krises*. When he came to the JAKSA—who caught the child's attention because he was more strikingly dressed than the others—that Chief seemed to point out something on little Max's head to the KLIWON, who sat next to him and who seemed to agree with his whispered remark on the subject.

'Go away now, Max,' said Havelaar, 'Papa has something to say to these gentlemen.'

The child ran off, throwing kisses with his hands by way of taking leave.

Whereupon Havelaar continued:

'Chiefs of LEBAK! We are all in the service of the King of the Netherlands. But He, who is just, and who requires us to do our duty, is far from here. Thirty times a thousand thousand souls, nay, more, are bound to obey his commands; but he cannot be near all those who depend on his will.

'The Great Lord at BUITENZORG is just, and requires everyone to do his duty. But he too, mighty though he is, and having authority over all who wield power in the towns and all who are elders in the villages, and having in his hand the forces of the army and of the ships that sail the seas—he too is unable to see where injustice is done, for it remains far from him.

'And the Resident at Serang, who is Lord of the region of Bantam, where five times a hundred thousand people dwell, requires justice to be done in his domain, and righteousness to reign in the lands that obey him. But when there is injustice, it is far from his dwelling. And whoever does evil hides from his face, for fear of punishment.

'And the Lord Adhipatti, who is Regent of South Bantam, desires that all shall live who practise goodness, and that no shame shall come to the land over which he is Regent.

'And I, who yesterday called upon Almighty God to witness that I would be just and merciful, that I would dispense justice without fear and without hate, that I would be "a good Assistant Resident"… I wish to do my duty.

'Chiefs of Lebak! We *all* wish to do our duty!

'But should there happen to be amongst us those who neglect their duty for gain, who sell justice for money, or who take the buffalo from the poor man and the fruits that belong to those who are hungry … who shall punish them?

'If one of you knew it, he would prevent it. And the Regent would not suffer such things to happen in his Regency. And I too shall stop it wherever I can. But if neither you, nor the Adhipatti, nor I should know it…

'Chiefs of Lebak! Who then would do justice in Bantan-Kidul?

'Listen to me, and I will tell you how justice would then be done.

'There comes a time when our women and children will weep as they prepare our shroud, and the passer-by will say: "Someone has died in that house!" Then whoever arrives in the villages will bring tidings of the death of the one that is no more, and whosoever harbours him will ask: "Who was the man that died?" And it will be said:

'"He was good and righteous. He administered justice, and drove not the injured from his door. He listened patiently to those that came to him, and restored to them what had been taken from them. And if a man could not drive the plough through the soil because his buffalo had been stolen from the stall, he helped him find the buffalo. And where the daughter had been taken from the house of the mother, he found the thief and brought back the daughter. And where the labourer had laboured he withheld not his wage from him, and he took not the fruit from him who had planted the tree. And he clothed himself not with the garment that should have covered another, nor did he feed himself with food that belonged to the poor."

'Then will they say in the villages: "Allah is great, Allah has taken him unto Himself. His will be done ... a good man has died."

'And again the passer-by will stop before a house, and ask: "Why is this, that the *gamelang* is silent, and the song of the maidens?" And again they will say to him: "A man has died."

'And he who travels through the villages will sit with his host at eve, and round about him will be the sons and daughters of the houses, and the children of those that live in the village, and he will say:

'"A man has died who vowed to be just; and he sold justice to whoever gave him money. He made his field fertile with the sweat of the labourer whom he had called away from his own field of labour. He withheld the wage from the worker, and fed himself on the food of the poor. He grew rich from the poverty of others. He had much gold and silver, and precious stones in abundance, but the husbandman who dwelt in his neighbourhood knew not how to still the hunger of his child. He smiled like a happy man, but there was gnashing of teeth from the plaintiff who sought redress. There was contentment on his face, but no milk in the breasts of the mothers who suckled."

'Then the dwellers in the villages will say: "Allah is great ... we curse no one!"

'Chiefs of LEBAK, death comes to us all!

'What will be said in the villages where we had power? And what by the passers-by who look on at our burial?

'And what shall we answer when, after our death, a voice shall

123

speak to our souls, and ask: "Why is there weeping in the fields, and why are the young men in hiding? Who took from the barn the harvest, and from the stall the buffalo that was to plough the field? What have you done with the brother whom I gave you, to be to him as a guardian? Why is the poor man sad, and why does he curse the fruitfulness of his wife?"'

Here Havelaar paused again; and after a few moments' silence he went on in the simplest manner possible, as though nothing whatever had been said that was meant to make an impression:

'I should like to live on good terms with you all, and so I ask you to look upon me as a friend. If anyone has erred, he may count on a lenient judgment from me, for, since I err only too often myself, I shall not be severe ... that is to say, not in the matter of ordinary offences of commission or omission in the service. Only when neglect of duty becomes a habit shall I seek to combat it. I will not speak of grosser misdemeanours ... of extortion and oppression. Nothing of that kind happens here, does it, ADHIPATTI?'

'Oh no, Sir, nothing of that kind happens in LEBAK.'

'Well, then, gentlemen, Chiefs of BANTAN-KIDUL, let us rejoice that our Division is so backward and so poor. We have noble work to do. If Allah preserves our lives, we shall see to it that prosperity comes. The soil is fertile, and the people are willing. If everyone is left in enjoyment of the fruit of his labours, there is no doubt that in a short space of time the population will increase both in numbers and in possessions and culture, for these things generally go hand in hand. Once more I ask you to look upon me as a friend whe will help you when he can, especially where injustice has to bo fought. And in this I shall be most grateful for your co-operation.

'In due course I shall return to you the Reports on Agriculture, Cattle-raising, Police and Justice, with my decisions.

'Chiefs of BANTAN-KIDUL! I have spoken. You may return, every one to his own house. My best wishes go with you all!'

He bowed, offered his arm to the old Regent, and conducted him across the compound to where Tina stood waiting on the front verandah.

'Come, Verbrugge, don't go home yet! Come on … what about a glass of Madeira? And … oh yes, there's something I *must* know. RADHEN JAKSA! Just a minute!'

Havelaar called this as all the Chiefs, with much bowing and scraping, were preparing to go home. Verbrugge was also on the point of leaving the compound, but now came back with the JAKSA.

'Tina, I'd like some Madeira, and so would Verbrugge. JAKSA, tell me, what was it you said to the KLIWON about Max?'

'*Mintah ampong,*[56] Sir, I looked at his head because you had spoken.'

'What the deuce has his head got to do with that? I've already forgotten what I said.'

'Sir, I told the KLIWON…'

Tina edged nearer; they were talking about little Max!

'Sir, I told the KLIWON that the *sienyo*[57] was a royal child.'

That pleased Tina. She thought so too!

The ADHIPATTI examined the head of the little boy and, to be sure, he too saw the *user-useran,* the double crown of hair which, according to Javanese superstition, means that its owner is destined eventually to wear a royal crown.

As etiquette did not permit of offering the JAKSA a seat in the presence of the Regent, the former took his leave, and for a while everyone talked without touching upon anything relating to 'the Service'. But abruptly—and therefore at variance with the Javanese native character, which is so extremely courteous—the Regent asked whether certain moneys which were down to the Tax Collector's credit could not be paid out?

'Of course not,' exclaimed Verbrugge. 'ADHIPATTI, you know it can't be done before the Collector's accounts have been passed.'

Havelaar was playing with Max. But that evidently did not prevent him from reading in the Regent's face that Verbrugge's answer did not please him.

'Come, Verbrugge, let's not be difficult,' he said. And he sent for a clerk from the office. 'We may as well pay this … the accounts are sure to be approved.'

When the ADHIPATTI had gone, Verbrugge, who was a stickler for the regulations, said:

'But, Mr Havelaar, this can't be done! The Collector's accounts are still at SERANG for examination ... suppose they're short?'

'Then I shall make it up,' said Havelaar.

Verbrugge simply could not see the reason for such excessive willingness to accommodate the Tax Collector. The clerk soon came back with some papers. Havelaar signed, and gave orders that the payment should be made without delay.

'Verbrugge, I'll tell you why I'm doing this! The Regent hasn't a penny in the house, his clerk told me so, and besides ... look at the brusque way he asked! It's as plain as a pikestaff. He wants that money *himself*, and the Collector is willing to lend it to him. I'd sooner break a regulation off my own bat than leave a man of his rank and years in embarrassment. And, Verbrugge, there's a scandalous abuse of authority in LEBAK. You ought to know that. *Do* you know it?'

Verbrugge was silent.

'*I* know it,' Havelaar went on, '*I know it*! Mr. Slotering died in November, didn't he? Well, the *day after his death* the Regent called up people to work on his *sawahs* ... without payment! You should have known this. *Did* you know it?'

Verbrugge did not know it.

'As Controleur, you *ought* to have known it! I do know it,' Havelaar continued. 'Here you have the monthly returns from the Districts'—and he showed him the packet of papers he had received at the meeting—'you see, I haven't opened anything. But in that packet you'll find the figures for the workers sent to the Divisional centre for statute labour. Well, are those figures correct?'

'I haven't seen them yet...'

'Nor have I! But I still ask you whether they are correct? Were the figures for the previous month correct?'

Verbrugge was silent.

'I'll tell you: they weren't! Because three times as many people had been summoned to work for the Regent as the regulations allow, and of course they didn't dare put *that* down in the returns. Is it true, what I'm saying? Or not?'

Verbrugge was silent.

'And the returns I've received to-day are false, too,' Havelaar went on. 'The Regent is poor. The Regents of BANDUNG and CHIANJUR are members of the family of which he is the head. He's an ADHIPATTI, and the Regent of CHIANJUR is only a TOMMONGONG, and yet, because LEBAK isn't suitable for coffee-growing, and consequently brings him in nothing extra, his income does not permit him to compete in pomp and circumstance with a humble DHEMANG in the PREANGER REGENCIES, who would have to hold the stirrup when our Regent's cousins mount their horses. Is that true?'

'Yes.'

'He has nothing but his salary, and that's reduced by a deduction to pay off an advance the Government made him when he... do you know?'

'Yes, I know.'

'—when he wanted to build a new mosque, which called for a lot of money. Besides, many of his family... do you know?'

'Yes, I know.'

'Many members of his family—who actually don't belong in LEBAK, and so aren't looked up to by the people either—swarm around him like a gang of thieves, and squeeze money out of him. Is this true? Or am I wrong?'

'It is the truth,' said Verbrugge.

'And when his coffers are empty, which is often the case, they rob the people *in his name* of everything that takes their fancy. Is this so?'

'It is.'

'So I'm correctly informed; but I'll say more about that later. The Regent's getting on in years, he's afraid of death and he's obsessed with the desire to win merit by gifts to the priests. He spends a lot of money paying the travelling expenses of pilgrims to Mecca, who bring him back all sorts of trash in the way of relics, charms and *jimats*.[58] Isn't that so?'

127

'Yes, that is so.'

'Well—it's because of all this that he's so poor. The DHEMANG of PARANG-KUJANG is his son-in-law. The Regent dare not help himself to other people's property, for fear of bringing discredit on his rank; but this DHEMANG does it for him—though he isn't the only one. He curries favour with the ADHIPATTI by extorting money and goods from the poor wretches, and by fetching them from their own rice fields and herding them to work on the Regent's *sawahs*, and the Regent... look, I'm willing to believe he would like it to be otherwise, but needs must when the devil drives. Isn't this all true, Verbrugge?'

'Yes, it's true,' said Verbrugge, who began to realize more and more that Havelaar had sharp eyes.

'I knew,' the other went on, 'that he has no money in the house. This morning you heard that I mean to do my duty. I will not put up with injustice, by God—*I will not put up with it*!'

And he sprang to his feet, and his tone was very different from that of the previous day, when he took his *official* oath.

'But,' he resumed, 'I want to do my duty gently. I don't want to know too much about what has happened in the past. But whatever happens from to-day is *my* responsibility, and *I* will answer for it! I hope to be here a long time. D'you realize, Verbrugge, that our calling's a magnificent one? But do you realize, too, that everything I said to you just now, I should really have heard from *you*? I know you as well as I know which people are making *garem glap*[59] on the south coast. You're an honest man... I know that too. But why didn't you tell me there was so much wrong here? You've been Acting Assistant Resident for the last two months, and you've been here as Controleur for much longer... so you must have known these things, mustn't you?'

'Mr Havelaar, I have never served under anyone like you. You're something out of the common, if you'll excuse my saying so.'

'Of course! I'm perfectly well aware I'm not like everyone else... but what has that got to do with it?'

'It has this to do with it: that you express conceptions and ideas that never existed before.'

'Oh yes they did! But they'd been lulled asleep by the damned official routine round which finds its style in "*I have the honour to be*" and its peace of mind in "*the great satisfaction of the Government*". No, Verbrugge! Don't slander yourself! You've nothing to learn from me. For instance, did I tell you anything new this morning at the *Sebah*?'

'No, not exactly new, but you spoke differently from others...'

'Yes, that is... because I've been rather badly brought up: I say just what comes into my head. But you ought to tell me why you've lain down under all that was wrong in LEBAK.'

'Until to-day I never got the impression of any *initiative* being taken. Besides, things have always been so in these parts.'

'Yes, yes, I know! Not everyone can be a prophet or an apostle... my word, if it was otherwise wood would become dear from all the crucifying! But I'm sure you'll help me to put everything right? I'm sure you'll do your *duty*?'

'Of course! Especially towards you. But not everyone would demand it so rigorously, or esteem it, or even take it in good part, and then a man so easily gets put down as someone who tilts at windmills.'

'No! That's the sort of thing which is said by people who love injustice because they live by it, saying that there *was* no injustice so as to have the pleasure of calling you and me Don Quixotes and at the same time keeping *their* windmills turning. But, Verbrugge, you needn't have waited for *me* before you did your duty! Mr Slotering was an able and honest man: *he* knew what was going on, he disapproved of it, and fought it ... look!'

Havelaar took from a file two sheets of paper, which he showed to Verbrugge, and asked: 'Whose writing is this?'

'Mr Slotering's...'

'Exactly! Well, these are rough notes, apparently on subjects he wished to discuss with the Resident. I read here ... look: "1. *On rice cultivation*; 2. *On the houses of the village chiefs*; 3. *On collection of the land taxes!! etc.*" After Number Three there are two exclamation marks. What did Mr Slotering mean by those?'

'How should *I* know?' exclaimed Verbrugge.

'*I* know! It means that far more money is paid in land tax than ever finds its way into the Treasury. But now I'll show you something we can both know, because it's written in letters and not in signs. Look here:

12. *On the exploitation of the people by the Regents and the lesser chiefs. (On the practice of keeping up several houses at the expense of the population, etc.)*

'Is this clear? You see, Mr Slotering *was* a man who knew how to take the initiative. So you could have joined forces with him. Listen again, there's more to come:

15. *That many members of the families and servants of the native chiefs appear on the payment sheets but take no part in the rice cultivation, so that they profit by it at the expense of the real participants. Moreover, they are illegally put in possession of sawahs, which by rights can only be given to active cultivators.*

'Here I find another memo, in pencil. Look—there's nothing vague about this one, either: "*The decline in the population of Parang-Kujang is solely due to the outrageous way in which the people are exploited.*" What do you say to that? Do you see now that I'm not so eccentric after all, when I try to do something about justice, and do you see now that others tried too?'

'It's true,' said Verbrugge, 'Mr Slotering often spoke to the Resident about all that.'

'And what was the result?'

'Then the Regent was called to the Residency. There was a *tête-à-tête*...'

'Exactly! And then?'

'The Regent usually denied everything. Then witnesses had to come ... no one dared to bear witness against the Regent ... Oh, Mr Havelaar, these things are so difficult!'

Before the reader has finished reading my book he will know as well as Verbrugge did, *why* these things were so difficult.

'Mr Slotering was very upset about it,' the Controleur went on. 'He wrote sharp letters to the chiefs...'

'I've read them ... last night,' said Havelaar.

'I often heard him say that if there was no change, and if the Resident did not take *vigorous* action, he would approach the Governor-General direct. And he said it to the Chiefs themselves at his last *Sebah*.'

'That would have been wrong of him. The Resident was his chief, and he should not have gone over his head, not under any circumstances. And why on earth should he? Surely it's not to be supposed that the Resident of BANTAM would approve injustice and tyranny?'

'Approve ... no! But no one likes to impeach a chief to the Government.'

'I don't like to impeach anyone, whoever he is, but if it *must* be done, then a chief as soon as anyone else. But here, thank God, there's no question of impeachment yet! Tomorrow I'll go and see the Regent. I shall point out to him how wrong it is to make illegal use of authority, especially where poor people's property is concerned. But, expecting that everything will come right, I shall help him in his difficulties to the best of my ability. You understand now, don't you, why I had that money paid to the Collector? I also intend to ask the Government to let him off paying the money he owes them. And to you, Verbrugge, I propose that together we do our duty scrupulously. As long as is possible, gently, but if *necessary*, without fear or favour! You're an honest man, I know, but you're timid. In future, say straight out how matters stand, *advienne que pourra*! Throw off that halfheartedness of yours, my dear chap... and now, what about staying to lunch? We have tinned Dutch cauliflower ... but everything is simple, because I have to be very economical ... I am much behind in my finances: that trip to Europe, you know! Come on, Max ... good Lord, lad, how heavy you're getting!'

And, with Max riding pickaback on his shoulders, he entered the inner gallery, accompanied by Verbrugge. Tina was waiting for them with the table laid for lunch; which, as Havelaar had said, was truly *very* simple! Duclari, who came to ask Verbrugge whether he meant to be home for the midday meal, was also invited to sit down with them; and if the reader would like a little variety in my story, he is referred to the next chapter, in which I shall relate all the things that were said during the lunch.

9

I would give a good deal, reader, to know exactly how long I could keep a heroine floating in the air while I described a castle, before your patience was exhausted and you put my book down, without waiting for the poor creature to reach the ground. If my tale called for such a caper, I should certainly take the precaution of choosing a first storey as starting-point for her to jump from, and a castle about which there was not much to say. But make yourself easy: Havelaar's house had no storeys, and the heroine of my book—good Heavens! Dear, true, *anspruchlose*[60] Tina, a heroine!—never jumped out of a window.

When I closed the last chapter with a hint of some variation in the next one, it was really more of a rhetorical trick, with the object of making an ending that 'clicked', than because I actually meant that the next chapter would be slipped in 'for variety's sake' and have no other value.

A writer is as vain as a ... man. Speak ill of his mother or the colour of his hair, say he has an Amsterdam accent—which no Amsterdammer will ever admit to—and maybe he will forgive you those things. But ... never touch the outside of the smallest part of a minor element of something that has lain anywhere near his writing ... for *that* he won't forgive you! So if you don't think my book marvellous and you should happen to meet me, kindly pass by as though we don't know each other.

So, through the magnifying glass of my writer's vanity, such a chapter merely 'for variety's sake' still seems to me highly important, even indispensable; and if you were to skip it and then failed to like my book as much as you ought, I should not hesitate to tell you that that skipping disqualified you from pronouncing an opinion on it, since the essential part of it was just the part you had not read. In this way, I should—for I am both man *and* writer—consider as *essential any* chapter which you had skipped with that unpardonable reader's irresponsibility of yours.

I can imagine your wife asking: 'Is there anything *in* that book?' And you will say, for instance—*horribile auditu* for my ears—with the volubility characteristic of married men:

'Hm ... well, rather ... I don't know yet.'

Why then, barbarian, read on! The all-important thing is just before the door! And I stare at you with trembling lips, and measure the thickness of the leaves turned over ... and in your face I search for the reflection of the chapter 'which is *so* beautiful'.

No, I say, he hasn't got to it yet. Presently he will jump up in ecstasy, he will embrace something ... perhaps his wife...

But you read on. You must have got past the 'beautiful chapter', I think. You haven't jumped up at all, you haven't embraced...

And ever thinner grows the volume of leaves under your right thumb, and ever fainter grows my hope of that embrace ... yes, honestly, I had even reckoned on a tear!

And you have read the novel right through, to 'where they get each other', and you say, with a yawn (yet another manifestation of the eloquence peculiar to the state of wedlock):

'Why ... well! It's the sort of book that ... hm! Oh, they write such a lot nowadays!'

But don't you know then, monster, tiger, *European*, reader—don't you know then that you have just whiled away an hour biting on my spirit like a toothpick? Gnawing and chewing flesh and bone of your own kind? Man-eater, it was my *soul*, that you have milled over for a second time, as cows eat grass! It was my *heart* that you have just swallowed as a titbit! For into that book I had poured both my heart and soul, and many tears fell on the manuscript, and my blood ebbed from my veins as I wrote on, and I gave you all this, and you bought it for a few pence, and all you can say is: 'Hm!'

But the reader will realize that I am not speaking of my own book here.

I only wish to say, in the words of Abraham Blankaart[61]...

'Who's Abraham Blankaart?' asked Louise Rosemeyer, and Frits told her—to my great delight, because it gave me an opportunity of getting up and putting an end to the reading, for that evening at any rate. As you know, I am a coffee broker—*37 Lauriergracht*—and my profession's my life. So anyone can understand how little satisfied I am with Stern's work. I had hoped for coffee, and he has given us ... Heaven knows what!

He has taken up our time with his composition for three of our social evenings already, and, what is worse, the Rosemeyers think it's nice! Whenever I criticize, he appeals to Louise. Her approval, he says, weighs more with him than all the coffee in the world, and, moreover: 'When my breast glows' ... etc.—Look up this tirade on page so-and-so; or rather, don't look it up—Well, then, here I am, and I don't know what to do! That parcel of Scarfman's is a Trojan horse, if ever there was one. Frits is also being corrupted by it. He's been helping Stern, I notice—that 'Abraham Blankaart' is much too Dutch for a German. They are such a couple of cocksure know-alls that I'm really getting concerned about the affair. The worst of it is, I've signed an agreement with Gaafzuiger for publication of a book on the *coffee auctions*—all Holland is waiting for it!—and now that confounded Stern goes off on a different tack altogether! Yesterday he said: 'Don't worry, all roads lead to Rome. Just wait for the end of the introduction'—is all this still only *introduction*?—'I promise you'—actually he said 'I forespeak you', in his German style—'that ultimately the business will boil down to coffee, coffee, nothing but coffee! Think of Horace,' he went on, 'hasn't he said: *Omne tulit punctum qui miscuit*[62] ... coffee with something else? Don't you act in the same way, when you put sugar and milk in your cup?'

And then I have to be silent. Not because he's right, but because I owe it as a duty to the firm of *Last & Co.* to see that old Stern doesn't fall into the hands of Busselinck & Waterman, who would serve him badly because they're tricksters.

To you, reader, I pour out my heart, and in order that after reading Stern's scribbling—have you really read it?—you should not pour out the vials of your wrath over an innocent head—for, I ask you, who would engage a broker who calls him a cannibal?—I insist on convincing you of my innocence. For, it's clear, I can't push Stern out of the 'firm' of my book now that things have gone so far that Louise Rosemeyer, when she comes out of church—apparently the boys wait for her—asks whether he'll come a bit early that evening, so that he can read them a *lot* about Max and Tina?

But since you will have bought the book or got it out of the library, banking on its respectable title, which promises something solid, I acknowledge your claim to value for money, and so I am again writing a couple of chapters myself. You don't go to the Rosemeyers' tea-parties, reader, and so you're better off than I am, who have to listen to it all. *You* are at liberty to skip the chapters that smell of German hysteria and pay heed only to what has been written by *me*, a man of standing and a coffee broker.

I am surprised to learn from Stern's scribblings—and he has shown me that it is true, from Scarfman's parcel—that no coffee is grown in that Division of LEBAK. This is a great mistake, and I shall consider my trouble amply rewarded if my book succeeds in drawing the Government's attention to that mistake. Scarfman's papers apparently prove that the soil in those parts is not suitable for coffee-growing. But that is absolutely no excuse, and I maintain that the Government is guilty of unpardonable neglect of duty towards Holland in general and the coffee brokers in particular, ay, even towards the Javanese themselves, for not either changing that soil—after all, the Javanese have nothing else to do anyway—or, if they think that's not practicable, for not sending the people who live there to other parts where the soil *is* good for coffee.

I never say anything I have not thoroughly considered, and I dare swear in this case that I am speaking with authority, as I have given mature reflection to the matter, especially since hearing Parson Blatherer's sermon at the special service for the conversion of the heathen.

That was last Wednesday night. You must know, reader, that I am strict in carrying out my duties as a father, and that the moral training of my children is a thing very near to my heart. Now, for some time past there has been something in Frits' stone and manner that doesn't please me—it all comes from Scarfman's pestilential parcel! So I gave him a good sound lecture that day, and said:

'Frits, I am not satisfied with you! I have always shown you the right path, and yet you will stray off it. You are priggish and tiresome, you write verses, and you have given Betsy Rosemeyer a kiss. The fear of the Lord is the beginning of wisdom, so you mustn't kiss the Rosemeyers, and you mustn't be such a prig. Immorality leads to perdition, my lad. Read the Scriptures, and mark that Scarfman! He left the ways of the Lord; now he is poor, and lives in a wretched garret ... lo, these are the consequences of immorality and misconduct! He wrote unseemly articles in the *Indépendance*, and he dropped the *Aglaias*. That's what you come to when you're wise in your own eyes. Now he doesn't even know the time, and his little boy has only half a pair of trousers. Remember that your body is the temple of the Holy Ghost, and that your father has always had to work hard for a living—it's the truth!— so lift up your eyes to Heaven, and try to grow up to be a respectable broker by the time I retire to Driebergen. And do take note of all those people who won't listen to good advice, who trample religion and morality underfoot, and let them be a warning to you. And don't put yourself on a level with Stern—his father is rich, and he'll have enough money in any case, even if he doesn't want to be a broker and even if he does do something wrong occasionally. Do remember that all evil is punished; again, take that Scarfman, who has no overcoat and looks like a broken-down actor. Do pay attention in church, don't sit there wriggling in all directions on your seat as if you were bored, my boy; what must God think of that? The church is *His* sanctuary, d'you see? And don't wait for young girls when the service is over, for that takes away all the edification. And don't make Marie giggle either, when I read the Scripture at breakfast time. All that sort of thing is out of place in a respectable household; oh, and you drew funny figures on Bastiaans's blotter, when he hadn't turned up again—because he's always having rheumatism—that keeps the men in the office from their work, and it says in Holy Writ that such follies lead to perdition. That fellow Scarfman also did wrong things when he was young; as a child, he struck a Greek in the Westermarkt... and now he is lazy, cocky and sickly, you see! So don't always be joining in Stern's jokes, my boy, *his* father is rich. Pretend not to see, when he's pulling faces at the book-keeper. And outside office hours, when he's busy making verses, just remark to him, casually-like, that he would be better employed in writing to his father to tell him he is very comfortable with us and that Marie has embroidered a pair of slippers for him with real floss silk. Ask him—quite spontaneously, you know!—whether he thinks his father is likely to go to Busselinck & Waterman, and tell him they're tricksters. You see, that way you'll put him on the right path ... one owes it to one's neighbour, and all that versifying is nonsense. Do be good and obedient, Frits, and don't pull the maid by her skirt when she brings the tea into the office and put me to shame, for then she spills the tea, and St Paul says a son should never cause his father sorrow. I've been on 'Change for twenty years, and I think I may say that I'm respected at my pillar there. So listen to my words of warning, Frits, and get your hat, and put on your coat, and come along with me to the prayer meeting, that will do you good!'

That was how I spoke to him; and I'm convinced I made an impression, especially as Parson Blatherer had chosen for the subject of his address: *The love of God, manifested by His rage against unbelievers*, with reference to Samuel's rebuke to Saul: I *Sam*. xv: *33*.

As I listened to that sermon, I kept thinking what a world of difference there is between human and divine wisdom. I have already said that in Scarfman's parcel, among a lot of rubbish, there were certainly one or two items which were conspicuous for their soundness of reasoning. But oh, of how little account are such things when compared with language like Parson Blatherer's! And it is not by his own power that he speaks thus—I know Blatherer, and believe me, he'll never set the Thames on fire; no—it is by the power that comes from above! The difference was all the more marked because he touched upon certain matters which had also been dealt with by Scarfman—as you have seen, there was a great deal in his parcel about the Javanese and other heathens. (Frits says the Javanese are not heathens, but I call anyone a heathen who has the wrong faith. For I hold to Jesus Christ, and Him crucified, and I have no doubt every respectable reader does the same.)

It is from Blatherer's sermon that I have drawn my conclusion about the wrongfulness of abandoning coffee cultivation in LEBAK, to which I shall revert presently. Moreover, as an honest man, I don't want the reader to receive absolutely nothing for his money. So I shall give him here a few passages from the sermon which were particularly striking.

Blatherer briefly proved the love of God from the words of the text, and very soon passed on to the real point at issue, the conversion of Javanese, Malays, whatever else those people call themselves. And this is what he said:

'Such, my Belovéd, was the glorious mission of Israel!'—he meant the extermination of the inhabitants of Canaan—'and such is also the mission of Holland! No, it shall not be said that the light which shines upon us will be hidden under a bushel, nor that we are niggardly in sharing with others the bread of eternal life! Cast your eyes upon the islands of the Indian Ocean, inhabited by millions upon millions of the children of the accursed son—the *rightly* accursed son—of the noble Noah, who found grace in the eyes of the Lord! There they crawl about in the loathsome snakepits of heathenish ignorance—there they bow the black, frizzy head under the yoke of self-seeking priests! There they pray to God, invoking a false prophet who is an abomination in the sight of the Lord! And, Belovéd! as though it were not enough to obey a false prophet, there are even those among them who worship another God, nay, other *gods*, gods of wood and stone, which they themselves have made after their own image, black, horrible, with flat noses, and devilish! Yea, Belovéd ... tears almost keep me from continuing; deeper even than this is the depravity of the Children of Ham! There are those among them who know *no* god, under whatever name! Who think it sufficient to obey the laws of civil society! Who deem a harvest song, wherein they express their joy over the success of their labours, sufficient thanks to the Supreme Being by Whom that harvest was allowed to ripen! Out there live lost ones, stray sheep, my Belovéd, who assert that it is enough to love wife and child, and not to take from their neighbour what is not theirs, in order to be able at night to lay down their heads to sleep in peace! Do you not shudder at that picture? Do your hearts not shrink with terror at the thought of what the fate will be of all those fools as soon as the trumpet shall sound, waking the dead for the sundering of the just from the unjust? Hear ye not?—yea, ye do hear, for from the text I have read ye have seen that the Lord thy God is a mighty God, and a God of righteous retribution—yea, ye hear the cracking of the bones and the crackle of the flames in the eternal Gehenna where there is weeping and gnashing of teeth! There, there they burn, and perish not, for their punishment is everlasting! There, with never-sated tongue, the flames lick at the screaming victims of unbelief! There the worm dieth not that gnaws their hearts through and through without ever destroying them, so that for ever there will be a heart to gnaw at in the breast of the godless! See how the black skin is stripped from the unbaptized child that, scarce born, was flung away from the breast of the mother into the pool of everlasting damnation...'

Here a woman fainted.

'But, Belovéd,' continued Parson Blatherer, 'God is a God of Love! He will not that the sinner shall be lost, but that he shall be saved *by* grace, *in* Christ, *through* Faith! And therefore our Holland has been chosen to save what may be saved of those wretched ones! Therefore has God, in His inscrutable Wisdom, given power to a land of small compass but great and strong in the knowledge of Him, power over the dwellers in those regions, that by the holy, ever-inestimable Gospel they may be delivered from the pains of hell! The ships of our Holland sail the great waters, to bring civilization, religion, Christianity, to the misguided Javanese! Nay, our happy Fatherland does not covet eternal bliss for itself alone: we wish to share it also with the wretched creatures on those distant shores who lie bound in the fetters of unbelief, superstition and immorality! Consideration of the duties that are laid upon us to this end shall form the seventh part of my address.'

(For what you have just read was the *sixth*.) The duties we had to perform on behalf of those poor heathens included the following:

1. *Making liberal contributions in money to the Missionary Society.*
2. *Supporting the Bible Societies, to enable them to distribute Bibles in Java.*
3. *Furthering prayer meetings at Harderwijk, for the benefit of the colonial army Recruiting Depot.*
4. *Writing sermons and hymns, suitable for our soldiers and sailors to read and sing to the Javanese.*
5. *Formation of a society of influential men whose task it should be to petition our gracious King:*
   a. To appoint as governors, officers and officials only such men as may be considered steadfast in the true faith;
   b. To have permission granted to the Javanese to visit the barracks, and also the men-of-war and merchantmen lying in the ports, so that by intercourse with Dutch soldiers and sailors they may be prepared for the Kingdom of God;
   c. To prohibit the acceptance of Bibles or religious tracts in public houses in payment for drink;
   d. To make it a condition of the granting of opium licences in Java that in every opium house there shall be kept a stock of Bibles in proportion to the

probable number of visitors to the institution, and that the licensee shall undertake to sell no opium unless the purchaser takes a religious tract at the same time;

e. To command that the Javanese shall be brought to God by labour.

6. Making liberal contributions to the Missionary Society.

I know I have already given this last item under No. 1; but he repeated it, and in the heat of his discourse such superfluity appears to me quite understandable.

But, reader, have you noticed No. 5e? Well, that proposal reminded me so strongly of the coffee auctions, and of the alleged unsuitability of the soil in LEBAK, that it will now no longer seem strange to you when I assure you that since Wednesday night point 5e has not been out of my thoughts for a moment. Parson Blatherer read out the missionaries' reports; so nobody can deny he has a thorough knowledge of these matters. Well then, if he, with those reports before him and his eye on the Almighty, maintains that much work will favourably influence the conquest of Javanese souls for the Kingdom of God, then surely I may conclude that I am not altogether wide of the mark when I say that coffee can perfectly well be grown in LEBAK and, furthermore, that it is even possible the Supreme Being has made the soil there unsuitable for coffee-growing for no other purpose than that the population of those parts shall be made fit for Heaven through the labour that will be necessary to transport different soil to them?

I can't help hoping my book will come to the eye of the King, and that soon bigger auctions will testify how closely the knowledge of God is connected with the proper interests of all respectable citizens! Just see how a simple and humble man like Blatherer, devoid of the wisdom of this world—the man has never been in the Exchange in his life—but enlightened by the Gospel, which is a lamp unto his path, has suddenly given *me*, a coffee broker, a hint which is not only important to all Holland but will enable me, if Frits behaves himself—he sat reasonably still in church—to retire to Driebergen five years earlier than I had expected. Yes, labour, labour, that's my watchword! Labour for the Javanese, that's my principle! And my principles are sacred to me.

Is not the Gospel our highest good? Is there anything more important than salvation? So isn't it our duty to bring those people salvation? And when, as a means thereto, labour is necessary—I myself have laboured on 'Change for twenty years—may we then refuse labour to the Javanese, knowing that his soul is so urgently in need of it to escape the everlasting fire hereafter? It would be selfishness, abominable selfishness, if we didn't make every effort to preserve those poor lost sheep from the terrible future Parson Blatherer so eloquently described. A lady fainted when he spoke of that black child ... perhaps she had a little boy with a rather dark complexion. Women are like that!

And why shouldn't I insist upon labour, I who do nothing but think of business from morning till night? Isn't this book, even—which Stern is making such a headache for me—a proof of the goodness of my intentions for the welfare of our Fatherland, proof of how I would sacrifice everything to that? And when _I_ have to labour so hard, I, who have been baptized—in the Amstelkerk—isn't it lawful, then, to demand from the Javanese that he, who still has to win his salvation, shall put his hand to the plough?

If that society—I mean the one in 5e—is formed, I'll join it. And I'll try to get the Rosemeyers to join as well, because the interests of sugar refiners are concerned too, though I don't think they're very sound in their principles—the Rosemeyers, I mean—for they keep a Roman Catholic maidservant.

Anyhow, _I_ intend to do my duty. I promised myself that when I went home from church with Frits. In _my_ house the Lord shall be served, _I'll_ see to that. And with all the more zeal because I realize more and more how wisely everything is ordered, how loving are the ways by which we are led at God's hand, and how He wishes to save us for both the eternal and the temporal life; for that soil in LEBAK can very easily be made suitable for coffee.

10

Although I spare nobody when principles are at stake, I can see that I shall have to try different tactics with Stern than with Frits. And, as it is to be feared that my name—the firm is *Last & Co.*, but I'm *Droogstoppel, Batavus Droogstoppel*—will be connected with a book containing matters which aren't in conformity with the respect that every decent man and broker owes himself, I deem it my duty to tell you how I endeavoured to bring young Stern back to the right path too.

I didn't speak to him of the Lord, because he's a Lutheran, but I made an appeal to his heart and his honour. Just see how I went about it, and note how much one can do when one knows men.

I had heard him say: 'On my word of honour', and I asked him what he meant by that.

'Well,' he said, 'I mean that I pledge my honour for the truth of what I say.'

'That's quite a mouthful!' I commented. 'Are you so sure you always tell the truth?'

'Yes,' he declared, 'I always tell the truth. When my breast glows…'

The reader knows the rest.

'That's certainly extremely fine,' said I, and I looked very innocent, as though I believed it.

But that was just the clever part of the trap I had set for him, with the object—without risking seeing old Stern fall into the hands of Busselinck & Waterman—of putting this young whippersnapper in his place for once, and making him feel what a gulf there is between an absolute beginner—even if his father *is* in business in a big way—and a broker who's been on 'Change for twenty years.

I must tell you that I knew he had learnt by heart—he says: 'outwardly', as a German would—all sorts of trumpery verses, and since verses always contain lies I was sure that sooner or later I should catch him telling an untruth. And it wasn't long before I did. I was sitting in the room opening off the drawing room, and he was in the drawing room ... for we have a suite.[63] Marie was knitting, and he was just going to tell her something. I listened closely, and when he had done I asked him whether he had the book with the thing in it which he had just been trolling out. He said yes, he had, and brought it to me. It was a volume of the works of one Heine. Next morning I gave him—Stern, I mean—the following:

Reflections on the love of truth in a person who recites trash by Heine to a young girl sitting knitting in the suite.

My wingéd song as it ranges,
My darling, shall bear you away,

My darling? Marie, your *darling?* Do your old people know that, or Louise Rosemeyer? Is it decent to say such a thing to a child who is quite likely to start disobeying her mother through it, as she may take it into her head that she's grown up because someone calls her *My darling?* And what's that about *bearing her on your wings?* You've got no wings, nor has your song. Just try crossing Lauriergracht that way, which isn't even very wide. But even if you had wings, are you at liberty to propose such things to a young girl who hasn't yet been confirmed? And even if she *had* become a full member of the Church, what *is* the meaning of that offer to fly away together? Shame on you!

Off to the plains of the Ganges,
To the loveliest place under day.

Go there by yourself, then, and rent a bungalow. But don't take a young girl with you whose duty is to help her mother in the household! You don't really mean it, though! In the first place, you've never seen the Ganges, so you can't know whether it's nice to live there or not. Shall *I* tell you how matters stand? It's all lies, which you only tell because in all this versifying you make yourself the slave of metre and rhyme. If the first line had ended in *home*, *work*, or *undone*, you would have asked Marie to go along with you to *Rome*, *New York*, *London*, and so on. You see, your proposed itinerary wasn't honestly meant, and it all comes down to an insipid jingle-jangle of words, with no head or tail to it. Suppose Marie really felt like making that crazy journey? I don't even speak of the uncomfortable mode of travelling you suggest! But, thank Heaven, she has too much sense to long for a country where, you say:

> A blossom-red garden lies shining
> Beneath the silent moon;
> The lotus flowers are pining
> For the sister promised soon;
> The giggling, gossiping violets
> Gaze up at the stars from their vales;
> In each other's ears the roses
> Whisper fragrant fairy tales.

Pray, what would you want to do with Marie in that garden in the moonlight? Is that moral, is it decent, is it respectable, Stern? Do you wish to put me to shame, like Busselinck & Waterman, whom no reputable firm will have anything to do with, because their daughter's run away and because they undercut? What answer could I make, if they were to ask me on 'Change why my daughter had stayed so long in that red garden? For surely you'll understand that no one would believe me if I said she had to be there to pay a visit to the lotus flowers, which, you say, have been looking out for her? And likewise, every sane person would laugh at me if I was silly enough to tell them: Yes, Marie is in that red garden over there—why *red*, by the way, and not *yellow*, or *mauve*? —listening to the violets chattering and giggling, or to the fairy tales the roses are secretly whispering into each other's ears. Even if such a thing *could* be true, what good would it do to Marie, if it all happened in whispers, so that she wouldn't catch a word of it anyway? But it's all lies, silly lies! And not even pretty lies either... just take a pencil and draw a rose with an ear, and see what it looks like! And what does it mean, that those fairy tales are so fragrant? Shall *I* just tell you, in good, round Dutch? It means there's something fishy about your idiotic fairy tales ... that's what it means!

> The gazelles, so pious and clever,
> Draw near to listen, bounding,
> And in the distance for ever
> The sacred stream is sounding...
> There shall we, softly sinking,
> Beneath the sheltering palm,
> The pleasures of rest and love drinking,
> Receive dream's blissful balm.

Can't you go to 'Artis'—you know I'm a member—if you absolutely *have* to see strange animals? Has it *got* to be those gazelles on the Ganges—which, in any case, are never so easy to observe in their wild state as in a neat enclosure of tarred iron? And why do you call those animals pious and clever? 'Clever,' I'll allow—at any rate they don't make such ridiculous verses—but... 'pious'? What does *that* mean? Isn't it misuse of a hallowed word that should only be applied to people of the true faith? And then, what about that 'sacred stream'? Are you justified in telling Marie things that would make her a heathen? Are you justified in shaking her conviction that there is no holy water but that of baptism, and no sacred river but Jordan? Isn't this sapping the foundations of morality, virtue, religion, Christianity and respectability? Think all this over, Stern, I implore you! Your father is a reputable firm, and I feel sure he would approve of my appealing in this way to your better nature, and that he prefers to do business with a man who stands up for virtue and religion. Yes, principles are sacred to me, and I've no hesitation in coming straight out with what I think. So you needn't make a secret of what I'm saying to you, you're welcome to write and tell your father that here you're staying in the bosom of a steady, respectable family and that this is how I'm showing you the path of righteousness. And just ask yourself what would have become of you if you'd fallen into the hands of Busselinck & Waterman! There, too, you would have recited just such verses; but there nobody would have appealed to your better nature, because they are tricksters. You are welcome to write that to your father too, for when principles are at stake I fear no one. *There* the girls *would* have gone along with you to the Ganges, and then you might now be lying under that tree in the wet grass, whereas now, since *I* have given you such a paternal warning, you can stay with us in a decent house. Write all that to your father, and tell him you are so grateful to have come to us, and that I look after you so well, and that Busselinck & Waterman's daughter has run away, and give him my kind regards, and tell him I'll take another 1/16 per cent less commission than they ask, because I can't bear those undercutters, taking the bread out of a competitor's mouth by offering more favourable conditions!

And, Stern, when you're reading at the Rosemeyers', do me the pleasure of serving up something more worth while! In Scarfman's parcel I've seen figures for coffee production over the last twenty years from all the residencies in Java: let's have something like *that*, for a change! And really, you mustn't go on at the girls, and all the rest of us, calling us cannibals who have swallowed something of yours ... that's not proper, my dear boy. Do take it from a man who knows the world! I served your father before he was born—his firm, I mean, no ... I mean *our* firm: *Last & Co.* It used to be *Last & Meyer*, but the *Meyers* have long been out of it—so you'll understand that my intentions towards you are of the best. And do urge Frits to behave better, and don't teach him to write verses, and pretend not to see it when he pulls faces at the book-keeper, and all that sort of thing. Set him a good example, because you're so much older, and try to get some sobriety and dignity into him, for he has to be a broker.

I remain,

Your fatherly friend,

Batavus Droogstoppel

(Messrs. *Last & Co., coffee brokers,*
37 Lauriergracht)

11

...I only wish to say, in the words of Abraham Blankaart, that I consider this chapter 'essential' because I think it gives the reader a better idea of Havelaar, and—there's no getting away from it—he seems to be the hero of the story.

'Tina, what sort of *ketimon*[64] do you call this? My dear girl, never add vegetable acid to fruit! You add salt to cucumbers, salt to pineapples, salt to grapefruit, salt to everything that grows in the ground. But vinegar to fish and meat ... there's something about it in Liebig...'

'Dear Max,' Tina inquired, laughing, 'how long do you think we've been here? That *ketimon* is from Mrs Slotering.'

And Havelaar had to make an effort to remember that he had only arrived the day before and that, with the best will in the world, Tina could not yet have arranged anything in the kitchen or the household. *He* had been at RANGKAS-BETUNG a long time! Had he not spent the whole night reading the Divisional archives, and had not too much gone through his mind already in connexion with LEBAK, for him to realize straightaway that he had hardly been there twenty-four hours? Tina understood that: she *always* understood him!

'Of course, you're perfectly right,' he said. 'But in any case, you really ought to read something by Liebig some time. Verbrugge, have *you* read much Liebig?'

'Who's he?' asked Verbrugge.

'He's a man who's written a lot about pickling gherkins. He's also discovered how you turn grass into wool ... you understand, don't you?'

'No, we don't,' said Verbrugge and Duclari in unison.

'Well, the thing itself, of course, has always been known: send a sheep into a field, and you'll see what happens! But Liebig's investigated the *way* in which it happens. Though others say he doesn't know much about it. Now they are trying to find out ways of omitting the sheep from the process altogether ... oh, those scientists! Molière knew all about them ... I'm very fond of Molière. If you like, we'll arrange a course of evening study, Tina will join us, when Max has gone to bed.'

Duclari and Verbrugge welcomed the idea. Havelaar said he had not many books, but among them were Schiller, Goethe, Heine, Vondel, Lamartine, Thiers, Say, Malthus, Scialoja, Adam Smith, Shakespeare, Byron...

Verbrugge said he could not read English.

'The deuce! You're over thirty, aren't you? What have you been doing all your life? But surely that must have made it difficult for you at PADANG, where so much English is spoken? Did you know *Miss Mata-api?*'[65]

'No, I don't recollect the name.'

'It wasn't her name, anyway. We called her that, in '43, because she had such sparkling eyes. She must be married by now ... it's so long ago! I never saw anything like her ... yes, I did, at Arles ... you ought to go *there* some time! That was the most beautiful thing I found in all my travels. There's nothing, I think, that brings before you so clearly beauty in the abstract, the visible image of *truth*, of *immaterial purity*, as a beautiful woman ... believe you me, just go to Arles or Nîmes...'

Duclari, Verbrugge, and—I have to admit it!—Tina too, could not help laughing loudly at the thought of just stepping over from the extreme western tip of Java to Arles or Nîmes in the South of France. Havelaar, no doubt standing in his imagination on the tower the Saracens built on the gallery round the *arena* at Arles, had some difficulty in understanding what they were laughing at. But then he went on:

'Well, you know what I mean ... if you should happen to be near there at any time. I never saw anything like it elsewhere. I had got used to being disappointed by all the things that are cracked up so much. For instance, take the waterfalls people never stop talking and writing about. Personally, I've felt little or nothing at

Tondano, Maros, Schaffhausen, Niagara. You have to consult your guidebook to get the right measure of admiration, for "so many feet high" and "so many cubic feet of water a minute", and if the figures are big, you have to say: "Ooh!" I never want to see any more waterfalls—at any rate not if I have to go out of my way for them. Those things say nothing to me! Buildings speak rather more loudly, especially when they are pages of history. But they appeal to feelings of a very different sort! You call up the past, and the shades of days gone by pass in review. Some of them are most horrible, and so, however remarkable such experiences may be at times, the emotions evoked do not always satisfy your sense of beauty ... never, at any rate, without alloy! And *without* the appeal of history there may be much beauty in some buildings, but it is usually spoilt by guides —whether of paper or flesh and blood, it's all one!—guides who filch your impressions from you with their sing-song: "This chapel was erected by the Bishop of Munster in 1423 ... the columns are 63 feet high, and rest upon" ... I don't know what, and I don't care either. That sort of babble is a bore, for one feels that one then has to get up exactly three-and-sixty feet of admiration in order not to be taken for a Vandal or a bagman ... Well, you may say ... keep your guide in your pocket if he's a printed one, and leave him outside or make him shut up in the other case. But often one really needs information in order to form a more or less correct judgment; and even if one could always do without the information, one would, anyway, seek in vain in any building for anything which satisfies the longing for beauty for more than a very brief moment, because a building doesn't *move*. I think this also applies to sculpture and painting. Nature is movement. Growth, hunger, thinking, feeling, are movement ... immobility is death! Without movement —no pain, no pleasure, no emotion! Just try to sit still without stirring, and you will soon find how quickly you make an eerie impression on everyone, and even on yourself. On seeing the most beautiful *tableau vivant* one soon longs for the next number, however dazzling the first impression may have been. Now, since our thirst for beauty is not slaked by one single glance at a beautiful thing, but requires a series of successive glances at the *movement of the beautiful*, we suffer from a sense of incompleteness, dissatisfaction, on contemplating *that* class of works of art; and for this reason I maintain that a beautiful woman—unless she's an oil-painting type without real movement—comes nearest to the ideal of the divine. You can see, to a certain extent, how great is the need for the movement I mean when a dancer, though she be an Elssler or a Taglioni, stands on her left leg after a dance, and grins at the public.'

'That doesn't count here,' said Verbrugge, 'because that is *absolutely* ugly.'

'I agree. Yet *she* offers it under the impression that it is beautiful and as the *climax* to all that preceded it, in which there may really have been much that was beautiful. She offers it as the "point" of the epigram, as the "*aux armes!*" of the *Marseillaise* she has sung with her feet, as the whisper of the willows on the grave of the love she has just portrayed in the dance. And that the spectators, who usually base their taste on custom and imitation (as we all do, more or less), consider *that* moment as the most thrilling is proved by the fact that it is *then* that they burst into applause, as if they wished to say "What went before was certainly very fine, but *now* I can really no longer contain my admiration!" You think that final pose is *absolutely* ugly. So do I. But why do we think so? I'll tell you ... it's because the *movement* ceased, and with it the *story* which the dancer told. Believe me, immobility is death!'

'But,' Duclari objected, 'you also refuse to admit waterfalls as an expression of beauty. But waterfalls *move*, don't they?!'

'Yes, only ... they tell no *story*! They move, but they don't get away from the place. They move like a rocking-horse, though without even the to-and-fro motion. They make a sound, but they don't speak. They cry: *hrroo ... hrroo ... hrroo ...* and never anything else! *You* cry *hrroo, hrroo* for six thousand years or more, and see how many people will regard you as entertaining company.'

'I shan't take the risk,' said Duclari. 'But I'm still not convinced that the movement you demand is so absolutely necessary. I'll grant you the waterfalls, but, I think, surely a good *painting* can express a great deal?'

'Undoubtedly, but only for a moment. I'll try to explain what I mean by an example. To-day is the eighteenth of February...'

'Oh no it isn't,' said Verbrugge, 'we're still in January...'

'No, no, to-day is the eighteenth of February, 1587, and you are locked up in Fotheringhay Castle...'

'*Me ?*' said Duclari, unwilling to believe his ears.

'Yes, you. You're bored, you seek diversion. There, in that wall, is an opening; it's too high up for you to see through it, but that's what you want to do. You put your table beneath it, and on that you put a chair, which has only three legs and one of those rather rickety. You once saw an acrobat at a fair who piled seven chairs on top of each other and then stood on them himself, on his head. Vanity and boredom spur you on to do something similar. Tottering, you climb that chair ... achieve your object ... cast a glance through the opening, and cry: "Oh God!" And you fall down! Now, can you tell me why you cried: "Oh God!" and why you fell?'

'I suppose the third leg of the chair broke,' said Verbrugge sententiously.

'Yes, no doubt the leg broke, but it wasn't that that made you fall. The leg broke because you fell. You would have held out on that chair for a whole year in front of any other opening, but now you *had* to fall, even if the chair had had thirteen legs, yes, even if you'd been standing on the floor!'

'I give in,' said Duclari. 'I can see you've made up your mind to bring me down, at all costs. Right, then ... I'm lying full-length on the floor ... but I couldn't for the life of me tell you why!'

'Well ... it's really *very* simple! You suddenly saw a woman dressed in black, kneeling before a block. And she bowed her head, and bright as silver was the neck that shone against the black velvet. And there stood a man with a great sword, and he held it high, and his eye gazed on that white neck, and he mentally measured the arc his sword must describe so that there ... there, between those vertebrae, it would be driven through with precision and force ... and then you fell, Duclari! You fell because you saw all that, and *that* was why you cried "Oh God!" Decidedly not because there were only three legs on your chair. And long after you had been let out of Fotheringhay—through the good offices of your cousin, I imagine, or because people got tired of giving you free board and lodging there like a canary, without being obliged to—long after, to this very day, you still dream waking dreams about that woman, and in your sleep even you start up, and fall heavily down on your couch again, because you are trying to seize the executioner's arm... isn't that so?'

'I'm prepared to believe it, but I can't be absolutely sure, because I've never looked through a hole in a wall at Fotheringhay.'

'All right, all right! Nor have I. But now I take a *painting* of the beheading of Mary Queen of Scots. Let's assume the representation is perfect. There she hangs, in a gilt frame, from a red cord if you like ... oh, I know what you're going to say! No, no, you don't see that frame, you've even forgotten that you gave up your walking-stick at the entrance to the picture gallery ... you forget your name, your child, the latest-model forage cap, you forget *everything*, in seeing, not a mere *picture*, but Mary Queen of Scots to the life, exactly as at Fotheringhay. The headsman stands there exactly as he must have stood in reality; I'll even go so far as to say that you throw out your arm to ward off the blow! I'll even go so far as to say that you exclaim: "Let the woman live, perhaps she'll mend her ways!" You see, I'm giving you fair play as far as the execution of the picture is concerned...'

'Yes, but what then? Isn't the impression just as striking as when I saw the real thing at Fotheringhay?'

'No, it certainly isn't; and only because this time you didn't climb on to a chair with three legs. You take another chair—on this occasion with four legs, and preferably well upholstered—you sit down in front of the picture, so as to enjoy it long and thoroughly

—strange though it seems, we do *enjoy* the sight of horrible things—and what impression do you think it will make on you?'

'Well… terror, fear, pity, tenderness… just as when I looked through the aperture in the wall. We have assumed that the painting is *perfect*, so it ought to make exactly the same impression on me as the real thing.'

'Oh no it doesn't! Within two minutes you feel a pain in your right arm, out of sympathy with the executioner who has to hold that heavy piece of steel up for so long without moving…'

'*Sympathy* with the *executioner*?'

'Yes! *Fellow-suffering, fellow-feeling*, you know! And also with the woman who has to kneel there in front of that block for such a long time, in an uncomfortable posture, and probably in an uncomfortable frame of mind, too. You are still sorry for her, but now not because she has to be beheaded, but because she is kept waiting for so long *before* she is beheaded, and in the end—assuming you still felt any impulse to interfere—if you were to say or call anything it would be no more than: "For goodness' sake strike, man, and get it over, the woman's waiting!" And if you were to see the picture again, and see it again *often*, then even your *first* impression would become: "Isn't that business finished yet? Is he still standing there, and is she still kneeling there?"'

'But what sort of movement is there in the beauty of the women at Arles, then?' asked Verbrugge.

'Oh, that's quite a different thing! They *enact* a whole history in their features. Carthage flourishes again and builds ships on their brows … listen to Hannibal's oath against Rome … there they are twisting strings for bows … here the town is on fire…'

'Max, Max, I really believe you left your heart in Arles,' teased Tina.

'Yes, for a moment … but I got it back: as you shall hear. Just imagine … I don't say: there I saw a woman, who was as beautiful as this or that. No: they were *all* beautiful, and so it was impossible to fall in love there for good and all, because the very next woman always put the previous one right out of your mind, and I honestly thought at the same time about Caligula or Tiberius—who is it, now, they tell that story about?—who wished the whole human race had only one head. For in this way I couldn't help wishing that the women of Arles...'

'Had only one head between them?'

'Yes...'

'To cut off?'

'Of course not! To ... kiss on the forehead, I was going to say, but that isn't it either! No, to gaze at, to dream about, and ... *to be good for* !'

No doubt Duclari and Verbrugge found this conclusion, again, *very* peculiar. But Max did not notice their surprise, and went on:

'Because the features were so noble I felt something like shame at being only a human being, and not a spark ... a ray—no, those would still be matter!—a thought! But ... then, all at once, a brother or a father would be sitting by the side of those women, and ... God help me, I saw one blow her nose!'

'I knew you would smudge the picture again!' said Tina sadly.

'Is that *my* fault? *I'd* sooner have seen her drop down dead! *May* such a woman desecrate herself?'

'But Mr Havelaar,' said Verbrugge, 'suppose she had a cold?'

'Well, she *shouldn't* have had a cold, with such a nose!'

'Yes, but...'

Just then, as ill-luck would have it, Tina suddenly felt she had to sneeze, and ... before she could stop herself, she had blown her nose!

'Max, dear Max, please don't be cross!' she begged, with a suppressed laugh.

He did not answer. And, however foolish it may seem or may be ... he *was* cross! And, what will also sound strange, Tina was pleased that he was cross, and that therefore he demanded more from *her* than from the Phocaean women of Arles,[66] even if it was not because she had reason to be proud of her nose.

157

If Duclari still thought the new Assistant Resident was 'a fool', he could not have been blamed for feeling confirmed in that opinion on noticing the momentary irritation which could be read on Havelaar's face after and because Tina blew her nose. But the former had got back from Carthage, and now read—with the speed with which he *could* read when his mind was not too far away—on his guests' faces that they were mentally laying down the following two propositions:

1. *He who does not wish his wife to blow her nose is a fool.*
2. *He who believes that a nose cut in beautiful lines may not be blown is mistaken in applying this belief to Mrs Havelaar, whose nose is slightly en pomme de terre.*

The first proposition Havelaar left undisputed, but ... the second!

'Oh!' he exclaimed, as if he had to reply, though his guests had been too polite to state their propositions aloud, 'I'll explain. Tina is...'

'Dear Max!' she said deprecatingly.

That meant: 'For Heaven's sake, don't tell these gentlemen why you consider I ought to be above colds!'

Havelaar seemed to understand what Tina meant, for he responded:

'All right, dear! But, gentlemen, do you know one is often mistaken in judging the rights of some people to physical imperfection?'

I am certain the guests had never heard of those rights.

'I knew a girl in Sumatra,' he continued, 'the daughter of a DA-TU.[67] Well now, I maintain that *she* had no right to such imperfection. And yet I saw her fall into the water during a shipwreck... just like anyone else. I, a mere mortal, had to help her ashore.'

'But ... ought she to have been able to fly like a seagull, then?'

'Of course, or ... no, she ought not to have had a body at all. Shall I tell you how I met her? It was in '42. I was Controleur of NA-TAL[68] ... were you ever there, Verbrugge?'

'Yes.'

'Well, then you know they grow pepper there. The pepper plan-

158

tations are on the coast at TALOH-BALEH, north of Natal town. I had to inspect them, and since I knew nothing about pepper I took with me in the proa a DATU, who knew more about it. His daughter, a child of thirteen, came along with us. We sailed along the coast, and were bored...'

'And then you were shipwrecked?'

'Oh no, it was fine weather, much too fine. The shipwreck took place a long time afterwards; otherwise I shouldn't have been bored. Well, we sailed along the coast, and it was stifling hot. A proa doesn't offer much opportunity for diversion, and on top of that I happened to be in a doleful mood, for many reasons. Firstly, I was having an unhappy love affair—an everyday occurrence with me at that time!—but, besides, I happened to be at a dead point between two attacks of ambition. I had made myself king, and been dethroned again. I had climbed a tower, and fallen back on to the ground... oh well, I shan't tell you how it all came about! Enough ... I was sitting in this proa with a sour face and a bad temper. I was what the Germans call *unenjoyable*. Among other things, I considered it was beneath my dignity to have to inspect pepper plantations, and that I should have been appointed governor of a solar system long ago. Then, again, it seemed to me a sort of moral murder to put a mind like mine in one proa along with that stupid DATU and his child.

'I must add, though, that otherwise I liked the Malay Chiefs, and got on very well with them. They have many qualities that make me prefer them to the grandees of Java. Yes, Verbrugge, I know you don't agree with me there, very few people do ... but we won't discuss that now.

'If I had made that trip on another day—with fewer mares' nests in my head, I mean—I should probably have got into conversation with the DATU at once, and perhaps I would have found it worth my while. Maybe I should then soon have got the girl to talk, and that might have entertained and amused me too, for a child usually has something original about it ... although I must admit that at that time I was still too much of a child myself to take an interest in originality. Now, things are different. Now I see in every girl of thirteen a manuscript in which as yet little or nothing has been crossed out. One surprises the author *en pantoufles*, and that's often quite nice.

'The child was threading beads on a string, and seemed to need all her attention for that. Three red ones, one black ... three red ones, one black: it was pretty!

'Her name was Si Upi Keteh. In Sumatra, that means something like *Little Miss* ... yes, Verbrugge, I know *you* know it, but Duclari has always served in Java. Her name was Si Upi Keteh, but I mentally called her "poor creature" or something of the sort, because in my estimation I was so infinitely exalted above her.

'Afternoon came ... evening almost, and the beads were put away. The land slid slowly past; Mount Ophir grew smaller and smaller behind us. To the left, in the west, above the wide, wide sea, which knows no limit until it reaches Madagascar, with Africa behind it ... the sun was sinking, and sent his beams playing ducks and drakes over the waves, at an angle that grew more and more obtuse. He sought coolness in the sea. How the devil did that thing go, now?'

'What thing ... the sun?'

'No, no ... I wrote verses in those days! Delicious ones ... just listen:

> You wonder why the ocean wave
> That washes Natal's shores,
> Though elsewhere amiable and calm,
> Here, venting all its power to harm,
> Ceaselessly pounds and roars?
>
> You ask, and the poor fisher-lad
> At once hears your request,
> And rolls an eye of dark distress
> Towards Ocean, stretching measureless
> Into the distant West.

He rolls his dark, his sombre eye,
To the West gazes he,
And shows you, as you stare around,
But water, without end or bound—
Sea, nothing but sea!

And that is why the ocean scours
So fiercely Natal's sand:
Where'er you look 'tis only sea.
Of water an infinity
To Madagascar's strand.

And many a sacrifice is made
The ocean to placate!
And many a cry chokes in the foam,
Unheard by wife, child, kin at home,
But heard at Heaven's gate!

And many a hand stretches its last,
Thrown upwards in its quest,
Gropes, clutches, splashes in despair,
Seeking to find support somewhere,
By cruel waves hard-pressed!
And I forget the rest...

'You could finish it if you wrote to Krygsman, who was your clerk at NATAL. He has it,' said Verbrugge.

'Where did *he* get it?' asked Max.

'Perhaps from your wastepaper basket. But he definitely has it. Isn't what follows the legend of the primal sin, which made the island sink that once protected the roadstead of NATAL? The story of JIVA and the two brothers?'

'Yes, that's right. The legend ... was no legend. It was a parable I made up, but it will be a legend in a few centuries' time ... if Krygs-

161

man goes around chanting it often enough. That was how *all* mythology began. JIVA is *soul*, as you know, *soul*, *spirit*, or something of the kind. I made it a woman, the indispensable, naughty Eve...'

'Well, Max, what's happened to our "Little Miss" and her beads?' asked Tina.

'The beads had been put away. It was six o'clock, and there on the Equator—NATAL lies a few minutes north of it: whenever I went overland to AYER-BANGIE, I made my horse step across it, more or less ... otherwise you could easily stumble over the thing, 'pon my honour!—Well, there on the Equator six o'clock was the signal for evening meditations. Now, it seems to me that at night one is always a little better, or less vicious at any rate, than in the morning, and this is only natural. In the morning one pulls oneself together—I know this is an Anglicism, but how am I to say it in Dutch?—one is ... bailiff or Controleur or ... no, that's enough to be going on with! A bailiff *pulls himself together*, to do his duty with a vengeance that day ... good God, what a duty! And what must *that* heart look like, *pulled together*! A Controleur—I don't mean you, Verbrugge!—a Controleur rubs his eyes, and realizes with distaste that he's got to meet the new Assistant Resident, who will put on absurd airs of superiority on the grounds of a few years' extra service, and of whom he has heard so many odd things ... in Sumatra. Or that day he has to measure fields, and wavers between his honesty—you may not know it, Duclari, because you're a soldier, but there really are honest Controleurs!—he stands dithering between that honesty of his and the fear that RADHEN DHEMANG such-and-such may ask him to return the white horse which is so good at *counting*. Or else, that day, he will have to give a firm *yes* or *no* in answer to memorandum number so-and-so. In short, when you wake up in the morning the whole world falls on your head, and that's heavy for any head, however strong. But at night you have a respite. There are ten full hours between then and the moment you will have to face your uniform jacket again. Ten hours: six-and-thirty thousand seconds in which to be a human being! That's a rosy enough prospect for anybody. That's the moment at which I hope to die, so as to arrive up yonder with an unofficial countenance. That's the moment at which your wife again finds in your face something of what *took* her when she let you keep that handkerchief with a coroneted E in the corner...'

'And when she hadn't yet acquired the right to have a cold,' said Tina.

'Oh, don't tease! All I want to say is, at night one feels more *gemüthlich*.'[69]

'Now when, as I said, the sun slowly vanished,' Havelaar went on, 'I became a better man. And you might reckon that the first sign of that betterment was my saying to Little Miss:

'"It will soon start getting cooler."

'"Yes, *Tuan*!" she replied.

'But I stooped in my majesty still lower to that "poor creature", and struck up a conversation with her. My merit was the greater because she said very little in reply. I found agreement with everything I said ... which also becomes tedious, however conceited one is.

'"Would you like to come to Taloh-Baleh with us next time, too?" I asked.

'"As the Tuan Kommandeur[70] shall decide."

'"No, I'm asking *you* whether *you* would enjoy another trip like this?'

'"If my father wishes it," she answered.

'I ask you, gentlemen, wasn't it enough to drive you crazy? Well, I didn't go crazy. The sun was down, and I felt *gemüthlich* enough not to be put off even by so much stupidity. Or rather I believe I began to take pleasure in hearing my own voice—there are few among us who are not fond of listening to themselves. But, after my taciturnity all day, I considered that, since I'd started speaking at last, I deserved something better than the altogether too silly answers of Si Upi Keteh.

'I'll tell her a fairy tale, I thought, then I shall hear it myself at the same time, and there's no need for her to answer me. Now you know that, just as when a ship is unloaded the last *kranjang*[71] of sugar put in will be the first to come out again, so we too have a habit of first unloading the thought or story which was put into our heads last. Shortly before, I had read a story by Jeronimus, "The Japanese Stonecutter", in the *Dutch East Indian Magazine* ... I say, that Jeronimus has written some nice things! Did you ever read his "Auction in the Houses of the Deceased"? Or his "Graves"? Or, best of all, "Pedatti"? I'll give it you.

'Well—I had just read "The Japanese Stonecutter"... Oh, now I remember what sent my thoughts straying off on to that poem in which I let the fisher lad roll his "dark eye" round in one direction till he must have squinted ... mighty silly! It was as association of ideas. My bad temper that day had to do with the dangers of the Natal roadstead ... As you know, Verbrugge, no warship is allowed to enter it, especially in July ... You see, Duclari, the south-west monsoon is strongest there in July, just the opposite of what it is here. Well, the dangers of those waters clamped themselves tightly on to my thwarted ambition, and that ambition, again, is linked with the poem about JIVA. I had repeatedly proposed to the Resident at NATAL that a breakwater should be made, or at any rate an artificial harbour in the mouth of the river, to bring trade to the Division of NATAL, which connects the vitally important Battak lands with the sea. A million and a half people in the interior didn't know what to do with their produce because the Natal roadstead was in such bad odour—and rightly so! Well, my proposals hadn't been approved by the Resident, or at least he maintained that the Government wouldn't approve them, and you know Residents never put forward anything but what they reckon will appeal to the Government anyway. Construction of a harbour at NATAL was contrary to the "closed door" policy, and so far from wishing to encourage ships to come there it was even forbidden—except in cases of emergency—to admit square-rigged vessels to the roadstead at all. If, in spite of this, a ship did happen to come—they were mostly American whalers or French ships that had loaded pepper in the little independent states at the northern point of Sumatra—I always got the captain to write me a letter asking leave to take on drinking water. My annoyance at the failure of my efforts to achieve something to the advantage of NATAL, or rather my wounded vanity... wasn't it hard for me, still to count for so little that I couldn't even have a harbour made where I wanted it? Well then, all this, in connection with my candidature for government of a solar system, was what had made me so unamiable that day. When the sunset had cured me a little—for discontent is an illness—it was that very illness which reminded me of "The Japanese Stonecutter", and perhaps I only thought that story aloud, making myself believe I was telling it to the child out of pure kindness, in order to tacitly take the last drop of the medicine I felt I needed. But she, the child, cured me—for a day or two, at any rate—better than my story, which, I think, went something like this:

'"*Upi*, there was a man who hewed stones from the rock. His labour was very hard, and he laboured much, but his wages were slender, and he was not content.

He sighed because his labour was hard. And he cried: 'Oh, that I were rich, that I might rest on a *baleh-baleh*[72] with a *klambu*[73] of silk!'

And there came an angel from heaven, who said: 'Be it unto thee as thou hast said.'

And he *was* rich. And he *did* rest on a *baleh-baleh*, and the *klambu* was of red silk.

And the king of the country passed by, with horsemen before his car. And behind his car there were horsemen, and the golden *payong* was held over the head of the king.

And when the rich man saw that, he was vexed that no golden *payong* was held over *his* head. And he was not content.

He sighed, and cried: 'I wish I were a king!'

And there came an angel from heaven, who said: 'Be it unto thee as thou hast said.'

165

And he *was* a king. And before his car rode many horsemen, and behind his car also there were horsemen, and over his head the golden *payong* was held.

And the sun shone with burning beams, and scorched the earth, so that the grassblades withered.

And the king complained that the sun burnt his face, and had more power than he. And he was not content.

He sighed, and cried: 'I wish I were the sun!'

And there came an angel from heaven, who said: 'Be it unto thee as thou hast said.'

And he *was* the sun. And he sent his beams upward and downward, to the right and to the left, and all round.

And he scorched the grassblades on the earth, and the faces of the kings that were on the earth.

And a cloud placed itself between him and the earth, and it threw back the beams of the sun.

And he grew wroth that his power was resisted, and he complained that that cloud had more power than he. And he was not content.

He wished to be the cloud, which was so powerful.

And there came an angel from heaven, who said: 'Be it unto thee as thou hast said.'

And he became a cloud, and placed himself between the sun and the earth, and caught the sunbeams, so that the grass grew green.

And the cloud rained in large drops on the earth, and made the rivers swell, and *banjirs* carried away the herds.

And the volume of his waters destroyed the fields.

And he fell upon a rock, which yielded not. And he plashed down in mighty streams, but the rock yielded not.

And he grew wroth because the rock would not yield, and because the strength of his streams was vain. And he was not content.

And he cried: 'To that rock, greater power has been given than to me! I wish I were that rock!'

And there came an angel from heaven, who said: 'Be it unto thee as thou hast said.'

And he *became* a rock, and moved not when the sun shone, nor when the rain fell.

And there came a man with a pickaxe and sharp chisel and heavy hammer, and he hewed stones out of the rock.

And the rock said: 'What is this, that this man has power over me, and can hew stones out of my bosom?' And he was not content.

He cried: 'I am weaker than this one ... I wish I were this man!'

And there came an angel from heaven, who said: 'Be it unto thee as thou hast said.'

And he was a stonecutter. And he hewed stones from the rock, with hard labour, and he laboured very hard for scanty wages, and he was content."'

'Charming,' exclaimed Duclari, 'but you still owe us the proof that little Upi ought to have been imponderable.'

'No, I never promised you that! I only wanted to tell you how I made her acquaintance. When my story was finished, I asked:

'"And you, Upi—what would *you* choose, if an angel from heaven came to ask you what you would like most?"

'"Sir, I should pray that he might take me back to Heaven with him."'

'Isn't that perfectly sweet?' asked Tina, turning to her guests, who perhaps thought it perfectly absurd...

Havelaar rose, and wiped his forehead.

12

'Dear Max,' said Tina, 'our dessert is *so* meagre. Couldn't you...
you know... Madame Geoffrin?'[74]

'—tell some more stories, instead of pudding? The deuce, I've no
voice left. It's Verbrugge's turn.'

'Yes, Mr Verbrugge! Do take over from Max for a while,' begged
Mrs Havelaar.

Verbrugge thought for a moment, and began:

'There was once a man who stole a turkey...'

'Oh, you scoundrel!' exclaimed Havelaar. 'You got that from
PADANG! And how does it go on?'

'That's all there is. Who knows the end of the story?'

'Well ... *I* do ... I ate it, along with ... someone else. Do you know
why I was suspended at PADANG?'

'They said your cash was short at NATAL,' replied Verbrugge.

'That wasn't altogether untrue, but it wasn't *true* either. For all
kinds of reasons, I'd been very careless about my accounts; they
were undoubtedly open to a lot of criticism. But that happened so
often in those days! Shortly after BARUS, TAPUS and SINGKEL were
taken, conditions in the north of Sumatra were so chaotic, everything was so unquiet, that no one could blame a young chap who
preferred being on horseback to counting money or keeping books
for the fact that everything wasn't in such apple-pie order as might
have been expected from an Amsterdam book-keeper with nothing
else to do. The Battak lands were in ferment, and you know, Verbrugge, how everything that happens there always reacts on NATAL.
I slept in my clothes every night, to be ready for emergencies, and
that was often necessary, too. Again, danger—some time before I
arrived a plot was discovered to assassinate my predecessor and
raise a rebellion—well, danger has something attractive about it, especially when you're only twenty-two. That attraction naturally
makes a man unfit at times for office work, or for the meticulous

precision which is necessary for the proper management of money matters. Besides, I had all sorts of follies in my head—'

'*Traussa !*'[75] Mrs Havelaar called to one of the servants.

'*What* don't you need?'

'I had told them to prepare something else in the kitchen … an omelette, or something of the kind.'

'I see! And that's no longer needed when I start talking about my follies? You're a naughty girl, Tina! Well, *I* don't mind, but these gentlemen have a voice in the matter too. Verbrugge, which will you have — your share of the omelette, or the story?'

'That's a difficult choice for a man of breeding,' said Verbrugge.

'And *I*'d rather not choose, either,' Duclari added, 'because it's a question here of deciding between husband and wife, and … *entre l'écorce et le bois il ne faut pas mettre le doigt.*'

'I'll help you out, gentlemen, the omelette is…'

'Mrs Havelaar,' said the courtly Duclari, 'the omelette will surely be worth as much as…'

'The story? Oh, certainly, if it was worth anything! But there is a difficulty…'

'I bet there's no sugar in the house yet,' exclaimed Verbrugge. 'Do please send to my place for anything you want.'

'There is sugar … from Mrs Slotering. No, that's not it. If the omelette was otherwise all right, sugar would be no difficulty, but…'

'What, has it fallen in the fire, then?'

'I wish it had! No, it can't fall in the fire. It's…'

'My dear Tina,' exclaimed Havelaar, 'what *is* the matter with it?'

'It's imponderable, Max, as your women of Arles … ought to have been! I've got no omelette, I've nothing more!'

'Then let's have the story, for Heaven's sake!' sighed Duclari, in comical despair.

'But we have coffee,' cried Tina.

'Good! We'll take coffee on the front verandah, and let's call Mrs Slotering and her girls to join us,' said Havelaar, whereupon the little company went outside.

'I expect she'll ask to be excused, Max. As you know, she prefers not to have her meals with us either, and I can't honestly blame her!'

'She'll have heard I tell yarns,' said Havelaar, 'and that's frightened her off.'

'Oh no, Max, that wouldn't bother her ... she doesn't understand Dutch. No, she's told me she wants to go on running her own household, and I can well understand that. Do you remember how you once translated my initials: E.H. v. W.?'

'Yes. *Eigen haard veel waard.*'[76]

'That's why! She's quite right! Besides, she seems to be a bit shy. Just imagine, she has all strange people who come into the compound sent away by the watchmen...'

'I want either the story or the omelette,' said Duclari.

'So do I!' exclaimed Verbrugge. 'No excuses accepted. We have a right to a full meal, and so I demand the tale of the turkey.'

'I've already given you that,' said Havelaar. 'I stole the bird from General Vandamme, and I ate it up ... with someone else.'

'Before that "someone else" was taken up to heaven,' said Tina archly.

'No, that's cheating!' cried Duclari. 'We must know *why* you stole the turkey.'

'Oh, because I was hungry, and that was the fault of General Vandamme, who had suspended me.'

'If I don't get to know more about this I'll bring my own omelette next time,' Verbrugge complained.

'Believe me, there's nothing more to it than that. He had a great many turkeys, and I had nothing. They drove the creatures past my door ... I took one, and said to the man who imagined he was looking after them: "Tell the General Max Havelaar is taking his turkey because he has to eat."'

'And what about that epigram?'

'Did Verbrugge tell you about that?'

'Yes.'

'It had nothing to do with the turkey. I wrote the thing because he suspended so many officials. At PADANG there were quite seven or eight whom he had suspended with varying justification. Several of them deserved it much less than I did. The Assistant Resident of PADANG, even, had been suspended, and for a quite different reason, I believe, from the one given in the Order. I don't mind telling you this, although I can't be absolutely sure I've got hold of the right end of the stick. I only repeat what the *Chinese Church*[77] at PADANG took to be the truth, and what in fact may well have been the truth, in view of the General's notorious character.

'You must know, he had married his wife to win a wager, and with it an anker of wine. So it was only natural that he often left home of an evening, to … gad about all over the place. On one occasion, in an alley near the Girls' Orphanage, a supernumerary, Valkenaar, is supposed to have respected his incognito so strictly that he gave him a thrashing, as though the General were an *ordinary* ruffian. Not far from there lived an English girl, Miss X. There was a rumour that this *Miss* had given birth to a child which had … disappeared. As chief of police, the Assistant Resident was obliged to go into the matter—and that was his intention, too, and he seems to have said something about it during a whist party at the General's house. But what do you think happened? Next day, he received orders to go to a certain Division, where the Controleur-in-charge had been suspended for dishonesty, in order to investigate certain matters on the spot and "submit a report" on them. The Assistant Resident was certainly surprised to be given an assignment which did not in the least concern his own Division. But, strictly speaking, he could consider the task as a mark of distinction, and since he was on such friendly terms with the General he had no cause to suspect a trap. So he accepted the job, and set out for … I prefer to forget where … to carry out his orders. Some time later he returned, and sent in a report which was not unfavourable to the Controleur. But, lo and behold! At PADANG, in the meantime, the public—that's to say, everyone and no one—had discovered that the Controleur had only been suspended to create an opportunity for getting the Assistant Resident out of the way for a while, to prevent his intended inquiry into the disappearance of Miss X's baby, or at least to postpone it for so long as to make it more difficult to clear the matter up. I repeat—I can't personally vouch for the truth of this. But, from the first-hand knowledge I acquired of General Vandamme afterwards, this version of the case seems quite credible to me. At PADANG there was no one who did not consider him quite capable of such a thing, in view of the depth to which his moral reputation had sunk. Most people would only allow him one good quality: courage in the face of danger. Well, I saw him in times of danger; and if I held the opinion that at least he was a *brave* man, that alone would prevent me from telling you this story now. I agree, in Sumatra he was responsible for a lot of "sabring"; but if you had seen anything of it from close quarters you would have felt inclined to discount that bravery of his, and ... it may seem strange, but I believe he owed his warrior's reputation largely to the love of contrast which all of us more or less have. We like to be able to say: "It's true that Peter or Paul is *this*, or *this*, or *this*, but ... he is also *that*: *that* can't be denied him!" And a man is never so certain of being praised as when he has a very conspicuous failing. You, Verbrugge, you're drunk every day...'

'Me?' said Verbrugge, who was a model of temperance.

'Yes, *I* am making you drunk now, every day! You forget yourself so far that Duclari falls over you on the verandah of an evening. He won't like that, but at once he'll recollect some good quality in you, though, to be honest, he hadn't noticed it so much in the past. And when *I* come on the scene, and find you so very ... *horizontal*, he will lay his hand on my arm, and exclaim: "Oh, but believe me, otherwise he's the best, the finest, the smartest fellow in the world!"'

'I say that of Verbrugge anyway,' said Duclari, 'even when he's *vertical*.'

'But not with such fire and conviction! Think how often one hears: "Oh, if *that* chap would only mind his Ps and Qs more, *wouldn't* he be somebody! But..." And then follows the tale of how he does *not* mind his Ps and Qs, and so he's *nobody*. I believe I know the reason for this. One always learns about good qualities in the dead, too, which we never saw in them when they were alive. And that's because they are *not in anyone's way*. All men are more or less rivals. We would like to tell the world we are above everyone else, *entirely* and in *everything*. But to do it is contrary not only to good form but also to self-interest, for very soon people would be so much on their guard that no one would believe a word we said, even when it was true. So a roundabout way has to be found, and this is how we go about it. When you, Duclari, say: "Lieutenant Spatterdash is a good soldier, he's a damn good soldier, I cannot tell you emphatically enough what a good soldier Lieutenant Spatterdash is ... but he's no good at theory..." Didn't you say so, Duclari?'

'I've never come across a Lieutenant Spatterdash in my life!'

'Very well, then create him, and say that about him.'

'All right, I've created him, and I say that about him.'

'Then do you know what you've really said? You've said that *you*, Duclari, are A1 on theory! I'm not a scrap better. Believe me, we're doing an injustice when we get so angry with a person who's very bad, for ... "there's so much bad in the best of us"! If we suppose perfection equals nought degrees and bad is a hundred, how wrong it is of us—us, wobbling between ninety-eight and ninety-nine!—to raise a hue and cry about a man who's made a hundred and one! Besides, I believe that many only fail to reach that hundredth degree for want of *good* qualities—for instance, lack of courage to be entirely what they are.'

'How many degrees am *I* at, Max?'

'I should want a magnifying glass to count the subdivisions, Tina.'

'I protest,' exclaimed Verbrugge—'No, Mrs Havelaar, not against your proximity to zero!—no, but officials have been suspended, a new-born child has disappeared, a General stands accused ... I demand the rest of the play!'

'Tina, for goodness' sake make sure there's something to eat in the house next time! No, Verbrugge, you're not going to get the rest of the play until I've done a little more riding around on my hobbyhorse about contrasts. I said every man sees in his fellow-man a kind of rival. We must not always be criticizing—that would become too noticeable! So we praise the other chap's good quality to the skies, in order to make a particular bad quality show up more without our appearing hostile. When someone comes and complains to me because I said: "His daughter is very beautiful, but he's a thief!" I answer: "What are you making such a fuss about? I said your daughter was a sweet girl, didn't I?" You see, I win all ends up! We're both shopkeepers—grocers: I take his customers off him, because they won't buy raisins from a thief, and ... at the same time people say I'm a kindhearted fellow, because I praise the daughter of a competitor.'

'No, but things aren't as bad as all that,' said Duclari. 'That's going a bit too far!'

'It only appears so to you because I made the comparison rather brief and blunt. We must wrap some mental cotton wool round that "he's a thief". But in essence the parable remains true. When we are compelled to admit that a person has qualities which give him a claim to esteem, respect or veneration, then it gives us pleasure to discover alongside those qualities something that relieves us partly or wholly from paying the tribute due. "To *such* a poet I would take my hat off but ... he beats his wife!" You see, we gladly use the woman's bruises as an excuse for keeping our hats on, and in the end we're even quite pleased that he clouts the poor creature, although that's otherwise a very nasty thing to do. As soon as we have to recognize that someone possesses virtues which entitle him to be put on a pedestal ... as soon as we can no longer deny his claim to it without being pronounced ignorant, insensitive or jealous, then at last we say: "Right, set him up!" But even while we're putting him there, and while he himself still thinks we are enchanted by his eminence, we are knotting the noose in the *lasso* which is to drag him down at the first favourable opportunity. The quicker the turnover among proprietors of pedestals, the more chance there is for everybody to have his little hour up on one in due course, and this is so true that, out of habit and for practice—just like a hunter potting at crows which he doesn't intend to pick up anyway—we love pulling down even those statues whose pedestal we shall never be able to ascend ourselves. Kappelman,[78] who lives on sauerkraut and small beer, seeks elevation in the complaint "Alexander was *not* great ... he was intemperate", though Kappelman will never have the slightest opportunity of competing with Alexander in conquering the world.

'However this may be, I am certain that many people would never have hit on the idea of General Vandamme being so brave if his bravery could not have served them as vehicle for the invariable rider: "but ... his morals!" And, again, that immorality of his would not have been taken so much amiss by many who weren't altogether unassailable on that score themselves if they hadn't needed it to counterbalance his renown for bravery, which kept some people from sleeping.

'One quality he really possessed to a very high degree: willpower. Whatever he made up his mind to do, had to be done, and usually was done. But—d'you see, once again I have the contrast ready to hand?—but then, in his choice of means he certainly was a little ... free, and, as Van der Palm said of Napoleon—in my opinion, unjustly: "Moral obstacles never deterred him!" Well, of course, in that way it is certainly easier to get where one wants to be than when one *does* consider oneself bound by such considerations.

'So, then ... the Assistant Resident of PADANG sent in a report that was favourable to the suspended Controleur, whose suspension thereby acquired a tinge of injustice. The PADANG gossip went on: the lost child was still the talk of the town. The Assistant Resident again felt called upon to take the matter up, but ... before he had been able to bring anything to light, he received an Order by which the Governor of the West Coast of Sumatra, General Vandamme, suspended him "for dishonesty in the execution of his office". It was said that he had presented the case of that Controleur in a false light, out of friendship or sympathy and against his better knowledge.

'I have not read the documents in the case. But I know that the Assistant Resident had no relations whatsoever with the Controleur, which would naturally follow anyway from the fact that he had been specially chosen to investigate the affair. I also know that he was a man of integrity, and the Government thought so too, as they showed by annulling the suspension after the case had been investigated elsewhere than on the West Coast of Sumatra. The Controleur was also rehabilitated eventually without a stain on his character. It was the suspension of those two that inspired me with the epigram which I had placed on the General's breakfast table by a man in his service who had previously been in mine:

> Walking Suspension-writ, who rules us by suspension,
> That werewolf of our days, Governor Suspend-all Jack,
> Would e'en have given his conscience suspensory attention
> Had it not long ago been firmly given the sack.'

'You must excuse me, Mr Havelaar, but I don't think your action was in order,' said Duclari.

'Nor do I ... but I had to do *something*! Put yourself in my place: I had no money, I received none, and I was afraid of dying of hunger any day, as, indeed, I very nearly did. I had few or no connexions at PADANG, and, besides, I had written and told the General that he would be responsible if I died from want, and that I would accept help from no one. There were people in the interior who heard about my circumstances and invited me to come and stay with them; but the General wouldn't allow a pass to be given to me. Nor was I allowed to leave for Java. Everywhere else I could have managed all right, and perhaps I could have got along even at PADANG if people hadn't been so afraid of the almighty General. It really looked as though he meant me to starve. That lasted nine months!'

176

'And how did you keep alive so long? Or had the General a lot of turkeys?'

'Yes, plenty! But that didn't help … you can only do a thing like that once, don't you think? What did I do all that time? Oh … I made verses, wrote plays … and so on.'

'And could you buy rice with those things at PADANG?'

'No, but *that* I never asked for them. I'd … rather not say how I lived.'

Tina squeezed his hand. *She* knew.

'I've read a few lines you are supposed to have written in those days, on the back of a bill,' said Verbrugge.

'I know the lines you mean. They described my position. At that time there was a magazine, *The Copyist*, for which I had a subscription. It was under Government patronage—the editor was an official in the General Secretariat in Batavia—and so the subscriptions were paid to the Treasury. I was presented with a bill for twenty guilders. Now, the money was dealt with in the Governor's office, and consequently the bill, if unpaid, had to go through that office to be returned to Java. So I took the opportunity of protesting about my poverty on the back of the bill:

Florins a score… what wealth! Letters, farewell to thee,
Farewell, my Copyist! Fate too unfortunate:
I die of hunger, cold, of thirst, disconsolate.
Those twenty coins would mean two months of food for me!
If I had such a sum I should be better shod,
Better fed, better housed, I should fare like a god…
The first thing is to live, be it in misery:
Crime is a cause for shame, not poverty![79]

'But when, afterwards, I called on the editor of *The Copyist* in Batavia to pay my twenty guilders, I found I owed him nothing. It appeared that the General himself had paid the money for me, so as not to have to return the embellished bill to Batavia!'

177

'But what did he do after you ... took that turkey? There's no denying it, it was ... theft! And after that epigram?'

'He punished me terribly! He might have put me on trial as guilty of disrespect to the Governor of the West Coast of Sumatra, which, in those days, by stretching a point, could have been interpreted as "*an attempt to undermine Dutch authority, and incitement to rebellion*" or "*larceny on the King's highway*". If he had done that, he would have shown himself to be a kind-hearted man. But, no, he punished me more effectively ... horribly! The man who had charge of the turkeys was ordered to take another road in future. And my epigram ... that was even worse! He said *nothing*, and did *nothing*! Look ... that was cruel! He grudged me the very least vestige of a martyr's crown, I was not allowed to become interesting through persecution, nor unhappy through excess of wit! Oh, Duclari ... oh, Verbrugge ... it was enough to sicken me once and for all of epigrams and turkeys! To receive *so* little encouragement quenches the flame of genius ... down to the very last spark! I never did it again!'

13

'And now may we hear the real reason why you were suspended?' asked Duclari.

'Oh, yes, with pleasure! I can vouch for the truth of all I have to say about it, and I can even partly prove it, so you will see from my story that I had some grounds for not rejecting the tittle-tattle of PADANG about the missing child as absolutely absurd. You'll find it highly credible after seeing the part played by our valiant General in *my* affairs.

'As I said, there were inaccuracies and gaps in my cash accounts at NATAL. You know perfectly well how every such slip is to one's own disadvantage: nobody has ever yet been in pocket through carelessness. The Head of the Accounts Branch at PADANG, who was not exactly a friend of mine, maintained that I was thousands of guilders down. But, look you ... my attention was not drawn to this while I was in NATAL.

'Quite unexpectedly, I received a transfer to the PADANG HIGH-LANDS. As you know, Verbrugge, in Sumatra a post in the PADANG HIGHLANDS is considered better and pleasanter than one in the northern residency. Only a short time before, I had had a visit from the Governor—you will hear why and how presently! And during his stay in the Division of NATAL, and in my own house, even, things happened in which I acted in what seemed to me a very proper and manly manner. So I took this posting as a mark of favour, and left NATAL for PADANG quite happily. I travelled on a French boat, the BAOBAB of Marseilles, which had loaded pepper in ACHIN and ... of course, "was short of drinking water" at NATAL.

'I arrived at PADANG with the intention of leaving for the interior at once. But I was in duty bound to pay my respects to the Governor, and I tried to do so. However, he sent me word that he could not receive me, and also that I was to postpone my departure for my new station until further orders. You will understand that I was very surprised at this, the more so since his mood when he left me at

NATAL had made me think he had rather a good opinion of me.

'I knew few people at PADANG, but from those few I heard—or rather I noticed it from their attitude—that the General was very annoyed with me. I say I *noticed* it, for, at an outpost such as PADANG was at that time, the amount of goodwill shown to you could be taken as a gauge, as barometer of the favour one had found in the eyes of the Governor. I felt that a storm was brewing, though I didn't know from what quarter the wind would blow. As I was in need of money, I asked this man and that to help me, and I was absolutely flabbergasted to meet with refusal everywhere! At PA-DANG, no less than elsewhere in the Indies, the attitude about giving credit was usually rather liberal. In any other case, people would willingly have advanced a few hundred guilders to a Controleur in transit who was held up somewhere unexpectedly. But to me all help was refused. I pressed some of those I spoke to to name the reasons for this, and little by little I at last got to know that errors and omissions had been discovered in my books at NATAL which laid me under suspicion of dishonest accounting. That there were errors in my accounts did not surprise me at all. I should have been surprised if there had 'nt been. But I did think it strange that the Governor, who had personally been witness to the fact that I had constantly had to fight, far away from my office, against the dis-content of the population and their persistent attempts at rebel-lion ... that he, who had praised me himself for what he called my "pluck", now labelled the errors in my books with the name of fraud or dishonesty. Surely no one knew better than he did that in such cases there never could be question of anything else but *force majeure*?

'And even if people denied this *force majeure*—even if they wished to hold me responsible for mistakes made when (often in deadly danger!) I was far from the cash box or anything like it, and had to entrust it to others—even if they demanded that when I was doing one thing I still had no business to leave the other undone—even then I could only have been guilty of a carelessness which had nothing to do with "dishonesty"! Besides, especially in those days, there were numerous cases in which the authorities had fully recognized the difficult position of officials in Sumatra in this respect; and it seemed to be an accepted principle that some allowance should be made. The Government contented itself with requiring the official concerned to make good the deficit, and the evidence had to be *very* strong before anyone uttered the word "dishonesty", or even thought it. In fact this had been so entirely the rule that at NATAL I had said myself to the Governor that I was afraid I should have a good deal to pay when my accounts were audited in the office at PADANG. His only answer was a shrug of the shoulders and "Oh... those money matters!" as though he felt himself that the less important things had to give way to the more important ones.

'Now I do admit that money matters can be important. But however important they are, in this case they were subordinate to other objects of concern. If I was several thousand guilders short in my books through carelessness or neglect, I should not have called this *in itself* a trifle. But those thousands were short because of my successful efforts to prevent a rebellion which threatened to set the whole district of MANDHÉLING ablaze and bring the Achinese back to the places from which we had only just expelled them at the cost of much money and many lives! So the importance of such a deficit sinks into insignificance; in fact, it even became rather unjust to require its repayment from someone who had preserved infinitely greater interests.

'And yet I was content to make such a repayment. For if they were not exacted, too wide a door would be opened to peculation.

'After waiting about for days—in what state of mind you can easily imagine!—I received a letter from the Governor's Secretariat informing me that I was suspected of dishonesty and had to answer a number of criticisms of my accounting.

'Some of them I was able to dispose of immediately. For others, however, I needed to examine certain documents, and it was especially important for me to be able to investigate these matters in

181

NATAL itself. There I could have asked my clerks about the causes of the discrepancies, and very probably I should have managed to clear everything up. The errors might have been due, for instance, to a failure to write off money sent to MANDHÉLING—you know, Verbrugge, troops in the interior are paid from the NATAL treasury —or other things of the sort, which I should very likely have discovered at once if I could have looked into things on the spot. But the General refused to let me go to NATAL. That refusal impressed me all the more with the strange manner in which that charge of "dishonesty" had been brought against me. *Why* had I been so suddenly transferred from NATAL with the appearance of doing me a kindness, when I was under suspicion of dishonesty? Why had this degrading suspicion only been made known to me when I was far from the place where I could have defended myself? And, above all, why had those matters, in my case, immediately been put in the most unfavourable light, contrary to accepted custom and equity?

'Before I had even been able to reply to all the criticisms as best I could without records or oral information, I learnt from an indirect source that the General was so angry with me *"because I had crossed him so much at Natal, in which indeed, people added, I had been very wrong."*

'Then a light dawned on me. Yes, I had crossed him; but all the time I had naïvely supposed he would respect me for it! I *had* crossed him; but when he left, nothing had made me suspect he was angry about it. Stupidly enough, I had looked upon my favourable posting to PADANG as a proof that he admired me for "crossing" him. You will see how little I knew him!

'But as soon as I learnt that this was the cause of the severity with which my financial management had been condemned, I was at peace with myself. I answered the charges point by point to the best of my ability, and ended my letter—I still have my draft—with the words:

I have answered the strictures passed on my accounts as far as I could do without access to records or the possibility of making local inquiries. I beg that Your Excellency will abstain from treating me with any indulgence. I am young, and insignificant in comparison with the power of the prevailing conceptions against which my principles compel me to take a stand. But I am nevertheless proud of my moral independence, proud of my honour.

'Next day I was suspended for "dishonest accounting". The Public Prosecutor—at that time, we still called him the Fiscal—was ordered to carry out his "office and duty" with regard to me.

'So there I stood at PADANG, scarce twenty-three years old, staring into a future that was to bring me dishonour! I was advised to plead my youth—I was still a minor when the alleged offences had taken place; but that I wouldn't do. I had already thought and suffered too much, and ... I venture to add: worked too much, to want to take cover behind my lack of years. You can see from the conclusion of the letter I've just quoted that I didn't wish to be treated as a child, when at NATAL I had done my duty towards the General as a man. And from that letter you can see at the same time how unjust the accusation was which they brought against me. A guilty man doesn't write like that!

'I wasn't put in jail, though I ought to have been if the authorities had been in earnest with their suspicion. But perhaps there was a reason for this ... "oversight". A prisoner has to be housed and fed, hasn't he? Since I was not allowed to leave PADANG, I was really a prisoner all the same, but a prisoner without a roof over his head and without bread to put in his mouth. I wrote repeatedly to the General, without result, telling him he wasn't justified in preventing me from leaving PADANG because, even if I were guilty of the worst of crimes, no offence may be punished with *starvation*.

'The Court was evidently at a loss as to how to act in the matter, and found a way out by declaring itself not competent because prosecutions for offences committed in performance of an office may only take place on authorization from the Government in BATAVIA. The General then detained me, as I said, at PADANG for nine months.

At last he received orders from above to allow me to go to BATA-
VIA.

'A few years later, when I had a little money—dear Tina, *you* had
given it me!—I paid a few thousand guilders to settle the NATAL
cash accounts for 1842 and 1843. And someone who can be considered as representing the Government of the Dutch East Indies
then said to me: "If I'd been in your place, I shouldn't have done
it ... they could have waited till doomsday!" That's the way of the
world!'

Havelaar was just going to begin the story which his guests expected from him, and which was to make clear why and how he had
so 'crossed' General Vandamme at NATAL, when Mrs Slotering appeared on her front verandah, and beckoned to the policeman who
was sitting on a bench at one side of Havelaar's house. He went
over to her, and then called out something to a man who had just
entered the compound, probably to go to the kitchen at the back of
the house. Our company would probably not have paid any attention to this if Tina had not said at table that afternoon that Mrs Slotering was so timid and seemed to keep a kind of check on everyone who entered the compound. The man whom the orderly had
called went up to her, and it seemed as if she was questioning him
and the result was not to his advantage. At any rate, he retraced his
steps, and left.

'I'm sorry, all the same,' said Tina. 'It may have been someone
with chickens for sale, or vegetables. I haven't a thing in the house
yet.'

'Well, send someone out for them, then,' Havelaar replied. 'You
know how fond these native ladies are of exercising authority. Besides, don't forget, her husband was the most important person
here, and however little an Assistant Resident may count in reality,
in his own Division he's king; and she hasn't got used to her de-
thronement yet. Don't let us rob the poor woman of her little pleasure. Pretend not to notice.'

184

That, Tina certainly did not find difficult: *she* was not fond of exercising authority.

Here it is necessary to make a digression, and this time I even want to make a digression about digressions. It is not always easy for a writer to sail without mishap between the Scylla and Charybdis of too much and too little; and the difficulty is aggravated when he has to describe conditions in spheres that are quite unknown to the reader. There is too close a connexion between places and events for him to leave those places altogether undescribed; and avoidance of the two dangers I have referred to becomes doubly difficult for anyone who has chosen the Dutch East Indies as the scene of his story. For whereas a writer who deals with European conditions can .ake many things for granted, the one who chooses the Indies as the setting for his drama constantly has to ask himself whether the non-Indies reader will really understand this or that. If the European reader should imagine Mrs Slotering to be 'staying' with the Havelaars, as would be the case in Europe, he must find it incomprehensible that she was not in the company which was taking coffee on the front verandah. It is true I have already said that she lived in a separate house; but for a correct understanding of this, and also of subsequent events, it is really necessary for me to give him some idea of the layout of Havelaar's house and compound.

The accusation so frequently made against the great master who wrote *Waverley*, i.e. that he often abuses the patience of his readers by devoting too many pages to describing places, seems unfounded to me; and I hold that, in order to judge the correctness of such a criticism, we must simply ask ourselves: is the description necessary to convey the impression which the author wishes to convey? If it is, then *he* should not be blamed for expecting *us* to take the trouble to *read* what he has taken the trouble to *write*. If it is not, then we may as well throw the book away. For the author who is empty-headed enough to give *gratuitous* topography instead of ideas is rarely worth the trouble of reading, even when his topography has finally come to an end. But we must not forget that the reader's opinion on the necessity or otherwise of a digression is often wrong because, before the 'catastrophe', he cannot know what is or is not requisite for a gradual unfolding of the circumstances. And if, after the 'catastrophe', he goes back to the book again—I am not speaking of books that one only reads once—and still holds that this or that digression could have been omitted without detriment to the impression made by the whole, it nevertheless always remains questionable whether he would have received exactly the same impression if the author had not more or less cleverly led him to it by those very digressions which now appear superfluous to him.

Do you think Amy Robsart's death would have moved you so much if you had been a stranger in Kenilworth's halls? And do you believe there is no connection—connection through contrast—between the rich attire in which the unworthy Leicester showed himself to her, and the blackness of his soul? Do you not feel that Leicester—everyone knows this who knows the man from sources other than the novel alone—was infinitely baser than he is depicted in *Kenilworth*? But the great novelist, who preferred to fascinate by artistic arrangement of shades rather than by coarseness of colours, deemed it beneath him to steep his brush in all the mud and blood that clung to Elizabeth's unworthy favourite. He wished to indicate only one speck in the pool of filth, but he knew the art of making such specks stand out by means of the tints he placed next to them in his immortal writings. Anyone who thinks he can throw overboard all that has thus been placed next to the main point loses sight completely of the fact that, in order to produce effects, one would then have to change over to the school which had such a long and successful run in France after 1830—although to the credit of that country I must say that the authors who sinned the most against good taste in this respect were more in vogue in other countries than in France itself. That school—I hope and believe it is now extinct—found it easy to grope in pools of blood and cast handfuls of it on to the canvas, so that the great splashes could be seen from afar! And, to be sure, it takes less effort to paint those crude streaks of scarlet and black than to pencil in the delicate touches in the calyx of a lily. For that reason, this school mostly chose kings as heroes for its stories, and preferably those belonging to the time before the nations had come of age. See, the sorrow of the king is translated on paper into the wailing of the people ... *his* wrath offers the author an opportunity of killing thousands on the field of battle ... *his* mistakes afford a pretext for painting famine and pestilence ... all this gives scope for coarse brushwork! If you are not moved by the mute horror of the corpse lying before you, then there is room in my story for another victim still writhing and screaming! You shed no tears for that mother vainly seeking her child?... very well then, I'll show you another mother watching her child being quartered! Your feelings are not harrowed by the martyrdom of that man?... then I will multiply your feelings a hundredfold by having ninety-nine other men tortured to death beside him! Are you so hardened as not to shudder at the sight of the soldier in the beleaguered fortress who devours his left arm from hunger?...

Epicurean! I propose to command: 'Every man is to eat the left arm of the man on his right ... Form a circle—right and left wheel, quick march!'

Yes, in this way artistic horrors turn to silliness ... which is what I wanted to prove *en passant*.

Yet this is what we should get if we were too hasty in condemning a writer for trying gradually to prepare us for his denouement without resorting to such screaming colours.

But the danger on the opposite side is even greater. You despise the efforts of a crude literature which holds that it must storm your feelings with such gross weapons, but ... if the author goes to the other extreme, if he offends by *too much* digression from his main theme, by too mannered a use of the brush, then you will be even angrier, and rightly so! For then he bores you, and that is unforgivable.

If you and I are out walking together, and you keep straying from the road and calling me into the brushwood with the sole object of lengthening our walk, I shall find that disagreeable and resolve to go out by myself next time. But if you are able to show me a plant in the undergrowth which I did not know before, or show me something about that plant which had hitherto escaped my notice ... if, from time to time, you point out a flower to me which I am pleased to pick and wear in my buttonhole, then I shall forgive you those departures from the road; in fact, I shall be grateful for them.

And even without flower or plant, as soon as you call me aside to show me through the trees the path which we shall be treading presently, but which still lies in front of us in the depths and winds through the fields down below as a scarcely perceptible line ... then, too, I shall not take your digression amiss. For when at last we shall have got so far, I shall know how our road has meandered through the mountains, what it is that has caused the sun, which was over yonder only just now, to have come round to the left of us, and why that hill, whose top we saw in front only a short while ago, is now behind us ... look, then your digression will have made it easy for me to understand my walk, and to understand is to enjoy.

In my story, reader, I have often left you on the high road when I was sorely tempted to take you off into the undergrowth. I feared that if I did the walk might vex you, since I did not know whether you would get any pleasure from the flowers or plants I wanted to show you. But because, this time, I believe it will eventually give you satisfaction to have seen the path we shall be following presently, I now feel I must tell you something about Havelaar's house.

You would be mistaken if you thought of a house in Java in European terms, and imagined a mass of stone with rooms large and small heaped on top of each other, with the street in front, neighbours to right and left whose *lares et penates* lean up against your own, and a puny garden behind containing three currant bushes. In nearly every case, houses in the East Indies have only one storey. This may appear strange to the European reader, for it is characteristic of civilization—or what passes as such—to think everything strange that is natural. East Indian houses are entirely different from ours, but it is not *they* that are strange, it is *our* houses. The first man to permit himself the luxury of not sleeping in one room with his cows did not place the second room of his house *on top* but *by the side* of the first; for building on one floor is simpler and also affords more comfort to the occupant. Our high houses were born of lack of space: we sought in the air what could not be found on the ground, and consequently every servant-girl who, of an evening, shuts the window of the attic she sleeps in is a living protest against overpopulation ... even if she herself thinks of something very different, as I am quite willing to believe.

In countries, therefore, where civilization and overpopulation have not yet squeezed humanity upward by compression from below, the houses are without upper storeys; and Havelaar's was not one of the rare exceptions to this rule. On entering ... but no, I will prove that I renounce all claims to picturesqueness. *Given*: An oblong rectangle which you are required to divide into twenty-one compartments, three across, seven down. We will number these compartments, beginning at the top left-hand corner and going from left to right, so that number 4 comes under number 1, number 5 under 2, and so on.

Numbers 1, 2 and 3 together form the front verandah, which is open on three sides and whose roof rests at the front on columns. From there you pass through double doors into the inner gallery, which is represented by compartments 4, 5 and 6. Compartments 7, 9, 10, 12, 13, 15, 16 and 18 are rooms, most of which have doors opening into the adjoining ones. The three highest numbers, 19, 20 and 21, form the open back verandah, and the numbers I have omitted—8, 11, 14 and 17—form a kind of corridor. I am really proud of this description!

I	2	3
4	5	6
7	8	9
10	11	12
13	14	15
16	17	18
19	20	21

I do not rightly know what expression would, in Europe, convey what is meant in the East Indies by the word 'compound'. A compound is neither garden, nor park, nor field, nor wood, but either something of each, or all these things together, or nothing of any of them. It is all the land which belongs to the house but is not covered by the house, so that the expression 'garden *and* compound' would be considered a pleonasm in the Indies. There, few if any houses are without such a compound around them. Some compounds contain woods and gardens and meadowland, and suggest a park. Others are flower gardens. Elsewhere, again, the entire compound is one large grass field. And finally there are some which, simple enough to begin with, have been converted into one plain macadamized square, which is perhaps less pleasing to the eye but promotes cleanliness in the houses because grass and trees attract all kinds of insects.

Havelaar's compound was very big—in fact, strange as it may sound, on one side it might have been called infinite, since it bordered on a ravine which extended to the banks of the Chiujung, the river that encloses RANGKAS-BETUNG in one of its many loops. It was difficult to say where Havelaar's grounds ended and where the common land began, since the boundaries between them were continually being altered by the great difference between high and low water levels in the Chiujung, which now withdrew its banks until they were almost out of sight and then again filled the ravine to a point very close to the Assistant Resident's house.

This ravine had always been a source of vexation to Mrs Slotering, as was very natural. The vegetation, which grows rapidly enough everywhere in the Indies, was especially rank there, owing to the constant accretion of ooze from the river. In fact it was so luxuriant that, even if the water had advanced or receded violently enough to uproot and carry off the brushwood, very little time would have been required to cover the ground again with all the scrubby plant life which made it so difficult to keep the compound clean, even in the immediate vicinity of the house. And that would have caused no small annoyance even to an occupant who was not the mother of a family. For, apart from all kinds of insects, which usually flew round the lamp in the evenings in such crowds as to make reading and writing impossible (a trouble encountered in many places in the East Indies), numerous snakes and other vermin lurked in the undergrowth, and did not confine themselves to the ravine but were also found, over and over again, in the garden beside and behind the house, or on the lawn in the front square of the compound.

This 'square' lay before you when you stood on the front verandah with your back to the house. To your left was the building containing the administrative offices, the Treasury, and the airy 'assembly room' in which Havelaar had addressed the Chiefs; and behind it extended the ravine, over which you could look out as far as the Chiujung. Right opposite the offices stood the old Assistant Resident's house, now temporarily occupied by Mrs Slotering; and since access from the highway into the compound was via two roads that skirted the two sides of the lawn, it follows that anyone entering the compound to go to the kitchen or stables, which were behind the main building, had to pass either the offices or Mrs Slotering's house. Beside and behind the main building lay the rather large garden which had appealed to Tina on account of the many flowers in it, and especially because little Max would so often be able to play there.

Havelaar had sent his excuses to Mrs Slotering for not having called on her yet. He intended to do so the next day; but Tina had been across in the meantime, and had made the lady's acquaintance. We have already heard that Mrs Slotering was a 'native child', who spoke no other language but Malay. She had intimated her wish to continue running her own household, an arrangement which Tina had gladly accepted. Her acceptance did not spring from lack of hospitality, but chiefly from the fear that, having only just arrived in LEBAK, she would not be able to make Mrs Slotering as comfortable as the particular condition of that lady made desirable. Admittedly, since she did not understand Dutch she would not be 'hurt' by Max's stories, as Tina had put it. But Tina realized that more was required than not to *hurt* the Slotering family, and the ill-stocked kitchen arising from her plans for economy made her genuinely welcome Mrs Slotering's resolve. Though even if circumstances had been different it is doubtful whether mutual pleasure would have resulted from Tina's associating with a person who spoke only one language, and that a language in which nothing has been printed that improves the mind. Tina would have kept Mrs Slotering company as much as possible, and talked to her a good deal about kitchen affairs, about *sambal-sambal*,[80] about pickling *ketimon* (without Liebig, ye gods!). But that kind of thing is and remains an inconvenience; and so it was all to the good that Mrs Slotering's voluntary self-segregation had settled matters in a manner which left both parties perfectly free. It was, however, strange that that lady had not only declined the Havelaars' offer that she and her children should eat in common with them, but would not even have her food prepared in the kitchen of their house. This, Tina said, was carrying discreetness a little too far, for there was room enough in the kitchen for both of them.

14

'I don't need to tell you,' Havelaar began, 'that our possessions on the West Coast of Sumatra border on a number of independent states in the north of the island, the most important of which is ACHIN. There is said to be a secret article in the Treaty of 1824 which imposes on us the obligation towards the British not to cross the River SINGKEL. General Vandamme, our pinchbeck Napoleon, was out to extend his dominion as far as possible; but he met with an insuperable obstacle in that direction. I am forced to believe the article exists, because otherwise it would be too odd that the Rajahs of TRUMON and ANALABU, whose territories are important to the pepper trade, shouldn't have become vassals of the Netherlands long ago. You know how easy it is to find a pretext for making war on such little states and annexing them. Stealing a country will always be easier than stealing a mill.[81] Though I believe General Vandamme would even have stolen a mill if he had felt like it, and that's why I think he must have had more solid grounds than justice and equity for sparing those places in the north.

'Anyway ... he turned his conqueror's eye not northwards but eastwards. The recently "pacified" Battak lands had been formed into the Assistant Residency of MANDHÉLING and ANKOLA. It's true, they hadn't yet been completely purged of Achinese influence—once fanaticism takes root, it's not easily extirpated; but at any rate the Achinese themselves were no longer there. However, this was still not enough for the Governor. He extended his authority to the east coast, and Dutch officials and Dutch garrisons were sent from MANDHÉLING to BILA and PERTIBIE, though, as you know, Verbrugge, those two posts were evacuated again later.

Well, a Government Commissioner arrived in Sumatra who considered this extension pointless and condemned it, especially since it ran counter to the heartbreaking thriftiness which the Motherland so urgently insisted on. But General Vandamme maintained that the extension need become no extra burden on the budget because the new garrisons were drawn from troops for which money had already been approved, so he had brought a very large area under Dutch rule without its having cost the home country a penny. And as far as the partial denudation of other places was concerned, in particular MANDHÉLING, he felt he could depend sufficiently on the loyalty and attachment to him of YANG DI PERTUAN, the principal chief in the Battak lands, for there to be no danger in this.

'The Commissioner gave in reluctantly, and even then only on the General's reiterated protestations that he *personally* went bail for YANG DI PERTUAN's fidelity.

'Now, the Controleur who administered the Division of NATAL before me was the son-in-law of the Assistant Resident of the Battak lands, who was on bad terms with YANG DI PERTUAN. Afterwards I heard a great deal about complaints that had been made against this Assistant Resident; but you had to take such accusations with a pinch of salt, because they originated with YANG DI PERTUAN and at a time when YANG himself had been charged with far more serious crimes, which may have forced him to look for his defence in the faults of his accuser ... as is not unusual. Anyway, the Controleur of NATAL sided with his father-in-law against YANG DI PERTUAN—perhaps all the more enthusiastically because he, the Controleur, I mean, was very friendly with a certain SUTAN SALIM, a NATAL chief who also had it in for YANG DI PERTUAN. There was a feud between the families of those two chiefs. Offers of marriage had been rejected, there was jealousy about influence, pride on the part of YANG DI PERTUAN, who was of better birth, and several other reasons, which all helped to keep NATAL and MANDHÉLING at odds with each other.

'All of a sudden, a rumour spread that a plot had been discovered in MANDHÉLING in which YANG DI PERTUAN was mixed up and which aimed at raising the sacred banner of rebellion and murdering all Europeans. The first news of it came from NATAL. This was only natural: people in neighbouring provinces are always better informed about such things than the people in the place itself, because many whose chief happens to be implicated are too much afraid of him to say what they know at home but will lose at any rate some of their fear as soon as they are in territory where he has no influence.

'Incidentally, Verbrugge, that's also the reason why I'm no stranger to the affairs of LEBAK, and why I knew a fair amount about what went on here before I ever thought I might be posted here. In 1846 I was in KRAWANG, and I have travelled around a good deal in the PREANGER REGENCIES, where I met fugitives from LEBAK as long ago as 1840. I also know some landowners in the BUITENZORG area, and in the districts around BATAVIA, and I can tell you that those gentry have always been delighted with the bad state of this Division, because it swelled the labour force on their estates.

'Well, that was how the conspiracy was said to have been discovered at NATAL, which conspiracy—*if* it ever existed, which I don't know—revealed YANG DI PERTUAN as a traitor. According to witnesses called by the Controleur of NATAL he was supposed, with his brother SUTAN ADAM, to have collected many Battak chiefs around him in a sacred wood where they had sworn they would never rest until the rule of the "dogs of Christians" had been wiped out in MANDHÉLING. It goes without saying that YANG had had divine inspiration for it all. As you know, this feature's never absent in such cases.

'Now, whether such a purpose was ever in YANG DI PERTUAN's mind, I cannot be certain. I have read the witnesses' statements, but you will see presently why these can't be a hundred-per-cent relied upon. One thing *is* certain: the man was such a fanatical Moslem that he may well have been capable of something of the sort. He and the rest of the Battak had been converted to the true faith by the *Padries*[82] only a short time before, and new converts are usually fanatics.

'The consequence of this real or supposed discovery was that YANG DI PERTUAN was arrested by the Assistant Resident of MANDHÉLING, and sent to NATAL. There the Controleur locked him up in the fort, and subsequently had him taken to PADANG as a prisoner on the first available ship, for onward transmission to BATAVIA. Naturally the Governor was supplied with all the documents which contained those incriminating testimonies and which had to justify the severity of the measures that had been taken.

'Our friend YANG DI PERTUAN left MANDHÉLING as a prisoner. At NATAL he was a *prisoner*. On board the man-of-war which transported him he was also, of course, a *prisoner*. So he expected also to be a prisoner at PADANG—whether guilty or not guilty makes no difference to the case, since he had been charged with high treason in due legal form by a competent authority. So he must have been mighty astonished on disembarking to learn that not only was he *free* but that the General, whose carriage was waiting for him, would count it an honour to receive him and offer him hospitality in his house! I am sure no man accused of high treason ever had a more pleasant surprise. Shortly after, the Assistant Resident of MANDHÉLING was suspended from office for a variety of offences on which I don't wish to pronounce an opinion here. But YANG DI PERTUAN, after staying for some time in the General's house at PADANG, and after being treated by him with the greatest distinction, went back via NATAL to MANDHÉLING, not with the self-assurance of a man whose name's been cleared, but with the arrogance of a man so exalted that his name doesn't need clearing. After all, the case hadn't even been *investigated*! Assuming that the charge against him was believed to be false, investigation would have been all the more necessary, in order to punish the false witnesses and especially the persons who had procured them. It appears that the General had his own reasons for not allowing this investigation to take place. The charge against YANG DI PERTUAN was treated as null and void, and I feel sure that the documents in the case were never brought to the attention of the Government at BATAVIA.

'Shortly after YANG DI PERTUAN's return I arrived at NATAL, to take over administration of that Division. My predecessor told me of course what had happened in MANDHÉLING, and gave me the nec-

197

essary information on the political relationship between that region and my Division. I couldn't blame him for complaining bitterly about the unjust treatment of his father-in-law, as he considered it to be, and about the incomprehensible protection which YANG DI PERTUAN was enjoying. Neither he nor I knew at that moment that for YANG DI PERTUAN to be sent to BATAVIA would have been a slap in the face for the General, who had very good reason to protect him at all costs against an accusation of high treason. This was all the more important for the General because, in the interval, the Government Commissioner I have just referred to had become Governor-General, and so would very likely have recalled him, being naturally angry over the unwarranted trust reposed in YANG DI PERTUAN and the consequent obstinacy with which the General had opposed evacuation of the East Coast.

'"All the same," the Controleur of NATAL said to me, "whatever may have induced the General to accept unquestioningly all the charges against my father-in-law, and not even to consider the much more serious accusations against YANG DI PERTUAN, the matter isn't finished yet! I suppose they have destroyed the witnesses' statements at PADANG; but I have something here that *can't* be destroyed!"

'And he showed me a judgment of the RAPPAT Court[83] at NATAL, of which he was President, sentencing a certain SI-PAMAGA to flogging and branding and—I think—twenty years' hard labour, for attempting to murder the TUANKU of NATAL.

'"Just you read the report of the trial," said the Controleur, "and judge for yourself whether my father-in-law won't be believed in BATAVIA, when he charges YANG DI PERTUAN with high treason *there*!"

'I read the report. According to the witnesses' statements and "*the confession of the accused*", this SI-PAMAGA had been paid to murder the TUANKU, the TUANKU's foster-father SUTAN SALIM, and the Dutch Controleur, at NATAL. To carry out this plan he had gone to the TUANKU's house and got into conversation about a *sewah*[84] with the servants sitting on the steps of the inner gallery, so as to spin out his stay until he should see the TUANKU. The TUANKU did, in fact, soon show up, accompanied by relatives and servants. PAMAGA had gone for the TUANKU with his *sewah*, but for some reason or other had not been able to execute his murderous project. The TUANKU had taken fright and jumped out of the window, and PAMAGA had fled. He hid in the woods, and was caught a few days later by the NATAL police.

'The accused, being asked *what had induced him to make this attack, and to plan the murder of Sutan Salim and the Controleur of Natal*, replied that he: "*was paid to do it by Sutan Adam, on behalf of the latter's brother, Yang di Pertuan of Mandhéling.*"

'"Is this clear or isn't it?" my predecessor asked. "The Resident confirmed the sentence; it's been carried out as regards the flogging and branding; and SI-PAMAGA's now on his way to PADANG, to be sent from there to Java and the chain gang. The documents in the case will reach BATAVIA at the same time as he does, and *there* they will be able to judge what sort of man it is on whose accusations my father-in-law has been suspended! The General can't annul *that* sentence, however much he may want to."

'I took over administration of the Division of NATAL, and the other Controleur left. Some time later I received word that the General would be visiting the north of Sumatra in a man-of-war, and would also call at NATAL. He stopped at my house with a large retinue, and immediately asked to see the original depositions regarding "that poor chap who had been so shockingly ill-treated".

'"They deserve the lash and the branding-iron themselves!" he added.

'I couldn't make head or tail of it. At that time I still knew nothing of the causes of the wrangle over YANG DI PERTUAN, so I couldn't imagine either that the previous Controleur would deliberately have condemned an innocent man to so severe a punishment, or that the General would shield a criminal against a just sentence. I was ordered to arrest SUTAN SALIM and the TUANKU. However, the young

TUANKU was much loved by the people, and we had only a small garrison in the fort, so I asked the General's permission to leave him at liberty, which was granted. But SUTAN SALIM, the special enemy of YANG DI PERTUAN, got no such mercy. There was great tension among the population. They suspected that the General was lowering himself to be the tool of MANDHÉLING hatred, and it was *those* circumstances that led me to act from time to time in a manner which he called "plucky"—and no wonder, for he didn't offer *me* the small force which could be spared from the fort, or the detachment of marines he had brought with him from the ship, for protection when I rode to the places where crowds of disaffected natives had assembled. It was then that I noticed that General Vandamme took very good care of his own skin, and that's why I can't subscribe to his renown for bravery until I have either seen more of it, or something different.

'In tremendous haste he formed what I might call an *ad hoc* tribunal. Its members were: two of his aides-de-camp, some other officers, the Public Prosecutor, whom he had brought with him from PADANG, and myself. This tribunal was to inquire into the way in which my predecessor had conducted the trial of SI-PAMAGA. I had to call a number of witnesses whose declarations were necessary for the purpose. The General, who of course presided, carried out the whole examination, and the depositions were written down by the Public Prosecutor. However, as this official understood little Malay —and absolutely nothing of the Malay spoken in the north of Sumatra—it was often necessary to interpret the witnesses' answers to him, which was mostly done by the General himself. The sessions of this tribunal produced documents which seem to prove unequivocally that SI-PAMAGA never intended to murder anyone whatever; that he had never seen SUTAN ADAM or YANG DI PERTUAN in his life; that he had *not* rushed at the TUANKU of NATAL; that the latter had *not* fled through the window ... and so on and so forth! Furthermore: that the sentence against this unfortunate SI-PAMAGA had been passed under pressure by the President of the Court—the ex-

Controleur of NATAL—and the Member of the Court SUTAN SALIM, who had jointly invented SI-PAMAGA's pretended crime in order to give the suspended Assistant Resident of MANDHÉLING a weapon of defence, and also to vent their hatred of YANG DI PERTUAN.

'Now, the manner in which the General examined the witnesses on this occasion reminded me of the game of whist played by a certain Emperor of Morocco, who said to his partner: "Play hearts or I'll cut your throat!" And the translations, as he dictated them to the Public Prosecutor, also left much to be desired.

'I *don't* know whether SUTAN SALIM and my predecessor exerted pressure on the Natal RAPPAT Court to get SI-PAMAGA declared guilty. But I *do* know that General Vandamme exerted pressure to get the man declared innocent! Without understanding the drift of it all at the time, I raised objections to these "irregularities", and went so far as to refuse to add my signature to some of the depositions; and ... it was in *that* that I had so "crossed" the General! *Now* you will also understand what I meant when I concluded my answer to the criticisms of my accounting by asking to be spared any indulgence.'

'That was certainly putting it very strong, for someone as young as you were!' said Duclari.

'*I* thought it quite natural. But one thing's sure: General Vandamme was not accustomed to anything like that! So I suffered a good deal from the consequences of the affair. Oh no, Verbrugge, I can see what you're going to say; but I certainly never *regretted* it. In fact, I'll even go so far as to add that I should not have confined myself to simply protesting against the way the General examined the witnesses, and to refusing my signature on some of the depositions, if I could have guessed at the time what I only found out afterwards—that is, that it was all a put-up job to make a case against my colleague. I had imagined that the General was so convinced of SI-PAMAGA's innocence that he was letting himself be carried away by a creditable desire to save an innocent man from a miscarriage of justice, in so far as that was still possible after the flogging and branding. It was in the light of this opinion that I took a stand against what seemed to me to be distortion of evidence; but I was not *so* indignant about it as I would have been if I had known that there was no question whatever of saving an innocent victim, but only of destroying evidence that inconvenienced the General, at the cost of my predecessor's honour and welfare.'

'And how did your predecessor get on?' asked Verbrugge.

'Fortunately for him, he had already left for Java before the General arrived back at PADANG. He appears to have been able to justify himself to the Government at BATAVIA; at any rate, he remained in the service. The Resident of AYER-BANGIE, who had signed the order for execution of the sentence, was—'

'Suspended?'

'Of course! You see, I wasn't so far wrong when I said in my squib that the Governor ruled by suspending us.'

'And what became of all the suspended officials?'

'Oh, there were many more! All of them were reinstated, sooner or later. Some of them have since occupied very important positions.'

'And SUTAN SALIM?'

'The General took him in custody to PADANG, and from there he was exiled to Java. In fact he is still at CHANYOR, in the Preanger Regencies. I paid him a visit when I was there in 1846. Tina, do you remember what I went to CHANYOR for?'

'No, Max, I've clean forgotten.'

'Well, one can't be expected to remember everything! I went there to get married, gentlemen!'

'But', said Duclari, 'while you're on the subject, tell me, is it true you fought so many duels at PADANG?'

'Yes, very many. I had a lot of provocation. As I have said, at an outpost like PADANG the Governor's favour is the measure by which many people dole out their goodwill. So most of them were very *ill*-willed towards me, often to the point of rudeness. I, for my part, was irritable and touchy. An unacknowledged greeting, a taunt about the "idiocy of a chap who wants to fight the General!", an allusion to my poverty, to my going hungry, to the "poor diet that seems to be attached to moral independence" ... you'll understand, all that embittered me. Many men, especially among the officers, knew that the General rather liked to hear that duels were being fought, especially with somebody as deeply in disgrace as I was. So maybe they deliberately needled me. I also sometimes fought a duel on behalf of someone else whom I considered had been wronged. Anyway, at that time and out there, duelling was the order of the day, and more than once I had two appointments in the same morning. Oh, there's something very attractive in duelling, especially with sabres, or "on" sabres as we call it in Dutch, why I don't know. But you will understand that I wouldn't indulge in that sort of thing now, even if there was as much occasion for it as there was in those days ... come here, Max—no, don't catch that butterfly, leave it alone—come here! Listen, you must never catch butterflies. That little creature first crawled about on a tree as a caterpillar for quite a long time: not at all a jolly life! Now it has just got wings, and wants to fly around in the air for a bit and enjoy itself, and search for food in the flowers, and it harms no one ... look, isn't it much nicer to see it flutter around like this?'

And so the conversation passed from duels to butterflies, then to the care the just man owes his beasts, to cruelty to animals, to the *Loi Grammont*,[85] to the National Assembly in Paris which passed that law, to the French Republic, and to goodness knows what else!

At last Havelaar rose. He excused himself to his guests, as he had business to attend to. When the Controleur called on him at his office next morning, that officer did not know that the new Assistant Resident, after the conversations on the front verandah the previous day, had ridden out to PARANG-KUJANG—the scene of the *'outrageous* abuses'—and had only got back a few hours before.

I beg the reader to believe that Havelaar was really too well-mannered to talk so much as I have made it appear in the last chapters, especially at his own table, as though he monopolized conversation with complete neglect of the duties of a host, which prescribe that guests should be allowed or given an opportunity to 'shine'. From the mass of material before me I have taken only a few random instances of his table talk; in fact, it would have been easier for me to make the colloquies much longer than to cut them short as I have had to do. I trust, however, that what has been said will go some way towards justifying the description I gave earlier of Havelaar's character and qualities, and that therefore the reader will not be completely uninterested in following the adventures that awaited him and his at RANGKAS-BETUNG.

The little family lived a quiet life. Havelaar was frequently out in the daytime, and sometimes spent half the night in his office. He was on the most cordial terms with the Commandant of the small garrison; and in familiar intercourse with the Controleur there was also not a trace to be seen of the difference in rank which so often renders relations between people stiff and disagreeable in the East Indies. Furthermore, Havelaar's love of helping wherever humanly possible was frequently most welcome to the Regent, who was therefore very much taken with his 'elder brother'. Finally, the sweet nature of Mrs Havelaar contributed in no small degree to pleasant relations with the few Europeans about the place, and with the native Chiefs. Official correspondence with the Resident at SE-RANG bore evidence of mutual friendliness. The Resident's orders were given courteously and carried out conscientiously.

Tina's household was soon to rights. After a long wait, the furniture arrived from BATAVIA, *ketimons* were salted, and when Max told stories at table it was no longer through lack of eggs for an omelette. Nevertheless, the family's way of life continued to show clearly that the economy they had planned was being scrupulously practised.

Mrs Slotering rarely left her house, and took tea with the Havelaars on their front verandah only a few times. She said little, and always kept a watchful eye on everyone who approached her own quarters or Havelaar's. They had, however, grown accustomed to what they had begun to call her *monomania*, and soon took no more notice of it.

Everything seemed to breathe a spirit of peace; for to Max and Tina it was a comparatively trifling business to accommodate themselves to the privations unavoidable at a post in the interior remote from the main road. As no bread was baked there, no bread was eaten. They could have had it brought from SERANG, but the cost of carriage would have been too high. Max knew as well as anyone else that there were many ways and means of having bread brought to RANGKAS-BETUNG without paying for it, but *unpaid labour*, that canker of the Indies, was an abomination to him. Numerous things of the sort were obtainable at LEBAK by the undue exercise of authority but were not to be bought at a reasonable price; and under such conditions Havelaar and his Tina submitted willingly to doing without them. They had suffered worse hardships in their time! Had not poor Tina spent months on board an Arab ship, with no other bed than the vessel's deck, with no other shelter from the heat of the sun and the showers of the south-west monsoon than a small table, between whose legs she had to wedge herself? Had she not then had to be satisfied with a small ration of dry rice and dirty water? And had she not, in those and many other circumstances, always been contented, so long as she might only be with her Max?

However, there was *one* circumstance at LEBAK which caused her vexation. Little Max could not play in the garden, because there were so many snakes in it. When Tina became aware of this and complained of it to Havelaar, he offered the servants a reward for every snake they caught; but in the first few days he paid out so much that he had to cancel his offer, for even under normal conditions, without his present urgent need to economize, the payments would soon have gone beyond his means. So it was decided that henceforth little Max was not to leave the house, and that, in order to get some fresh air, he would have to content himself with playing on the front verandah. In spite of this precaution Tina was always anxious, particularly in the evening, as it is well known that snakes will then often creep into houses and conceal themselves for warmth in the bedrooms.

Admittedly, snakes and suchlike vermin are to be found everywhere in the East Indies. But at the larger centres of population, where the people live closer together, they are naturally more rare than in wilder places such as RANGKAS-BETUNG. If Havelaar could have had his compound cleared of weeds right to the edge of the ravine, the snakes would no doubt still have appeared from time to time in the garden, but they would never have been found there in such numbers as was now the case. The nature of snakes makes them prefer darkness and seclusion to the light of open spaces, and so if Havelaar's compound had been kept in proper order those reptiles would not have left the wild luxuriance of the ravine except, as it were, in spite of themselves, when they lost their way. But Havelaar's grounds were not kept in proper order, and I must tell you why, since it affords a further glimpse of the abuses that prevail almost everywhere in the Dutch East Indian possessions.

The houses of governing officials in the Indies stand on ground which belongs to the community, in so far as it is possible to speak of communal property in a country where the Government appropriates everything. Suffice it to say that that ground, that compound does not belong to the occupying official himself. If such were the case, he would be careful not to buy or rent ground which it was beyond his means to look after. Now, when the compound of the house assigned to the official is too large to be properly tended, it soon degenerates into a wilderness, owing to the luxuriant growth of vegetation in the tropics. And yet you seldom, if ever, see such a compound in neglected condition. In fact, the traveller is often amazed by the beautiful park surrounding a Resident's dwelling. No East Indian civil servant has a big enough income to have the requisite labour performed for adequate payment. Nevertheless, a stately appearance is essential for the residence of the officer in authority, to prevent the population, so much impressed by outward show, from finding cause for contempt in such neglect; and hence the question arises: how, then, is this managed? In most places these officials have the use of a chain gang, i.e., of criminals under sentence from elsewhere; but this form of manpower was not available in BANTAM, for more or less valid political reasons. Yet even in places where there are such convicts, there are seldom enough of them to do the work required for decent maintenance of a large compound, especially in view of the need of labour for other purposes. So other means have to be found; and the summoning of workers for the performance of 'statute labour' seems the most obvious one. The Regent or the DHEMANG who receives a summons of this kind hastens to respond to it, for he knows only too well that afterwards it will be difficult for the official who so abuses his authority to punish a native Chief for doing likewise. And thus the offence of the one becomes the licence of the other.

Yet it seems to me that *in some cases* errors of this kind on the part of a man in authority must not be judged too severely, and especially not by European standards. For the population itself—perhaps from habit—would think it very odd if, *ever* and *always*, he kept strictly to the regulations which prescribe the number of those liable to perform statute labour in his compound, because circumstances may arise which were not foreseen when those regulations were framed. But once the limit of what is strictly legal has been exceeded, it becomes difficult to fix a point where such excess becomes exploitation, and the greatest circumspection becomes all the more necessary when one knows that the Chiefs are only waiting for a bad example in order to follow it on a much larger scale. There is a story of a certain king who would not allow even one grain of salt, which he had taken with his frugal meal when passing through the country at the head of his army, to remain unpaid for, because, he said, that would be a beginning of injustice which would eventually ruin his whole empire. That fable—or, if it isn't a fable, the case—must be of Asiatic origin, whether the king in question was called TAMERLANE, NUREDDIN or GENGHIS KHAN. And just as the sight of dikes suggests the possibility of floods, we may assume that there is a tendency to *such* abuses in a country where *such* lessons are conveyed.

Now, the small number of people who were legally at Havelaar's disposal could only keep weeds and undergrowth from a very small part of his compound, in the immediate vicinity of the house. The rest was a complete jungle within a few weeks. Havelaar wrote to the Resident about means of remedying this, either by a financial allowance or by proposing to the Government that chain gangs should be assigned to labour in the Residency of BANTAM, just as in other places. He received a negative reply, with the remark that persons sentenced by him in the police court to 'labour on the public roads' could be put to work in his compound, if he liked. Havelaar knew that, of course—or at any rate he was well aware that such disposal of condemned offenders was universally looked upon as the most natural thing in the world. But he had never wanted to make use of this presumed right, either at RANGKAS-BETUNG, or in AMBOINA, or in MENADO, or at NATAL. It went against the grain with him to have his garden kept in order as a penalty for minor offences, and he had often asked himself how the Government could permit the continued existence of regulations which might tempt an official to punish petty, excusable misdemeanours in proportion not to their magnitude but to the condition or the extent of his compound! The mere idea that an offender, even when justly punished, might imagine that self-interest lurked in the sentence passed on him made Havelaar, when he had to punish, always give preference to imprisonment, however objectionable that was otherwise.

And this was why little Max was not allowed to play in the garden, and why Tina did not get as much pleasure from the flowers as she had expected to do on the day of her arrival at RANGKAS-BETUNG.

It goes without saying that this, and similar small vexations, had no influence on the frame of mind of a household that possessed so much material for building itself a happy home life, and it was certainly not such trifles as these that sometimes caused Havelaar to come in with a clouded brow, after having been on a journey or after hearing someone who had asked to speak to him. We know from his address to the Chiefs that he meant to do his duty, that he meant to fight injustice; and I also trust that, from the conversations I have recorded, the reader has learnt to know him as a man who was well able to get to the bottom of a thing and bring to light that which was hidden from the sight of *some* others or was lying in darkness. It might therefore be assumed that not much of what happened in LEBAK would escape his notice. Then, too, we have seen that that Division had had his attention many years earlier, so that on the very first day, when Verbrugge met him in the *pendoppo* where my story begins, he proved that he was no stranger to his new sphere of activities. By investigations on the spot he found confirmation of many things he had surmised; and the Assistant Residency files, in particular, had shown him that the region whose administration had been entrusted to him was really in a most deplorable state.

From the letters and notes of his predecessor, Mr Slotering, he found that that official had made the same observations. The correspondence with the Chiefs contained reproach upon reproach, threat upon threat, and made it quite understandable that the former Assistant Resident was supposed to have finally said that he would appeal direct to the Government if no end came to this state of affairs.

When Verbrugge had told Havelaar this, Havelaar had answered that his predecessor would have acted very wrongly in doing so, since the Assistant Resident of LEBAK had no right, under any circumstances, to go over the head of the Resident of BANTAM, and he had added that that would have been in no way justified either, since it was surely unthinkable that so high an official would support exploitation and extortion?

And such support *was* really inconceivable, in the sense meant by Havelaar—that is to say, with the idea that the Resident should derive any advantage or profit from the offences concerned. Nevertheless, there was undoubtedly a reason which made him most reluctant to do justice with regard to the complaints made by Havelaar's. predecessor. We have seen how that predecessor had repeatedly spoken to the Resident about the prevailing abuses—in a *tête-à-tête*, as Verbrugge said—and how little good that had done. It is therefore not without interest to inquire why so highly placed an official—who, as head of the entire Residency, was at least as much bound as the Assistant Resident to see that justice was done— nearly always judged that he had reasons for arresting the course of justice.

At SERANG, when Havelaar was staying in the Resident's house, he had spoken to Mr Slymering about the abuses in LEBAK, and had been told 'that this was more or less the case everywhere'. That, of course, Havelaar could not deny. After all, who would maintain that he had seen a country where no wrong was ever done? But Havelaar held that this was no reason for allowing abuses to continue where one found them, especially when one was explicitly called upon to resist them; also that, from everything he knew of LEBAK, there was no question of *more* or *less* there but of *an excessive degree*. To which the Resident replied, amongst other things, that in the Division of CHIRINGIEN, also belonging to BANTAM, things were still worse.

Now assuming, as may be assumed, that a Resident derives no direct advantage from extortion and from arbitrary use of the population, the question arises: what, then, induces so many people, contrary to sworn oath and duty, to allow such abuses to persist without notifying the Government of them? And anyone who reflects on this question must find it very, very strange that the existence of these abuses is so calmly recognized, as though it were a matter beyond any man's reach or competence to remedy. I will endeavour to unfold the reasons for this.

In general, the mere task of carrying evil tidings is an unpleasant one, and it really seems as though something of the unfavourable impression they make sticks to the man whose depressing duty it is to convey them. Now, if this fact alone is sufficient reason for some people to deny, against their better knowledge, the existence of something disagreeable, how much more must it be the case when there is a risk, not only of incurring that disfavour which seems to be the lot of the bearer of ill news, but of being actually looked upon as the *cause* of the adverse situation which duty compels one to reveal!

The Government of the Dutch East Indies likes to write and tell its masters in the Motherland that everything is going well. The Residents like to report that to the Government. The Assistant Residents, who, in their turn, receive hardly anything but favourable reports from their Controleurs, also prefer not to send any disagreeable news to the Residents. All this gives birth to an artificial optimism in the official and written treatment of affairs, in contradiction not only to the truth but also to the personal opinion expressed by the optimists themselves when discussing those affairs orally, and—stranger still!—often even in contradiction to the facts in their own written statements. I could quote many examples of reports which extolled to the skies the favourable conditions in a Residency and belied themselves in the same breath, especially when *figures* spoke. If the ultimate consequences did not make the matter too serious, these examples would arouse laughter and ridicule, and one can only be amazed at the naïveté with which, in such cases, the grossest lies are often maintained and ... accepted, although the writer himself, a few sentences further on, proffers the weapons for combating those lies. I shall confine myself to one single instance— which, however, I could multiply many times over. Among the documents before me I find the Annual Report of a Residency. The Resident speaks in glowing terms of the flourishing trade there, and asserts that the greatest prosperity and activity are to be seen throughout the whole region. But a little later he has to talk about the slender means at his disposal for foiling smugglers, and acts immediately to prevent a disagreeable impression from being made on the Government by the conclusion that a great deal of import duty is therefore being evaded in his Residency:

'No,' he says, 'there is no need to fear that at all! Little or nothing is smuggled into my Residency, because ... there is so little doing in these parts that no one would risk his capital in commerce here!'

I have read a similar report which began with the words: 'During the past year the peace in the area has remained peaceful.' Such sentences certainly bear witness to a very confident confidence in the Government's indulgence towards anyone who spares it unpleasant news or who, as the saying goes, 'does not embarrass it' with depressing reports!

Where the population does not increase, the fact is attributed to the inaccuracy of the censuses of previous years. Where the revenue from taxes does not rise, it is counted a merit: the intention is to encourage agriculture by low assessments, since it is only *now* beginning to develop and will soon—preferably when the writer of the report has left the district—yield fabulous results. Where riots have taken place that *cannot* remain concealed, they are the work of a few ill-disposed persons, who need no longer be feared, since there is now *general* contentment everywhere. Where distress or famine has thinned out the population, it is owing to failure of crops, drought, heavy rains, or something of the sort, but never to misgovernment.

Before me lies the note by Havelaar's predecessor in which he ascribed 'the decline in the population of PARANG-KUJANG' to '*outrageous*' abuses. That note was *un*official, and contained points which the writer was to *talk* over with the Resident of BANTAM. But in vain did Havelaar search in the records for evidence that he had frankly reported the matter in so many words in an *official memorandum*.

In short, the official reports from the functionaries to the Government, and consequently also those based upon them which the

Government sends to the Motherland, are mostly and for the most important part *untrue*.

I know this is a grave charge, but I stand by it, and am in a position to support it with proofs. Anyone who is put out by my expressing my opinion so uninhibitedly should consider how many millions of pounds and how many human lives England would have been spared if someone there had succeeded in opening the eyes of the nation to the true state of affairs in India, and how beholden everyone would have been to the man who had had the courage to be a Job's messenger before it was too late to repair the damage in a less sanguinary manner than subsequently became inevitable.

I have said I can prove my charge. Where necessary, I can show that there was often famine in regions which were praised as models of prosperity, and that frequently a population which was reported to be peaceful and contented was on the point of exploding in revolt. It is not my intention to produce these proofs in *this* book, though I feel sure that no one will lay it down without believing that they exist.

For the moment I will confine myself to one more example of the absurd optimism of which I have spoken—an example which anyone, whether he is *au fait* with Dutch East Indian affairs or not, can easily grasp.

Each month, every Resident renders a return of the amount of rice imported into or exported from his Residency. In this return, trade is split into two parts, namely, that with the outside world and that with the rest of Java. Now, if one takes note of the quantity of rice exported according to the latter returns *from* Residencies in Java *to* Residencies in Java, it will be seen that the quantity amounts to many thousands of pikols *more* than the rice which, according to the same returns, is imported *into* Residencies in Java *from* Residencies in Java.

I shall at present refrain from saying what one must inevitably think of the intelligence of a Government that accepts such statements and publishes them. I only wish to draw the reader's attention to the *object* of this deceit.

The percentage bonus paid to European and native functionaries for products to be sold in Europe had such a detrimental effect on rice cultivation that some regions were ravaged by a famine which could *not* be conjured away from the sight of the Motherland. I have already said that instructions were then issued to the effect that things must not be allowed to go quite so far again. The many consequences of these instructions included the returns of imports and exports of rice I have mentioned, so that the Government could constantly keep an eye on the ebb and flow in supply of that article of food. *Export* from a Residency means prosperity; *import* into it means want.

Now, when those returns are examined and compared, it will be seen that rice is so abundant everywhere *that all the Residencies combined export more rice* than *all the Residencies combined import*. I repeat that here there is no question of export overseas, for which a separate statement is rendered. The conclusion of all this is therefore the absurd thesis *that there is more rice in Java than there is*. That's prosperity, *if* you like!

I have already said that the desire never to send other than good news to the Government would be comic if the results of it all were not so tragic. For what correction of so much wrong can be hoped for in the face of a predetermined purpose to twist and distort everything in the reports to the authorities? What, for instance, may be expected from a population which, by nature gentle and submissive, has complained of oppression for years and years, when it sees one Resident after another retire on furlough or pension, or be called away to another post, without the *slightest thing* being done to redress the grievances under which it suffers? Must not the bent spring eventually recoil? Must not the long-suppressed discontent —suppressed so that the Government can continue to deny its existence!—finally turn to rage, desperation, madness? Is there not a *Jacquerie* at the end of this road?

And where, then, will the officials be who succeeded one another for so many years without ever stumbling on the idea that there might be something higher than the 'favour of the Government'? Something higher than the 'satisfaction of the Governor-General'? Where will they be then, the writers of empty reports who throw sand in the eyes of the administration with their untruths? Will they, who previously lacked the courage to put one bold word on paper, suddenly fly to arms and save the Dutch possessions for the Netherlands? Will they restore to the Netherlands the treasure that will be required to quell insurrection, to prevent revolution? Will they restore to life the thousands who will have perished through *their* guilt?

And those officials, those Controleurs and Residents, are not the *most* guilty parties. It is the Government itself which, as though struck with incomprehensible blindness, encourages, invites and rewards the submission of favourable reports. And this is particularly the case where there is question of oppression of the people by native Chiefs.

Many attribute this unofficial protection of the Chiefs to the ignoble calculation that the latter, who have to display pomp and circumstance in order to exercise over the population that influence which the Government needs in order to uphold *its* authority, would require a much higher remuneration than they receive now if they were not left at liberty to supplement it by unlawful use of the property and labour of the people. However this may be, it is certain that the Government only applies the provisions which are supposed to protect the Javanese against extortion and robbery when such application is unavoidable. Considerations of high policy transcending ordinary judgment, which are often sheer fabrications, are usually adduced as reasons for sparing *this* Regent or *that* Chief; and, in fact, there is an opinion so general as to be a proverb in the Indies that the Government would rather dismiss ten Residents than one Regent. And when such pretended political reasons have any foundation at all they are usually based on false information, since every Resident has a personal interest in giving an exalted impression of his Regents' influence over the people, to cover himself in case he should eventually be criticized for excessive lenience towards those Chiefs.

For the present I will pass over the disgusting hypocrisy of the humane-sounding provisions—and of the oaths!—which protect the Javanese ... on paper ... against tyranny, and request the reader to remember how Havelaar had repeated those oaths in a manner that suggested disdain. At the moment, I would only point to the difficult position a man is in who considers himself bound to perform his duty by something entirely different from a spoken formula.

And for Havelaar this difficulty was even greater than it would have been for many others, because he was gentle by nature, in complete contrast to his powers of penetration, which the reader will by now have discovered to be uncommonly keen. He therefore had to wrestle not only with the fear of men or with anxiety about his career and promotion, or merely with the duties devolving on him as a husband and father—he also had to conquer an enemy in his own heart! He could not see sorrow without suffering personally. It would take too long to give examples of the way in which he would protect an opponent against himself, even where he had been injured and insulted. He had told Duclari and Verbrugge that he had found something alluring in duelling with the sabre in his youth, and that was true ... but he did not add that, after wounding his antagonist, he generally wept, and would tend his former enemy like a sister of mercy until he had recovered. I might tell you how at NATAL, when a chained convict had shot at him, he called the man before him, spoke to him kindly, and had him fed and gave him more liberty than any of the others because he concluded that the prisoner's exasperation was due to the fact that his sentence, which had been passed elsewhere, was too severe. As a rule, his tenderheartedness was either denied or pronounced ridiculous. Denied by those who confounded his heart with his head; pronounced ridiculous by those who could not understand how a sensible person could take the trouble to save a fly which had got tangled in a spider's web. Denied again, then, by everyone—except Tina—who, after this, heard him abusing those 'stupid insects' and 'stupid Nature' that created such insects.

But there was yet another way of dragging him down from the pedestal on which those around him—whether they liked him or not—felt bound to place him. 'Yes, he *is* witty, but ... he is superficial.' Or: 'He *is* brainy, but ... he doesn't use his brains properly.' Or: 'Yes, he *is* kindhearted, but ... he makes a show of it!'

Here I shall not stick up for his wit or his brains; but what about his heart? Poor, struggling flies which he saved when there was no one near, will *you* not defend that heart against the charge of 'making a show'?

But you have flown away, and have not troubled about Havelaar —you, who could not know that some day he would be in need of your testimony!

Was it 'show' on Havelaar's part, when he jumped into the estuary of the river at NATAL after a dog—SAPPHO was the animal's name—because he feared that, since she was still no more than a pup, she could not swim well enough to escape the sharks that swarm there? It seems to me more difficult to believe that this was 'making a show' of kindheartedness than that it was kindheartedness itself.

I summon you, you, the many who have known Havelaar, if you have not been frozen by winter's cold and are dead ... like the rescued flies, or dried up by the heat yonder, below the Line! I summon you to bear witness to his heart, all you that have known him! Now, especially, do I summon you with confidence, because now you no longer need to look for the place to fix the rope in order to drag him down from whatever little eminence he may have occupied!

Meanwhile, I will make room here for some verses from his hand which will perhaps render your testimony superfluous, no matter how incoherent they may make my book appear. Max was once far, very far, away from wife and child. He had been compelled to leave them behind in the Indies, and was in Germany. With the mental agility which I attribute to him, but which I will not insist upon if anyone should wish to contest it, he had mastered the language of the country in which he had been staying only a few months. Here, then, are the lines he wrote in German—lines which, at the same time, paint the devotion that bound him to those dear to him.

'My child, that is the ninth hour striking—hark!
The night wind whispers, and the air grows cool,
Too cool for you, perhaps: your forehead glows!
You have so wildly played the livelong day,
You must be tired, so come, your *tikar*[86] waits.'

'Oh Mother, let me stay a moment more!
I lie so softly resting now ... and there,
Inside upon my mat, I sleep at once,
Not knowing even what I dream! But here,
Here I can tell you forthwith what I dream,
And ask you what it means ... oh listen, Mother,
What was that?'

     '—'twas a *klappa*[87] which fell down.'

'And does that hurt the *klappa*?'

        'No, I think not,
For neither fruit nor stone, they say, has feeling.'

'And flowers, then—do they feel nothing?'

          'No,
They're said to have no feeling either.'

                                    'Mother,
Yesterday, when I broke the *pukul ampat*,[88]
Why did you say then that it hurt the flower?'

—'My child, the *pukul ampat* was so fair,
You roughly tore apart its tender leaves,
And I was sorry for the poor sweet flower.
Even if the flower itself feels nothing of it
I felt it for the flower, it was so fair.'

'But Mother, are you also fair?'

                                    'No, child,
I do not think so.'

'But *you* have "feeling"?'

'Yes, people have that ... but not all alike.'

'And can something hurt *you*? Do you feel pain
When my head rests, so heavy, in your lap?'

'No, that gives me no pain!'

                            'And, Mother, I...
Do *I* have "feeling"?'

                            'Certainly! Remember
How once you tripped, and cut your little hand
Upon a stone, and wept most bitterly.
You also wept when *Saudien* told you how
Up there among the hills a little lamb
Fell in a deep ravine and died. And then
You wept for a long time. Look, *that* was feeling.'

'But, Mother, is this "feeling" pain, then?'

'Yes,
Quite often, but... not always, sometimes not! You know,
When little sister clutches at your hair,
And crowing pulls your face close down to hers,
Then you laugh merrily, and that's also feeling.'

'And little sister, then ... she cries so often,
Is it for pain? Has she, then, "feeling" too?'

'Perhaps, my dear, but we cannot know that,
Because she is too small to tell us so.'

'But, Mother... listen, what was that?'

'A deer
Belated in the woods, and hurrying now
To reach its home, and find its longed-for rest
With other deer it loves.'

'Mother, has a deer
Like that a little sister too? Has it
A mother like mine?'

'Child, I do not know.'

'That would be sad indeed, if it had not!
But Mother, look... what shines there in that bush?
See how it hops and skips... is it a spark?'

'It is a firefly.'

'May I try to catch it?'

'You may, but the small insect is so soft
That surely you will hurt it, and as soon
As you do roughly touch it with your fingers,
The creature sickens, dies and glows no more!'

'Oh, that would be a pity. No, I'll leave it!
See, now it disappears... no, it comes here...
But I won't catch it! Now it's flying on,
Happy because I have not caught it.
There it goes... high! High, up there... what is *that*,
Are all those little fireflies too?'

                                        'Those are
The stars.'

                'Look, one! And ten! A thousand!
However many are there?'

                                'I have no idea,
Nobody yet has counted all the stars.'

'But tell me, cannot even *He* do that?'

'No, love, not even *He*.'

                                'Is it far off,
Up yonder where the stars are?'

                                        '*Very* far!'

'But have they got this "feeling" too, those stars?
And would they, if I touched them with my hand,
Sicken at once, and die, and lose their gleam,
Just like the firefly? See, it hovers still!
Say, would I also hurt the stars?'

                                                'Oh no,
You could not hurt the stars! Besides, they are too far
For your small hand: you cannot reach so high.'

'Can *He* stretch out his hand and catch the stars?'

'No, dear, not even *He*; nobody can!'

'Oh, what a pity! How I should have loved
To give you one! But wait until I'm big,
And I will *love you so much that I can*!'

The child fell off to sleep, and dreamt of "feeling",
Of stars it clutched and caught with little hands...
Long was it ere the mother slept! But she
Dreamt too, thinking of Him far off...

Yes, at the risk of seeming to write a chaotic book, I have given a
place here to these lines. I wish to neglect no opportunity of making
known the man who plays the leading role in my story, so that he
may be of some interest to the reader later, when dark clouds gather
over his head.

15

Havelaar's predecessor had certainly wanted to do the right thing, but he also appeared to have been somewhat afraid of the Government's high displeasure (the man had many children and no money behind him). So he had preferred to *speak* to the Resident about what he himself called *outrageous* abuses rather than name them openly in an official report. He knew that a Resident does not like to receive a written statement, which remains in his files and can be produced later as evidence that his attention had been drawn in good time to this or that irregularity, whereas an oral communication brings no such risk upon him but leaves him the choice between dealing with a complaint or ignoring it. These oral communications usually resulted in an interview with the Regent, who of course denied everything and demanded proof. Then the Resident summoned the people who had had the temerity to complain; and, crawling at the feet of the ADHIPATTI, they prayed for pardon. 'No, the buffalo had not been taken from them for nothing; they felt sure that double the price would be paid for it.' 'No, they had not been called away from their fields to labour in the *sawahs* of the Regent without payment—they knew perfectly well that the ADHIPATTI would afterwards have liberally rewarded them.' 'They had made their accusation in a moment of groundless resentment... they must have been mad, and they begged to be duly punished for such gross disrespect!'

The Resident knew perfectly well what to think of these retractions; but nevertheless they gave him a splendid opportunity of maintaining the Regent in office and honour, and he was spared the unpleasant task of 'embarrassing' the Government with an unfavourable report. The rash accusers were punished with *rattan* canings; the Regent had triumphed; and the Resident returned to the Divisional centre with the pleasant consciousness of having 'fixed' things so nicely yet again.

But what was the *Assistant* Resident to do when other aggrieved parties came to him next day? Or—as frequently happened—when the same parties returned to *him* and retracted their retraction? Was he *again* to make a note of the matter, *again* to speak about it to the Resident, *again* to see the same tragic farce enacted, and all this at the risk of eventually being set down as a man with a mania for bringing stupid and malicious accusations which always had to be dismissed as unfounded? What would become of the vitally necessary friendly relations between the principal native Chief and the senior European official when the latter appeared to be continually lending an ear to trumped-up charges against that Chief? And, above all, what happened to the poor plaintiffs once they had returned to their village and were back in the power of the District or Village Chief they had impeached as instruments of the Regent's tyranny?

What did happen to them? Those that were able to flee, fled. That was why so many Bantammers were wandering around in the neighbouring provinces! That was why there were so many men from LEBAK among the insurgents in the LAMPONG Districts! That was why Havelaar, in his address to the Chiefs, had asked: 'What is this—that so many houses stand empty in the villages? And why do many prefer the shade of alien woods to the coolness of the forests of BANTAN-KIDUL?'

But not everyone *could* flee. The man whose body was seen drifting down the river on the morning following the night when, secretly, reluctantly, anxiously, he had asked for an audience with the Assistant Resident ... *he* no longer needed to flee. Perhaps it should be considered humane, to have saved him by sudden death from living a little longer. For he was spared the ill-treatment that awaited him on his return to his village, and the *rattan*-scourging which was the penalty for all who might imagine for a moment that they were not beasts, not inanimate blocks of wood or stone. The penalty for him who, in a fit of madness, had believed that there was Justice in the land, and that the Assistant Resident had the wish and the power to uphold that Justice...

Was it not indeed better to prevent the man from returning next day to the Assistant Resident—as the latter had told him to do—and to stifle his complaint in the yellow waters of the CHIUJUNG, which would carry him gently down to its mouth, accustomed as it was to being the bearer of such fraternal offerings from the sharks inland to the sharks in the sea?

And Havelaar knew all this! Can the reader feel what torment his heart endured when he remembered that he was called upon to do justice and in this was responsible to a higher power than a Government which might prescribe justice in its laws but did not always care to see that justice enforced? Can the reader feel how he was torn by doubt, not of *what* he should do, but of *how* he should do it?

He had begun gently. He had spoken to the ADHIPATTI as an 'elder brother' should; and if anyone thinks that I, captivated by the hero of my story, may be trying to exalt unduly the manner in which he spoke, they should know that after one such talk the Regent sent his PATTEH to Havelaar to thank him for his kind words. And this is not all. Long afterwards—when Havelaar had ceased to be Assistant Resident of LEBAK, that is to say when nothing more was to be either hoped or feared from him—the PATTEH was talking to Controleur Verbrugge; and the remembrance of what Havelaar had said affected him so deeply that he exclaimed: 'Never yet has any lord spoken like him!'

Yes, he wished to save, to set right, not to destroy! He was sorry for the Regent. He knew how oppressive lack of money can be, especially when it leads to humiliation and insult; and he sought excuses for him. The Regent was old, and the head of a family whose members lived in opulence in the neighbouring provinces, where much coffee was produced and therefore large bonuses were enjoyed. Was it not galling for him to have to lead so much more modest a life than his younger relatives? Besides, swayed by fanaticism, the man fancied that, as his years increased, he might purchase the salvation of his soul by subsidizing pilgrimages to Mecca and by giving alms to prayer-droning idlers. The officials who had preceded Havelaar in LEBAK had not always set good examples. And finally, the size of the Regent's family there, who lived entirely at his expense, made it difficult for him to return to the right path.

In this way Havelaar looked for reasons for postponing severe measures, and for trying again, and yet again, to see what could be accomplished by gentleness.

And he even went further than gentleness. With a generosity reminiscent of the errors that had made him so poor, he continually advanced money to the Regent on his own responsibility, so that need might not be too powerful an incentive to transgression; and, as usual, he ignored his own interest to such an extent that he was prepared to reduce himself and his to the barest necessities in order to succour the Regent with what little he might still be able to spare from his income.

If it should still seem essential to prove the kindliness with which Havelaar carried out his difficult duty, this proof could be found in an oral message he once gave the Controleur when the latter was leaving for SERANG for a few days: 'Tell the Resident that, when he hears of the abuses that take place here, he must not think I am indifferent to them. I only refrain from officially reporting them at once because I am sorry for the Regent and I want to save him from too great severity by first seeing what persuasion can do to bring him to a sense of his duty.'

Havelaar was often away for days on end. When he was at home, he was usually to be found in the room which we have represented as compartment 7 on our plan. There he sat writing, and received the persons who asked to see him. He had chosen that room in order to be near his Tina, who was generally in the next one. For they were so wrapped up in each other that Max, even when he was busy with some task that demanded concentration and effort, constantly felt the need to see her or hear her. It was often comical to see how he would suddenly address a word to her which arose in his mind in connexion with the subjects that occupied him, and how quickly she, without knowing what he was doing, was able to follow the drift of his thoughts—which, in fact, he usually did not even explain to her, as though it went without saying that she would know what he meant. Often, too, when he was dissatisfied with his own work, or with depressing news he had just received, he would jump up and say something unkind to her, although she was in no way responsible for his dissatisfaction! But she liked to hear that, because it was just one more proof of how much Max confused her with himself. Nor was there ever any question of regret for such seeming harshness, or of forgiveness from the other side. To them, this would have seemed like someone begging his own pardon for hitting himself on the head in irritation.

Indeed, Tina knew him so well that she knew exactly when she had to be by to give him a moment's relaxation; exactly when he needed her advice; and no less exactly when she had to leave him alone.

It was in that room that Havelaar was sitting one morning when the Controleur came in holding a letter which he had just received.

'This is a difficult matter, Mr Havelaar,' he said, almost before he had got through the door. 'Very difficult!'

Now when I say that the letter merely contained a request by Havelaar that he should explain a change in costs of timberwork and labour, the reader will think that Controleur Verbrugge very soon considered a thing difficult. So I hasten to add that a good many others would have found it just as difficult to answer that simple question.

Some years before, a prison had been built at RANGKAS-BETUNG. Now, it is generally known that officials in Java are adepts in the art of erecting buildings that are worth thousands of guilders without expending more than as many hundreds in doing so. This gives them a reputation for efficiency and zeal in the service of the country. The difference between the moneys spent and the value of what is obtained for them is made up by unpaid-for supplies or unpaid labour. For some years there have been regulations prohibiting this. Whether they are observed is not our concern here. Nor, either, whether the Government *wishes* them to be observed with a strictness that would embarrass the budget of the Public Works Department. I suppose these regulations are in the same case as many others that look so philanthropic on paper.

But a lot more buildings were needed at RANGKAS-BETUNG, and the experts responsible for preparing the plans had requested quotations for local rates of wages and prices of material. Havelaar had instructed Controleur Verbrugge to make careful inquiries, and had advised him to give the true prices, without reference to what had happened in the past. When Verbrugge had carried out his instructions, it appeared that the prices did not tally with the quotations of a few years before. The Resident had now written to ask the reason for the difference; and that was what Verbrugge found so difficult.

Havelaar, who knew perfectly well what lay behind this seemingly simple matter, said he would give Verbrugge his views on the 'difficulty' in writing; and among the documents before me, I find a copy of the letter which seems to have been the result.

If my reader should complain that I am wasting his time with correspondence about the prices of timberwork, which do not appear to have anything to do with him, I beg him to consider that the real point at issue is quite a different one, viz., the condition of the East Indian Government economy, and that the letter which I reproduce below not only casts another ray of light on the factitious optimism I have already mentioned but also indicates the difficulties confronting anyone who, like Havelaar, wants to go straight ahead without constraint.

No. 114   *Rangkas-Betung*, 15 March 1856
To the Controleur of Lebak

When I referred to you the letter from the Director of Public Works No. 271/354, dated 16 February ult., I requested you to answer the questions asked therein, after consultation with the Regent and with due observance of what I wrote in my memorandum No. 97 of the 5th inst.

That memorandum contained some general indications regarding what may be considered equitable and just in fixing the prices of materials to be supplied by the population on the orders of the Government.

In your memorandum No. 6 of the 8th inst., you complied with my request—I believe, to the best of your knowledge. Hence, relying on your local experience and that of the Regent, I submitted the quotations to the Resident exactly as you supplied them.

This was followed by a letter from that senior official, No. 326 of the 11th inst., requesting information on the cause of the difference between the prices quoted by me and those paid in 1853 and 1854 for the building of a prison.

I, of course, forwarded that letter to you, and instructed you orally to justify your quotations. This should have been all the easier for you since you were able to refer to the instructions given you in my letter of the 5th inst., which instructions we have also repeatedly discussed orally.

So far, all was plain sailing.

But yesterday you came to my office with the Resident's letter in your hand, and began to say how difficult it was to deal with it. I again observed in you a sort of reluctance to call a spade a spade, an attitude to which I have already drawn your attention several times, for instance recently in the presence of the Resident—an attitude which, for short, I would call halfheartedness, and against which I have often given you friendly warning.

Halfheartedness leads to nothing. *Half* good is *no* good. *Half* truths are *un*truths.

For full salary, for full rank, after a clear and *full* oath, one must do one's *full* duty.

If courage is sometimes required to do it, one must possess that courage.

For my part, I should not have the courage to lack that courage. Because, in addition to the dissatisfaction with oneself which arises from neglect of duty or lukewarmness ... the search for easier detours, the desire to avoid conflict always and everywhere, the penchant to 'fix' things, inevitably cause more anxiety, and actually more danger, than will be encountered on the straight and narrow path.

As regards a very important matter which is now under consideration by the Government and in which you should really be officially concerned, I have tacitly left you, so to speak, neutral, and have only alluded to it jokingly now and again.

Recently, for example, your report on the causes of hardship and famine among the population reached me, and I wrote on it: '*All this may be the truth but it is not the* WHOLE *truth, nor the* MAIN *truth. The chief cause lies deeper*.' You admitted that frankly, and I did not avail myself of my *right* to demand that, in the circumstances, you should then *name* that chief cause.

I had many reasons for such forbearance, amongst them this one ... that I felt it would be unjust to suddenly demand from *you* something which many others in your place would also be incapable of—to force *you* suddenly to jettison the habits of secretiveness and fear of other people which are not so much *your* fault as that of the leadership you have been given. Finally, I wished first to set you an example of how much simpler and easier it is to do one's *whole* duty than only half of it.

Now, however, having had the privilege of supervising your work for so many days longer, and having repeatedly given you the opportunity of becoming acquainted with principles which—unless I am greatly mistaken—will triumph in the end, I would ask you to adopt these principles. I would ask you to summon up the strength which is not lacking in you but has fallen into disuse, and which seems indispensable if one is to say what has to be said with frankness and to the best of one's knowledge; and I would therefore ask you to renounce altogether this unmanly shrinking from telling the plain truth about a case.

Accordingly, I now expect from you a simple but *complete* statement of what you think is the cause of the difference in prices between *now* and 1853–54.

I earnestly trust that you will not look upon any passage in this letter as written with the intention of hurting your feelings. I hope you know me well enough now to understand that I always say neither more nor less than what I mean; and in addition I again assure you that my remarks actually apply less to *you* personally than to the school in which you have been trained as an East Indian civil servant.

This extenuating circumstance would, however, lose all force if, still being with me and serving the Government under my guidance, you continued to follow the bad old routine which I am opposing.

You will have noticed that I have dropped addressing you as '*Uweledelgestrenge*':[89] I was sick of it. Please do the same by me, and let our 'right-nobility' and, when necessary, our 'severity', appear elsewhere and, more particularly, *otherwise* than in these tiresome, nonsensical titles.

The Assistant Resident of Lebak
Max Havelaar

Verbrugge's answer incriminated some of Havelaar's predecessors, and proved that the latter was not far wrong when he included 'bad examples in the past' among the circumstances pleading in favour of the Regent.

In communicating this letter I have run on ahead of my story, to emphasize in advance how little help Havelaar could expect from the Controleur as soon as it became necessary to call entirely different, more important 'spades' by their proper names, considering that this official, who was unquestionably a right-minded man, had to be thus addressed to make him tell the truth where it was merely a matter of quoting the prices of timber, stone and mortar, and wages. It will therefore be realized that Havelaar not only had to fight the power of the persons with a vested interest in criminality, but also the cowardice of those who—though condemning that criminality as much as he—did not regard themselves as called upon or able to take the necessary courageous stand against it.

Perhaps, too, after reading that letter, the reader will have rather less contempt for the slavish submissiveness of the Javanese who, faced with his Chief, cravenly withdraws the charge he has made, however justified it is. For if one reflects that there was so much cause for fear even on the part of the European official, who, after all, might be considered to be not so much exposed to vengeance, what, then, awaited the poor native who, in a village far from the main Government centre, fell back completely into the hands of the oppressors he had accused? Is it surprising that those poor wretches, terrified at the consequences of their temerity, sought to evade or mitigate those consequences by abject submission?

And Controleur Verbrugge was not the only one who did his duty with a nervousness more appropriate to dereliction of duty. When the JAKSA, the native Chief who performs the office of Public Prosecutor in the Divisional court, had to visit Havelaar, he preferred to do so by night, unseen and unattended. He, who was supposed to prevent theft ... he, whose task it was to catch the sneak thief ... sneaked on tiptoe, as though he himself were the thief who feared to be caught, in at the back of the house, after first assuring himself that no other visitors were there who might later betray him as guilty of doing his duty.

Was it surprising that Havelaar was dejected, and that it was more necessary than ever for Tina to go into his room and cheer him up, when she saw how he sat there resting his head on his hand?

And yet for him the greatest obstacle was not the timidity of his assistants, or the accessory cowardice of those who had begun by appealing to him for help. He was prepared to do justice entirely alone if need be, without the help of others, yes, *against* all others, even against the very persons who were in need of that justice! For he knew the influence he had on the people, and that—if the poor oppressed ones should be called upon to repeat aloud and before a court what they had whispered to him in privacy, in the evening or the night—he knew that he had the power to work on their feelings, that the strength of his words would be greater than dread of the revenge of District Chief or Regent. So it was not fear that his protégés would desert their own cause which restrained him. No ... but it cost him so much to accuse the old ADHIPATTI: *that* was the reason for his struggle with himself! For again, on the other hand he was not at liberty to yield to this reluctance, since the entire population, apart even from its claim to justice, had as good a claim to pity as the Regent.

Fear of trouble for himself had no part in his hesitation. He knew how unwilling the Government was to see a Regent impeached, and how much easier it was for some authorities to reduce a European official to beggary than to punish a native Chief. But he had a reason for believing that at that particular moment principles different from the usual ones would prevail in judging such a matter. It is true that he would have done his duty even without this belief—in fact he would have done it all the more readily if he had considered the danger to him and his to be greater than ever before. We have said that difficulties attracted him, and that he had a craving for self-sacrifice. But he felt that the lure of such a sacrifice did not exist here, and feared that if, in the end, he had to engage in a serious battle against injustice, he would have to forego the chivalrous pleasure of beginning the battle as the weaker party.

Yes, he *feared* that. He believed that the head of the Government was a Governor-General who would be his ally, and it was one further peculiarity in his character that this conviction restrained him from stern measures; longer, in fact, than anything else would have restrained him, because it was repugnant to him to attack Injustice at a moment when he took the cause of Justice to be stronger than usual.

Have I not said, in my attempt at describing his character, that he was naïve for all his acumen?

Let me try to make it clear how Havelaar had come to hold this belief.

Very few European readers can form a correct conception of the moral altitude at which a Governor-General must stand in order not to be below the eminence of his office; and it must, therefore, not be taken as too severe a judgment when I say I consider that very few persons—perhaps not one—have ever been equal to so exalted a task. I will not now enumerate all the qualities of head and heart that are necessary to it, but would ask the reader only to cast a glance at the vertiginous height on which the man is suddenly placed who, yesterday still a simple citizen, today wields power over millions of subjects. He who until recently was lost in his environment, without rising above it in rank or authority, finds himself all at once, most often unexpectedly, elevated above a multitude infinitely larger than the circle which, small as it was, nevertheless hid him entirely from view in earlier days; and I believe that I do not exaggerate when I call the height vertiginous, since it does indeed call to mind the dizziness of someone who unexpectedly sees an abyss before him, or the blindness that strikes us when we are rapidly brought from deep darkness into dazzling light. However strong they may be, the nerves of sight or brain are not proof against such transitions.

If, then, an appointment as Governor-General often carries in itself the seeds of corruption even for men who possess outstanding mental and moral capacities, what is to be expected from persons who start their term of office handicapped by many shortcomings? And assuming for a moment that the King is always correctly informed when he appends his exalted name to the deed in which he professes to be convinced of the '*loyalty, zeal and ability*' of his appointed Lieutenant; and assuming that the new Viceroy *is* loyal, zealous and able ... the question still remains whether that zeal, and more especially that *ability*, are present in him to a *degree* sufficiently raised above *mediocrity* to meet the requirements of his high calling.

For the question cannot be whether the man who leaves the King's council chamber in The Hague as a newly-made Governor-General *then* possesses the ability which will be necessary for his new office ... that is *impossible*! The expression of confidence in his ability can only amount to the opinion that at a given moment, in an entirely new sphere of activity he will know, as it were by inspiration, what he cannot have learnt in The Hague. In other words: that he is a genius, a genius who must all at once know and be able to do what he did not know and could not do before. Such geniuses are rare, even among persons who enjoy the favour of kings.

As I am speaking of geniuses, it will be realized that I wish to pass over what might be said about a great many Governors-General. Also, I should be loth to introduce into my book pages which would jeopardize its serious purpose by exposing it to the suspicion of scandalmongering. I shall therefore not give particulars that would refer to specific persons; but I think I can give the following diagnosis of the condition of Governors-General in *general*. *First stage*. Giddiness. Intoxication with incense. Conceit. Immoderate self-confidence. Disdain for others, especially 'old Indies hands'. *Second stage*. Exhaustion. Fear. Dejection. Craving for sleep and rest. Excessive confidence in the Council of the Indies. Homesickness for a country house in Holland.

In between these two stages—perhaps even as the cause of the transition—there are attacks of dysentery.

I am sure that many in the Indies will be grateful to me for this diagnosis. It is of good practical use, for it may be taken virtually for granted that the patient who, in his euphoria, would strain at a gnat in the first period, will subsequently—i.e., after the stomach troubles!—be able to swallow camels without inconvenience. Or, to speak more plainly: an official who 'accepts gifts, *not with the object of enriching himself*'—for instance, a bunch of bananas worth a few farthings—will be dismissed with opprobrium and ignominy in the *first* period of the illness, but a man who has the patience to wait for the *second* and last period will, in perfect tranquillity and with no fear of punishment, be able to appropriate the garden where the bananas grew, together with the gardens adjoining... and the houses in the neighbourhood... and everything in those houses ...and a few more things beside, *ad libitum*.

Everyone is welcome to profit by this pathologico-philosophical observation of mine, keeping my advice to himself, of course, to prevent excessive competition...

The devil! Why must indignation and sorrow so often masquerade in the motley of satire? The devil! Why must a tear be accompanied by a grin, in order to be understood? Or is it the fault of lack of skill on my part, that I can find no words to probe the depth of the wound that eats into the body politic of our State like a cancer, without looking for my style in *Figaro* or *Punch*?

Style ... yes! Before me lie documents in which there is style! Style which shows that there was a *man* about, a *man* who would have been worth shaking hands with! And what good has that style done poor Havelaar? *He* did not translate his tears into grins, *he* did not jeer, *he* did not seek to make his effect by a garish variety of colours, or by the jests of a barker before a tent at a fair ... what good has it done him?

If I could write like him, I should write otherwise than he did.

Style? Did you hear how he spoke to the Chiefs? What good has it done him?

If I could speak like him, I should speak otherwise than he did.

Away with kindly language, away with gentleness, frankness, clarity, simplicity, feeling! Away with all that savours of Horace's *justum ac tenacem*![90] Let trumpets sound, and the sharp clash of cymbals be heard, and the hiss of rockets, and the screech of untuned strings, and now and then a word of truth, that it may steal in like contraband under cover of all the drumming and fifing!

Style? *He* had style! He had too much soul to drown his thoughts in the 'I-have-the-honours' and the 'noble-severities' and the 'respectfully-submitted-for-considerations' which are the delight of the little world he moved in. When he wrote, something went through you who read it which made you feel that real clouds were driving across the sky during that thunderstorm, and that it was not merely the rattle of tin stage-thunder which you heard! When he struck fire from his ideas, you felt the heat of that fire, unless you were a born penpusher, or a Governor-General, or a writer of most nauseating Reports on 'peaceful peace'. And what good has it done him?

If, then, I want to be heard—and, above all, understood!—I must write otherwise than he did. But, if so—*how*?

Reader, I am looking for the answer to that *how*, and that is why my book is such a hotchpotch. It is a tradesman's pattern card… make your choice! Later, I will give you yellow or blue or red, as you have chosen.

Havelaar had observed Governor-General-disease so often, and in so many patients—and frequently among lower animals, too, for there are analogous Resident-, Controleur-, and Supernumerary-diseases, which are to Governor-General-disease as measles to small-pox. And, finally, he had suffered from that kind of ailment himself! He had observed it all so often that the symptoms were pretty familiar to him. And he had found the then Governor-General less giddy at the outset than most of the others had been, and thought he might conclude from that that the further course of the illness would also be different.

It was for this reason that he feared he would be the stronger when, in the end, he would have to stand up for the rights of the inhabitants of Lebak.

237

16

Havelaar received a letter from the Regent of CHANYOR in which the Regent said that he wished to visit his uncle, the ADHIPATTI of LEBAK. This was very unwelcome news. Havelaar was aware that the Chiefs in the PREANGER REGENCIES were accustomed to display great luxury, and that the TOMMONGONG of CHANYOR would not make such a journey without a retinue of many hundreds of people, who, with their horses, would all have to be housed and fed. He would therefore gladly have prevented this visit but, try as he would, he could not think of any way of doing so without hurting the feelings of the Regent of LEBAK, who was very proud and would have been deeply offended if his comparative poverty had been put forward as a reason for not visiting him. Yet if the visit could *not* be avoided, it was bound to lead to aggravation of the burden that already weighed so heavily on the people.

It is to be doubted whether Havelaar's address had made a lasting impression on the Chiefs. With many, this was certainly not the case and, indeed, he had not expected it himself. But just as certainly, word had gone round the villages that the *tuan* in authority at RANGKAS-BETUNG wished to do justice; and so, even though his words had lacked the power to check crime, they had undoubtedly given its victims the courage to complain, albeit only hesitantly and secretly.

They would creep up through the ravine at nightfall, and as Tina sat in her room she would often be startled by sudden rustling sounds, and through the open window she would see dark figures stealing past with timorous steps. Soon she no longer jumped, for she knew what it meant when those shapes wandered so spectrally round the house, seeking the protection of her Max! She would beckon him, and he would rise to call the insulted and injured before him. Most of them were from the District of PARANG-KUJANG, of which the Regent's son-in-law was Chief. That Chief was certainly not backward in taking his share of the booty, but it was common knowledge that he nearly always practised his extortions in the name and on behalf of the Regent. It was touching to see how those poor wretches relied on Havelaar's chivalry, and were convinced that he would not call them to repeat publicly next day what they had said privately the night before in his room. For this, of course, would have meant ill-treatment for all of them, and death for many! Havelaar noted down what they told him, and then bade them return to their villages. He promised that justice would be done provided they did not rebel, or, as most of them intended, flee from the Division. As a rule, he was at the scene of the crime shortly afterwards; in fact, he had frequently been there and investigated the case—usually during the night—before the complainer had been able to get back himself. In this way Havelaar visited, in that extensive Division, villages which lay twenty hours' journey away from RANGKAS-BETUNG, without either the Regent or Controleur Verbrugge even knowing that he was absent from the Divisional headquarters. It was his intention thus to shield the complainants from the danger of reprisals and at the same time to spare the Regent the ignominy of a public inquiry which, under the present Assistant Resident, would certainly *not* have ended in the complaint's being withdrawn. He still hoped the Chiefs might turn from the dangerous road they had trodden so long, and in that case he would have been content to demand compensation for the victims of robbery.

But every time he spoke to the Regent he found that the promises of amendment had been vain, and he was bitterly distressed by the failure of his efforts.

We shall now leave him for a while to this distress and to his difficult work, in order to tell the reader the story of the Javanese SAÏJAH from the *dessah* of BADUR. I have picked out the names of that village and that Javanese from Havelaar's notes. It is a story of extortion and robbery; and if anyone wishes to regard it—that is to say, the substance of it—as fictitious, I can supply the names of *thirty-two* persons in the District of PARANG-KUJANG alone from whom, in one month, *thirty-six buffaloes* were forcibly taken on behalf of the Regent. Or rather, to be more precise, I can name thirty-two persons from that District who, in one month, *had the courage to complain*, and whose complaints were *investigated and found justified* by Havelaar.

There are *five* such Districts in the Division of LEBAK...

Now, if anyone chooses to assume that the number of stolen buffaloes was less high in the places that did not have the honour of being ruled by the ADHIPATTI's son-in-law I shall not dispute the point, however open to doubt it remains whether the shamelessness of other Chiefs was not based on grounds as solid as exalted kinship. For instance, in the absence of a dreaded father-in-law the District Chief of CHILANGKAHAN, on the south coast, could bank on the difficulty of lodging complaints which confronted poor people who had to travel from *forty* to *sixty* miles before they could hide at dusk in the ravine beside Havelaar's house. And if, then, we also remember the many who set out for that house and never reached it... the many who never even left their village, frightened by their own past experience or by contemplation of the fate that befell other complainers—then I believe we should be wrong in imagining that to multiply the number of buffaloes stolen in one district by *five* would yield too high a figure for the total number of buffaloes which were stolen every month in the combined *five* districts in order to satisfy the needs of the Regent of LEBAK's Court.

And it was not only buffaloes that were stolen, nor, even, was theft of buffaloes the principal evil. Especially in the East Indies, where *statute labour* still exists, less effrontery is needed to summon the people unlawfully for unpaid work than is needed to steal their property. It is easier to make them believe that the Government requires their labour but will not pay for it than that it would demand their buffaloes for nothing. And even if the timid Javanese *dared* to try to find out whether the so-called *statute labour* exacted from him was really in accordance with the regulations, he would still be quite unable to do so since, in these isolated, self-contained communities, the right hand does not know what the left hand is doing, and hence he could not calculate whether twice, ten or fifty times the permitted number of persons had been called up. If, then, the more dangerous, more readily detected crime of buffalo theft is carried out so brazenly, what can be expected as regards abuses that are more easily practised and less liable to detection?

I said I was going to tell the story of the Javanese SAÏJAH. But before I start I am obliged to make one of those digressions which are so hard to avoid in describing conditions entirely foreign to the reader. And this will also give me an opportunity to touch on the reasons why it is so extremely difficult for outsiders to form a correct opinion on East Indian affairs.

In alluding to the people of Java, I have repeatedly called them the 'Javanese'. This may appear natural enough to the European reader; but the name will have sounded wrong to those with first-hand knowledge of Java. The western residencies of BANTAM, BATAVIA, PREANGER, KRAWANG and part of CHERIBON, which are collectively called the SUNDA LANDS, are not regarded as belonging to Java proper. Here we leave out of account, of course, that portion of the population which consists of foreigners from overseas, and consider only the original inhabitants; but they are certainly quite different from the people in Middle or East Java. Costume, tribal character and language are so totally unlike those further east that the SUNDANESE or ORANG GUNUNG, the man from the mountains, differs more profoundly from the real Javanese than an Englishman from a Dutchman. These differences often lead to disagreement in judging East Indian affairs. For since Java itself is already so sharply divided into two dissimilar parts, without even considering the many subdivisions of those parts, the reader can imagine how great the difference must be between tribes that live farther from each other and are separated by the sea. The man whose acquaintance with the Dutch East Indies is confined to Java can no more have a correct idea of the MALAY, the AMBOINESE, the BATTAK, the ALFURO, the TIMORESE, the DAYAK, the BUGI, or the MACASSAR than if he had never left Europe; and to anyone who has had opportunities of observing the differences between these groups it is frequently amusing to hear the conversations—and depressing to read the speeches!—of persons who acquired their knowledge of East Indian affairs at BATAVIA or BUITENZORG. I have often marvelled at the audacity with which, for instance, an ex-Governor-General has tried to give weight to his words in Parliament by a fictitious claim to local knowledge and experience. I attach great value to knowledge obtained by serious study in the library, and I have more than once been astonished by the extensive familiarity with Dutch East Indian affairs shown by people who never set foot on East Indian soil. As soon as an ex-Governor-General gives evidence of having acquired such knowledge in *that* manner, we owe him the respect due to long, conscientious, and fruitful labour. In fact we owe even greater respect to him than to the scholar, who has had fewer difficulties to overcome because, at a great distance away, *without* immediate contact, he runs less risk of making the errors that result from a *defective* contact, such as must inevitably have fallen to the share of the ex-Governor-General.

I said that I marvelled at the audacity displayed by some persons during discussions of Dutch East Indian affairs. For they must know that their words are heard by others besides those who imagine that a few years spent at BUITENZORG are sufficient in order to know the Indies. They must be aware, after all, that their words are also read by those persons in the Indies who were witnesses to their incapacity when they were there, and who, like myself, are astounded at the temerity of a man who, engaged until quite recently in the vain endeavour to conceal his inadequacy under the high rank conferred on him by the King, now suddenly makes bold to speak as if he really knew something about the affairs he is dealing with!

And, indeed, we hear complaints about non-competent interference over and over again. Over and over again, this or that line in colonial policy is combated by denying the competence of him who represents that line, and perhaps it would be worthwhile instituting a thorough inquiry as to the qualities which render a person competent to… judge competence. More often than not, an important question is decided, not by reference to the matter itself, but by the value attached to the opinions of the man who talks about it. And as he is usually a person who passes for an *Expert*, and preferably a man 'who had such an important post in the Indies', it follows that the result of a parliamentary vote is generally coloured by the errors that always seem to be part and parcel of those 'important posts'. If this is already the case where the influence of such an expert is only exercised by a Member of the House of Representatives, how much greater must be the bias towards warped judgment when that influence is backed by the trust of the King who allowed himself to be persuaded into placing such an expert at the head of his Ministry for the Colonies?

It is a strange phenomenon—perhaps springing from a kind of inertia which shirks the trouble of judging for itself—that people give their confidence so lightly to persons able to create the impression of possessing superior knowledge, whenever such knowledge can *only* be drawn from sources not accessible to everybody. The cause may be that one's self-esteem is less injured by having to acknowledge such superiority than it would be if one might have used the same resources oneself, in which case something like rivalry might come into play. The people's representative experiences no difficulty in relinquishing his opinion as soon as it is contested by someone whose judgment may be considered as better-founded than his own, provided such a judgment need be ascribed not to personal superiority—confession of which would be harder!—but merely to the special circumstances in which such an opponent has had the good fortune to be.

And, leaving out of account those who 'had such *important posts* in the Indies', it is indeed strange how often people attribute value to the opinions of persons who have absolutely nothing to justify it except the 'memory of so-and-so many years spent in those parts'. This is the more peculiar, since the people who respect such an argument would probably be the last to accept everything they were told, say, about the Dutch national economy by someone who could prove that he had spent forty or fifty years in Holland. There are persons who have spent over thirty years in the Dutch East Indies without ever coming into contact either with the common people or with the native Chiefs, and it is pitiful to reflect that the Council of the Indies is often entirely or largely composed of such persons—indeed, that means have even been found to persuade the King to approve the appointment as Governor-General of men belonging to *this* class of expert.

When I said that the ability imputed to a newly appointed Governor-General necessarily implied that he was taken to be a genius, it was in no way my intention to recommend the appointment of geniuses. For, in addition to the drawback that this important post would constantly remain unfilled, there is another argument against such a proposal. A genius could not possibly work under the Ministry for the Colonies, and would therefore be unemployable... as geniuses usually are.

It might perhaps be desirable if the principal defects I have enumerated as a clinical diagnosis should attract the attention of those called upon to choose successive Governors-General. We shall take it for granted that all persons who are considered for the position are honest and possess enough brains to learn what they will have to know. I next consider it essential that we should be able to expect them to avoid not only that presumptuous pedantry at the outset but also, and more particularly, that apathetic somnolence in the last years of their administration. I have already said that Havelaar believed he could rely on the help of the Governor-General in doing his difficult duty, and I added that that belief was just another proof of his naïveté. The Governor-General concerned was already awaiting his successor: rest in the Netherlands was at hand!

We shall see what consequences this tendency to sleep brought to the Division of LEBAK, to Havelaar, and to the Javanese SAÏJAH, whose monotonous story—one of very many!—I shall now relate.

Yes, monotonous it will be! Monotonous as the tale of the labour of the ant that has to drag its contribution to the winter store up a clod of earth—a mountain—which lies on the way to the storehouse. Time and time again it falls back with its burden, and time and time again it tries once more to see whether it can possibly reach that small stone up there ... the rock which crowns the mountain. But between it and that summit there is an abyss which has to be negotiated ... a gulf which not a thousand ants would fill. For this purpose the tiny creature, with scarcely the strength to drag its load along on level ground—a load many times heavier than its own body—has to raise that load above its head while still staying upright on an unstable spot. It must keep its balance as it rises erect with its burden between its forefeet. It must swing that burden upwards and to one side, so that it will come down on a point jutting out from the wall of rock. It totters, staggers, starts, collapses, tries to hold on to the half-uprooted tree whose top points down into the depths—a grass-blade!—it misses the support it seeks; the tree swings back—the grass-blade gives way under it! Alas! The drudge has fallen down the precipice with its load. It is still for a moment, for quite a second ... which is long in the life of an ant. Is it stunned by the pain of the fall? Or is it yielding to some grief because so much effort was in vain? Anyway, it has not lost courage. Once more it seizes its load, and once more it drags it upwards, presently to fall again, and yet again, down the precipice into the depths.

So monotonous is my story. But I shall not speak of ants, whose joy or sorrow is beyond our perception, owing to the coarseness of our senses. I shall speak of men and women, of creatures who live and move and have their being as we do. To be sure, those who shun emotion and wish to avoid the pain of pity will say that these men and women are yellow, or brown—many call them black; and for those people, the difference in colour is reason enough for turning their eyes away from such misery, or, if they deign to look down at it at all, to look down at it without emotion.

My tale is therefore addressed only to those who are capable of holding the difficult belief that a heart beats beneath that dark epidermis, and that he who is blessed with the possession of a white skin, and with the breeding, generosity, knowledge of business and of God, and virtue, that go along with it ... that he might apply his 'white' qualities otherwise than has so far been the experience of those less blessed in their colour and spiritual excellence.

However, my hopes for sympathy with the people of Java do not go so far as to make me expect that the description of the theft, in broad daylight, of the last buffalo from the *kendang*,[91] stolen without scruple under the protection of Dutch authority ... the description of the owner and his weeping children following the animal as it is driven off ... of that owner sitting down on the steps of the robber's house, speechless and stunned and sunk in sorrow ... the description of him chased away with insults and scorn, with the threat of *rattan* stripes and prison in fetters ... no, I neither expect nor demand, O fellow-Dutchmen, that such a picture will move you as much as if I were to sketch for you the lot of a Dutch peasant whose cow has been taken from him. I ask for no tear to flow with the tears on such dusky faces, no noble indignation when I speak of the despair of the victims. Nor do I expect you to rise and go to the King with my book in your hand, and say: 'See, O King, this is what happens in *your* Empire, in your lovely Empire of Insulinde!'

No, no, no, I do not expect any of that! Too much of your sympathy is absorbed by suffering close at hand to leave you so much to spare for what is so far off! Is not your whole nervous system kept on the rack by the distressful task of choosing a new Member of Parliament? Is not your torn soul tossed between the world-renowned merits of Nonentity A and Nobody B? And do you not require your precious tears for more serious matters than ... but what more need I say? Weren't things slack on 'Change yesterday, and isn't oversupply threatening the coffee market with a slump?

'I hope to goodness you don't write such stupid things to your papa, Stern!' I said, and perhaps I said it a bit hotly, for I can't bear untruth: that has always been a firm principle of mine. The very same evening I wrote to old Stern, telling him to make haste with his orders, and to be on his guard against false rumours, for coffee prices are very steady.

The reader will realize what I have again had to put up with in listening to these last chapters. In the children's playroom I found a game of solitaire, which I shall take with me to the Rosemeyers in future. Wasn't I right when I said that that Scarfman had sent them all mad with his parcel? I ask you, in all this scribbling of Stern's—and Frits takes a hand in it too, that's a fact!—would you recognize young people who had been brought up in a genteel household? What's the meaning of those stupid sallies against a 'disease' which manifests itself in longing for a country house? Is that a hit at me? Aren't I to be allowed to go to Driebergen, then, when Frits is a broker? And whoever talks about stomach complaints in the presence of women and girls? It's a firm principle of mine always to keep calm—I consider this useful in business—but I must admit I've often found it mighty difficult lately, listening to all the nonsense Stern reads out. What on earth does he want? Where is all this to end? When are we ever going to get something solid and worthwhile? What do I care whether this Havelaar fellow keeps his garden tidy, and whether people come into his house at the front or at the back? At Busselinck & Waterman's you have to go in through a narrow passage, next to an oil warehouse, where it's always terribly dirty. And then, all that moaning and groaning about buffaloes! What do they want buffaloes for, those niggers? *I've* never had a buffalo, and I'm satisfied enough. Some people are always complaining. And as for all that railing against forced labour, you can easily see that he didn't hear Parson Blatherer's sermon, or he would know how useful such labour is for the spread of God's Kingdom. But, of course, Stern's a Lutheran.

Oh, to be sure, if I had guessed *how* he was going to write the book which is going to be so important to all coffee brokers—and others—I'd sooner have done it myself. But he's backed up by the Rosemeyers, who are in sugar, and it's that that makes him so bra-

zen. I said straight out—for I'm outspoken in things of this kind—
that we could perfectly well do without the story of that *Saïjah*, but
suddenly I got Louise Rosemeyer against me. Apparently Stern
told her there's to be some love in it, and girls dote on that sort of
thing. I shouldn't have let myself be put off by her, though, if the
Rosemeyers hadn't told me they would like to make the acquaintance of Stern's father. The idea, of course, is to use the father in
order to reach the uncle, because the uncle's in sugar. Now, if I
come out too strongly for common sense against young Stern, I
may make the impression of wanting to draw them away from him,
and that's certainly not the case, because they're in sugar.

I can't for the life of me understand what Stern is driving at with
all this rigmarole. There have always been discontented people in
the world; and, I ask you, *is* it nice of him to abuse the Government
when he enjoys so many benefits in Holland—only this week my
wife made him some camomile tea! Is he out to feed the general discontent? Does *he* want to be Governor-General? Well, he's conceited enough ... I mean, to *want* to be. The day before yesterday I
asked him whether he wanted to be Governor-General, and told
him candidly that his Dutch was still so very imperfect! 'Oh, that's
no obstacle,' he answered. 'Apparently it's only very rarely that
they send a Governor-General out who understands the language
of the country!' What on earth can you do with such a prig? He has
not the slightest respect for my experience! When I told him that I
had been a broker these seventeen years, and had been on 'Change
for twenty years, he instanced Busselinck & Waterman, who have
been brokers for eighteen years, 'so they have one year more experience than you have!' he said. He had me there, because I must admit, since I'm a man of truth, that Busselinck & Waterman know
little about business for all that, and they're tricksters.

Marie's head has been turned, too. Just fancy, this week—it was
her turn to read aloud at breakfast, and we'd got to the story of Lot
—she suddenly stopped, and refused to read on. My wife, who sets
as much store by religion as I do, tried to coax her to be obedient,

248

because of course it isn't proper for a young girl to be so self-willed. All in vain! Then I, as father, had to intervene and give her a good scolding, because her obstinacy spoilt the breakfast edification, and that always has a bad effect on the whole day. But nothing was any use, and she went so far as to say that she would rather be beaten to death than read on. I punished her by shutting her up in her room for three days, on nothing but coffee and bread, and hope it will do her some good. And so that the punishment might also be conducive to her moral improvement, I ordered her to copy out the chapter she would not read ten times over. My main reason for resorting to such severity was because I have noticed that latterly—I don't know whether Stern's at the bottom of it or not—she has got ideas into her head that seem to me to be dangerous to the morality my wife and I prize so highly. Amongst other things, I have heard her sing a French song—by *Béranger*, I believe—pitying a poor old beggarwoman who sang on the stage in her youth; and yesterday she came down to breakfast without stays—Marie, I mean—and that's not respectable, is it now?

Oh, and while I'm about it I must also admit that the prayer meeting has not done Frits much good. I was fairly satisfied with the way he sat still in church. He didn't stir, he never took his eyes off the pulpit; but later on I heard that Betsy Rosemeyer had been sitting close beneath it. I said nothing about that, one mustn't be too hard on young people, and the Rosemeyers are a reputable firm. They gave their eldest daughter quite a tidy little portion when she married Bruggeman, who's in drugs, and so I believe that that kind of thing keeps Frits away from the Westermarkt, which pleases me greatly, because I set so much store by morality.

But that doesn't prevent my being vexed when I see Frits hardening his heart even as Pharaoh, who was really less guilty than Frits because he had no father who was constantly showing him the right path, for the Scriptures say nothing about Pharaoh Senior. Parson Blatherer complains about his conceit—I mean Frits's—at the confirmation class, and the boy seems to have acquired—out of that parcel of Scarfman's again!—an amount of pert priggishness which drives poor dear old Blatherer to distraction! It's touching to see how the worthy man, who often lunches with us, tries to work on Frits's good feelings, and how the young rascal always has new questions ready which show the rebelliousness of his heart. It all comes from that accursed parcel of Scarfman's! With tears of emotion rolling down his cheeks, the zealous servant of the Gospel—Blatherer, I mean—seeks to persuade him to renounce the wisdom of this world, and to be inducted into the mysteries of God's wisdom. Gently and tenderly he beseeches him not to reject the bread of eternal life and so to fall into the clutches of Satan, who dwells with his angels in the fire that has been prepared for him unto all eternity. 'Oh!' he said yesterday—Blatherer, I mean—'Oh, my young friend, do open your eyes and your ears, and hear and see what the Lord gives you to see and to hear from my lips! Mark the testimony of the saints who died for the true Faith! Observe St Stephen, as he sinks under the stones that crush him! See how his eye still seeks heaven, how his tongue still sings psalms...'

'I'd sooner have chucked some stones back at them!' said Frits. Reader, what am I to do with that boy?

A moment later, Blatherer started again, for he is a zealous servant of the Lord and does not cease from labouring. 'Oh,' said he, 'my young friend, do open...' the beginning was the same as before. 'But,' he continued, 'can you remain unmoved at the thought of what will become of you when once you shall be numbered among the goats on the left side...'

Here the reprobate—I mean Frits—roared with laughter, and Marie began to laugh too. I even thought I perceived the beginnings of a smile on my wife's face. But now I thought it high time to come to Blatherer's aid, and I punished Frits with a fine from his money-box, to be paid to the Missionary Society.

Oh, reader, reader, all this cuts me to the heart! I ask you ... how can a man, suffering such pangs, take pleasure in listening to yarns about buffaloes and Javanese? What is a buffalo compared with

Frits's salvation? How can I bother about the affairs of those far-off people when I have grounds for fearing that Frits by his unbelief will ruin my own affairs, and that he will never make a sound broker? For Blatherer himself has said that God ordains everything in such a way that right-mindedness leads to riches. 'Lo and behold!' says he, 'is there not much wealth in Holland? That is because we have the Faith. Are not battle, murder and sudden death the order of the day in France? That is because they are Catholics. Are not the Javanese poor? They are heathens. The longer the Dutch have to do with the Javanese, the more wealth there will be here and the more poverty there will be there. It is God's will that it should be so!'

I am amazed at Blatherer's business acumen. For it is true that I, who am strict in my religious observances, see my business growing more prosperous year by year, whilst Busselinck & Waterman, who are a godless lot, will never be anything but petty tricksters till the day they die. The Rosemeyers, too, who are in sugar and have a Papist maidservant, recently had to accept five shillings in the pound from a Jew who had gone smash. The more I think on things, the more I discover the inscrutable ways of God. Recently it appeared that thirty million guilders clear profit had again resulted from the sale of products supplied by the heathens, and that didn't even include what *I* made out of them, or the many others who earn a living in this line of business. Doesn't it seem as though the Lord had said: 'Here, here are thirty million to reward your belief'? Isn't it clearly the finger of God, who makes the wicked labour to preserve the just? Isn't it a hint to us to continue in the right path? A hint to get much produced over there and to stand firm in the true faith here? Isn't that why we're told to 'work and pray', meaning that *we* should pray and have the work done by that black scum which doesn't know its 'Our Father'?

Oh, how right Blatherer is when he calls God's yoke easy! How light is the burden made for all that believe! I am not much past forty, and I could retire if I liked, and go to Driebergen; but just see what others come to, who forsake the Lord! Yesterday I saw Scarfman with his wife and his little boy. They looked like ghosts. He is as pale as death, his eyes bulge out, and his cheeks are hollow. He walks with a stoop, although he is younger than I am. *She* was very shabbily dressed, too, and she seemed to have been crying again. Well, I had noticed immediately that she was the discontented sort—I only have to see anyone once to get their measure. That comes of experience. She had on a short, thin mantle of black silk, although it was pretty cold. Not a sign of a crinoline. Her thin dress hung slack around her knees, and was frayed at the hem. He wasn't even wearing his scarf this time, and looked as if it was summer. And yet he still seems to have pride of a sort, for he gave something to a poor woman who was sitting on the *lock* (Frits calls it a *bridge*. But when the thing's of stone, and can't be raised or lowered, I call it a *lock*),[92] and anyone who has so little himself commits a sin if he gives some of it away to another. Besides, I never give alms in the street—that's a principle of mine—for I always think, when I happen to see poor people: who's to say it isn't their own fault? And I should do wrong to harden them in their perversity. On Sundays I give twice in the collections, once for the poor, and once for the church. That's the way to do it! I don't know whether Scarfman saw me, but I walked on quickly, looking up at the sky, and meditated on the justice of the Almighty, who certainly wouldn't let him go about like that without a winter overcoat if he had behaved better and wasn't lazy, cocky and sickly.

Now, as to my book ... I really do owe the reader an apology for the unforgivable way in which Stern abuses our contract. I must admit that the prospect of the next evening party, and the love story of this *Saïjah*, make my heart sink. The reader already knows what healthy views I have about love ... you only need to turn up my verdict on Stern's outing to the Ganges. That young girls should find things of that sort nice, I can well understand; but it beats me how men of riper years can listen to such rubbish without feeling sick. I am certain I shall find the triolet of my game of solitaire during the next party.

I shall do my best to stop my ears to SAÏJAH, and hope the man soon gets married, that's to say if *he* is the hero of the love story. It's rather kind of Stern to have warned me in advance that it's going to be a monotonous tale. As soon as he goes on to something else, I'll start listening again. Though all this running down the Government bores me almost as much as love stories do. It all goes to show that Stern is young and hasn't had much experience. To judge things properly, you have to see them from close quarters. When I got married I went to The Hague, the seat of government, myself, and saw the pictures in the Mauritshuis gallery with my wife. In The Hague I came into contact with all ranks of society, for I saw the Minister of Finance driving past, and we bought flannel together in Veenestraat—me and my wife, I mean—and nowhere did I see the least sign of dissatisfaction with the Government. The woman in the shop looked prosperous and contented enough, and so in 1848, when some people tried to tell us that things in The Hague weren't all they should be, I said my piece about that discontent straight out at our weekly party. And people believed me, too, for everyone knew I spoke from experience, and on the journey back—from The Hague, I mean—the guard played the old song 'Get some fun out of life' on his horn, and the man wouldn't have done that if there'd been so much to grouse about, would he? In this way I took note of everything, and so I knew at once what to think about all the grumbling in '48.

Opposite us lives a woman whose nephew's out East running a *toko*, as they call a shop there. Now, if everything was going as badly as Stern says, she would be bound to know about it too, and yet the woman appears to be very satisfied with things, for I never hear her complain. On the contrary, she says her nephew lives in a country house there, that he is a member of the vestry, and that he sent her a cigar case ornamented with peacock's feathers which he made himself out of bamboo. All this, I should think, shows plainly how groundless those complaints about bad government are. And you can also see from it that anyone who minds his Ps and Qs has a chance of earning quite a bit in that country, and so Scarfman must have been lazy, cocky and sickly there too, otherwise he would not have come back so poor and be walking around here without a winter coat. And the nephew of that woman opposite isn't the only one who's made his fortune in the East. In *Poland* I see a good many men who have been there, and they are very smartly dressed indeed. But it's understandable, people must look to their business out there, just as much as here. Money doesn't grow on trees in Java either: you have to work! And anyone who doesn't want to do that is poor and stays poor, that goes without saying.

17

SAÏJAH's father had a buffalo with which he worked his field. When this buffalo was taken from him by the District Chief of PARANG-KUJANG he was very sad, and said not a word for many days. For ploughing-time was drawing near and it was to be feared that, if the *sawah* was not prepared soon enough, sowing-time would also pass by, and in the end there would be no paddy to cut and to store in the barn.

For the benefit of readers who know Java but do not know BAN-TAM, I must point out here that in this Residency there is such a thing as personal ownership of land, which is not the case elsewhere.

Well then, SAÏJAH's father was greatly distressed. He feared that his wife would lack rice, and also SAÏJAH, who was still a child, and the little brothers and sisters of SAÏJAH. Moreover, the District Chief would report him to the Assistant Resident if he was behind-hand in paying his land tax. For that is punishable by law.

Then SAÏJAH's father took a *kris* which was *pusaka*[93] left him by *his* father. The kris was not a very beautiful one, but there were sil-ver bands round the sheath, and a small silver plate at the tip of the sheath. He sold this kris to a Chinaman who lived in the Divisional capital, and came home with twenty-four guilders, which is about two pounds in English money, for which sum he bought another buffalo.

SAÏJAH, who was then about seven years old, soon struck up a friendship with the new buffalo. Not inadvisedly do I use the word 'friendship'; for it is indeed touching to see how attached the Java-nese buffalo becomes to the little boy who minds and takes care of him. Presently I shall give an example of this attachment. The great strong animal meekly bends his heavy head to right or left or down-ward, in response to the pressure of the finger of the child whom he knows, whom he understands, with whom he has grown up.

And such friendship, then, did little SAÏJAH rapidly inspire in the newcomer, and SAÏJAH's encouraging child's voice seemed to give even greater power to the powerful shoulders of the animal as it tore open the heavy clay soil and marked its passage in deep, sharp furrows. The buffalo turned docilely round when it reached the end, and lost not an inch of ground in ploughing the new furrow, which always lay right next to the old one as though the rice field were a garden plot which had been raked by a giant.

Beside this *sawah* lay those of ADINDA's father, the father of the child who was to marry SAÏJAH. And when ADINDA's little brothers reached the border between the fields, at the same moment that SAÏ-JAH was there too with his plough, they called out to each other merrily, and in friendly rivalry bragged of the strength and obedience of their respective buffaloes. But I believe SAÏJAH's was the best, perhaps because he knew how to speak to it better than the others did. For buffaloes are very susceptible to kind words.

SAÏJAH was nine years old, and ADINDA already six, when that buffalo was taken from SAÏJAH's father by the District Chief of PA-RANG-KUJANG.

This time SAÏJAH's father, who was very poor, sold to a Chinaman two silver *klambu*-hooks—*pusaka* from the parents of his wife —for eighteen guilders. And with that money he bought a new buffalo.

But SAÏJAH was sick at heart. For he knew from ADINDA's brothers that the last buffalo had been driven off to the Divisional centre, and he had asked his father whether he had not seen the animal when he was there selling the *klambu*-hooks? To which question SAÏJAH's father had not chosen to reply. And therefore SAÏJAH feared that his buffalo had been slaughtered, like the other buffaloes which the District Chief took from the people.

And SAÏJAH wept much when he thought of the poor buffalo with which he had lived so intimately for two years. And he could not eat for a long time, because his throat was too tight when he tried to swallow.

You must remember that SAÏJAH was only a child.

The new buffalo got to know SAÏJAH and very soon took the

place of the old one in the child's affections ... too soon, really. For, alas, the impressions made on the wax of our hearts are so easily smoothed out to make room for other writing! Anyway, even though the new buffalo was not so strong as the old one ... even though the old yoke was too wide for its shoulders ... yet the poor animal was as tractable as its predecessor which had been slaughtered; and though SAÏJAH could no longer boast of the strength of his buffalo when he met ADINDA's brothers at the edge of the fields, he still maintained that no other buffalo surpassed his in willingness. And when the furrows did not run as straight as before, or when the animal walked round clods of earth, leaving them unbroken, SAÏJAH gladly remedied all that with his *pachol*, to the best of his ability. Besides, no buffalo had such an *user-useran* as SAÏJAH's buffalo! No less an authority than the *penghulu*[94] had said that there was *ontong*[95] in the pattern of those whorls of hair on its withers.

One day when they were out in the field, SAÏJAH shouted in vain to his buffalo to get a move on. The beast had stopped dead. SAÏJAH, annoyed at such great and, what was more, such unusual insubordination, could not refrain from insulting it. 'A-s-!' he exclaimed. Anyone who has been in the Indies will know what I mean, and those who do not know what I mean can only benefit by my sparing them the explanation of a coarse expression.

SAÏJAH meant no harm by it. He only said it because he had so often heard it said by others when they were dissatisfied with their buffaloes. But he need not have said it, for it was of no avail: his buffalo did not budge. The animal shook its head, as though to throw off the yoke ... you could see the breath steaming from its nostrils ... it snorted, trembled, shook ... there was fear in its blue eye, and its upper lip was drawn back baring the gums...

'Run, run!' ADINDA's brothers suddenly cried. 'SAÏJAH, run! There's a tiger!'

And all unyoked their buffaloes, swung themselves on to the animals' broad backs, and galloped away over *sawahs*, across *galangans*,[96] through mud, through scrub and bush and *allang-allang*,[97] by fields and roads. But when they rode panting and sweating into the village of BADUR, SAÏJAH was not with them.

For when he had freed his buffalo from the yoke and mounted it like the others, in order to flee as they had done, the buffalo suddenly leapt forward, throwing SAÏJAH off his balance. He fell to the ground. The tiger was very near...

SAÏJAH's buffalo, carried on by its own speed, rushed several leaps past the place where his little master waited for death. But only through its own speed, and not through its own will, had it gone farther than SAÏJAH. For scarcely had it overcome the momentum that propels all matter even after cessation of the cause that set it in motion than it turned back, planted its clumsy body on its clumsy feet above the child like a roof, and turned its horned head to the tiger. The tiger sprang ... but for the last time. The buffalo caught it on its horns, and only lost some flesh ripped from its neck. The aggressor lay on the ground with its belly torn open, and SAÏJAH was saved. There had indeed been *ontong* in that buffalo's *user-useran*!

When this buffalo was taken from SAÏJAH's father and slaughtered...

I told you, reader, that my story is monotonous.

...When this buffalo was killed, SAÏJAH had already seen twelve summers, and ADINDA was already weaving *sarongs*, and *batiking* geometrical designs on the *kepala*, the wide band across one end of the *sarong*.[98] She already had thoughts to express in the pattern she traced on the fabric with her little cup of wax, and she drew sorrow, for she had seen SAÏJAH very sorrowful.

And SAÏJAH's father was also deeply grieved, but his mother most of all. For it was she who had healed the wound on the neck of the faithful animal that had brought home her child unhurt, after she had thought, from hearing the tidings of ADINDA's brothers, that SAÏJAH had been carried off by the tiger. So often had she contemplated that wound, thinking how deep the claw that had penetrated so far into the tough thews of the buffalo would have been driven into the tender body of her child; and every time she had laid fresh healing herbs on the wound she had stroked the buffalo, and spoken kind words to it, so that the good, faithful animal should know how grateful a mother can be! She now hoped with all her heart that the buffalo might have understood her, for then it would also have understood why she wept when it was taken away to be killed, and it would have known that SAÏJAH's mother was not the one who had ordered it to be killed.

Eventually, SAÏJAH's father fled the country. For he was much afraid of being punished for not paying his land tax, and he had no more *pusaka* with which to buy a new buffalo as his parents had always lived in PARANG-KUJANG and had therefore had little to leave him. And the parents of his wife had also always lived in that same District. Nevertheless, after the loss of his last buffalo he still kept going for a few years by ploughing with hired animals. But that is a very thankless kind of labour, and especially galling to a man who once had buffaloes of his own. SAÏJAH's mother died of a broken heart; and it was then that his father, in a moment of despondency, ran away from LEBAK, and from BANTAM, to look for work in the BUITENZORG region. He was flogged with *rattan* for leaving LEBAK without a pass, and brought back to BADUR by the police. There he was thrown into jail, because they took him to be mad (which would not have been beyond all comprehension) and because they were afraid that, in a fit of insanity, he might run *amok* or commit some other offence. But he was not a prisoner for long, as he died soon afterwards.

What became of SAÏJAH's little brothers and sisters I do not know. The hut in which they lived at BADUR stood empty for a while, but soon collapsed, since it was only built of bamboo roofed with palm leaves. A little dust and dirt covered the spot which had seen much suffering. There are many such spots in LEBAK.

SAÏJAH was fifteen when his father left for BUITENZORG. He did not go with him, because he had bigger plans in his head. He had been told that in BATAVIA there were so many gentlemen who rode in *bendies* and hence he would easily find a place there as *bendie* boy, for which someone is usually chosen who is still young, not full-grown, so that he will not upset the balance of the light, two-wheeled vehicle by adding too much weight at the back of it. He had been assured that there was much to be earned in such service, provided one behaved oneself. In fact, in this manner he might even save enough money in three years to buy two buffaloes. The prospect looked rosy to him. With proud step, the step of a man with great affairs on hand, he entered ADINDA's house, after his father had gone, and informed her of his scheme.

'Just think,' he said, 'when I return, we shall be old enough to get married, and we shall have two buffaloes!'

'That is very good, SAÏJAH! I shall be pleased to marry you when you come back. I shall spin, and weave *sarongs* and *slendangs*, and *batik* cloths, and be very industrious all that time.'

'Oh, that I believe, ADINDA! But ... suppose I find you married?'

'SAÏJAH, you know perfectly well that I shall marry no one else. My father promised me to your father.'

'But what do *you* think?'

'I shall marry you, rest assured of that!'

'When I come back, I shall call from afar...'

'Who can hear that, when we are pounding rice in the village?'

'That is true. But ADINDA ... oh yes, I have a better idea: Wait for me near the *jati* wood, under the *ketapan* tree, where you gave me the *melati* flower.'

'But, SAÏJAH, how shall I know when I must go and wait for you at the *ketapan*?'

SAÏJAH thought for a moment, and said:

'Count the moons. I shall be away thrice twelve moons ... not counting this one. Look, ADINDA—cut a notch in your rice block at the coming of every new moon. When you shall have cut thrice twelve notches, I shall arrive under the *ketapan* on the following day. Will you promise to be there?'

'Yes, SAÏJAH! I shall be under the *ketapan* near the *jati* wood when you return!'

Then Saïjah tore a strip from his blue turban, which was very threadbare. And he gave that scrap of linen to Adinda, to keep as a pledge. And then he left her and Badur.

He walked for many days. He passed Rangkas-Betung, which was not yet the administrative centre of Lebak, and Warung-Gunung, where the Assistant Resident then lived, and the following day he saw Pandeglang, lying as in a garden. Yet another day and he arrived at Serang, and stood amazed at the splendour of so large a place, with so many houses, built of stone and roofed with red tiles. Saïjah had never seen anything like it before. He stayed there for a day because he was tired, but at night, when it was cool, he went on, and next day he came to Tangérang, before the shadow had descended to his lips, although he wore the big *tudung* which his father had left behind for him.

At Tangérang he bathed in the river near the ferry, and then rested in the house of an acquaintance of his father's, who showed him how to plait straw hats like those that come from Manila. He stayed one day to learn this, because he thought he might be able to earn some money at it later if he should not succeed in Batavia. The following day, towards nightfall, as it grew cool, he thanked his host heartily, and travelled on.

As soon as it was quite dark and no one could see, he took out the leaf in which he kept the *melati* that Adinda had given him under the *ketapan* tree. For the thought that he would not be seeing her again for such a long time had made him heavyhearted. On the first day, and even on the second, he had not felt his loneliness so deeply, because his soul had been wholly wrapped up in the idea of earning money with which to buy two buffaloes—a grand design indeed, since his father had never had more than one; and his thoughts had been too strongly concentrated on seeing Adinda again to leave room for very great sadness about parting from her. He had bidden her farewell with over-exalted hopes, and his thoughts had linked that farewell with the ultimate reunion under the *ketapan*. For so great a part did the prospect of that reunion play in his heart that he felt quite cheerful when he passed the tree on leaving BADUR, as though they were already past, those six-and-thirty moons which separated him from that moment. It had seemed to him that he only had to turn round, as if coming back from the journey, to see ADINDA waiting for him under the tree.

But the further he went from BADUR, and the more he felt the terrible length of only one day, the longer he began to find the six-and-thirty moons that lay before him. There was something in his soul that made him stride along less quickly. He felt a sadness in his knees, and, though it was not despondency that came over him, still it was melancholy, which is not far removed from despondency. He thought of turning back; but what would ADINDA have said to such faintheartedness?

So he walked on, although less swiftly than on the first day. He held the *melati* in his hand, and often pressed it to his breast. In those three days he had grown much older, and could no longer understand how he could have been so calm in the past, when ADINDA had lived so close to him and he could see her as often and as long as he liked! For *now* he would not be calm, if he could have expected that presently she would stand before him! Nor did he understand why, after their leavetaking, he had not turned round and gone back again to gaze on her just once more. And also he remembered how, only recently, he had quarrelled with her about the cord she had spun for her brothers' *lalayang*,[99] which had broken because, he maintained, there had been a flaw in her weaving, and that had lost them a wager with the children from CHIPURUT. 'How in the world,' he thought, 'could I have got angry with ADINDA over that? For even if she *had* spun a flaw in the cord, and if the match between BADUR and CHIPURUT *had* been lost through that, and not through the piece of glass so naughtily and dexterously thrown by little JA-MIN, hidden behind the *pagger*[100]—was I, even then, justified in behaving so harshly towards her and calling her ill names? Suppose I die in BATAVIA without having asked her pardon for such gross rudeness? Shan't I be remembered as an evil man, who flung abuse at girls? And when they hear that I died in a strange land, will not everyone at BADUR say: "It is a good thing SAÏJAH died, for he gave ADINDA the rough edge of his tongue"?'

Thus his thoughts took a course that differed widely from their previous exaltation; and involuntarily they found expression, first in broken words that were scarcely audible, but soon in a monologue, and finally in the sorrowful chant the translation of which I give here. My original intention was to introduce some metre and rhyme into my version, but, like Havelaar, I think it will be better without such a corset:

'I do not know where I shall die.
I have seen the great sea on the South Coast, when I was there making salt with my father;
If I die on the sea, and they throw my body into the deep water, sharks will come.
They will swim round about my corpse, and ask: "Which of us shall devour this body, descending through the water?"
I shall not hear.

I do not know where I shall die.
I have seen the burning house of PA-ANSU, which he had set on fire himself because he was demented.
If I die in a burning house, the flaming timbers will fall down on my corpse,
and outside the house there will be a hue and cry of people, throwing water to kill the fire.
I shall not hear.

I do not know where I shall die.
I have seen little SI-UNAH fall from the *klappa* tree, when he was picking a *klappa* for his mother.
If I fall from a *klappa* tree I shall lie dead at its foot, in the bushes, like SI-UNAH.

My mother will not cry out for me, for she is dead. But others
will cry with loud voices: "Lo, there lies SAÏJAH!"
I shall not hear.

I do not know where I shall die.
I have seen the dead body of PA-LISU, who had died of old age,
for his hair was white.
If I die of old age, with white hair, the keening women will stand
round my body.
And loudly they will lament, like the keening women round PA-
LISU's body. And the grandchildren will also weep, very loudly.
I shall not hear.

I do not know where I shall die.
I have seen many at BADUR who had died. They were wrapped in
a white garment, and were buried in the earth.
If I die at BADUR, and they bury me outside the village, eastward
against the hill, where the grass is high,
then will ADINDA pass that way, and the hem of her *sarong* will
softly sweep the grass in passing...
And I shall hear.'

SAÏJAH arrived in BATAVIA. He asked a gentleman to take him into
his service as groom, which the gentleman promptly did, because
he did not understand SAÏJAH's language, Sundanese. For in BATA-
VIA people like to have servants who have not yet learnt Malay, and
consequently are not yet so corrupted as others who have been
longer in contact with European civilization. SAÏJAH soon learned
Malay, but he behaved in an exemplary manner, for he never ceased
to think of the two buffaloes he wanted to buy, and of ADINDA. He
grew tall and strong because he ate every day, which was not always
possible at BADUR. He was popular in the stables, and would certainly not have been rejected if he had asked the hand of the coachman's daughter in marriage. And his master, too, liked SAÏJAH so

much that he soon promoted him to the position of house boy. His wages were raised, and he was constantly being given presents, for people were extremely satisfied with his work. The mistress of the house had read *Sue*'s novel *The Wandering Jew*, that nine days' wonder, and could not help thinking of Prince DJALMA when she saw SAÏJAH. And the young ladies also understood better than before why the Javanese painter RADHEN SALEH had had such a vogue in Paris.

But they thought SAÏJAH ungrateful when, after nearly three years' service, he gave notice and asked for a certificate of good conduct. However, they could not refuse him this; and SAÏJAH set out for his native village with a joyful heart.

He passed PISING, where Havelaar had once lived, long before. But that SAÏJAH did not know. And even if he had known, he carried in his soul quite different things to occupy him. He counted the treasures he was taking home. In a bamboo roll he had his pass and his master's testimonial. In a small cylindrical case, attached to a leather strap, something heavy seemed to be constantly nudging his shoulder, but he liked to feel it ... and no wonder! In it were thirty Spanish dollars, enough to buy three buffaloes. What would ADINDA say?! And that was not all. On his back could be seen the silver-mounted sheath of a kris which he carried in his belt. The hilt was undoubtedly of finely carved *kamuning*,[101] for he had wrapped it most carefully in a piece of silk. And he had still more treasures. In the knot of his loin-cloth he was keeping a woman's girdle of broad silver links with a gold *ikat-pendieng* or clasp. To be sure, the girdle was short, but then she was so slender ... ADINDA!

And hanging from a thin cord round his neck, beneath his vest, he carried a little silk bag containing some dried *melati*.

Was it surprising that he tarried no longer at TANGÉRANG than was necessary to visit the friend of his father who made such fine straw hats? Was it surprising that he had little to say to the girls he met on the road, who asked him 'Whither and whence?', which is the customary greeting in those parts? Was it surprising that he no longer thought SERANG so splendid, now that he had come to know BATAVIA? That he no longer crept away into the *pagger* as he had done three years before, when the Resident drove past, now that he had seen the much greater Lord who lives at Buitenzorg and is the grandfather of the SUSUHUNAN of SOLO?[102] Was it surprising that he paid little attention to the stories of the fellow-travellers who walked part of the way with him and were full of all the news of BAN-TAN-KIDUL? That he scarcely listened when they told him that the attempts to grow coffee had been entirely abandoned, after much fruitless labour? That the District Chief of PARANG-KUJANG had been sentenced to fourteen days' detention in his father-in-law's house for highway robbery? That the Divisional centre was now RANGKAS-BETUNG? That a new Assistant Resident had arrived because the previous one had died a few months before? And how that new official had spoken at the first *Sebah* meeting? How for some time now nobody had been punished for complaining, and how the people hoped that all that had been stolen would be returned or made good?

No ... he had sweeter visions before his mind's eye. He scanned the clouds for the *ketapan* tree, as he was still too far off to see it at BADUR. He clutched at the surrounding air as though wishing to embrace the form he would find waiting for him under that tree. He pictured to himself ADINDA's face, her head, her shoulder ... he saw the heavy *kondeh*, so black and glossy, caught in its own snare, hanging down her neck ... he saw her great eyes, lustrous in dark reflection ... the nostrils she had so haughtily wrinkled as a child whenever he teased her—how was it possible!—and the corner of her mouth, in which she stored a smile. He saw her breast, which by now would be swelling under the *kabaya* ... he saw how the *sa-rong*, which she herself had woven, tightly sheathed her hips and, following the curve of the thigh, descended past the knee in exquisite undulation to her small foot...

No, he heard but little of what people said to him. He heard quite different tones. He heard ADINDA say: 'Welcome to you, SAÏJAH!

I have thought of you while spinning and weaving, and while pounding rice in the block that carries thrice twelve notches made by my hand. Here am I, under the *ketapan*, on the first day of the new moon. Welcome to you, SAÏJAH: I will be your wife!'

That was the music which sounded so delicious in his ear, and made him deaf to all the news the people told him on his way.

At last he saw the *ketapan*. Or rather, he saw a great dark patch which hid many stars from his eyes. That could only be the *jati* wood, near the tree where he was to see ADINDA again, at sunrise tomorrow. He searched in the dark, feeling with his hands the trunks of many trees. It was not long before he found a familiar roughness on the south side of one, and he put his finger into the slit which SI-PANTEH had hacked in it with his *parang*,[103] to exorcize the *pontianak*[104] who was responsible for the toothache of PANTEH'S mother, shortly before his little brother was born. This was the *ketapan* SAÏJAH sought.

Yes, this was indeed the spot where he had seen ADINDA for the first time with other eyes than the rest of his playfellows, because there she had refused for the first time to take part in a game which she had played with all the children—boys and girls—only a little while before. And it was there that she had given him the *melati*.

He sat down at the foot of the tree, and looked up at the stars. And when one shot across the sky, he took it to be a greeting to him on his return to BADUR. And he wondered whether ADINDA would now be asleep? And whether she had correctly marked the moons in her rice block? It would grieve him so deeply if she had missed one, as though they had not been enough ... six-and-thirty! And he wondered whether she had *batiked* pretty *sarongs* and *slendangs*? And he also asked himself, with some curiosity, who might now be living in his father's house? And his childhood came back to him, and his mother, and how that buffalo had saved him from the tiger, and he could not help musing on what might have become of ADINDA if the buffalo had been less staunch.

He paid close attention to the setting of the stars in the west, and with every star that vanished below the horizon he calculated how much nearer the sun was to rising in the east, and how much nearer he was himself to seeing ADINDA again.

For she would be sure to come at the first gleam, yes, she would already be there in the grey of early dawn … oh why had she not come to the tree the day before?

It grieved him that she had not anticipated it — the glorious moment which had shone before him with ineffable radiance for three long years. And, unjust as he was in the selfishness of his love, it seemed to him that ADINDA should have been there, waiting for *him*, who now complained—and before the appointed time, at that! —because he had to wait for *her*.

He complained without cause. For the sun had still not yet risen, the Eye of Day had still not cast a first glance on the plain. To be sure, the stars were paling up there above his head, mortified over the approaching end of their reign … to be sure, strange colours streamed across the summits of the mountains, which looked darker the more sharply they were outlined against a lighter background… to be sure, something glowing fleeted hither and thither through the clouds in the east—arrows of gold and fire were being shot to and fro, following the skyline. But they vanished again, seeming to drop down behind the incomprehensible curtain that continued to veil the day from SAÏJAH's eyes.

And nevertheless it gradually grew lighter and lighter around him. He could already see the landscape, and he could already make out the tufted crest of the *klappa* wood in which BADUR lies hidden… there slept ADINDA!

No, she slept no longer! How could she sleep? Did she not know SAÏJAH would be waiting for her? Assuredly she had not slept at all that night! Doubtless the village watchman had knocked at the door to ask why the *pelitah*[105] was still burning in her little house; and with a sweet laugh she had told him that a vow was keeping her up to finish weaving the *slendang* she was working on, which had to be ready for the first day of the new moon…

Or she had spent the night in darkness, sitting on her rice block and counting with eager fingers to make sure there really were six-and-thirty deep notches carved in it, side by side. And she had amused herself with a pretence of fright, imagining she might have miscounted and that perhaps one of them was still wanting ... so that again, and yet again, and over and over again, she could revel in the glorious certainty that without a shadow of doubt thrice twelve moons had passed since she had last seen SAÏJAH.

She, too, because it was already growing so light, would strain her eyes in a vain endeavour to send her glances down over the horizon, that they might meet the sun, the laggard sun, which tarried ... tarried...

There came a streak of bluish red that fastened on to the clouds, and their rims lit up and glowed. And lightning flashed, and once again fiery arrows shot through the air, but this time they did not fall, they fixed themselves firmly on the dark background, and shed their glow around them in wider and wider circles, and met, crossing, swinging, winding, wandering, and they fused together in fiery sheaves, and flashed and shimmered in golden gleams on a ground of nacre, and there was red, and blue, and yellow, and silver, and purple, and azure in it all ... Oh God! That was the dawn; that was the coming of ADINDA!

SAÏJAH had never learnt to pray, and it would have been a pity to teach him, for holier prayer and more fervent thanksgiving than were found in the speechless ecstasy of his soul could not have been expressed in human language.

He did not want to go to BADUR. To *see* ADINDA again appeared to him less glorious than to be *sure* of seeing her again. He made himself comfortable at the foot of the *ketapan*, and let his eyes stray over the countryside. Nature smiled on him, and seemed to bid him welcome as a mother welcomes her returning child. And just as the mother depicts her joy by deliberately recalling past sorrow, by showing what she had preserved as a keepsake during her child's absence, so did SAÏJAH delight himself by looking again at so many spots that had witnessed episodes in his short life. But however much his eyes or his thoughts might wander round, his gaze and his longing returned every time to the path that leads from BADUR to the *ketapan* tree. All that his senses perceived bore the name ADINDA. He saw the precipice on the left, where the earth was so yellow and where a young buffalo had once slid into the depths: there the villagers had come together to save the animal—for it is no trivial matter to lose a young buffalo!—and they had let each other down on strong *rattan* cords. ADINDA's father had been the bravest ... oh, how ADINDA had clapped her hands!

And over there, on the other side, where the clump of coconut palms waved above the huts of the village, somewhere there SI-UNAH had fallen from a tree and died. How his mother had wept: 'because SI-UNAH was still so small,' she wailed ... as though she would have grieved less if he had been bigger! But it was true, he *was* small, for he was smaller and more fragile even than ADINDA...

No one came along the path that led from BADUR to the *ketapan*. But she would come by and by; it was still very early.

SAÏJAH saw a *bajing*[106] darting to and fro about the trunk of a *klappa* tree, with frisky nimbleness. The little creature—a plague to the owner of the tree, but so charming in its appearance and movements—clambered tirelessly up and down. SAÏJAH saw it and forced himself to keep looking at it, because that gave his mind some rest from the hard labour in which it had been engaged since sunrise... rest from the exhausting strain of waiting. Anon his impressions took the form of words; and he sang of what was passing in his soul. I would sooner *read* his song to you in Malay, that Italian of the East; but here is the translation:

'See how the *bajing* seeks food to sustain him in the *klappa* tree.
He climbs, descends, darts to left and right,
he goes round the tree, leaps, falls, rises and falls again:
he has no wings, and yet is swift as a bird.

Happiness to you, my *bajing*, may bliss befall you!
You will certainly find the food you seek...
but I sit alone by the *jati* wood,
waiting for the food of my heart.

Long has the belly of my *bajing* been filled...
Long has he been back in the comfort of his nest...
But ever my soul
and my heart are bitterly sad... ADINDA!'

And still there was no one on the path leading from BADUR to the *ketapan*...

SAÏJAH's eye fell on a butterfly, that seemed to rejoice at the growing warmth of the day:

'See how the butterfly flits hither and thither.
His tiny wings gleam like a many-tinted flower.
His little heart loves the blossom of the *kenari*:
surely he is seeking his fragrant belovéd!

Happiness to you, my butterfly, may bliss befall you!
You will certainly find what you seek...
But I sit alone by the *jati* wood,
waiting for the love of my heart.

Long ago has the butterfly kissed
the *kenari* blossom he so much adores...
But ever my soul
and my heart are bitterly sad... ADINDA!'

And there was no one on the path leading from BADUR to the *ketapan*.

The sun was already high... there was already heat in the air.

'See how the sun glitters yonder: high,
high above the hill of *waringin* trees!
She feels too warm, she would sink down,
to sleep in the sea, as in the arms of a spouse.

Happiness to you, O sun, may bliss befall you!
What you seek you will certainly find...
But I sit alone by the *jati* wood,
waiting for rest for my heart.

Long will the sun have gone down,
and sleep in the sea, when all is dark...
And ever my soul
and my heart will be bitterly sad... ADINDA!'

Still there was no one on the path leading from BADUR to the *ketapan*.

'When butterflies no longer flit hither and thither,
when the stars no longer twinkle,
when the *melati* is no longer fragrant,
when there are no more sad hearts,
nor wild beasts in the wood...
when the sun shall stray from her path,
and the moon forget what east and west are...
if then ADINDA has still not come,
then shall an angel with dazzling wings
come down to earth, seeking what stayed behind.
Then shall my body lie here, under the *ketapan*...
My soul is bitterly sad... ADINDA!'

And still, still there was no one on the path leading from BADUR to
the *ketapan*.

'Then shall my body be seen by the angel.
He will point it out to his brothers, and will say:
"See, there a man has died and been forgotten!
His cold, stiff mouth kisses a *melati* flower.
Come, let us lift him up and take him to heaven,
him, who waited for ADINDA till he died.
Surely *he* should not be left behind here,
whose heart had strength to love so deeply!"

Then shall once more my stiff, cold mouth open
to call ADINDA, love of my heart...
Once more, once more shall I kiss the *melati*
given to me by *her* ... ADINDA ... ADINDA!'

There was no one on the path leading from BADUR to the *ketapan*.

Oh, she had undoubtedly fallen asleep towards dawn, worn out with watching through the night, with watching through many long nights! She had probably not slept for weeks: that was it!

Should he arise, and go to BADUR? No! Was it to seem as though he doubted she would come?

Suppose he called to the man yonder, who was driving his buffalo to the field? But the man was too far away. And besides, SAÏJAH did not want to *talk about* ADINDA, did not want to *ask after* ADINDA ... He wanted to *see* her, her only, her first! Oh surely, surely she would come soon!

He would wait, wait...

But what if she were ill, or ... dead?

Like a wounded deer, SAÏJAH flew up the path that leads from the *ketapan* to the village where Adinda lived. He saw nothing and heard nothing, and yet he could have heard something, for there were people standing in the road at the entrance to the village who called 'SAÏJAH, SAÏJAH!'

But ... was it his haste, his passion, which prevented him from finding ADINDA's house? In his headlong dash he had reached the

273

end of the road, where the village stops, and like a madman he returned, and smote his forehead because he had been able to pass *her* house without seeing it! But again he was back at the entrance to BADUR, and—God, God, was it a dream?—again he had not found ADINDA's house! Once more he flew back, and all at once he stood still, grasped his head with both his hands as though to press out of it the frenzy that overcame him, and cried loudly: 'Drunk... drunk... I am drunk!'

And the women of BADUR came out of their houses, and with pity they saw poor SAÏJAH standing there, for they recognized him and realized that he was looking for ADINDA's house, and they knew that there was no house of ADINDA's in the village of BADUR.

For, when the District Chief of PARANG-KUJANG took the buffalo of ADINDA's father...

I told you, reader, that my tale is monotonous.

...then ADINDA's mother had died of heartbreak. And her youngest sister had died, because she had no mother to suckle her. And ADINDA's father, who was afraid of being punished for not paying his land tax...

I know, I know, my tale *is* monotonous!

...ADINDA's father had fled the country. He had taken ADINDA with him, and her brothers. But he had heard how SAÏJAH's father had been punished with *rattan* stripes at BUITENZORG because he had left BADUR without a pass. And therefore ADINDA's father had not gone to BUITENZORG, nor to KRAWANG, nor to the PREANGER nor to the BATAVIAN DISTRICTS ... He had gone to CHILANGKAHAN, the District of LEBAK which borders on the sea. There he had hidden in the woods and awaited the arrival of PA-ENTO, PA-LONTAH, SI-UNIAH, PA-ANSIU, ABDUL-ISMA and a few more who had been robbed of their buffaloes by the District Chief of PARANG-KUJANG and were all afraid of being punished for not paying their land tax. During the night they had seized a fishing proa there, and had put out to sea. They had steered a westerly course, keeping the land to starboard as far as JAVA HEAD. Thence they had steered northwards, until they sighted TANAH-ITAM, which European sailors call PRINCES ISLAND. They had skirted the eastern coast of that island, and then they had made for KAISER'S BAY, taking their bearings by the high peak in the LAMPONG DISTRICTS. That, at any rate, was the route which people in LEBAK whispered into each other's ears whenever there was talk of 'official' buffalo-theft and unpaid land tax.

But the dazed SAÏJAH did not clearly understand what was said to him. He did not even quite grasp the news of his father's death. There was a buzzing in his ears, as though someone had beaten a gong in his head. He felt the blood being forced in jerks through the veins at his temples, which threatened to burst under the pressure. He did not speak, and stared dully about him, without seeing any of the things that were near him; and at last he burst into ghastly laughter.

An old woman took him along to her hut, and tended the poor crazy wretch. It was not long before he stopped laughing so horribly; but still he did not speak. Only during the night were those who shared the hut with him startled into wakefulness by his voice, when he sang tonelessly: '*I do not know where I shall die.*' And some of the inhabitants of BADUR put money together to pay for a sacrifice to the crocodiles of the CHIUJUNG for the recovery of SAÏJAH, whom they looked upon as demented.

But he was not demented.

For one night, when the moon was shining brightly, he rose from his *baleh-baleh* and stole softly out, and searched for the place where ADINDA had lived. It was not easy to find, because so many houses had fallen into ruins. But he seemed to recognize the place from the width of the angle which certain beams of light through the trees formed in meeting his eye, as the mariner takes his bearings from lighthouses or prominent mountain peaks.

Yes, it must be *there* ... ADINDA had lived *there*!

Stumbling over half-decayed bamboo and fragments of the fallen roof, he cleared a way for himself to the sanctuary he sought. And indeed, he still found portions of the upright wall beside which

ADINDA's *baleh-baleh* had stood, and stuck in that wall there was still the bamboo peg on which she had hung her dress when she lay down to sleep...

But the *baleh-baleh* had collapsed like the house, and was almost gone to dust. He picked up a handful of that dust, pressed it to his open lips, and drew a deep, deep breath...

Next day he asked the old woman who had looked after him where the rice block was that had stood in the compound before ADINDA's house. The woman was delighted to hear him speak, and went all round the village to find the block. When she was able to tell SAÏJAH who the new owner was, he followed her in silence, and, when he had been taken to the rice block, he counted on it two-and-thirty notches...

Then he gave the old woman as many Spanish dollars as would buy a buffalo, and left BADUR. At CHILANGKAHAN he bought a fisherman's proa, and in it, after a few days' sailing, he reached the LAMPONG DISTRICTS, where rebels were resisting the Dutch Government.

He joined a group of Bantammers, not so much in order to fight as to find ADINDA. For he was gentle by nature, and more suscepti-ble to sorrow than to rancour.

One day, when the rebels had again been defeated, he wandered about in a village that had just been taken by the Dutch army and was therefore in flames. SAÏJAH knew that the band which had been annihilated there had consisted largely of men from BANTAM. Like a ghost he roamed around in the huts which had not yet been en-tirely destroyed by the fire, and found the corpse of ADINDA's father, with a *klewang*-bayonet wound in the chest. Beside him SAÏ-JAH saw the three murdered brothers of ADINDA, youths, hardly more than children still; and a little farther away, the body of ADIN-DA, naked, horribly abused...

A narrow strip of blue linen protruded from the gaping wound in her breast that seemed to have ended a long struggle...

Then SAÏJAH rushed towards some Dutch soldiers who, with

levelled rifles, were driving the last surviving rebels into the fire of the blazing houses. With open arms he ran on to the broad sword-bayonets, pressed forward with all his might, and by a final effort even pushed the soldiers back, until the hilts of the bayonets grated against his breastbone.

And there was great rejoicing in BATAVIA over the latest victory, which had added fresh laurels to those already won by the Dutch East Indian Army. And the Governor-General wrote to the Mother-land to say that peace had been restored in the LAMPONG DISTRICTS. And the King of the Netherlands, advised by his Ministers, once again rewarded so much heroism with many decorations.

And doubtless, at Sunday service or prayer meeting, hymns of thanksgiving rose to heaven from the hearts of the godly on learn-ing that the 'Lord of Hosts' had again fought under the Dutch banner...

> 'But, moved by so much woe, that day
> God turned their offerings away!'[107]

I have made the end of SAÏJAH's story shorter than I need have done if I had felt inclined to depict horrors. The reader will have noticed how I lingered over my hero's sojourn under the *ketapan* as though unwilling to face the tragic denouement, which I touched on only superficially, with aversion. And yet that was not my intention when I started to write about SAÏJAH. At first I feared I should need stronger colours if I was to move the reader when describing such strange conditions. Little by little, however, I realized that it would be an insult to my public to believe that they would like to have *more* blood spilt in my picture.

And yet I *could* have done so, for I have documents before me... but no: I would sooner make a confession.

Yes, a confession! Reader ... I do not know whether SAÏJAH loved ADINDA. Nor whether he went to BATAVIA. Nor whether he was murdered in the LAMPONG DISTRICTS by Dutch bayonets. I do not know whether his father succumbed as a result of the *rattan* flogging he received for leaving BADUR without a pass. I do not know whether ADINDA counted the moons by notches in her rice block.

I do not know all this!

But I know *more*. I know, *and I can prove*, that there were *many* ADINDAS and many SAÏJAHS, and that *what is fiction in particular is truth in general*. I have already said that I can give the names of persons who were driven from their homes by oppression, like the fathers of SAÏJAH and ADINDA. It is not my purpose in this work to make statements such as would be required by a tribunal sitting to pronounce judgment on the manner in which Dutch authority is exercised in the East Indies—statements which would only have power to convince those who had the patience to read through them with an attention and interest not to be expected from a public that reads for pleasure. Hence, instead of bare names of persons and places, with dates—instead of a copy of *the list of thefts and extortions which lies before me*—instead of these, I have tried to give a sketch of what *may* go on in the hearts of poor people robbed of their means of subsistence, or, more precisely: I have only *suggested* what may go on in their hearts, fearing that I might be too wide of the mark if I firmly delineated emotions which I never felt myself.

But ... as regards the *underlying truth*? O that I were summoned to substantiate what I have written! O that people would say: 'You have invented this SAÏJAH ... he never sang that song ... no ADINDA ever lived at BADUR!' But then, again ... O that such might be said by those with the power and the desire to do justice as soon as I had proved I was no slanderer!

Is the parable of the Good Samaritan a lie because perhaps no despoiled traveller was ever received into a Samaritan house? Is the parable of the Sower a lie because—as everyone realizes—no husbandman would ever cast his seed on stony ground? Or—to come down to a level nearer that of my book—may one deny the truth which underlies *Uncle Tom's Cabin* because LITTLE EVA never existed? Shall it be said to the authoress of that immortal plea—immortal not on account of art or talent, but because of its *purpose* and the *impression* it makes—shall it be said to her: 'You have lied, the slaves are not ill-treated, for ... not all of your book is true: it's a novel!'? Was not she, too, compelled to give, instead of an enumeration of dry facts, a story embodying those facts, so that the realization of the need for reform might penetrate the hearts of her readers? Would her book have been read if she had given it the form of a court deposition? Is it her fault—or mine—that truth, in order to find an entrance, so often has to borrow the guise of a lie?

And to others, who will perhaps contend that I have idealized SAÏJAH and his love, I must put the question: 'How do you know?' For it is a fact that very few Europeans think it worth their trouble to stoop and observe the emotions of those coffee- and sugar-producing machines we call 'natives'. But, even supposing this objection was well-founded, he who brings it forward as evidence against the main thesis of my book gives me a great victory. For, translated, these considerations are as follows: 'The evil you combat does not exist, or is not so very bad, *because* the native is not like your SAÏJAH ... the ill-treatment of the Javanese is not so great an evil as it would be if you had drawn your SAÏJAH more accurately. The Sundanese does not sing such songs; does not love like that; does not feel like that; and therefore...'

No, Minister for the Colonies ... No, Governors-General (retired) ... *that* is not what you have to prove! You have to prove that the people are not ill-treated, irrespective of whether there are sentimental SAÏJAHS among them or not. Or would you dare maintain that it is lawful to steal buffaloes from people who do not love, who sing no melancholy songs, who are not sentimental?

If I were attacked on literary grounds I should defend the accuracy of my picture of SAÏJAH. But in a political context I would at once concede the truth of any strictures on that accuracy, in order to prevent the main argument from being shifted on to a wrong basis. It is all the same to me whether I am considered an incompetent artist, provided the admission be made that the ill-treatment of the native is: OUTRAGEOUS! For that was the word used in the note by Havelaar's predecessor, as shown to Controleur Verbrugge—*a note which I have before me*.

But I have other evidence! And that is just as well, for Havelaar's predecessor might also have been wrong.

Alas! If *he* was wrong, he paid very dearly for it!

18

It was afternoon. Havelaar came out of his room and found his Tina on the front verandah, waiting with the tea. Mrs Slotering emerged from her house, and seemed to be coming across to the Havelaars; but all at once she went towards the gate, and made quite vehement signs to a man, who had just that moment entered, to go away. She stood still until she was sure he had gone; and then she returned along the grass plot, towards Havelaar's house.

'I'm going to find out the meaning of this, once and for all!' said Havelaar; and, after welcoming her, he asked, in a jocular manner, so that she might not think he begrudged her that remnant of authority in a compound which had formerly been hers:

'Well, Mrs Slotering, I wish you would tell me why you always send away anyone who enters the compound? Suppose, now, that man who just came in had had chickens for sale, or something else which we could do with in the kitchen?'

Mrs Slotering's face took on a pained expression, which did not escape Havelaar's eye. 'Oh,' she exclaimed, 'there are so many bad people about!'

'Quite, that's the case everywhere. But if we make things so difficult, the good ones will stay away too. Come now, Mrs Slotering, do tell me quite frankly why you keep such a strict watch on the compound?'

Havelaar looked at her, and tried in vain to read the answer in her moist eyes. He pressed a little harder for an explanation… the widow burst into tears, and said that her husband had been poisoned at PARANG-KUJANG, at the house of the District Chief.

'He wanted to be just, Mr Havelaar,' the poor woman went on, 'he wanted to put a stop to the ill-treatment under which the people suffer so much. He admonished and threatened the Chiefs, at meetings and in writing … you must have found his letters in the files?'

That was true. Havelaar had read those letters, *copies of which are lying before me.*

'He talked to the Resident about it over and over again,' the widow continued, 'but always to no purpose. Everybody knew that these things were done on behalf of the Regent and under his protection, and that the Resident didn't want to impeach the Regent to the Government, so the interviews all led to nothing but further ill-treatment of the people who had complained. As a result my poor husband said that if there was no improvement by the end of the year he would go straight to the Governor-General about it. That was in November. Shortly afterwards he set out on a tour of inspection, had lunch at the house of the DHEMANG of PARANG-KUJANG, and was brought hime in a pitiful state. He did nothing but point to his stomach and cry: "Fire, fire!" and a few hours later he was dead. And he had always been the picture of health!'

'Did you get the doctor from SERANG?' asked Havelaar.

'Yes, but my husband died soon after the doctor arrived, so he only treated him for a very short time. I didn't dare to tell the doctor what I suspected, because I knew that, in my condition, I should not be able to leave this place for some time, and I was afraid whoever had done it might take revenge on me and the children if I opened my mouth. I have heard that, like my husband, you are opposing the abuses that are rampant here, and that is why I don't have a minute's peace. I wanted to keep all this from you, in order not to alarm you and Mrs Havelaar, and so I simply watched the compound, to make sure no strangers got to the kitchen.'

And now it became clear to Tina why Mrs Slotering had continued to maintain a separate household, and had not even wished to make use of the kitchen 'which was so big, after all'.

Havelaar retired to his room and wrote a letter to the doctor at SERANG, asking for details of the symptoms observed at Slotering's death. The answer he ultimately received was not in accordance with the suspicions of the widow. The doctor said Slotering had died from an 'abscess of the liver'. I have not been able to ascertain whether such a complaint can manifest itself suddenly and cause death in a few hours. I think that serious consideration must be given here to Mrs Slotering's statement that her husband had always enjoyed good health up till then. But even if we attach no value to such a statement—seeing that the conception of what constitutes health is very subjective, especially among non-medical persons— the important question still remains as to whether a man who dies today of an 'abscess of the liver' could yesterday have *mounted a horse* with the intention of inspecting a mountainous region so large that it takes twenty hours to cross it in some directions. The doctor who treated Slotering may have been a capable physician and yet still have been mistaken in judging the symptoms of the illness, unprepared as he was to suspect foul play.

However this may be, I cannot prove that Havelaar's predecessor was poisoned, since Havelaar was not allowed the time to clear up the matter. But I can certainly prove *that those about him considered he had been poisoned*, and that they linked their suspicion with his desire to resist injustice.

Meanwhile Havelaar sent for Controleur Verbrugge.

Verbrugge entered the room. Havelaar asked him curtly:

'What did Mr Slotering die of?'

'I don't know.'

'Was he poisoned?'

'I don't know, but...'

'Speak up, Verbrugge!'

'He tried to stamp out the abuses here, Mr Havelaar, like you, and ... and ... and...'

'Well? Go on!'

'I am convinced that he ... *would* have been poisoned if he had stayed here longer.'

'Write that down!'

Verbrugge wrote down what he had said: *it lies before me*!

'Another thing. Is it true, or is it *not* true, that people are oppressed and exploited in LEBAK?'

Verbrugge did not answer.

'Answer me, Verbrugge!'

283

'I ... don't dare.'

'Write it down, then, that you don't dare!'

Verbrugge wrote it down: *it lies before me*.

'Good! Now another thing: you don't dare answer my last question, but recently, when there was talk of a case of *poisoning*, you told me you were the sole support of your sisters in BATAVIA, didn't you? Isn't *that* perhaps the reason for your fear, the root of what I've always called your *halfheartedness*?'

'Yes!'

'Write that down.'

Verbrugge wrote it down: *his statement lies before me*.

'Right,' said Havelaar, 'now I know enough.' And Verbrugge could go.

Havelaar went out on to the verandah and played with little Max, whom he kissed more tenderly even than usual. When Mrs Slotering had gone he sent the child away, and called Tina into his room.

'Darling Tina, I have a favour to ask you. I should like you and Max to go to BATAVIA: today I am bringing a charge against the Regent.'

She threw her arms around his neck, and refused to obey him for the first time, sobbing:

'No, Max, no, Max, I won't ... I *won't*! *We will eat and drink together!*'

Had Havelaar been wrong when he maintained that she had as little right to blow her nose as the women of Arles?

He wrote and sent off to the Resident the letter which I reproduce here. Since I have given some idea of the circumstances in which this letter was written, I do not think it necessary to emphasize the resolute devotion to duty which shines through it, or the kindheartedness which moved Havelaar to try to protect the Regent from too severe a punishment. But it will not be so superfluous to draw attention to Havelaar's cautiousness, which kept him from uttering a word about the discovery he had just made concerning Slotering's death in order that the positive nature of his present case should not be weakened by uncertainty about an accusation which, though important, was as yet unproved. He intended to have the body of his predecessor exhumed and scientifically examined as soon as the Regent had been got out of the way and his adherents rendered powerless for evil. But, as I have said, he was not given the opportunity.

In my transcriptions of official documents—transcriptions which otherwise correspond word for word with the original—I think I may be allowed to replace the silly formal titles by simple pronouns. I expect my readers to possess enough good taste to approve this alteration:

No. 88. *Secret*
Urgent   *Rangkas-Betung,* 24 February 1856
To the Resident of Bantam

Since I took up my duties here, a month ago, I have been mainly occupied in investigating the manner in which the native Chiefs discharge their obligations towards the population as regards *statute labour*, *pundutan*[108] and similar matters.

I very soon discovered that the Regent called up people on his own authority and for his own benefit in numbers greatly exceeding his legally permitted number of *panchens* and *kemits*.[109]

I hesitated between formally reporting the matter at once and the desire to turn this senior native official from his ways by kindliness, followed by threats if necessary. But ultimately I took the second course, for two reasons: I wanted to put a stop to the malpractices concerned and at the same time to avoid excessive severity at the outset in dealing with such an old servant of the Government, especially in view of the bad examples which, I gather, he has often had before his eyes. Furthermore, I took into consideration the particular circumstance that he is expecting a visit from two relatives, the Regents of BANDUNG and CHANYOR (at any rate the latter, who, I believe, is already on the way with a large retinue), so that he had been even more tempted than usual to break the law in order to

285

make the requisite preparations for those visits—was, in fact, *compelled* to do so, by the straitened condition of his finances.

All this disposed me to take a lenient view of things that had already happened, but not at all to indulgence for the future.

I insisted on immediate cessation of every illegal practice.

I have already notified you privately of this provisional attempt on my part to bring the Regent to a sense of his duty by treating him gently.

It has, however, become evident that he sets everything at naught with barefaced insolence, and by virtue of my official oath I feel obliged to inform you:

That I *accuse the* REGENT OF LEBAK, RADHEN ADHIPATTI KARTA NATTA NAGARA, of abuse of authority by illegal use of the labour of his subjects, and that I *suspect* him of extortion by requisitioning goods in kind either without payment or for arbitrarily fixed, inadequate payment;

Further, that I suspect his son-in-law, the DHEMANG of PARANG-KUJANG, of complicity in the aforementioned acts.

In order that both indictments may be properly prepared, I propose that you instruct me:

    1. to send the Regent of LEBAK with the utmost speed to SERANG, taking care that neither before his departure nor during the journey shall he be given the opportunity of influencing, by bribery or otherwise, the testimonies I shall have to obtain;

    2. to detain the Dhemang of PARANG-KUJANG in custody until further notice;

    3. to take similar measures against such persons of lesser rank who, since they belong to the Regent's family, may be expected to influence the objectivity of the proposed inquiry;

    4. to hold this inquiry at once, and to give a full report on the result.

I would also suggest for your consideration that the visit of the Regent of CHANYOR be countermanded.

Finally, I beg to assure you—no doubt superfluously, since you know the Division of LEBAK better than I have yet been able to get to know it—that, from a *political* point of view, there is no objection whatever to a strictly just treatment of this case, but that, on the contrary, I greatly fear the consequences if it is *not* cleared up. For I am informed that the people who, as a witness told me, are desperate from their troubles, have long been looking out for deliverance.

I am partly sustained in the difficult duty I perform in writing this letter by the hope that I shall be permitted, in due time, to urge certain extenuating circumstances on behalf of the old Regent, for whose plight, however much it may be due to his own fault, I nevertheless feel deep sympathy.

The Assistant Resident of Lebak
Max Havelaar

Next day he received a reply from ... the Resident of BANTAM? Oh no—from Mr Slymering, in his *private* capacity!

This reply is a priceless contribution to knowledge of the way in which the business of government is carried on in the Dutch East Indies. Mr Slymering complained 'that Havelaar had not first acquainted him orally with the matters dealt with in letter No. 88.' Of course ... because there would then have been a better chance of '*fixing*' things. And furthermore: 'that Havelaar *disturbed him in his pressing occupations*'!

The man was no doubt occupied with an annual report on peaceful peace! I have his letter before me, and can hardly believe my eyes. I reread the letter from the Assistant Resident of LEBAK ... I place *him* and the Resident of BANTAM, Havelaar and Slymering, side by side...

That Scarfman is a common blackguard! You must know, reader, that Bastiaans has again taken to not turning up at the office because of his rheumatism. Now I make it a matter of conscience not

to squander the funds of the firm—*Last & Co.*—for where principles are at stake I am adamant; and a couple of days ago I recollected
that Scarfman really writes quite a good hand and, since he looks so
shabby, he could probably be got for not much money. So I felt it
was my duty to the firm to provide for a replacement for Bastiaans
in the cheapest manner possible. Off I went, then, to the Lange-
Leidsche-dwarsstraat. The woman was out in her junk shop this
time, but did not seem to recognize me, although it was not so long
ago that I had told her I was Mister *Droogstoppel, Coffee broker of Lauriergracht*. There is always something a bit insulting about that not
recognizing a person. But since it is a little less cold now, I wasn't
wearing my fur-trimmed coat, as I had been on the previous occasion, so I put it down to the coat and shan't take it too much to
heart ... the insult, I mean. Well, I told her once more that I was
Mister *Droogstoppel*, of *Lauriergracht, Coffee broker*, and asked her to
go and see whether that Scarfman chap was at home (I didn't want
to deal with his wife, as I had done last time, she's always discontented). But would you believe it, my rag-and-bone woman refused! She couldn't be climbing up and downstairs all day for that
poverty-stricken lot, she said, I'd better go and see for myself. And
then I again got a description of the stairs and landings, which I
didn't need at all, for I always know how to get to a place when I've
been there once, because I always take such careful note of everything. I've made a habit of doing that in business. So I climbed the
stairs, and knocked at the door I knew, which opened at my touch.
I entered and, since there was no one in the room, I had a good look
round. Not that there was much to see. A pair of short child's trousers, with an embroidered strip running down them, was hanging
over a chair ... why do such people have to wear embroidered trousers? In a corner stood a suitcase, not very heavy, which I absent-
mindedly lifted by the handle, and on the mantelpiece lay some
books, which I quickly glanced into. A queer collection! Some volumes of BYRON, HORACE, BASTIAT, BÉRANGER, and ... guess! A Bible, a complete Bible, with the *Apocrypha* and all! That was some-

thing I *certainly* hadn't expected to find at Scarfman's. And it seemed to have been read, too, for I found a lot of notes relating to the Scriptures, on odd scraps of paper—all in the same handwriting as the papers in that cursed parcel. He seemed to have made a special study of the Book of Job, for the Bible fell open easily at that place. I suppose he is beginning to feel the hand of the Lord, and so he's trying to make his peace with Him by reading the Good Book. I don't object to that. But, while I was still waiting, my eye happened to fall on a lady's workbox which was standing on the table. I looked through it unthinkingly. It contained a pair of half-finished child's stockings and a lot of silly verses, and also a letter to Scarfman's wife, as could be seen from the address. The letter was open, and looked as if it had been crumpled up in anger. Now, it is a firm principle with me never to read anything that is not addressed to me, because I don't think that's good form. So I never do it when it's not to my advantage. But now something told me it was my duty to take a look at that letter, because it might perhaps afford me guidance in the philanthropic plan that had led me to visit Scarfman. I reflected how surely the Lord is always near His own, since now He had unexpectedly give me a chance of getting to know something more about this man, and thus protected me against the danger of doing a kindness to an immoral person. I pay careful attention to such hints from the Lord, and this has often come in very useful in business. To my great surprise I saw that this wife of Scarfman's was of very good family—at any rate, the letter was signed by a relative whose name is of high repute in Holland and, I must say, I was really enchanted by the beauty of it all. The writer seemed to be one who laboured diligently for the Lord, for he said that Scarfman's wife ought to obtain a separation from such a wretch, who let her suffer poverty, who couldn't earn his living, and who was a scoundrel into the bargain, because he was in debt... that the writer of the letter was concerned over her lot, although she had brought it on herself, as she had forsaken the Lord and followed Scarfman ... that she must return to the Lord, and that then perhaps the whole family would join forces to find her some needlework to do. But, first and foremost, she had to get away from that Scarfman, who was a real disgrace to them all.

In short, there was not more edification to be found in church than there was in that letter.

I knew enough, and was grateful for having been warned in so marvellous a manner. For without that warning I should certainly again have become the victim of my own kind heart. I decided to give Bastiaans another chance until I found a suitable replacement, for I hate putting anybody into the street, and at present we can't spare one man, there's so much doing.

The reader will no doubt want to know how I got on at the last party, and whether I found the *triolet*. Well, I never went to that party! Wonderful things have come to pass: I have been to Drie-bergen with my wife and Marie. My father-in-law old Last, the son of the first Last—who was there when the Meyers were still in the firm, but they've long been out—old Last had repeatedly said he would like to see my wife and Marie. Now it happened to be quite nice weather, and my dread of the love story Stern had been threatening us with suddenly made me recall that invitation. I spoke about it to our book-keeper, who is a man of much experience; and after mature deliberation he suggested I should sleep on the matter. I at once decided to do that, for I am always quick to act. The very next morning I realized how sensible the book-keeper's advice had been, for night had given me the idea that I could not do better than postpone my decision until Friday. In short, after having fully weighed all the pros and cons—there was much to be said for our plan, but much against it, too—we went on Saturday afternoon and returned on the Monday morning. I should not tell you all this in such detail if it were not closely connected with my book. In the first place, I am anxious that you should know why I do not protest against the idiocies Stern is sure to have served up again last Sunday. (What kind of a tale is that, about somebody who would hear something when he was dead? Marie mentioned it. She got it from the young

Rosemeyers, who are in sugar.) Secondly, I have once more become absolutely convinced that all those yarns about distress and unrest in the East are sheer lies. This shows how travel gives you the opportunity of going into things properly.

You must know that my father-in-law had accepted an invitation for Saturday night to visit a gentleman who used to be a Resident in the East and now lives in a big country house near Driebergen. *That's* where we've been; and truly I cannot speak highly enough of the kind reception we had. The gentleman sent his carriage to fetch us, and his coachman wore a red waistcoat. It was certainly rather too cold as yet to look round the grounds properly, though they must be splendid in summer. But the house itself left nothing to be desired, it had in abundance everything that makes life enjoyable: a billiard room, a library, a conservatory of iron and glass, and the cockatoo had a silver perch to sit on. I've never seen anything like it, and at once remarked that good conduct always brings its reward. The man had been careful in looking to his business, that was obvious, for he had no fewer than three high decorations. He owned this delightful country seat, and a house in Amsterdam besides. At dinner everything was cooked with truffles, and the servants at table also wore red waistcoats, just like the coachman.

As I take a great interest in East Indian affairs—because of the coffee—I brought the conversation round to that subject, and very soon saw what I ought to think of it all. This Resident told me that he had always done very well in the East, and therefore there is not a word of truth in all those tales about discontent among the people. I mentioned Scarfman. He knew him, and took a very unfavourable view of him. He assured me they had done quite right to sack the fellow, for he was a very discontented person, who was always finding fault with everything although there was a lot to be criticized in his own behaviour. For instance, he was always carrying off girls and taking them home to his wife, and he didn't pay his debts, which, there's no denying it, is very disreputable. Now, as I knew so well from the letter I had read how true all these charges were, it pleased me greatly to see how right I had been in my judgment of the case, and I was very satisfied with myself. Though, I must say, I am well known for that at my pillar on 'Change ... I mean, for always judging things so correctly.

That Resident and his wife were charming, hospitable people. They told us a lot about their manner of life in the East. You know, it must really be very pleasant there. They said their Driebergen estate was not half as big as their 'compound', as they called it, in the interior of Java, which needed quite a hundred people to keep it in order. But—and this is a clear indication of how popular they were —those people did it entirely gratis, purely for love! They also said that, when they left, the sale of their furniture brought them quite ten times its value, because the native Chiefs like to buy a souvenir of a Resident who has been good to them. I told this to Stern later, and he contended it was done by coercion, and that he could prove that from Scarfman's parcel. But I told him his Scarfman was a slanderer, that he abducted girls—like that young German at Busselinck & Waterman's—and that I attached no value whatever to his opinion, because now I had heard from a Resident personally how matters stood, and so had nothing to learn from Mister Scarfman.

Other people from the East were there that evening, among them a gentleman who was very rich and made a lot of money out of tea, which the Javanese produce for him for little money and the Government buys from him at a high price, in order to encourage the industry of those Javanese. That gentleman was also very angry with all the malcontents who are everlastingly talking and writing against the Government. He could not praise the Colonial Office highly enough, for he said he was convinced they lost a lot of money on the tea they bought from him, and that therefore it was true generosity on their part to go on paying so high a price for an article which actually had little value and which, incidentally, he himself did not even like (he always drank Chinese tea, not Javanese). He also said that the Governor-General who had extended the tea contracts, in spite of the calculation which proved that the country lost so much by them, was such an able, right-thinking fellow, and, above all, such a loyal friend to those who had known him in earlier days. For that Governor-General had taken no notice of the talk about losses on tea, and when the cancellation of the contracts was mooted, in 1846 I believe, had done the gentleman personally a great service, by decreeing that they should still continue to buy his tea. 'Yes,' he exclaimed, 'my heart bleeds when I hear such noble people slandered! If it hadn't been for him, I and my wife and children would now have to *walk*.' Then he had his *barouchet* brought round, and it was so spick and span, and the horses looked so well fed, that I could easily understand how a man can burn with gratitude for a Governor-General like that one. It warms the cockles of your heart to contemplate such sweet emotions, especially when you compare them with the cursed grumbling and whining of Scarfman and his sort.

Next day the Resident paid us a return visit, and so did the gentleman for whom the Javanese make tea. They both asked at the same time what train we intended to take back to Amsterdam. We didn't understand the meaning of this, but afterwards it became clear, for when we arrived in town on the Monday morning there were two servants at the station, one in a red waistcoat and one in a yellow waistcoat, who told us in unison that they had received a telegram ordering them to meet us with a carriage. My wife was quite overcome, and I thought of what Busselinck & Waterman would have said if they had seen it ... I mean, that there were two carriages waiting for us. But it wasn't easy to make a choice, for I could not bring myself to offend one of the two parties by declining so charming an attention. What a dilemma! But, as usual, I managed to extricate myself from that exceedingly delicate situation. I put my wife and Marie in the red carriage—the red waistcoat, I mean—and got into the yellow one myself ... I mean the carriage.

How those horses tore along! In Weesperstraat, which is always so dirty, the mud flew up to right and left as high as the houses and, as Fate would have it, there we passed that vagabond of a Scarf-

man, walking hunched up with his head bent, and I saw how he tried
to wipe the splashes from his pale face with the sleeve of his threadbare jacket. I have rarely had a pleasanter outing, and my wife
thought the same.

19

In the private note Mr Slymering sent to Havelaar he said that, in spite of his 'pressing occupations', he would come to RANGKAS-BE-TUNG the next day, in order to discuss what ought to be done. Havelaar knew only too well what such discussions meant—his predecessor had had so many '*tête-à-têtes*' with the Resident of BANTAM! So he wrote the following letter, which he despatched to meet the Resident, to ensure that the latter read it before reaching LEBAK. Comment on this document is superfluous:

No. 91. *Secret*
Urgent   *Rangkas-Betung,* 25 February 1856
                                                  11 p.m.

Yesterday at noon I had the honour to send you **my urgent** memorandum No. 88, to the effect that:

After long investigation, and after having vainly sought to turn the person concerned from the error of his ways by gentle means, I felt obliged by my official oath to *charge* the Regent of LEBAK with abuse of authority, and that I *suspected* him of extortion.

In that letter I took the liberty to suggest that you should summon this native Chief to SERANG, in order that an examination of the justice both of my charge and of my suspicion should be instituted *after his departure from Lebak and after neutralization of the corrupting influence of his numerous family.*

Long, or rather *deeply*, had I reflected before I decided upon this course.

I had taken care to let you know that I have tried, by exhortations and warnings, to save the old Regent from misfortune and ignominy, and myself from the deep sorrow of being the cause of it—albeit only the immediate cause.

But I saw on the other hand the *sorely oppressed* population, *who have been exploited for years*; I thought of the urgent need to make an example—for I have *many other scandals* to report to you, at least if

295

the reaction to *this* case does not put a stop to them; and, I repeat, *after mature consideration* I did what I took to be my duty.

At this moment I am in receipt of your kind and esteemed private letter, informing me that you will be here tomorrow and at the same time hinting that I would have done better to have dealt with this matter in private first.

Tomorrow, therefore, I shall have the honour of seeing you, and this is why I take the liberty of sending this letter in time to reach you on the road, so that I may make the following statement before we meet:

All my investigations into the actions of the Regent have been strictly secret. The only people who knew about them were *himself* and the PATTEH, for I had given him fair warning. Even the Controleur still knows only part of the result of my inquiries. This secrecy had a twofold object. First, when I still hoped to turn the Regent from the path of error, I wished, *if* I was successful, not to compromise him. On his behalf the PATTEH thanked me expressly for my discretion (on the 12th instant). But afterwards, when I began to despair of the success of my efforts—or rather, when the cup of my indignation ran over *on hearing of yet another incident*[110]—when further silence on *his* account would have become *complicity*, then this secrecy had to be observed on *my* account. For I have also duties to fulfil to myself—duties to me and mine.

After writing my letter of yesterday, should I not be unworthy to serve the Government if its contents were idle, baseless, or a figment of the imagination? And should, or shall, I be able to prove that I have acted '*as behoves a good Assistant Resident*'—prove that I am not unworthy of the position given me—prove that I do not thoughtlessly and rashly hazard seventeen hard years of service, and, what is more, the interests of wife and child ... shall I be able to *prove* all this, if no profound secrecy shrouds my investigations and prevents the guilty man from *covering himself*, as the saying goes?

At the slightest alarm the Regent will send an urgent message to his nephew, who is on the way to him and is interested in his uncle's retaining his position. He will ask for money, money at all costs, and will scatter it lavishly among those whom he had lately wronged. And the result might be—I trust I shall not have to say: *will* be —the opinion that *I* have passed a frivolous judgment; in brief that I am a useless official, to put it no worse than that.

It is in order to safeguard myself against such an eventuality that I am writing this letter. I have the highest respect for you; but I know the spirit which one might call 'East Indian official's spirit', and I do not have that spirit!

Your intimation that it would have been better if the case had first been dealt with *in private* makes me fear any *tête-à-tête*. What I said in yesterday's letter is *true*. But it might *appear* untrue if the case were treated in a manner that could lead to my charge and my suspicion being revealed *before the Regent has gone from here*.

I cannot but admit to you that even your sudden arrival, in connexion with the special messenger I sent to SERANG yesterday, makes me fear that the guilty party, who has hitherto refused to yield to my admonitions, will *now* awake too soon, and do what he can, be it ever so little, to exculpate himself.

I take the liberty, for the present, to abide literally by my memorandum of yesterday; but I beg to point out that that memorandum *also* contained the proposal: *to remove the Regent before the inquiry, and to render his followers powerless for the time being*. I consider myself bound to answer for the statements I made only if you agree to my proposal concerning the *manner* of the inquiry, i.e.: that it shall be impartial, open, and above all, *free*.

This freedom does *not* exist until the Regent has been removed and, in my humble opinion, there is no danger in removing him. For he can be told that it is *I* who accuse and suspect him, and that it is *I*, not he, who is in danger if he is innocent. For I myself consider that I deserve to be dismissed the service if it should be shown that I have acted frivolously, or even only precipitately.

Precipitately! After *years, years*, of abuse of authority!

Precipitately! As though an honest man could sleep, live, enjoy life, as long as those whose well-being he is called upon to watch over, those who are in the highest sense his *neighbours*, are robbed and exploited!

I admit, I have not been here long. But I trust that the question asked one day will be *what* I did, and whether I did it *well*, not whether I did it in *too short a time*. To me, any time is too long when it is marked by extortion and oppression, and on me every second would weigh heavy which, owing to *my* negligence, *my* dereliction of duty, *my*' spirit of compromise', had been spent in misery by others.

I regret the days which I allowed to pass before reporting officially to you, and I ask pardon for that neglect.

I beg to request that I may be given the opportunity to substantiate my letter of yesterday, and safeguarded against the failure of my efforts to free the Division of LEBAK from the worms which have been gnawing at its welfare since time immemorial.

It is for these reasons that I again presume to ask you: kindly to approve my actions in this matter—which, I would point out, have consisted only in *inquiry*, *report* and *recommendation*; to remove the Regent of LEBAK from here without any previous *direct* or *indirect* warning; and further, to order an inquiry to be made into the facts I communicated to you in my letter No. 88 of yesterday's date.

The Assistant Resident of Lebak
Max Havelaar

This appeal to the Resident *not to give protection to the guilty* reached him when he was still en route for RANGKAS-BETUNG. An hour after he arrived there, he called on the Regent and asked him two questions: what charges he could make against the Assistant Resident, and whether *he, the Adhipatti, was in need of money*!

To the first question the Regent replied: 'None, I swear!' To the second question he replied in the affirmative, whereupon the Resident gave him a couple of banknotes which he took out of his waistcoat pocket, having brought them for the purpose!

It will be understood that Havelaar was completely ignorant of this, and presently we shall see how he got to know of the Resident's disgraceful action.

When Mr Slymering alighted at Havelaar's house he was paler than usual and his words were farther apart than ever. And, indeed, it was no trifling ordeal for one who was so brilliant at 'fixing' things and in compiling annual peace reports to suddenly receive letters in which there was not a trace of 'optimism' or skilful twisting of facts or fear of displeasing the Government by 'embarrassing' it with unfavourable tidings. The Resident of BANTAM had had a fright; and if I may be pardoned the lowness of the image for the sake of its appositeness, I should like to compare him with a street arab who complains of the violation of time-honoured customs because someone has hit him without the usua lpreliminary invective.

He began by asking the Controleur why he had not tried to restrain Havelaar from making his charge. It was the first poor Verbrugge had heard about the charge, and he said so, but found no credence. For Mr Slymering could not conceive how anyone could possibly have proceeded to such unheard-of performance of duty all by himself, on his own responsibility, and without long-drawn-out deliberations and 'consultations'. Since, however, Verbrugge persisted in asserting his ignorance of Havelaar's letters—and he spoke the truth—the Resident had to concede the point, and began by reading the letters aloud to him.

What Verbrugge suffered in listening to them is not to be described. He was an honest man, and would not have lied if Havelaar had appealed to him to confirm their truth. But quite apart from this, in many written reports he had also not always been able to avoid telling the truth, even when the truth was dangerous. What would happen if Havelaar made use of those reports?

After reading the letters the Resident stated that it would please him if Havelaar would take them back, so that they could be considered as not having been written. This proposal was declined with polite firmness.

After trying in vain to persuade his subordinate to change his mind, the Resident said he now had no alternative but to institute an inquiry into the truth of the complaints, and that he therefore had to ask Havelaar to call the witnesses who could substantiate his accusations.

Poor people who had torn your flesh on the thorn bushes in the ravine! How anxiously your hearts would have throbbed if you could have heard that!

Poor Verbrugge! You, first witness, chief witness, witness *ex officio*, witness by virtue of office and oath! Witness who had already borne witness, in writing! In writing that lay there, on the table, under Havelaar's hand...

Havelaar answered:

'Resident, *I* am Assistant Resident of LEBAK, *I* have undertaken to protect the population from extortion and tyranny, *I* accuse the Regent and his son-in-law of PARANG-KUJANG, *I* shall prove the truth of my charge as soon as I am given the opportunity which I proposed in my letters, and if my charge is false it is *I* who am guilty of slander!'

How freely Verbrugge breathed again!

And how strange Havelaar's words seemed to the Resident!

The meeting lasted a long time. With great courteousness—for courteous and well-bred he certainly was—the Resident urged Havelaar to relinquish such mistaken principles. But, with equal courteousness, Havelaar remained adamant. The end was that the Resident had to yield, and said by way of a threat what for Havelaar was a triumph: *that he would now be compelled to bring the letters in question to the attention of the Government.*

The session was closed. The Resident visited the ADHIPATTI— we have already seen what his business was there!—and then sat down to lunch at the Havelaars' frugal board. Immediately afterwards he returned to SERANG, with great despatch: Because. He. Was. So. Terribly. Busy.

Next day Havelaar received a letter from the Resident of BAN-

TAM, the contents of which may be inferred from his answer, which I give here:

No. 93. *Secret*   *Rangkas-Betung*, 28 February 1856

I beg to acknowledge receipt of your urgent *secret* memorandum ref. La. O of 28th inst., to the following effect:

That you have reasons for not acting on the proposals made in my official letters Nos 88 and 91 of 24th and 25th inst.;

that you would have preferred to receive a previous confidential communication from me on the matter;

that you do not approve my actions as described in those two letters;

and finally, some orders.

I now have the honour to assure you once more—just as I did orally at our conference of the day before yesterday:

That I bow completely to your authority, where the point at issue is the acceptance or otherwise of my *proposals*: and

that the *orders* I have received will be carried out strictly, and if need be with self-abnegation, as though you were a witness of all I do or say, or rather of all I do *not* do and do *not* say.

I know you have confidence in my loyalty in this respect.

But I take the liberty to protest most solemnly against the least hint of disapproval on your part with regard to *any* action, *any* word, *any* phrase which I have performed, spoken, or written in the matter in question.

I am convinced that I have done my *duty* ... in intention and in manner of execution, *my whole duty* ... *and nothing but my duty*, without the slightest deviation.

I reflected a long time before I acted—i.e.: before I *investigated*, *reported*, and *proposed*—and if I have erred at all in anything ... I did not err through overhastiness.

In similar circumstances I should again do and not do exactly the same, literally exactly the same—though rather more quickly.

And even if a higher authority than yours disapproved of anything I did—excepting perhaps the idiosyncrasy of my style, which is part of myself, a fault for which I am as little responsible as a stammerer is for his—even if that happened ... but no, it is out of the question; yet, even if that did happen—*I have done my duty*!

I am certainly grieved—though not surprised—that you think differently about this; and, if my person only was concerned, I should resign myself at once to being, as I think, misjudged. But there is a *principle* at stake, and my conscience demands that the question of whose opinion is correct, *yours* or *mine*, should be decisively settled.

I cannot serve otherwise than I have served at LEBAK. So if the Government wishes to be served differently, honesty compels me respectfully to proffer my resignation. In that case, at the age of thirty-six, I shall have to try to begin a new career. In that case, after seventeen years, after seventeen *arduous, difficult* years of service, after having devoted my life's best powers to what I held to be my duty, I shall again have to ask society whether it will give me bread for wife and child, bread in exchange for my brains ... bread in exchange, maybe, for labour with a wheelbarrow or spade, if the strength of my arm should be judged of greater value than the strength of my soul.

But I cannot and will not believe that your opinion will be shared by His Excellency the Governor-General, and therefore, ere I am driven to the bitter extremity I have described in the previous paragraph, I am bound to request respectfully that you will advise the Government:

to instruct the Resident of BANTAM to approve the actions of the Assistant Resident of LEBAK relative to the latter's memoranda Nos. 88 and 91 of the 24th and 25th inst.

Or otherwise:

to call upon the aforesaid Assistant Resident to answer grounds for disapproval to be formulated by the Resident of BANTAM.

In conclusion, please allow me to give you the grateful assurance that if *anything* could have made me go back upon my principles in this matter, long considered and soberly but ardently adhered to as they are ... it would indeed have been the courteous and charming manner in which you contested those principles at our conference two days ago.

The Assistant Resident of Lebak
Max Havelaar

Without pronouncing a verdict as to the truth of the widow Slotering's suspicion about what had made her children orphans, and accepting only what can be proved, namely, that in LEBAK there was a close connexion between devotion to duty and poison—even if this connexion, too, only existed in people's minds ... I hardly need to say that Max and Tina passed wretched days after the Resident's visit. It is surely unnecessary for me to portray the torturing anxiety of a mother who, when giving food to her child, continually has to ask herself whether she may not be murdering her darling. And if any child had been prayed-for it was little Max, who had been seven years in coming after the Havelaar's marriage, as though the rogue knew it was not exactly an advantage to enter the world as the son of such parents!

Twenty-nine long days did Havelaar have to wait before the Governor-General informed him ... but we are not yet so far.

Shortly after Mr Slymering's vain efforts to persuade Havelaar to take back his letters, or to give the names of the poor wretches who had trusted in his magnanimity, Verbrugge came to his house. The worthy man was as white as a sheet, and had difficulty in speaking.

'I've been with the Regent,' he said... 'It's infamous—infamous... but don't betray me!'

'What? What is it I am not to betray?'

'Will you give me your word not to make use of what I am going to say to you?'

'Halfheartedness again!' said Havelaar. 'But ... all right! I give you my word.'

And then Verbrugge told him what the reader already knows—

303

that the Resident had asked the ADHIPATTI whether he could say anything against the Assistant Resident, and had also, quite unexpectedly, offered and given him money. Verbrugge had heard it from the Regent himself, who asked him what reasons the Resident could have had for this? Havelaar was indignant, but ... he had given his word.

Next day Verbrugge returned, and said that Duclari had pointed out to him how mean it was to leave Havelaar, who had to fight *such* opponents, so entirely alone; and Verbrugge had therefore come to release him from his word.

'Good!' Havelaar exclaimed. 'Write it down!'

Verbrugge wrote it down. That statement also lies before me.

The reader must long ago have understood why I can so readily relinquish all claims to *detailed* authenticity for the history of SAÏJAH?

It is very striking to observe how the timorous Verbrugge, before Duclari's reproaches goaded him into changing his mind, had dared to rely on Havelaar's word in a case which would tempt a man so strongly to break it!

And ... another thing. Years have passed since the events I am relating. In that time, Havelaar has suffered much, he has seen his family suffer—the documents before me testify to that!—yet he appears to have waited ... I give here the following note from his hand:

I see from the newspapers that Mr Slymering has been made a Knight of the Order of the Netherlands Lion. Apparently he is now Resident of Jokjakarta. So I could now bring the Lebak affair up again without danger to Verbrugge.

20

It was evening. Tina sat reading in the inner gallery, and Havelaar was drawing an embroidery pattern. Little Max was conjuring a jig-saw puzzle together and losing his temper because he could not find 'that woman's red body'.

'Do you think it will be all right like this, Tina?' asked Havelaar. 'Look, I've made this palm tree a trifle bigger ... It's exactly Ho-garth's "line of beauty", don't you think?'

'Yes, Max! But the lace holes are too close together.'

'Oh? And what about the other strips, then? Max! Let's have a look at your knickers! Hallo, are you wearing *that* strip? Why, I still remember where you worked that one, Tina!'

'I don't. Where was it, then?'

'It was in The Hague, when Max was ill, and we were so scared because the doctor said his head was such an unusual shape and that we had to be so careful to prevent congestion of the brain... it was then that you were embroidering that strip.'

Tina got up and kissed little Max.

'I've *got* her tummy, I've *got* her tummy!' the child cried exultant-ly, and the red woman was complete.

'Who can hear a *tontong*?'[111] the mother asked.

'I can,' said her son.

'And what does that mean?'

'Bedtime! But ... I haven't had any supper yet.'

'You shall have your supper first, of course.'

And Tina rose, and gave him his simple meal, which she ap-parently took from a secure cupboard in her room, for the click of several locks was heard.

'What are you giving him?' asked Havelaar.

'Oh, don't worry! It's rusks from a tin I got in BATAVIA. And the sugar's always been locked up, too.'

Havelaar's thoughts returned to the point where they had been interrupted.

'Do you know,' he went on, 'we haven't paid that doctor's bill yet ... oh, it's very hard!'

'My dear Max, we're living so carefully here, we shall soon be able to pay them all! Besides it won't be long now before you're made a Resident, and then everything will be settled in no time.'

'It's that that troubles me,' said Havelaar. 'I should be so very sorry to leave LEBAK ... look, I'll explain. Don't you think we loved our Max even more after he'd been so ill? Well, it seems to me that that's how I shall feel about this poor place LEBAK, after it's been cured of the cancer it's been suffering from all these years. The thought of promotion dismays me—I can't be spared from here, Tina! And yet ... on the other hand ... when I think of our debts...'

'Everything will come right, Max! Even if you had to go away from here now, you would still be able to help LEBAK later, when you're Governor-General.'

Savage streaks appeared in Havelaar's embroidery pattern! There was fury in that floral motif ... those lace holes became angular, sharp, they bit each other...

Tina realized she had said something amiss.

'Darling Max...' she began gently.

'Curse it! Do you want those poor wretches to starve for *so* long? Can *you* live on sand?'

'Darling Max!'

But he jumped up. There was no more drawing that evening. He strode angrily up and down the inner gallery, and at last he burst out, in a tone that would have sounded rough and harsh to any stranger but was very differently interpreted by Tina:

'Damn this laxness, this shameful laxness! Here have I been sitting waiting for justice for a month, and meanwhile the poor people are suffering terribly! The Regent seems certain that no one dares to touch him! Look...'

He went into his office, and came back with a letter in his hand... a letter which lies before me, reader!

'Look! In this letter he has the audacity to make proposals to me about the *kind* of labour he wants done by the people he has unlawfully called up! Isn't this carrying impudence too far? And do you know who those people are? They are women with small children, with babies at the breast, pregnant women who have been driven here from PARANG-KUJANG in order to work for *him*! There are no more men left anyway! And they've nothing to eat, and they sleep in the road, and eat sand! Can *you* eat sand? Must they eat sand until I'm Governor-General? God damn!'

Tina knew very well whom Max was *really* angry with when he spoke like this to her, whom he loved so deeply.

'And,' Havelaar continued, 'all this is done on *my* responsibility! At this very moment, if some of those poor wretches are wandering about outside there and see the glow of our lamps, they'll say: "There's where the scoundrel lives who's supposed to protect us! There he sits peacefully with wife and child, drawing embroidery patterns ... and we lie starving in the road with our children, like outcast dogs!" Yes, I hear it, I hear it, the crying for vengeance on my head! Max, come here!'

And he kissed his son with a wildness which frightened little Max.

'Child, when they tell you I was a rascal who hadn't the courage to do justice... that so many mothers died through my fault... when they tell you that your father's neglect of duty filched the blessing from your head ... oh, Max, Max, tell *them* what I suffered!'

And he burst into tears, which Tina kissed away. She took little Max to his bed—a mat of straw—and when she returned she found Havelaar in conversation with Verbrugge and Duclari, who had just come in. They were talking about the expected decision by the Government.

'I can well understand that the Resident's in a fix,' said Duclari. 'He can't advise the Government to comply with your proposals, because if they did, *too much* would come to light. I've been in BANTAM a long time, and I know a good deal about it, even more than you do, Mr Havelaar! I was in these parts when I was still an N.C.O.,

307

and in that position you get to know things the native doesn't rush to tell the officials. But if there was a public inquiry and all that should come out, the Governor-General would call the Resident to account, and ask him why he didn't discover in two years what you saw at once! So, of course, Slymering has to try to prevent an inquiry from being made...'

'I realize that,' answered Havelaar. 'I was shaken by his attempt to get the ADHIPATTI to make allegations against me—which seems to indicate that he'll try to stage a diversion, for instance by accusing me of ... I don't know what. So I "covered myself" by sending copies of my letters direct to the Government. In one of them I asked to be called upon for an explanation if a pretence should be made that *I* had done something amiss. Now, if the Resident attacks *me*, in common justice no decision can be taken without first giving me a hearing. Even a criminal is entitled to that, and since I've done nothing wrong...'

'There's the post!' exclaimed Verbrugge.

Yes, it was the post! The post, which brought the following letter ... from the Governor-General of the Dutch East Indies to the *ex*-Assistant Resident of LEBAK, Max Havelaar:

The Office of the Governor-General
No. 54   *Buitenzorg*, 23 March 1856

The manner in which you have proceeded since your discovery or supposition of malpractices on the part of Chiefs of the Division of LEBAK, and the attitude taken by you in this towards your superior officer the Resident of BANTAM, have incurred my extreme dissatisfaction.

Your above-mentioned actions reveal an absence as much of the calm deliberation, tact and prudence so essential in an officer vested (*sic*) with the administration of authority in the interior, as of a proper conception of subordination to your immediate superior.

Only a few days after you had entered upon your new duties, you thought fit to make the Chief of the Native Administration of LE-

BAK the object of incriminating investigations, without previously consulting the Resident (*sic*).

In those investigations, without even substantiating your charges against that Chief by facts (*sic*), let alone proofs, you found cause to recommend measures which would have subjected a native Official of the stamp of the Regent of LEBAK, a sixty-year-old but still zealous servant of the State, kin to important neighbouring families of Regents and about whom reports have invariably been favourable, to a treatment that would have meant his complete moral ruin.

Moreover, when the Resident showed himself indisposed to give immediate effect to your proposals, you refused to comply with the reasonable demand of your Chief, that you should make a full disclosure of all that was known to you regarding the actions of the native Administration in LEBAK.

Such conduct merits every condemnation, and would readily give cause to suspect your *unfitness* to occupy a post in the East Indian Civil Service.

I am therefore compelled to relieve you of your duties as Assistant Resident of LEBAK.

In view, however, of the favourable reports formerly received concerning you, I have not wished to regard what has occurred as a reason for depriving you of the prospect of another appointment in the Service. I therefore entrust you provisionally with performance of the function of Assistant Resident of NGAWI.

Your future behaviour in that position will wholly determine whether it will be possible to retain you in the East Indian Civil Service.

And below this was written the name of the man on whose '*zeal*, *ability* and *loyalty*' the King had said he could rely when signing his appointment as Governor-General of the Dutch East Indies.

'We're going, Tina dear,' said Havelaar resignedly; and he handed the memorandum to Verbrugge, who read it together with Duclari.

Verbrugge had tears in his eyes, but said nothing. Duclari, a particularly refined man, burst out in a savage oath:

'Jesus Christ! I've seen rogues and thieves in Government service here ... they left with full honours, and *you* get a letter like this!'

'It's nothing,' said Havelaar. 'The Governor-General is an honest man: he must have been misled ... though he could have guarded against that by hearing me first. He's got tangled in the web of Buitenzorg bureaucracy. We know what that's like! But I'll go to him and show him how matters stand here. He'll see justice done, I'm certain!'

'But ... if you go to NGAWI...?'

'Quite—I know! The Regent of NGAWI is related to the Court of JOKJA. I know NGAWI, I was two years in BAGLEN, which isn't far from there. In NGAWI I should be forced to do exactly what I've done here: that would mean nothing but useless travelling to and fro! Besides, it's impossible for me to serve on probation, as though I had misbehaved myself! And, finally, I realize that I must not be an official if I'm to put an end to all this corruption. As long as I'm an official there are too many persons between me and the Government who are interested in denying the misery of the population. And there are still more reasons why I shouldn't go to NGAWI! The post wasn't open ... they made it vacant specially for me, look!'

And he showed them in the *Javasche Courant*, the newspaper which had come by the same post, that in the same Government Order in Council which assigned the administration of NGAWI to him the Assistant Resident of that Division was transferred to another Division that *was* vacant.

'Do you know why it's NGAWI they want to send me to and not the Division that was vacant? I'll tell you! NGAWI's part of the Residency of MADIUN, and the Resident of MADIUN is the *brother-in-law of the last Resident of Bantam*. I said that there always have been such scandalous goings-on here ... and that the Regent has had such bad examples in the past...'

'Aha!' Verbrugge and Duclari ejaculated simultaneously. They understood now why NGAWI had been chosen as the scene of Havelaar's term of trial, to see whether he would mend his ways!

'And there's yet another reason why I can't go there,' he continued. 'The Governor-General will soon be retiring ... I know his successor, and I know there's nothing to be expected from him. So, if anything is to be done in time for the wretched people of LEBAK, I shall have to see the present man before he goes, and if I went to NGAWI now that would be impossible. Tina ... listen!'

'Yes, dear Max?'

'You've plenty of courage, haven't you?'

'Max, you know I've plenty of courage, when I'm with you!'

'Very well!'

He rose, went to his room and wrote the following request—in my opinion a model of eloquence:

Rangkas-Betung, 29 March 1856
To the Governor-General of the Dutch East Indies

I have had the honour to receive Your Excellency's memorandum No. 54 of the 23rd inst.

In reply to that document, I feel constrained to beg Your Excellency to grant me an honourable discharge from the service of the State.

Max Havelaar

Not so much time was required at BUITENZORG to accept Havelaar's resignation as appeared to have been necessary to decide how his accusation could be parried. For that had taken a month, and the requested discharge reached LEBAK within a few days.

'Thank Heaven!' Tina exclaimed. 'At last you can be yourself!'

Havelaar received no instructions to hand the administration of his Division over to Verbrugge *ad interim*, and therefore assumed he was to wait for his successor. That official was a long time in art riving, because he had to come from an entirely different part of Java. After waiting for nearly three weeks, the ex-Assistant Residen-

of LEBAK, who, however, had still functioned as Assistant Resident all the time, wrote the following letter to Controleur Verbrugge:

No. 153   *Rangkas-Betung,* 15 April 1856
To the Controleur of Lebak

As you know, by Government Decree No. 4, of the 4th inst., I have been honourably discharged from the service of the State at my own request.

On receipt of that decision, I might perhaps have been justified in giving up my duties as Assistant Resident at once, since it seems anomalous to fill an office when one is not an official.

However, I received no instructions to surrender my charge, and partly from a sense of my obligation not to leave my post without having been properly relieved, partly for reasons of minor importance, I awaited the arrival of my successor, imagining that that officer would be here before long—at any rate in the course of this month.

I have just learnt from you that my replacement cannot be expected quite so soon—you heard this, I believe, at SERANG—and also that the Resident was surprised that I, in view of the very peculiar position in which I find myself, have not yet asked to be allowed to transfer the duties of administration to you.

Nothing could please me more than this news. For I need not assure you that I, who have declared that I could not serve otherwise than I have done here ... I, who for this way of serving have been punished with censure and with a ruinous and discreditable transfer ... with the order to betray the poor people who trusted to my good faith—with the choice, therefore, between dishonour and destitution!—that, after all this, I have still had, with pains and care, to examine in the light of my duty every case that arose, and that even the simplest matter has been trying to me, torn as I am between my conscience and the principles of the Government, to whom I owe loyalty so long as I have not been relieved of my office.

The difficulty of my position has become especially apparent whenever I have had to answer a *complaint*.

For I *had* promised not to deliver anyone up to the rancour of his Chiefs! I had—imprudently enough!—pledged my word for the uprightness of the Government.

The people of LEBAK cannot know that his promise and this pledge have been disavowed, and that I stand alone, poor and powerless, in my desire for justice and humanity.

And all the time, the complaints have continued!

Since I received the Governor-General's memorandum of 23 March, it has been intensely painful for me to sit here as a *supposed* refuge—as an *impotent* protector.

It has been heartrending to listen to complaints about maltreatment, exploitation, poverty, hunger ... while I myself am now going to face hunger and poverty, with wife and child.

And yet I am not at liberty to betray the Government either. I am not at liberty to tell these poor people: "Go, and suffer still, for the Administration *wishes* you to be exploited!" I am not at liberty to confess my impotence, coupled as it is with the shame and unscrupulousness of the Governor-General's advisers.

This is what I have answered:

"I cannot help you immediately! But I shall go to BATAVIA, and I shall speak to the Great Lord there about your misery. *He* is just, and *he* will stand by you. For the time being, go quietly home... do not rebel ... do not leave the place yet ... wait in patience: I think ... I hope ... that justice will be done!"

In this way, ashamed of the breach of my promise of assistance, I thought to reconcile my personal views with my duty towards the Government, *since it still pays me this month*; and I should have gone on like this until my successor arrived if a particular occurrence today had not necessitated my putting an end to this equivocal relation.

Seven people had complained. I gave them the above reply. They returned to their homes. On the way, they met their village chief.

313

He is supposed to have forbidden them to leave their *kampong* again, and—so I hear—has taken their clothes away from them to force them to stay at home. But one of them escaped, came to me *again*, and declared *that he dared not return to his village*!

I am at my wit's end to know what to say to this man!

I *cannot* protect him ... I *must not* confess my impotence to him... I *will not* prosecute the village chief concerned, since that would look as though I had raked up such a case to serve my cause. I no longer know *what* to do...

Subject to further approval by the Resident of BANTAM, I charge you with administration of the Division of LEBAK with effect from tomorrow morning.

The Assistant Resident of Lebak
Max Havelaar

After this, Havelaar left RANGKAS-BETUNG with his wife and child. He refused to have any escort. Duclari and Verbrugge were deeply moved by the leavetaking. Havelaar was also touched, especially when, at the first staging post, he found a large crowd of people, who had stolen away from RANGKAS-BETUNG to salute him for the last time.

At SERANG the family alighted at Mr Slymering's house, where they were received with the customary East Indian hospitality.

That night the Resident had many visitors. They said as significantly as possible that they had come *to meet Havelaar*, and Max was given many an eloquent handshake...

But he had to go to BATAVIA, to see the Governor-General...

On his arrival there, he asked for an audience. That was denied him, because His Excellency had a whitlow on his foot.

Havelaar waited until the whitlow was better. Then he again asked for an audience.

His Excellency '*had even had to refuse an audience to the Director-General of Finance, owing to pressure of business*', and consequently he could not see Havelaar either.

Havelaar waited until His Excellency should have struggled through all his business. Meanwhile, he felt something like jealousy of the persons who assisted His Excellency in his labours. For he himself liked to work hard, and rapidly, and as a rule such 'pressures' melted away under his hands. But there could be no question of this now, of course. Havelaar's labour was harder than labour: he *waited*!

He waited. Finally he sent in another application for an audience. He received the answer *that His Excellency could not receive him because he was too busy with the preparations for his impending departure.*

Max earnestly requested His Excellency to grant him the favour of one half-hour interview as soon as a small space of time should occur between two bouts of busy-ness.

At last he learnt that His Excellency was to depart next day!

This news hit him like a thunderbolt. He still clung desperately to the belief that the retiring Viceroy was an honest man, and... had been deceived. A quarter of an hour would have been sufficient for Havelaar to prove the justice of his cause, but it seemed that this quarter of an hour was to be denied him.

Among his papers, I find the file copy of a letter he seems to have written to the departing Governor-General the night before that official left for the mother country. In the margin there is a note in pencil: 'Not exact', from which I conclude that Havelaar must have altered some sentences or phrases in the letter as sent. I draw attention to this so that the fact that *this* document is not *word for word* the same as the actual letter may give no grounds for doubting the authenticity of the other *official* papers which I have quoted and which have all been signed by another hand as *Certified true copies*. Perhaps the man to whom the letter was addressed feels like publishing the *exact* text of it. Comparison would then show to what extent Havelaar had deviated from his draft. *In essence*, the letter was as follows:

Your Excellency!

My official request, made by letter dated 28 February, for an audience in connexion with the affairs of LEBAK, has met with no response.

Your Excellency has likewise not been pleased to comply with my subsequent repeated requests for an audience.

Your Excellency has therefore ranked an official *who was favourably known to the Government* (these are Your Excellency's own words!) —one who has served the State in these parts for seventeen years, one who had not only done no wrong but had even, with unprecedented self-abnegation, striven to do right, and was ready to stake everything for honour and duty ... such a man Your Excellency has ranked below a criminal. For a criminal is at least given a *hearing*.

I can understand that Your Excellency has been misled with regard to me. But I cannot understand why Your Excellency has not taken the opportunity to escape from being misled.

Tomorrow Your Excellency departs from here, and I cannot let you leave without having said once more *that I have done my* DUTY, MY WHOLE DUTY, AND NOTHING BUT MY DUTY, *with discretion, with restraint, with humanity, with gentleness and with courage*.

The grounds of the condemnation expressed in Your Excellency's memorandum of 23 March are *fictitious and mendacious from beginning to end*.

This I can *prove*, and I should already have done so if Your Excellency had been pleased to grant me half an hour's audience. If Your Excellency had been able to spare one half hour *in which to do justice*!

Such has not been the case! As a result, a respectable family has been reduced to beggary...

However, it is not this that I complain about.

Your Excellency has *sanctioned*: THE SYSTEM OF ABUSE OF AUTHORITY, OF ROBBERY AND MURDER, UNDER WHICH THE HUMBLE JAVANESE GROANS, and it is that that I complain about.

That cries to heaven!

Your Excellency, there is blood on the pieces of silver you have saved from the salary you have earned *thus*!

Once more I ask for a moment's hearing, be it this night or be it early tomorrow morning! And—also once more—I do not ask it for myself, but for the cause I stand for, the cause of justice and humanity, which is at the same time the cause of enlightened self-interest.

If Your Excellency can reconcile your conscience to leaving without hearing me, mine will be clear through the conviction that I have done everything possible to prevent the sad and bloody events which will soon result from the ignorance in which the Government chooses to be left concerning what is going on among the people.

Max Havelaar

Havelaar waited that evening. He waited the whole night.

He had hoped that anger at the tone of his letter might bring about what persuasion and patience had not been able to bring about. His hope was in vain! The Governor-General departed without having heard Havelaar. Another Excellency had retired to rest in the Motherland!

Havelaar wandered about, poor and forsaken. He sought...

Enough, my good Stern! I, Multatuli, take up the pen. You are not required to write Havelaar's life story. I called you into being... I brought you from Hamburg ... I taught you to write fairly good Dutch in a very short time ... I let you kiss Louise Rosemeyer, who's in sugar ... It is enough, Stern, you may go!

That Scarfman and his wife...

Halt, wretched spawn of sordid moneygrubbing and blasphemous cant! I created you ... you grew into a monster under my pen ... I loathe my own handiwork: choke in coffee and disappear!

Yes, I, Multatuli, 'who have borne much', take up the pen. I make no apology for the form of my book. That form seemed suitable to me for the attainment of my object.

That object is a dual one.

In the first place, I wanted to body forth something that may be kept as a sacred heirloom, as *pusaka*, by little Max and his sister when their parents shall have perished from hunger. I wanted to give those children a patent of nobility from my own hand.

And in the second place: *I want to be read!*

Yes, I want to be read! I want to be read by politicians who are obliged to keep an eye on the signs of the times ... by literati, who 'would just like to have a look, all the same' at the book everyone is running down ... by merchants who have an interest in the coffee auctions ... by ladies' maids who will borrow me for a few pence... by ex-Governors-General in retirement ... by Ministers in office... by the lackeys of those Excellencies ... by praying preachers, who will say *more majorum* that I am attacking Almighty God whereas I am only rising against the petty idol *they* have made in their own image ... by thousands and tens of thousands of specimens of the tribe of Droogstoppel, who—continuing to grind their own little axes in the well-known fashion—will be the loudest in joining in the chorus about the 'prettiness' of my writings ... by the members of the House of Representatives, who ought to know what is going on in the great Empire beyond the seas which belongs to the Realm of the Netherlands.

Yes, I *will* be read!

When this object is attained, I shall be satisfied. For it was not my intention to write *well* ... I wanted to write in such a way as to be heard. And, just as someone who yells 'Stop thief!' troubles little about the style of his improvised address to the public, so am I quite indifferent to the judgments people will pass on the way in which I have yelled *my* 'Stop thief!'

'The book is chaotic ... disjointed ... striving for effect ... the style is bad ... the writer lacks skill ... no talent ... no method...'

Right, right ... all right! But ... THE JAVANESE IS MALTREATED! For: *the* SUBSTANCE *of my work is irrefutable!*

Moreover, the more loudly my book is condemned the better I shall be pleased, for so much the greater will be my chance *of being heard*. And that is what I *want*!

But you whom I disturb in your 'pressure of business' or in your peaceful 'retirement'—you Ministers and Governors-General ... if I were you I should not bank too much on my pen's lack of skill. It could practise, you know, and with a little effort it might even become proficient enough to make the people believe the truth! Then I should ask that People for a place in its Parliament, were it only for the purpose of protesting against the certificates of integrity which East Indian experts present to each other—perhaps to give the world the extraordinary idea that they themselves *value* that quality...

For the purpose of protesting against the endless expeditions and deeds of derring-do against poor miserable creatures who have first been goaded to rebellion by ill-treatment...

For the purpose of protesting against the shameful cowardice of circulars that besmirch the honour of the Nation by *invoking public charity* for the *victims* of *chronic piracy*!

I agree, those rebels are starved skeletons, and the pirates are able-bodied men!

And if that place in Parliament were refused me ... if people persisted in not believing me...

Then I should translate my book into the few languages I know, and into the many languages I can still learn, in order to ask from Europe what I have failed to find in the Netherlands.

And in all the capital cities songs would be sung with refrains like this: *A pirate state lies on the sea, Between the Scheldt and Eastern Friesland!*

And if even this did not avail?

Then I should translate my book into *Malay, Javanese, Sundanese, Alfuro, Buginese, Battak*...

And I should hurl *klewang*-whetting war songs into the hearts of the poor martyrs to whom I have promised help, I, Multatuli.

Deliverance and help, by legal means, if *possible* ... by the *legitimate* means of force, if *necessary*.

And *this would react most unfavourably on the* 'Coffee Auctions of the Dutch Trading Company'!

For I am no fly-rescuing poet, no half-baked dreamer, like the downtrodden Havelaar, who did his duty with the courage of a lion and now starves with the patience of a marmot in the winter.

This book is only a beginning...

I shall wax in power and keenness of weapons, in proportion as shall be necessary...

God grant that it may not be necessary!

No! It will *not* be necessary! For I dedicate my book to You, William the Third, King, Grand Duke, Prince ... more than Prince, Grand Duke and King ... EMPEROR of the glorious realm of INSULINDE, that coils yonder round the Equator like a girdle of emerald...

You I dare ask with confidence whether it is Your Imperial will:

that the *Havelaars* be spattered with the mud of *Slymerings* and *Droogstoppels*?

and that yonder Your more than *thirty million* subjects be MALTREATED AND EXPLOITED IN YOUR NAME?

NOTES

The text for this translation is that of the edition of 1875, from which the long introductory note has also been taken. The remaining notes by Multatuli come from the edition of 1881, the last the author was able to revise. Only a selection of the notes is given, and these have been abridged in the places marked with square brackets.

INTRODUCTORY NOTE (ABRIDGED) BY MULTATULI TO THE EDITION OF 1875

The delay in the appearance of this edition must be blamed on me, and certainly not on my very energetic publisher. Though it is doubtful whether the word *blame* is correct here. Blame presupposes *guilt*; and I wonder whether this can be applicable to my almost unconquerable aversion to experiencing once more page by page, word by word, letter by letter, the sad drama that gave birth to this book? This *book*! ... the reader sees no more in it than that. But to *me* these pages are a chapter of my life ... to me their correction was torment, one long torment! Over and over again the pen dropped from my hand, over and over again my eyes swam as I read the—incomplete and toned-down!—sketch of what happened twenty years ago in that formerly unknown spot on the map called LEBAK. And I felt even more wretched when I looked back on what has taken place since the publication of *the book* Havelaar, fifteen years ago now. I repeatedly threw the printer's proofs aside and tried to fix my mental eyes on less tragic subjects than those which Havelaar's still fruitless struggle called to mind. Weeks, sometimes months—my publisher can vouch for it!—went by without my having the courage to look at the proofs. But somehow or other I have managed to stagger through the work of correction—correction which has taken more out of me than the writing of the book did. For in the winter of 1859, when I wrote my *Havelaar* in Brussels, partly in a little room without a fire, partly at a rickety, dirty table in a tavern amid good-natured but rather unaesthetically minded beer-drinkers, I thought I should *accomplish something, achieve something, bring something about*. Hope gave me courage, hope made me eloquent now and then. I still remember the mood that inspired me when I wrote and told *her*:* 'My book's finished, my book's finished! Now everything will soon come right!' I had struggled through—and wasted, alas!—four long, four difficult years in trying, without publicity, without commotion, above all without scandal, to do something that might improve the situation in which the Javanese languishes. The wretched Van Twist,** who would have been my natural ally if any idea of honour and duty could have been found in him, was not to be induced to lift a finger. The letter I addressed to him has been published innumerable times, and contains virtually all the points that form the gravamen of the Havelaar case. The man has never replied, never shown a sign of wanting to do what could be done to repair the damage he has caused. I was *forced* at last, by his unprincipled indifference, to publication—to the choice of a path other than that I had been treading up to then. Indignation finally showed me how to obtain what had seemed unobtainable: *a moment's hearing*. What lazy Van Twist would not grant me, I managed to extort from the Nation: *Max Havelaar* was read. I was ... heard. Alas, hearing is one thing, reading another. The book was 'lovely', they assured me, and if I happened to have any more pretty tales like that one ...

Oh certainly, people found 'amusement' in reading it, and never thought —or pretended not to think—that it was not for 'amusement' that *I*, in middle age, threw up my career, which had promised to be a brilliant one. That *I* had not aimed at 'amusement' in defying death by poison for myself, for my staunch and true wife, and for our dear child! *Havelaar* was such an entertaining book, people had the face to say to me; and these eulogists included persons who would scream with terror if confronted with the slightest, most ordinary danger—not, I would add, to life and limb but to a small part of their comfort. Most of my readers seem to think I exposed myself and mine to poverty, degradation and death in order to provide them with some pleasant reading-matter.

This error ... but let us say no more about it. One thing is certain: I had no idea that such a naïvely cruel *jocrissiade**** lay before me when I cried with such exultation 'My book's finished, my book's finished!' My conviction that I spoke truth, that I had brought to a conclusion what I had been busy writing, and my obliviousness of the extent to which the read-

* His wife, the 'Tina' of *Max Havelaar*. *Tr.*
** Governor-General of the Dutch East Indies at the time of the events narrated in *Havelaar*. *Tr.*
*** From Jocrisse, a type in sixteenth-century French comedy. He is a stupid, clumsy servant, or a henpecked husband who does the housework. *Tr.*

ing and listening public has grown accustomed to *cant* (sic—*Tr*), to empty talk, to almost perpetual contradiction between words and deeds ... all this filled me in 1859 with so much hope as had indeed been *necessary* to make the painful writing of *Havelaar* possible. But *now*, fifteen years later, when I have seen only too well that the Nation takes the part of Van Twist and Co—i.e. the part of rascality, robbery and murder—against me, i.e. against Justice, Humanity and Enlightened Self-interest—now, it has been infinitely harder for me to deal with these pages than in 1859, albeit even then painful bitterness repeatedly threatened to get the upper hand. And here and there it breaks through in the book, however much I should have liked to repress it. [...]

And ... to all the grief over the continuing failure of my endeavours has been added my grief over the loss of *her* who stood shoulder to shoulder with me so heroically in the struggle against the world, and who will not be there when the hour of triumph shall finally come.

The hour of triumph, reader! For, whether you think it strange or not, I *shall* triumph! Despite the tricks and intrigues of the statesmanikins to whom the Netherlands entrusts its most vital concerns. Despite our stupid Constitution, which puts a premium on mediocrity or, worse, on an attitude of mind that excludes everything which might arrest the universally recognized decay of our body politic. Despite the many who have a vested interest in Injustice. Despite mean jealousy of my 'writing talent' ... isn't that what it's called? (I'm not a writer—do believe me, gentlemen scribblers who are determined to see a colleague and competitor in me!) Despite coarse slander which considers nothing too gross or too ridiculous if it will serve to smother my voice and break my influence. And finally, despite the pitiful laxity of the Nation, which goes on tolerating all this ... I shall triumph!

Of late, writers have risen to reproach me with not achieving anything, or not enough, with changing nothing or not enough, with bringing about nothing or not enough. I shall have something more to say presently about the source of such reproaches. As regards the point itself ... I fully acknowledge that nothing has *improved* in the Indies. But ... *changed*? The individuals who took advantage of the furore made by *Havelaar* to hoist themselves into the saddle, first immediately after the book's publication and then by means of our wretched constitutional seesaw-system, have done nothing else but change things. They had no alternative, had they? Their profession of political acrobat required it. The partly incapable, partly not very honest little bunch of politicians that 'fell upwards through lack of weight' after '60 realized that something had to be *done*, though they preferred not to do the right thing, which, if it comes to

323

that—I can see their point there!—would have been tantamount to sui-cide. Justice for the ill-used Javanese would have meant elevating him; and that would have been a death sentence for most of our politicians. Nevertheless, a show had to be put up of activity in a new direction, and the People, 'shuddering' with indignation, had a succession of bones thrown to them, not really to appease their hunger for reform but to keep their jaws busy, even if it was only with blathering about what passed for economics and politics. The men in power threw titbits to their party caucuses, newspaper fabricators, and the rest of their coffee-house public, one after the other—a policy to which I gave the definitive name of *duitenplaterij*.* For many years, even before *Havelaar*, freedom of labour had been the main dish, the *pièce de résistance* on the highly danger-ous *menu*. By way of a change the gentlemen served to their unsuspecting guests trumped-up questions about the East Indian coinage. Then follow-ed the land registration question, the Preanger question, the plantation-crop bonus question, the accountability question, the agricultural law question, the private ownership of land question, and a few more of the sort. One new law trod on the heels of another, and the men in office— whether conservative or liberal made not the slightest difference!—suc-ceeded every time in hoodwinking the people into believing that the only possible solution *to the universally recognized difficulty* now lay really and truly and entirely in the very latest remedy to be proposed. Honestly, they cried, *this* one will work!

Thus every discredited experiment was followed by a new experiment. After each used-up quack medicine, a new quack medicine. With each new ministry, a new panacea. For each new panacea, new ministers, usu-ally destined to burden the overburdened pension list for more years than they had burdened the throne of office for months. And the Second Chamber orating the while! And the party caucuses cracking-up or cry-ing-down! And the People listening! All the novelties were examined, tested, adopted, applied. In the Indies the Chiefs, the European officials, and most of all the Population, were made dizzy by the ceaseless turning about ... and nothing *changed* after *Havelaar*? Owing to *Havelaar*? Come off it! After and because of that book, the Indies suffered the same fate as Punch's watch. Someone told this philosopher that its works were dirty, and that was why it did not go right. He promptly threw it into the gut-

---

* In connexion with a new coinage for the Indies, the Government pre-pared and discussed pictures (*platen*) of the new coins (*duiten*). Such '*duiten-platerij*' was for Multatuli a ruse to distract attention from the fundamen-tals of the situation. *Tr.*

ter and cleaned it with a stable broom. According to another tradition of the Hague puppet theatre our politician planted the heel of his wooden shoe on it. I can assure the reader that a great deal really has *changed* in that watch!

The Netherlands has not chosen to do justice in the Havelaar case. As sure as eggs are eggs, this omission—this *crime!*—will mark the starting-point of the loss of its East Indian possessions. Anyone who doubts this prophecy because today, i.e. only fifteen years after my *very reluctant* action, the Dutch flag still waves at Batavia, betrays the narrowness of his political vision. Do you think upheavals such as those in store for Insulinde, and which, in fact, have already begun—don't you see this, Dutchmen?—can take place in the same period of time as a commonplace incident in private life? In the life of States, fifteen years is less than a moment.

Nevertheless, the catastrophe will be consummated relatively quickly. The reckless war with ACHIN was one of the last *duitenplaterijen* a certain minister needed in order to divert attention from his incompetence, and it will prove as disastrous in outcome and influence as it was rash and criminal in plan. The precarious authority of the Netherlands is not proof against such setbacks as we are suffering there. But, even before the manifestation of the more remote consequences which this piece of cruel stupidity is *bound* to entail ... where, in this case, is the highly extolled *ministerial responsibility* to be found? Must the Nation simply resign itself to the fact that one Fransen van de Putte has thought fit to get it into a situation which is costing it so many millions of money, so many human lives—not to mention a shameful loss of prestige in the Malay Archipelago? Of course it must! *That* man's name is also on the pension list! Apparently the Dutch taxpayer has so much money he doesn't know what to do with it.

As regards the war with ACHIN, I shall presently be compelled to revert to it now and again in the notes to *Havelaar*. But before going any further I should like to say that in this context, too, I have noticed how carelessly people read the book. Hardly if ever have I had evidence that anyone had connected the present war, and my prediction of it elsewhere, with the contents of Chapter 13. In view of the wide circulation of *Havelaar* it is indeed strange that when, in September '72, my letter to the King appeared, and war was declared against ACHIN in the following spring, so few remembered that I had referred to our strained relations with that State as long before as '60, and given proof of knowing more about these matters than our hack journalists and Members of Parliament. If people *had* remembered, my well-meant warning of September '72 might have borne better fruit! Old Jupiter still makes the Kings and Nations he wishes to destroy blind, deaf, mad and conservative or ... liberal, it's all the same. The main thing is and always will be: *to search for the truth, to recognize its importance, and, above all, to act on the information which, obtained thus, can be considered true*. All else is wrong, and Holland will lose the Indies because no justice was done to me in my endeavours to protect the Javanese against ill-treatment.

There are still people who cannot grasp the connexion between these two things. But is that my fault? The smothering of my complaints comes down to protection of untruth, encouragement of lying. Is it really so difficult to understand that in the long run such vast possessions cannot be administered when the powers that be are unwilling to receive any but untrue reports about the country and the population? Surely, in order to regulate, to administer, to govern something, the people responsible must first *know* in what condition the affairs concerned are? And so long as they disregard the information given in *Havelaar* they do *not* know!

And another thing. It appears from that book that the existing laws are not enforced. Then, pray, what is the good of behaving, in The Hague and during elections, as though there were any point in making *new* laws? I maintain that the old laws *in the main* were not so bad. But people chose not to observe them. *There* is the crux of the matter. There, and not in endless speechifying on subjects of supposed or simulated political importance, wranglings that undoubtedly serve to provide newspaper scribblers with texts for leading articles, keep ministers in power for one week longer, and occupy the entirely otiose imitation talents of Chamber debaters, but bring us not one step nearer to the only true goal: *protection of the Javanese against the rapacity of his Chiefs in complicity with a corrupt Dutch Administration.*

As regards this new edition [...] the pestilential dots with which Mr Van Lennep thought fit to spoil my work (e.g. P ... K ... ng for *Parang-Kujang*) have here, of course, been replaced by *readable words*. I have left unaltered the pseudonyms Slymering, Verbrugge, Duclari and Slotering because those names have become common property. My murdered predecessor was called Carolus. The real names of Controleur Verbrugge and Commandant Duclari were Van Hemert and Collard. The Resident of BANTAM was Brest van Kempen, and the petty Napoleon at PADANG was General Michiels. You may ask: what led me to change these names in the manuscript I entrusted to Mr Van Lennep? Let it suffice for me to refer to the end of Chapter 19 and say that I wanted to safeguard the honest but unheroic Controleur against victimization. He may not have supported me, but he had not opposed me either, and he had even supplied frank statements when I asked for them. That was already a great deal, and could have cost him dear. To continue ... the name Slymering served to characterize my model. And finally, the change of the names of Carolus and Collard into Slotering and Duclari followed automatically from the other substitutions. I was certainly not out to observe secrecy—as, if it comes to that, is apparent from the whole purport of my book—but I found it distasteful to expose certain persons to criticism by the *lay* reading public. I considered that in the *official* world—and the matter was *their* concern—people would know whom they had to approach for further information on the facts I revealed. And they *did* know; for, after *Havelaar* had reached the Indies, Governor-General Pahud went post-haste to Lebak 'to investigate complaints about abuses there'. [...]

NOTES

1. *(Tr):* This dedication is to Multatuli's first wife, the 'Tina' of *Max Havelaar*.

2. *(Tr):* This fragment, written by Multatuli himself, is probably all that ever existed of the 'Unpublished play' from which it is supposed to have been taken. '*Barbertje moet hangen*' (= 'Babbie must hang') has now become proverbial in Dutch to describe a situation in which a particular scapegoat is to be made to suffer at all costs. As in other cases (e.g. 'Frankenstein'), the phrase is incorrect: it is Lothario who must hang, not Babbie. 'Babbie must hang' is paralleled by 'No matter, the Jew shall burn!' —the invariable answer made by the Patriarch of Jerusalem to all pleas for mercy on the saintly Nathan, in Lessing's play *Nathan the Wise*; hence the reference to his 'judgment'!

3. *(M):* The book was divided into chapters by Mr Van Lennep. I was not enough of a professional writer, especially in 1860, to bring so much order into my argument, and I still think this division could be dispensed with without harming the book from a literary point of view.
The abrupt alternation of the parts by Droogstoppel and Stern has that touch of piquancy about it which keeps the reader from going to sleep, or ... wakes him up. But experience has taught me that the numbering of the chapters makes it easier to look up particular passages, so I have left things as they are.

4. *(Tr):* Lauriergracht = literally 'Laurel *Canal*'.

5. *(Tr):* Hieronymus van Alphen (1746–1803) wrote three small volumes of *Little Poems for Children*—comparable in English with Ann and Jane

Taylor's *Original Poems for Infant Minds*—which were enormously popular in their day.

6. *(Tr)*: Batavierstraat = 'Batavier' *Street*, after the Batavi, the inhabitants of the Netherlands at the time of the Romans (singular 'Batavus', as in Droogstoppel!).

7. *(Tr)*: The Netherlands Royal Zoological Society *Natura Artis Magistra*, founded 1838; also its Zoological Gardens at Amsterdam.

8. *(Tr)*: A pretty village not far from Utrecht, with many country houses and villas. It is a favourite place of retirement for well-to-do people.

9. *(M)*: The *Poolsche Koffiehuis* was, perhaps still is, a very busy café in Kalverstraat, Amsterdam, and a favourite meeting-place for a certain type of businessman connected with the stock and produce exchanges.

10. *(Tr)*: This is one of Multatuli's 'Dickensian' names, which would lose all their savour in 'translation'. 'Batavus', referring as it does to the Batavi, the savage tribe which inhabited Holland at the beginning of the Christian era, suggests so many things: ancient virtues, sturdy John Bull-like common sense, parochialism, crass materialism, block-headed stupidity, a 'backwoodsman's' attitude to life's problems, etc. 'Droogstoppel' means literally 'Drystubble' (*cf.* 'Dryasdust').

11. *(Tr)*: The opening words of Homer's *Iliad*.

12. *(Tr)*: This statement comes from the beginning of Book II of Herodotus's *Histories*.

13. *(Tr)*: In the Netherlands until very recently all women of the working and lower middle classes were addressed as 'Juffrouw' = Miss, whether they were single or married. 'Mevrouw' = Mrs was reserved for their married betters!

14. *(Tr)*: Refers to *Don Quixote at the Wedding of Camacho*, a play by Pieter Langendijk (1683–1756). At the beginning of Act II, the professional poet Master Jochem describes himself, saying 'I rhyme while I sleep, I rhyme while I eat, And even on the privy I think out my rondeaux.'

15. *(Tr)*: The *Nederlandsche Handel-Maatschappij, N.V.* (= 'Dutch Trading Company, Ltd.') was founded in 1825 at Amsterdam, largely at the instance of King William the First of the Netherlands. It was originally an export/import organization especially for the Dutch overseas possessions, with particular interest in East Indian products, but is now essentially a banking concern.

16. *(M)*: I am far from disagreeing with *everything* I put into Droogstoppel's mouth. He 'normally never had anything to do' with verses of the

kind that follow here. Well, neither have I! The difference lies in our respective reasons for disliking such verses. It is not only excusable, but even positively essential, that a young heart with a burning thirst after *poetry*, mesmerized by a self-assertive dilettantish literature unworthy of the name, should fail in its first attempts at self-expression and take for real something which ultimately proves to be nothing but empty noise—'jingle-jangle' as I called it in the Postscript to my play *The Bride Above*. *Il faut passer par là!* The oak which is destined to yield sound, dry wood must begin life as a green sapling. But the Droogstoppels never did have overmuch sap in the first place, and did not need to change to become what they are: desiccated and useless. They are not above but below making the mistake of the others, and, moreover, they would start attaching value to 'verses and suchlike' fast enough if those trumpery products were listed on 'Change.

If Droogstoppel's down-to-earth outpourings should serve to put a damper on *false poetry* in the minds of our young people, I would heartily recommend them to the attention of parents, pedagogues and reviewers. For my part, if I had to choose between him and a certain sort of versifier ... well, I still wouldn't choose him! But I admit I should find my act of justice hard.

17. *(Tr):* Something of everything, nothing in all.

18. *(Tr):* Many matters but not much matter.

19. *(Tr):* *Horror vacui* ('Nature abhors a vacuum') is the ancient explanation for the fact that (owing actually to atmospheric pressure) tubes devoid of air fill with the liquid in which they are placed.

20. *(Tr):* Felice Orsini tried to kill Napoleon III in 1858 by throwing three bombs at him while he was on his way to the theatre in his carriage.

21. *(Tr):* This name for the former Dutch East Indies was coined by Multatuli ('insula' = island, and 'Ind(i)ë').

22. *(Tr):* Right of the first possessor.

23. *(Tr):* *Jus talionis* = right of retaliation ('an eye for an eye ...'). In a note to the edition of 1875 Multatuli gives such a poem as the one referred to—a bloodthirsty prophecy, ostensibly written by a rebel Javanese chief, of the end of Dutch rule in the East Indies and the retribution in store for the Dutch.

24. *(Tr):* Gaafzuiger literally means gift- or talent-sucker, i.e. exploiter.

25. *(Tr):* Van Speyk, a lieutenant in the Dutch Navy, was a hero of the

brief war of 1830 between Belgium and the Netherlands which ended in Belgium's achieving independence.

26. *(Tr)*: See note 13.

27. *(Tr)*: Cologne Cathedral was begun in 1248 but left unfinished in 1509, at the onset of the Reformation, which Multatuli gives as the reason for the cessation of work on it. It is not known for certain whether the architect Erwin von Steinbach (d. 1318) was associated with it.
In 1842 work was resumed, and the Cathedral was finally completed in 1880.

28. *(M)*: RADHEN ADHIPATTI KARTA NATTA NEGARA. The three last words are the *name*, the two first are the *title*. It stands to reason that such a title is difficult to translate exactly. Nevertheless, old Valentyn tried to do so in his works on the East Indies, where he speaks of 'Dukes' and 'Counts'. To anyone who knows the native Chiefs, there is something odd in this.
After the diverse titles of those rulers who appear to be more or less independent, PANGÉRANG ranks the highest. This title can be fairly accurately rendered as 'Prince', because it is based on kinship with one of the two ruling houses of Solo (Surakarta) and Jokja (Jokjakarta), though I believe there are exceptions, which do not concern us here. The title next below this is ADHIPATTI or, in full: RADHEN ADHIPATTI. RADHEN by itself indicates a rank which is lower but nevertheless still fairly high above the common run of people. The TOMMONGONGS come somewhat lower than the ADHIPATTIS. [...]

29. *(M)*: Types of rice field, differentiated according to physical situation and mode of cultivation, especially as regards the possibility or otherwise of providing them with water. The *sawah* is artificially irrigated, whereas *gagahs* and *tipars* are directly dependent on rainfall for their water supply.

30. *(M)*: Rice in the husk.

31. *(M)*: Village. Elsewhere called *negrie*, and also *kampong*.

32. *(M)*: The *alun-alun* is an extensive open space in front of the group of buildings which form the Regent's residence. As a rule there are two noble *waringin* trees in this square, and the age of these trees shows that they were there before the *alun-alun* and that therefore the Regent's dwelling has been built near them, probably *in order* to be near them. [...]

33. *(M)*: Native official whose function can be approximately described as that of 'Overseer'.

34. *(Tr):* Multatuli originally wrote 'Bluebeard's wife', but Van Lennep 'edited' this into 'Mrs Bluebeard's sister' and the mistake remained unaltered in all the published editions of *Max Havelaar*.

35. *(Tr):* See note 98.

36. *(Tr):* A kind of turban.

37. *(Tr):* Ingredients in betel-chewing.

38. *(Tr):* Medium-sized deer.

39. *(M):* Hold the Commandant's horse!

40. *(M): Ini apa tuan-tuan datang!* = There come the gentlemen! The *tudung* is the plaited straw hat of the Javanese, shaped like a big round plate. It protects the native not only against the sun but also against the rain, of which he is ludicrously afraid. A kind of hat which was recently fashionable among Dutch ladies for wear in the garden looked exactly like a *tudung*.

41. *(M):* A small white flower with a strong jasmine-like perfume. It plays a great part in ballads and legends, just as the rose does with us.

42. *(M):* A 'bun' of hair at the back of the neck. It is never held together by a separate ribbon or cord but always hangs suspended in a loop of the hair itself. If a *chignon* consists specifically of *false* hair, the *kondeh* is *not* a *chignon*.

43. *(Tr):* Robinson Crusoe novels. Defoe's famous book gave rise to dozens of imitations all over Europe, including Holland. The Italian poet Silvio Pellico (1787–1854) spent years in Austrian prisons for his nationalist principles. His account of his experiences, *My Prisons*, was an international best seller, as was also *Picciola*, by 'Saintine' (Boniface Xavier, 1795–1865), the tale of a captive who keeps his soul alive by tending a flower.

44. *(M):* Golden *payong*. In accordance with Javanese custom the rank of a Chief is indicated by the colour of the umbrella carried along behind him. The colour is determined by official rules; a plain gilt *payong* is reserved for the most exalted Chiefs.

45. *(Tr):* A palanquin or litter.

46. *(M):* Fugitives in CHIKANDI and BOLANG. The private estates in the BATAVIA and BUITENZORG regions are largely worked by refugees from LEBAK. 'When the people aren't being squeezed in Lebak,' I heard a landowner say, 'we're short of labour.'

47. *(Tr):* Banana.

48. *(M): Hollander.* To the natives, every white man is an *orang hollanda, wolanda, belanda,* indiscriminately. In the main centres of population they occasionally make an exception to this rule by speaking of *orang ingris* or *orang pranchies,* i.e. Englishman or Frenchman. The German is sometimes called *orang hollanda gunung*—'mountain Hollander', 'Hollander from the interior'.

49. *(M):* Native Chiefs. The PATTEH helps the Regent as secretary, messenger, factotum. The KLIWON is the intermediary between the Administration and the village headmen. He usually supervises municipal public works, the posting of watchmen, organization of statute labour, etc. The JAKSA is Public Prosecutor and in charge of the police.

50. *(M): Gongs* and *gamelangs.* The *gong* is a heavy metal cymbal suspended from a cord. The *gamelang* is played like our glass harmonica or the well-known 'wood and straw' instrument. At this point in the text I could also have mentioned the *anklung,* a grid-shaped instrument of plates lying on stretched cords. It is worth noting that all these names are onomatopes. The *gong* sounds deep and strong. The *anklung* and *gamelang,* on the other hand, are soft and sweet but very melancholy.

51. *(Tr):* Name of a French warship.

52. *(M):* A kind of mattock.

53. *(Tr):* Spates, inundations.

54. *(M):* The *kris* is the traditional weapon of the Javanese and, as such, is an indispensable part of his 'full dress', as the sword used to be of ours. It is a flat dagger with a serpentine blade and a very small handle. As a rule, *krises* are made of one piece of forged mild steel—i.e. damascened? —which is hardened by buffalo's hooves. The *kris* is preserved from rust by being rubbed with *jeroke* (a kind of lemon), and with arsenic, which gives the metal a strange dull colour. There is a superstition to the effect that anyone who wishes to look at a *kris* must draw it *completely* out of the sheath; if he removes it only partly he is liable to meet with great misfortune. There are innumerable tales in circulation about magic *krises,* etc. *(Tr): Klewang* = a short sabre which broadens towards the end and can also be used as a chopping-knife.

55. *(M): Maniessan* = sweetmeats, candied fruits. The custom in the Indies of eating such things while taking tea is of Chinese origin.

56. *(M):* Excuse me.

57. *(Tr):* Young gentleman.

58. *(M): Jimats* are letters or other objects that fall down from heaven to furnish fanatics and charlatans with credentials. [...]

59. *(Tr): Garem glap* = salt made illegally, salt being then a Government monopoly.

60. *(Tr): anspruch(s)los(e)* = German for unassuming, unpretending, modest, etc.

61. *(Tr): Abraham Blankaart.* Uncle and guardian of Sara Burgerhart, eponymous heroine of a Dutch novel by Elisabeth Wolff and Agatha Deken which appeared in 1782. *'Sara Burgerhart'* is a story in letter form on the model of those by Samuel Richardson, and was a great success.

62. *(Tr): Omne tulit punctum qui miscuit utile dulci.* 'Acclaimed by all is he who mixes ... the useful with the pleasant' (in this case ... 'coffee with something else' !).

63. *(Tr): Suite.* In Dutch houses the 'centre piece' was normally a set of two rooms used, for instance, as morning-room and drawing-room, or dining-room and drawing-room, separated from each other by large, usually sliding, glass doors. Possession of a 'suite' was the acme of bourgeois respectability. On this occasion Stern and Marie were sitting in one room of the suite and Droogstoppel was sitting in a room opening off it.

64. *(M):* Gherkins.

65. *(M): Miss Mata-Api* = Miss Fire-Eye.

66. *(M):* ARLES is considered to have been an inland colony of people from MASSILIA (MARSEILLES), which was founded by the Phoenicians. The fact that the truly characteristic beauty of the women of ARLES has been preserved better there than at MARSEILLES may be due to the fact that there was less opportunity for intercourse with foreigners at ARLES. In coastal towns such as MARSEILLES, races lose their purity very quickly. Whether the women at NÎMES—another outpost of MARSEILLES—are as beautiful as those at ARLES, I do not know.

67. *(M):* Native Chief.

68. *(Tr):* Natal in Sumatra, of course, not South Africa.

69. *(Tr): Gemüthlich* (German) = genial, sociable, well-disposed, 'at peace with the world'.

70. *(M):* In those places in Sumatra which were formerly English strong points, the natives still call the governing officials Kommandeurs—*commodore* (? Commander—*Tr*). [...]

71. *(M):* Basket in which sugar is shipped to the Netherlands. The plaited bamboo of these *kranjangs,* usually coated with tar, can nowadays be seen far inland in Europe, where it is used for fences and the like.

72. *(M):* Bamboo couch.

73. *(Tr):* Mosquito curtain.

74. *(M): Madame Geoffrin.* My manuscript read *Madame Scarron*, and I think Mr van Lennep made a mistake in altering it. *Madame Geoffrin*, being very rich, did not need to supplement a frugal table by telling stories. Moreover, I am certain that some writers connect this well-known anecdote with *Madame Scarron.*

(Tr): Cf. Alexandre Dumas, *Marie Giovanni, Journal de Voyage d'une Parisienne* (1855), Ch. VI. 'When there was no roast meat at the poet Scarron's, his wife told a story.'

75. *(M):* No need, not necessary!

76. *(Tr):* Literally 'one's own hearth is worth much'. Cf. 'There's no place like home'.

77. *(M):* The *Tout-Paris* of the chief towns in the East Indies—'everyone who counts'. This term appears to owe its origin to the gossiping sessions that used to take place among people lingering after the service at the exit from the Protestant church in or near the Chinese camp at Batavia.

78. *(Tr):* Multatuli's typification of the small-minded petty bourgeois.

79. *(Tr):* The original is in French.

80. *(Tr):* The many kinds of side dishes, sweet and sour, often highly spiced, which accompany the main meal in the Indies, the 'rijsttafel' (= 'rice table').

81. *(Tr):* This refers to the story of Frederick the Great and the miller of Sans Souci, whose mill stood on ground that was wanted for the King's garden. Frederick's agent first tried to buy the mill and then, when the miller refused to sell, threatened to take it. To which the miller answered 'Haven't we the law court in Berlin?' and the agent gave up.
In 1838 Multatuli had made a translation of the poem on the subject by Andrieux, which ends:

> 'See: a province is stolen
> And a mill is spared.'

82. *(M):* PADRIES was the familiar name we gave to the Achinese tribe that had converted the BATTAK to ISLAM a short time before. Doubtless the term ought to be PEDIRESE, after PEDIR, one of the most insignificant states of ACHIN. [...]

83. *(M):* The RAPPAT Court at NATAL consisted of the principal native Chiefs of the Division, with the senior Dutch official as President. The

Court dealt not only with civil and criminal cases but also with political matters. As appears from the text, the 'fiat' of the Resident of AYER-BANGIE was all that was required for execution of the sentences passed by the Court. I do not know the derivation of the word RAPPAT. Apparently it is only used in SUMATRA.

84. *(M)*: The traditional weapon of the inhabitants of those parts, like the *kris* in Java. The *sewah* is a somewhat curved dagger with a very small hilt and the cutting edge on the inside of the curve. The original purpose of giving it this shape was doubtless to enable the hilt to be entirely hidden in the hand while the very blunt back of the weapon lies against the wrist and is covered by the arm. In this way the victim does not notice that his assailant has a weapon at all before the latter has struck him, with three peculiar, swift movements of wrist and arm. Quite apart from its suitability for murder, the *sewah* is a symbol of freedom and manliness. Anyone who takes a Malay Chief prisoner—as was my painful duty under the circumstances described on p. 199 *et seq.*—requires him to give up his *sewah*. [...]

85. *(Tr)*: A French law against cruelty to animals (1850), for which the politician J.-P. D. de Grammont was responsible.

86. *(M)*: Small straw mat.

87. *(Tr)*: Coconut.

88. *(M)*: *Pukul ampat* = 'Four o'clock', the name of a flower which opens at that time in the afternoon and closes again towards morning. [...]

89. *(Tr)*: One in the hierarchy of titles still used in the Netherlands in addressing officials, etc. This one means literally 'Your right noble severe ...' But, as Alphonse Nahuys pointed out in his translation of this book, such English titles as 'Right Worshipful' could likewise not be translated into Dutch without becoming ridiculous.

90. *(Tr)*: Just and determined.

91. *(M)*: Enclosure of rough stakes.

92. *(M)*: '*Sluis*' (= *lock*), meaning a stone bridge, is typical Amsterdam usage. [...]

93. *(M)*: Heirloom, here—as often—with all that that implies in the way of veneration.

94. *(M)*: Village priest.

95. *(M)*: Happiness, good fortune.

96. *(M):* Low, narrow dykes which keep the water in the *sawahs*.

97. *(M):* Reeds, giant or prairie (sic—*Tr*) grass. It is often so high that a man on horseback can hide in it. [...]

98. *(M): Sarong. Batik. Kepala.* The *sarong* is the characteristic garment of the Javanese, and is worn by men and women alike. It is a length of woven *kapok*, the ends of which are sewn together. A *sarong* of silk is a rarity. One of the two ends is called the *kepala* (i.e. 'head'), and ends in a broad band which is painted, usually with a pattern of triangular motifs fitting into each other. This 'painting' is called *batik*, and is done by hand. The fabric is stretched on a frame and the paint is applied in a little vessel of tin, shaped like a miniature teapot or Aladdin lamp. (*Tr:* This is not quite correct. The 'paint' is actually molten wax, which is poured on to those parts of the *sarong* that are to be kept free from the dye in which the material is later immersed, i.e. those parts that are meant to show up as designs.) A *sarong* without a *kepala* and not joined at the ends is called a *slendang*. This garment is worn round the hips, and the men sometimes have it short, or roll it up to a greater or lesser extent. [...]

99. *(M):* Kite. In Java it is not only children who play with this toy. The *lalayang* has no tail, and describes all kinds of gyrations, which can be controlled to a certain extent by the person holding the cord. The object of the game referred to is to cut the opponent's cord in the air. The efforts made to do this result in a sort of fight, which is very entertaining to watch and stimulates the onlookers into taking sides enthusiastically. SAÏJAH's supposition that 'little Jamin' could have cheated is just another (commonly held) East Indian delusion, in view of the skill in throwing that would have been required to cut the cord in this way.

100 *(M): Pagger* (by rights *pagar*) means *hedge*. [...]

101. *(M): Kamuning.* A choice, yellow-grained wood, which is produced only by the root of the small tree of that name, and consequently is never found in large pieces. It is very costly.

102. *(M):* SUSUHUNAN of SOLO. The Emperor of SURAKARTA. In his official correspondence he calls the Governor-General by a number of titles, including that of 'Grandfather'.

103. *(Tr):* Chopping-knife.

104. *(M):* A spirit that dwells in trees and has a bitter grudge against women, especially pregnant women. [...]

105. *(M):* Small lamp.

106. *(Tr):* Javanese squirrel.

107. *(Tr):* Last two lines of a pompous Dutch religious poem, used here ironically.

108. *(M):* Food and other items levied from the people without payment. [...]

109. *(M):* Unpaid watchmen and other servants.

110. *(M):* The poisoning of Mr Carolus.

111. *(M): Tontong (tomtom, tamtam)* is a large, hanging, hollow wooden block, on which the hours are struck. The name is yet another onomatope.

READ MORE IN PENGUIN

In every corner of the world, on every subject under the sun, Penguin represents quality and variety – the very best in publishing today.

For complete information about books available from Penguin – including Puffins, Penguin Classics and Arkana – and how to order them, write to us at the appropriate address below. Please note that for copyright reasons the selection of books varies from country to country.

In the United Kingdom: Please write to *Dept. EP, Penguin Books Ltd, Bath Road, Harmondsworth, West Drayton, Middlesex UB7 0DA*

In the United States: Please write to *Consumer Sales, Penguin USA, P.O. Box 999, Dept. 17109, Bergenfield, New Jersey 07621-0120*. VISA and MasterCard holders call 1-800-253-6476 to order Penguin titles

In Canada: Please write to *Penguin Books Canada Ltd, 10 Alcorn Avenue, Suite 300, Toronto, Ontario M4V 3B2*

In Australia: Please write to *Penguin Books Australia Ltd, P.O. Box 257, Ringwood, Victoria 3134*

In New Zealand: Please write to *Penguin Books (NZ) Ltd, Private Bag 102902, North Shore Mail Centre, Auckland 10*

In India: Please write to *Penguin Books India Pvt Ltd, 706 Eros Apartments, 56 Nehru Place, New Delhi 110 019*

In the Netherlands: Please write to *Penguin Books Netherlands bv, Postbus 3507, NL-1001 AH Amsterdam*

In Germany: Please write to *Penguin Books Deutschland GmbH, Metzlerstrasse 26, 60594 Frankfurt am Main*

In Spain: Please write to *Penguin Books S. A., Bravo Murillo 19, 1° B, 28015 Madrid*

In Italy: Please write to *Penguin Italia s.r.l., Via Felice Casati 20, I–20124 Milano*

In France: Please write to *Penguin France S. A., 17 rue Lejeune, F–31000 Toulouse*

In Japan: Please write to *Penguin Books Japan, Ishikiribashi Building, 2–5–4, Suido, Bunkyo-ku, Tokyo 112*

In South Africa: Please write to *Longman Penguin Southern Africa (Pty) Ltd, Private Bag X08, Bertsham 2013*

READ MORE IN PENGUIN

A CHOICE OF CLASSICS

Molière	**The Misanthrope/The Sicilian/Tartuffe/A Doctor in Spite of Himself/The Imaginary Invalid**
	The Miser/The Would-be Gentleman/That Scoundrel Scapin/Love's the Best Doctor/ Don Juan
Michel de Montaigne	**An Apology for Raymond Sebond**
	Complete Essays
Marguerite de Navarre	**The Heptameron**
Blaise Pascal	**Pensées**
	The Provincial Letters
Abbé Prevost	**Manon Lescaut**
Rabelais	**The Histories of Gargantua and Pantagruel**
Racine	**Andromache/Britannicus/Berenice**
	Iphigenia/Phaedra/Athaliah
Arthur Rimbaud	**Collected Poems**
Jean-Jacques Rousseau	**The Confessions**
	A Discourse on Inequality
	Emile
Jacques Saint-Pierre	**Paul and Virginia**
Madame de Sevigné	**Selected Letters**
Stendhal	**The Life of Henry Brulard**
	Love
	Scarlet and Black
	The Charterhouse of Parma
Voltaire	**Candide**
	Letters on England
	Philosophical Dictionary
Emile Zola	**L'Assomoir**
	La Bête humaine
	The Debacle
	The Earth
	Germinal
	Nana
	Thérèse Raquin

READ MORE IN PENGUIN

A CHOICE OF CLASSICS

Honoré de Balzac	**The Black Sheep**
	César Birotteau
	The Chouans
	Cousin Bette
	Cousin Pons
	Eugénie Grandet
	A Harlot High and Low
	Lost Illusions
	A Murky Business
	Old Goriot
	Selected Short Stories
	Ursule Mirouët
	The Wild Ass's Skin
J. A. Brillat-Savarin	**The Physiology of Taste**
Charles Baudelaire	**Selected Poems**
Pierre Corneille	**The Cid/Cinna/The Theatrical Illusion**
Alphonse Daudet	**Letters from My Windmill**
Denis Diderot	**Jacques the Fatalist**
	Selected Writings on Art and Literature
Alexandre Dumas	**The Count of Monte Cristo**
Gustave Flaubert	**Bouvard and Pécuchet**
	Flaubert in Egypt
	Madame Bovary
	Salammbo
	Sentimental Education
	The Temptation of St Antony
	Three Tales
Victor Hugo	**Les Misérables**
	Notre-Dame of Paris
Laclos	**Les Liaisons Dangereuses**
La Fontaine	**Selected Fables**
Madame de Lafayette	**The Princesse de Clèves**
Lautréamont	**Maldoror and Poems**